The Sting

Kimberley Chambers lives in Essex and has been, at various times, a disc jockey, cab driver and a street trader. She is now a No.1 *Sunday Times* bestselling author of fourteen novels.

Join Kimberley's legion of legendary fans online:

www.kimberleychambers.com

/kimberleychambersofficial

@kimbochambers

@kimberley.chambers

By the same author

KIMBERLEY CHAMBERS
The Sting

HarperCollins*Publishers*

HarperCollins*Publishers* Ltd
1 London Bridge Street,
London SE1 9GF

www.harpercollins.co.uk

This paperback edition 2019
2

First published by HarperCollins*Publishers* 2019

A catalogue record for this book
is available from the British Library

ISBN: 978-0-00-814480-7

Typeset in Sabon LT Std by
Palimpsest Book Production Ltd, Falkirk, Stirlingshire

Printed and bound in the UK by CPI Group (UK) Ltd, Croydon CR0 4YY

MIX
Paper from
responsible sources
FSC™ C007454

This book is produced from independently certified FSC™ paper
to ensure responsible forest management.

For more information visit: www.harpercollins.co.uk/green

In memory of my brave friend Suzanne's son
Ricky Paul Hayden
14.05.89—13.09.16

Cruelly taken far too soon
RIP Ricky xxx

ACKNOWLEDGEMENTS

Big love and thanks to my fab agent, Tim Bates, and my exceptionally brilliant editor, Kimberley Young. Thanks also to the hardworking team at HarperCollins who are an absolute joy to work with. Charlotte Brabbin, Sarah Shea, Hannah O'Brien, and the whole of the amazing Sales team.

A special mention to my lovely publicist, Felicity Denham. Also Charlie Redmayne, Laura Meyer, Pat Fletcher (second Mum), Rosie de Courcy and the wonderful Sue Cox. And a special mention to my policeman pal, Ron, and his lovely wife, Maz. Thanks so much for all your help, I'm really glad you smashed my door down now. ☺

An author is a nobody without their readers and mine are the best! A huge thank you to each and every one of you for your loyal support, reviews and lovely comments regarding my work. It's very much appreciated.

And last, but certainly not least, RIP Chas Hodges. A musical genius.

'Every saint has a past,
and every sinner a future'

Oscar Wilde

PROLOGUE

New Year's Eve 1972

'Should auld acquaintance be forgot,
And never brought to mind.
Should auld acquaintance be forgot,
And auld lang syne.
For auld lang syne, my jo,
For auld land syne,
We'll take a cup o' kindness yet,
For auld lang syne.'

I'm in the middle of the circle holding hands with my sisters Hazel and Linda. My mum, dad and Nanny Noreen are all singing at the top of their voices. My mum looks happy, even though she still has the remainder of a black eye that my dad gave her on Christmas Eve.

'Open the front door, Tommy,' orders my dad. He calls New Year's Eve Hogmanay after an oatcake.

I do as I'm told. Old Mr Cleaver across the road is banging two dustbin lids together. I feel something brush past my leg and then I scream when I realize what it is. It's a black cat and it's obviously been run over. It collapses in the hallway right in front of me.

Nanny Noreen goes ballistic and blames me. She's very religious and believes in Scottish folklore. 'You stupid boy,' she bellows. 'You know the first to step through the door after midnight affects the fortunes of everyone who lives in the house. I've told you that enough times, so what do you invite in, a dying black cat. Now we're going to have bad luck all year. You wait and see.'

I stare at the cat as it takes its last breath. Little did I know at that point Nanny Noreen was speaking the truth.

In a few days' time, my life as I'd known it would no longer be. Everything was about to change for the worse.

My name is Tommy Boyle and this is my story . . .

PART ONE

When sorrows come,
they come not single spies,
but in battalions.

William Shakespeare

CHAPTER ONE

Christmas 1972

Tommy Boyle pressed his nose against the cold glass of his bedroom window. The weather had taken a turn for the worse this week. It was literally freezing, but Tommy didn't care about the cold. All he was bothered about was his father coming home from the oil rigs. He was so excited; he'd barely slept last night.

Hearing his sisters squabbling over the record player, Tommy sighed. Three months at a time his father worked away for, and it was difficult being surrounded by females. He missed the simple things: such as watching *The Big Match* or *Match of the Day* and discussing the games. Girls knew nothing about football. Nor Cowboys and Indians, or Battleship.

'Not this rubbish again. Turn it off,' shouted twelve-year-old Tommy. His younger sister had obviously got her way. Linda was obsessed with little Jimmy Osmond, reckoned she would marry him one day. 'Long-Haired Lover from Liverpool' was one of only two songs Linda ever played. Benny Hill's 'Ernie (The Fastest Milkman in the West)' was the other and Tommy hated both. He thought they were silly songs.

'Breakfast's ready, kids.'

Tommy ran down the stairs, but slipped, landing in a heap at the bottom.

Valerie Boyle picked her son up. 'What did you do? You silly sausage. Have you hurt yourself?'

Tommy had hurt himself. His knee was throbbing, but he was determined not to cry. 'Boys don't cry,' his dad had always told him. 'I'm all right. My pyjamas are too long. I fell over the bottoms of 'em.'

Valerie had only bought her son the fleecy pyjamas the previous day. They were meant to fit a twelve-year-old, but Tommy was small for his age. 'I'll get the machine out in a bit, alter them for you. You'll live, eh?' Valerie smiled, ruffling her son's mousy blond hair.

'Where's Rex?' Tommy enquired. Rex was the Alsatian his father had purchased to protect the family in his absence. Tommy loved Rex and the feeling was mutual. He would often take the dog out with him. Rex was too strong on his lead for Tommy, but he would walk happily by his side and never went into the road.

'Rex is having his breakfast in his kennel, love. You know your dad doesn't allow Rex indoors while he's here, and he'll be home soon, won't he?'

'Yeah, but it's cold. Rex can't sleep in his kennel this time of year. He'll freeze.'

'I've put some blankets in there, Tommy. He'll only be out there for ten days, until your dad goes back to work. Then he can come inside again,' Valerie replied, wishing her husband wasn't coming home for Christmas at all. She didn't love Alexander any more, hadn't for a long time. But the children did, so she put their happiness first. For all Alexander's faults, he was a hard worker and good provider. They lived in a nice three-bedroom house: private, not council. Working on those oil rigs paid extremely well.

A deafening scream filled the air, followed by ten-year-old Linda holding two halves of a seven-inch single in her hands. 'Hazel snapped Jimmy in half,' she cried.

'No, I never. It was an accident,' lied fourteen-year-old Hazel. 'I wanted to play Alice Cooper and she—'

'Enough.' Valerie Boyle held her hands in the air while eyeing her eldest daughter with suspicion. Hazel had a nasty streak at times, just like her father. 'Go eat your breakfast, now!'

'I loved that record, Mummy,' Linda whimpered.

Valerie held her youngest child close to her chest. 'I know you did, darling. Don't worry. Mummy will go to the record shop after breakfast and buy you another one.'

Tommy Boyle stared out of the front-room window nervously chewing at his fingernails. His father had been due home at lunchtime and it was now teatime.

'Sausage rolls are ready. Who wants one?' Valerie yelled, trying to keep her voice sounding jovial. Alexander had promised her faithfully he would come straight home, what with it being Christmas Eve. Him stopping off at a pub for this length of time would only lead to one thing. Arguments. Alexander was a horrible drunk, would always drag up the past.

'Will Dad bring us presents too? Or is Father Christmas bringing them all?' enquired Linda.

Hazel sniggered. 'Father Christmas doesn't exist, divvy.'

'Yes, he does. He eats the mince pies we leave outside and his reindeers drink the milk.'

'No, he doesn't. Rex does.'

'Stop it, Hazel. Christmas is meant to be a time of joy, not disagreements. And if I catch you breaking your sister's records again, you'll get no pocket money for a month,' warned Valerie.

His stomach churning like it always did when he feared his dad might come home drunk, Tommy continued to stare forlornly out of the window.

It was gone midnight when Tommy was awoken by shouting and what sounded like glass smashing. He immediately started to shake. His mum was only five foot two, his dad a whole foot taller, and he knew who would end up with the cuts and bruises.

Linda appeared in his bedroom, tears streaming down her face. 'They're fighting, Tommy.'

'Get in my bed and put the quilt over your head.'

'Dad won't hurt Mum, will he?' Linda asked fearfully.

'No. I'll sort it. You stay here,' Tommy replied bravely.

Sitting on the top of the stairs rocking to and fro was Hazel. Tommy sat next to his sister and put a comforting arm around her shoulders. The argument was loud, but muffled in parts.

'You lying whore. I know you've been with Terry Fletcher because you were seen in the fucking pub with him,' bellowed Alexander Boyle.

Tommy winced as he heard something else smash. It sounded like china. 'I'm gonna make sure Mum is OK.'

'No, Tommy. Don't go down there,' Hazel pleaded, grabbing her brother's arm. 'He'll only hit you again, like he did last time. Don't get involved.'

Remembering the time he'd got a clump for intervening, Tommy sat down. For as long as he could remember, his parents had argued. His dad was a tall, broad-shouldered man with black hair and blue eyes. He was from Glasgow originally and spoke with a deep Scottish accent. So much so, some of Tommy's friends struggled to understand what he was saying. At forty-five, he was thirteen years older than Tommy's mum.

'Who is Terry Fletcher?' Hazel asked. 'Is he Billy Fletcher's dad?'

Tommy shrugged. Billy Fletcher was older than him and in Hazel's year at school. Tommy thought he was a flash git and steered well clear of him. Whoever this Terry Fletcher was, it was clear he was the cause of the argument. From what he could gather, his dad was accusing his mother of fornicating with Terry while he'd been away.

Tommy didn't know too much about his parents' past. They never really spoke about it. The snippets he had learned mostly came via his dad's mum, Nanny Noreen. She reckoned his father was happily married to a good Catholic girl before he'd been forced to travel to London to find work. According to Nanny Noreen, his mother was working as a barmaid back then and she'd trapped his father by falling pregnant with Hazel.

'A laughing stock you've made me, you no-good slut. Parading around with another man while I'm working my balls off to provide for you. Have you any idea how that makes me feel? You're a prostitute, same as your mother was,' bellowed Alexander.

'Do you think our dead nan really was a prostitute?' asked Linda.

Not realizing Linda had snuck out of his bedroom, Tommy leapt up and held her in his arms. 'Nah, take no notice. Mum says when Dad is drunk he doesn't know what he's saying.' Tommy had actually heard Nanny Noreen say that his other nan had been a brass and had died while having an illegal abortion, but he liked to protect his sisters from such horrible gossip.

'Mum has been going out lots of an evening lately and she has been wearing her best frocks and shoes. Do you think Dad could be telling the truth? Perhaps she hasn't been going to the bingo?' Hazel suggested.

Once again, Tommy shrugged. The boys at school were all infatuated with his mother. She was short, very pretty and blonde. The boys insisted she was a ringer for the actress Barbara Windsor, but Tommy reckoned that was because of the size of her boobies. She did look a bit like Barbara, he supposed, but to him she was plain old 'Mum'. He had heard a few rumours though, that she was a 'Good Time Girl'. Tommy hadn't really understood what that meant at the time, but he was kind of getting the gist now.

Hearing more shouting, then a loud scream, Tommy decided enough was enough and bolted down the stairs.

'No, Tommy. No,' Hazel shrieked, running after her

brother. Linda followed suit. As siblings, they often had disagreements. But whenever their parents fought, the three of them stuck together like glue.

'What you doing? Leave Mum alone,' Tommy ordered. His mother was lying on the kitchen floor and his father was crouched over her with his hands around her throat.

'Go back to bed, you,' Alexander hissed, without even looking around.

'None of us are going back to bed. Not until you leave Mum alone,' Hazel bravely defied him.

The sound of his first-born's voice was enough to jolt Alexander Boyle back to reality. He loosened his grip around his wife's throat and gingerly stood up. He grinned at Hazel. A stupid, drunken grin. 'You going to give your dad a hug then?'

Knowing it would be better for her mother if she did, Hazel walked towards him and put her arms around his waist.

'Daddy's home. Come on you two. Give your old man a hug.'

Linda was hiding behind her brother's back, but when Tommy squeezed her hand and led her over to their father, she also guessed playing normal was the right thing to do.

Valerie stood up. Her left eye socket was throbbing where the bastard had given her a right-hander. Alexander had his back towards her, so she brushed herself down and locked eyes with her beloved son. 'Thank you,' she mouthed.

* * *

Unable to sleep, Tommy thought about his family. They were happy most of the time and all parents argued, he supposed.

His mum was from Poplar originally. She was bubbly and laughed a lot. She had sea-blue eyes and her smile could light up a room. There'd been rows in the past caused by other men chatting to his mum. His father had hit a man at Old Mother Flynn's daughter's wedding because he said the man was taking liberties with his mother.

Since his dad had gone to work on the oil rigs things had got better. His last few visits home had been such good fun and there hadn't been a cross word. Tommy wasn't sure why Nanny Noreen wasn't a fan of his mum. Hazel reckoned that was because their mother wasn't Catholic and she had liked their dad's first wife. She was very religious, Nanny Noreen, and his mum didn't believe in religion. His dad did though, especially when it came to football. He was a big Celtic fan and hated Glasgow Rangers with a passion. He called them 'Protestant scum' and had been raging when they'd won the UEFA Cup Winners Cup at the Nou Camp earlier this year. His dad's sorrow had turned to joy when Rangers had got banned from defending the trophy thanks to a pitch invasion from their fans. 'Serves the Protestant scum right, lad,' he'd chuckled, doing a jig of unbridled joy.

Unlike most of his friends, Tommy had no cousins. His dad had a brother who lived in Scotland, but they didn't speak. Tommy had no idea why they'd fallen out because nobody ever wanted to talk about such things.

His mum also had a brother, but he had no children and they rarely saw him anyway. Uncle Ian lived in South London and Tommy's dad said he was a 'weirdo'. Even his mum didn't seem to like Uncle Ian very much.

Tommy liked the house he lived in. It was ever so modern with brown and orange patterned wallpaper. Apparently, when he was little they'd lived in a house in Seven Kings. Tommy didn't remember that, the one they lived in now in Barking was all he could recall. Unlike most of his pals, Tommy had his own bedroom that he'd decorated with posters of his favourite footballers. He was a Celtic fan like his father, but Tottenham Hotspur was his English team. He had decided to become a Spurs fan after watching them win the UEFA Cup Final in May. Martin Chivers and Alan Mullery had scored the goals. Chivers was Tommy's favourite player.

Hearing Rex howling outside, Tommy prayed that he wouldn't wake his dad. He had heard his father come up to bed about an hour ago, but not his mum.

Linda stirred as her brother got out of bed. She could never sleep alone if her parents had been fighting. 'Where you going, Tommy? Has Father Christmas arrived?'

'No. You go back to sleep. I'm going to check on Rex. I won't be long.'

Aware his father was snoring like a pig, Tommy tiptoed down the stairs. It wasn't just Rex he wanted to check on. Sleep would not come unless he was sure his mother was all right.

Valerie Boyle was sitting by the lit-up Christmas tree wrapping the last of the children's presents. She could barely see out of her left eye now, the socket was so swollen.

Tommy crouched next to her. 'Are you OK, Mum?' he asked softly.

Willing herself not to cry, Valerie forced a smile. 'Of course I am. Tough as old boots, me.'

'Is Dad still angry?'

'No. I don't think so.'

'Who is Terry Fletcher, Mum?'

No way could Valerie tell her son the truth. Not only would it break his heart, she would hate him to think badly of her. She shrugged. 'I have no idea, Tom. You know what your father is like when he gets a bee in his bonnet, especially if he's been drinking.'

Satisfied his mother would never lie to him, Tommy nodded. 'Rex is howling. I think he must be cold. Can I bring him in the kitchen? I will sleep with him and I promise I'll put him outside before Dad gets up in the morning.'

Valerie reached her arm out and stroked her son's cheek. Tommy was a good boy with a big heart. 'Go on then. I'm going to sleep on the sofa tonight anyway, so I'll hear your dad getting up.'

Valerie finished wrapping the presents, then went to check on Tommy. He was fast asleep on the lino and so was Rex. She covered them both with a blanket, then glanced at her face in the bathroom mirror. She looked a mess and she would have to endure her bastard of a husband's sanctimonious mother tomorrow. 'You're an animal, Alexander Boyle,' she mumbled. 'Merry bloody Christmas.'

CHAPTER TWO

Christmas morning started out like any other. The kids opened their presents, then watched *Clapperboard's Christmas Cracker* and *Play School* while munching on home-made sausage rolls. Considering the events of the previous evening, the atmosphere was relatively normal. The only telling sign of the drama was their mother's swollen eye.

Alexander poked his head around the lounge door. Hazel was engrossed in her *Jackie* annual, Tommy in his *Roy of the Rovers* and Linda's head was in a *St Trinian's* book. 'Look what I found in the dining room,' Alexander grinned.

Realizing they had more presents, all three children jumped up excitedly.

'Wow! A real Celtic kit, like the actual players wear. Look, Mum,' Tommy gabbled, taking his tank top and shirt off and putting the top on. 'Can I wear it today? Please can I, Dad?'

Alexander chuckled. 'I don't see why not – do you, Mum?'

Valerie forced a smile. She loved Christmas as a rule, always decorated the house with a huge tree, paper chains, tinsel, and put all the cards up on the wall either side of the fireplace. She even blew up an enormous inflatable snowman; he stood in the corner next to the glass cabinet she kept her collection of china dolls in. This year, however, apart from enjoying the children's excitement when opening their gifts, Valerie was only going through the motions. She was counting down the days until her husband went back to work and she could spend time with the man she truly loved.

'Oh my God! It's those yellow dungarees we saw in Rathbone market,' Hazel exclaimed. 'I love them. Can I put them on now?'

'Go on then,' Alexander laughed.

'Barbie and Ken! And they're wearing cords like you made me, Tommy and Hazel, Mum.' Linda was over the moon.

Valerie smiled. She was a dab hand with a sewing machine. Not only did she make lots of pretty frocks for herself, whenever the kids spotted one of their idols on *Top of the Pops* or in a magazine wearing something they desired, Valerie would find a pattern and make them an identical version. 'Your father and I wrote to Father Christmas ourselves because we knew how much you wanted Barbie and Ken, didn't we, Alex?'

'We sure did. And this is for you,' Alexander replied, handing Valerie a gift. He hadn't forgiven her. Would never forgive her for the past. But he only had Irish Tony's word on seeing her out with Terry Fletcher and, to be fair, Irish Tony was always pissed and rarely knew what day it was. Valerie had sworn to him last night that the only times she had been out of an evening while he was working away was to the bingo with her mate Lisa, so for the children's sake Alexander had chosen to believe that. For now, at least.

'Thank you, Alex. They're beautiful,' Valerie said, darting off to the bathroom mirror to secure the knotted gold hoops to her ears. She didn't like them much, preferred dangly earrings, but she was determined to play the dutiful wife for the sake of her kids. She had quite liked the perfume Alex had given her earlier, which was a bonus. Aliage by Estée Lauder. She'd been amazed he'd got that right. Every year he bought her scent and he usually got it so very wrong. She liked musky perfumes and no matter how many times she told Alexander that, she always ended up with something with a sickly sweet aroma.

Having already received numerous presents from his wife and children, Alexander was surprised when Tommy ran out of the room then returned with another. 'I chose this and bought it out of my pocket money, Dad.'

Alexander ripped off the wrapping paper. It was a small framed photo of the victorious Celtic side who had won the league last season.

'I thought you could take it to the oil rig with you,' Tommy suggested.

Alexander stood up and ruffled the boy's head. Tommy was a lovable kid, but Alexander could never love him, not properly anyway. He glared at Valerie. 'I'm off to the pub now. I'll pick my mum up on the way home.'

'What pub you going to?' Valerie asked, her heart in her mouth.

Alexander liked to drink back in his old stamping ground Seven Kings, rather than Barking. 'The Joker,' he replied. 'Why?'

Valerie breathed a sigh of relief and smiled. Terry Fletcher wouldn't be in there. 'No reason. Have fun. Dinner will be ready at half three.'

'Why isn't David on here? He's so much better than Chuck Berry. "My Ding-A-Ling" is a stupid song,' Hazel complained.

Tommy rolled his eyes. What was it with girls? His eldest sister was in love with David Cassidy. 'Because David's a poofta.'

Hazel punched her brother in the arm. 'No, he is not.'

Watching *Top of the Pops* was a ritual in the Boyle household. Tommy liked David Bowie, but he would never admit that to the lads at school because David wore make-up and he would get ribbed for it.

'Yes! Jimmy's on,' Linda squealed, jumping up and down with excitement.

'They didn't even have the Shangri-Las on there,' Hazel moaned. 'Leader of the Pack' was her current favourite record. It reminded her of Jimmy Young, who lived across the road. He was a bad boy who rode a motorbike. He was also very handsome.

Valerie was singing along, merrily basting the potatoes when she heard Alexander arrive home. Her heart beat rapidly and she said a silent prayer he wasn't half-cut. She would hate him to spoil the kids' Christmas by kicking off again. 'Did you have a nice time?' she shouted out. She could hear the nervousness in her own voice.

'So-so. Come and say hello to Mum then,' Alexander bellowed. Irish Tony had wound him up again. 'I'm more than ninety-nine per cent sure it was your Valerie with Terry Fletcher, Alex. I'm a hundred per cent. I saw 'em holding hands.'

'Hello, Noreen. Merry Christmas,' Valerie said, wiping her hands on her apron before kissing the old cow on the cheek. She could tell Alexander had heard more gossip due to the sneer on his face.

'Oh dear! Looks nasty, that eye. Walk into another door, did you?' Noreen knew full well her son clumped Valerie at times and she didn't have an ounce of sympathy for the woman. Valerie was a born flirt and, unfortunately for Alexander, she couldn't keep her knickers on. Noreen would never forgive her for how she'd treated her son and she rued the day Alexander ever met the whore. His first wife Mary had been a lovely lady.

'Dad's still got the hump with Mum. You don't think they'll fight again, do you?' Hazel whispered in her brother's ear.

Tommy shrugged. He'd been doing a lot of shrugging lately.

Valerie Boyle was a good cook and had gone to town as per usual with the Christmas dinner. The turkey was succulent, the stuffing crispy, the parsnips just on the right side of burnt and the vegetables not too soft.

'Bit soggy, these roast potatoes,' Noreen complained, pushing the spuds to one side of her plate.

Tommy glared at his grandmother. She wasn't a loving woman and he could tell Hazel was her favourite. 'I like the potatoes. It's a nice dinner, Mum.'

'You would say that, wouldn't you? You're your mother's son all right,' Noreen spat.

'What's that supposed to mean?' Tommy asked.

'Don't answer your grandma back, eat your dinner, boy,' Alexander ordered.

'You never answered my question, Valerie. What happened to your face?' Noreen pried. Her son hadn't mentioned anything was amiss on the journey.

Aware of her children's eyes on her, Valerie cleared her throat. 'I tripped and fell down the stairs.'

Noreen pursed her lips. She knew Valerie was lying, guessed she'd been hawking her mutton again. 'Best you be more careful in future then, eh?'

'Hello, Rex. Look what I got for you, boy. You'll like this. It's turkey,' Tommy said, stroking his best mate. Rex looked so forlorn living in his kennel, it broke Tommy's heart. But his dad wouldn't budge, not even when he'd begged to let Rex inside for Christmas Day. 'It's a dog, Tommy. Dogs live in kennels and humans live in houses. Fact.'

Rex nuzzled his head inside Tommy's navy blue Parka. He hated being out in the cold, alone.

Alexander dropped his mother home early evening, then drove back towards Barking with a face like thunder. Irish Tony's words had been on his mind all day and it had been an effort playing happy families.

He was far too embarrassed to admit the truth to his mother. She'd warned him not to leave Mary for Valerie in the first place, and he felt like a bloody fool.

'How could you do this to me, you bitch?' Alex mumbled under his breath. He loved Valerie with a burning passion. She was an absolute stunner and the thought of another man even touching her filled him with rage. He'd always been insanely jealous, couldn't help himself. Perhaps he should hand in his notice? Quit the oil rigs and stay at home where he could keep a watchful eye on her. Trouble with that idea was, local jobs paid nowhere near what he earned on the rigs and they had a very expensive mortgage. Only other option was to pay this Terry Fletcher a visit and warn him off. Alexander didn't know the bloke personally but had heard through the grapevine he was married and lived in Barking with his wife and two kids. Alexander didn't want to turn up at Terry's door in case the wife chucked him out. That would only push him and Valerie closer together.

Alexander punched his steering wheel in frustration. 'Slag.'

Valerie Boyle put the Party Susan on the dining table. 'Supper's ready, kids. Would you like me to bring a plate of sandwiches in the lounge to you, Alex?' she shouted out. Her husband was sitting in his favourite armchair, knocking back the Scotch like it was going out of style.

'I'm not hungry,' Alexander replied.

'Whassa matter with Dad, Mum?' Linda asked. It

was clear to all three children that after dropping their nan off their father had arrived home in a foul mood.

'He's probably just tired and winding down from work. Why don't you three take your sandwiches and pickles upstairs, eat them in your bedrooms. You don't have to go to sleep yet. You can play with your toys upstairs too.' Valerie was a protective mother, would hate her children to witness any more violence. She had always tried to hide that from them.

'No. I'm staying downstairs with you,' Tommy replied. He was determined not to leave his mother alone with his father. That thought scared him.

The girls went to their bedroom and Tommy sat next to his mother on the sofa. His dad had a film on, but Tommy could tell he wasn't really watching it. His mood was tense and you could cut the atmosphere with a knife. 'What's this film about, Dad?' Tommy asked.

'It's about a slag, son. A slag who has affairs while her old man is working away.'

Valerie felt her heart lurch. 'Please don't say such things to Tommy, Alex. I have done nothing wrong. I told you that last night.'

'That isn't what Irish Tony says. He's seen you out with your fancy man, holding hands. How often does your mother go out of a night, Tommy?'

'Not much. Once a week usually, to the bingo,' Tommy lied.

'Hazel, Linda, get down here a minute,' Alexander bellowed.

'For goodness' sake, Alex. Please don't do this, not

on Christmas Day. If you want to argue with me, then fine. But leave the children out of it,' Valerie urged.

Hazel precariously poked her head around the lounge door. 'What's up?'

'Come in the room properly,' Alexander ordered. 'Stand in front of me and look me in the eyes, love.'

'Why?'

'Because I want to ask you something.'

'Me too?' Linda enquired, looking at Tommy, who stared at her, willing her not to put her foot in anything.

Alexander held his eldest daughter's hand. 'Don't you dare lie to me, Hazel, this is important. I want to know how often your mother goes out of a night?'

Hazel didn't know how to respond. She didn't want to get her mum into trouble but neither did she want to lie to her dad. 'Sometimes she goes out,' Hazel mumbled.

'Yes, but how many times? Think back to, say, last week. You can remember that clearly, can't you?'

Hazel nodded.

'How many times did your mother go out of an evening last week? Mind, I will check with the neighbours and if I find out you've fibbed to me, you'll get no pocket money for a whole year. Do you understand?'

Valerie squeezed Tommy's trembling hand. 'Please stop this nonsense, Alex. The children don't deserve it.'

Hazel chewed nervously on her lower lip. She got far more pocket money than any of her friends and she would hate not to be able to buy her records, favourite magazines and sweets. 'Five times, Dad. Mum went out five times last week in the evening.'

'Thank you, Hazel. You and Linda can go back upstairs now.'

Alexander waited until the front-room door was shut, then leapt up and whacked Tommy hard around the head. 'That's for fucking lying to me. Now get your arse up them stairs and I won't be taking you to football tomorrow either.'

Tommy burst into tears and ran from the room. He had been so excited about attending his first ever proper football match, had been bragging about it at school before he broke up. What was he meant to say to his pals now?

Valerie winced as Alexander moved closer to her. She knew what was coming next and had little choice but to take it.

Alexander punched his wife in the side of the head, then pinned her to the carpet. His breath smelled of Scotch, his face etched in a sneer. 'You're my woman. Nobody else's. You belong to me,' he spat as he ripped her knickers off. Seconds later he raped her, brutally.

CHAPTER THREE

The rest of the festive season went quite quickly with no more major drama. Tommy had heard his parents doing naughties as his bedroom was next to theirs, so he guessed they must have made up.

On 3 January, Alexander hugged his family and said his goodbyes. 'I meant what I said, Valerie. I am paying someone to watch you,' he warned before strolling down the path with his case.

'You OK, Mum?' Tommy asked, as his father disappeared in the distance.

'I am now. Go and let Rex in, love.'

'You look nice, Mum. You going out?' Linda asked, later that afternoon. Her mum was wearing a pretty green flowery frock she hadn't seen before.

'Yes. Only popping round Lisa's. I haven't seen her all over Christmas and want to give her her present. I won't be late. Don't forget to get all your stuff ready for school. I'll be back before you go to bed.'

'You not going bingo?' Hazel asked suspiciously.

'Not sure. We might.'

Tommy gave his mother a hug. 'Me and Rex will look after the girls. Have a nice time.'

'I'm the oldest. So it's me who looks after you,' Hazel argued.

Valerie kissed her son on the forehead. 'Be good. Love you.'

As Tommy waved his mother goodbye at the front door, he had no idea he would never see her again.

Terry Fletcher opened a Babycham for Valerie and a can of bitter for himself. He didn't have a lot of spare cash, especially at Christmas, but he'd scraped together enough to book himself and Valerie a hotel room today. Usually they would do the deed in the back of his Ford Cortina, but it was bloody freezing and Terry had wanted to treat the woman he loved.

'So, how was your Christmas?' Valerie asked. She'd just been telling Terry what a dreadful time she'd had with Alexander.

'Same old, same old. Susan was her usual miserable self,' Terry replied, referring to his wife.

'Your kids enjoy it?'

'Yeah. Kids always enjoy Christmas, don't they? Did yours have fun?'

'No. To be honest, they didn't. They're getting older now, sense what is going on more. Which is why I've come to a decision.'

Terry was the total opposite to Alexander in every way imaginable. He was blond, had a cheeky grin, sparkling blue eyes and a bubbly personality. He worked as a docker and at thirty was two years younger than Valerie. He'd been married for fourteen years though, had got Susan pregnant when she was sweet sixteen and was forced into a shotgun wedding by her father. 'What you decided, my love?'

'That I'm leaving him, Terry. I hate him with a passion. It's you I want to be with.'

Terry puffed his cheeks out. He hadn't been expecting this. 'I do love you, Val, more than anything, you know that. But where we going to live? And what about the kids? It's awkward, isn't it?'

'There's stuff you don't know, Terry. About Alexander.'

Terry knew that Alexander knocked Valerie about and would have done something about it ages ago if he could. But for obvious reasons, he couldn't. He squeezed his lover's hand. 'Tell me.'

Tears streaming down her face, Valerie admitted the one thing she had vowed never to admit to anybody. 'He gets off on our arguments and fights, Terry. Then afterwards, he rapes me.'

'You fucking what! I'll kill the bastard.'

The roads were treacherous, thanks to the snow and freezing conditions. 'This is a joke, Val. No way are we going to get home in this. We're going to have to turn around and go back to the hotel,' Terry said. The hotel he'd booked was in Canvey, miles away from Barking, and it was becoming impossible to steer the car. The roads were like an ice rink.

'I can't leave the kids alone, Terry. They'll be worried sick. I've never left them all night before.'

'Can't you call them from the hotel? I can't drive back to Barking in this. It's too dangerous.'

Imagining her beloved children looking out of the window, wondering where she'd got to, Valerie shook her head. 'No. I have to get back, Terry. Tonight.'

Tommy Boyle stared out of the window. There was a kind of eeriness about the stormy weather; nobody was about and a dog was howling in the distance. He was getting worried now as his mother always came home when she said she would.

Hazel and Linda were sitting next to the blazing coal fire with Rex. 'Where do you reckon she is, Tom?' Hazel asked.

'I told you a hundred times already, I don't know,' Tommy snapped. 'Go look for her address book again, see if you can find Lisa's number,' Tommy ordered.

'I looked everywhere already. Linda reckons she put it in her handbag.'

'I'm sure I saw her put it in her handbag earlier, Tommy,' Linda insisted.

'I'm going to get dressed and walk to Lisa's house. You two stay here and do not answer the door to anyone,' Tommy ordered. He was ready for bed, had his pyjamas on.

'You can't go out this time of night on your own, Tommy,' Linda warned. 'If Mum comes home and you're not here, she will be furious.'

'Linda's right. Besides, you'll freeze to death. There was ice on the inside of our bedroom window earlier,' Hazel stated.

'I'll be fine. I'll take Rex with me.'

* * *

Hazel and Linda waited anxiously for their brother to return home.

'He's back, Haze,' Linda squealed.

Hazel bolted to the front door and yanked it open. 'Did you see Lisa? Is Mum with her?'

Teeth chattering, Tommy sat by the fire rubbing his frozen hands together. 'Mum was with Lisa earlier, then she went to visit another friend. She said the weather must've stopped Mum getting home and we're not to worry. Mum told Lisa if she wasn't able to get home, we were to go to school as normal tomorrow.'

'Thank God for that,' Linda sighed.

Tommy and Hazel went to the same school, but usually walked separately with friends. Today, however, Hazel was waiting outside Tommy's classroom for him and the pair of them ran home together.

Their mum kept a key they all used under the plant pot, and it was Tommy who did the honours. 'Mum, Mum,' he shouted.

Hazel ran up the stairs, then reappeared, crying. 'She ain't been home, Tommy. Mum's make-up is still on the dressing table like it were yesterday. No way would she come home, then go out again without putting her make-up on fresh.'

By teatime, all three children were extremely worried and at a loss what to do. Hazel had warmed up the stew their mother had cooked the day before, but nobody was very hungry. Their mum was a good mum, their world, and she never left them for long periods of time. Even when she went to the bingo she was always back by 9.30 p.m. at the latest to tuck them into bed.

'What we gonna do, Tommy?' asked Linda.

'I'm going to ring Nanny Noreen. She will know what to do,' Hazel replied.

Tommy leapt up. 'No. Don't ring her. Nanny Noreen hates Mum. If you call her, it will only cause more trouble between Mum and Dad.'

'What we meant to do then?' Hazel shrieked.

When his eldest sister began howling louder than Rex ever did, Tommy went outside to get more coal for the fire. He didn't know what to do, he was only twelve, but he was the man of the house and he would decide what was best.

By 10 p.m., Tommy was in panic mode himself, but was trying not to show it as he didn't want to upset his sisters.

'Shall we all walk round to Lisa's house? See if she knows where Mum's other friend lives,' Hazel suggested.

'No. Not tonight. But if Mum isn't back by tomorrow afternoon, then we will,' Tommy replied.

'I'm scared. I think we should call the police,' Linda stated.

'The weather is still really bad. Hopefully, Mum will be home as soon as the ice and snow has thawed,' Tommy said. He sounded far more reassuring than he actually felt.

Hazel's eyes welled up again. 'I got a bad feeling in my tummy about all this.'

Tommy clapped his hands excitedly. 'I know what we can do: pray to that man Nanny Noreen always prays to when she loses something. What's his name? Saint something.'

'Saint Anthony,' Hazel sneered. Her grandmother drove her mad, spouting her religious claptrap. Hazel thought it was rubbish. 'How's he meant to find Mum?'

'I don't know. But he found Nan's wedding ring that time, and her back-door key. It's got to be worth a try, surely?'

'Tommy's right, Hazel,' Linda added. 'If we pray, Mum might come home tonight.'

Hazel shrugged. 'OK then. Do we have to kneel and clasp our hands together?'

'Yes. Let's do it properly. Shut your eyes too,' Tommy ordered. He waited until his sisters were in position, then closed his eyes. 'Please, Saint Anthony, can you find our mum and send her home for us. We will be ever so grateful. Her name is Valerie Boyle. Amen.'

It was the following morning, during history, when Tommy's headmaster entered the classroom. He whispered something in Mrs Jeffries' ear, then she looked directly at him. 'Tommy, do you want to go with Mr Andrews, love.'

'Why?' Tommy mumbled. All the boys were scared of Mr Andrews, who often caned them. As far as Tommy was aware, he'd done nothing wrong.

'Come along, boy,' the headmaster urged.

Outside the classroom was Tommy's next-door neighbour, Mrs Talbot. 'Hello. What you doing here?

Have you seen my mum?' Tommy asked, hoping Saint Anthony had found her.

'I'll get Hazel,' the headmaster said.

'What's going on, Mrs Talbot?' Tommy asked. He had a terrible feeling of unrest in his stomach.

'Your nan's at home, love, with Linda. She'll explain everything to you.'

'What! Nanny Noreen? She's at our house?'

'Yes, Tommy.'

It was at that precise moment Tommy knew something was dreadfully wrong. Nanny Noreen wouldn't set foot in the house unless his dad was at home.

Mrs Talbot said very little on the short journey, then came inside the house with them. The mood was sombre. Nanny Noreen had a face like thunder and Linda was sobbing.

'Whassa matter? Where's Mum?' Tommy asked, dreading the answer.

Linda flung herself at her brother. 'Mum's dead, Tommy. She died.'

Tommy had no idea what being struck by lightning felt like, but he should imagine it was similar to this.

Hazel sank to her knees, screaming blue murder. Even Mrs Talbot was crying and Tommy had never seen her cry before. 'When? How? What happened?' Tommy muttered. They had been studying Jack the Ripper in history and he fleetingly visualized his mum being murdered, like those poor victims had.

'Sit down, children,' Nanny Noreen ordered.

Tommy lifted Hazel off the carpet and all three sat on the sofa, holding hands.

'Your mother was involved in a fatal car crash. She died, along with her fancy man. I've managed to get a message to your father and he's on his way home.'

'Fancy man! Dead! No. She can't be. Mum was visiting her friend Margaret,' Tommy insisted.

'Your mother was a hussy and a liar, boy. She was having it off with a man called Terry Fletcher. He was driving the car when it crashed. How your father will ever live down the shame, I do not know. May your mother's soul burn in hell.'

'Don't say that. We love our mum,' Linda cried.

Hazel was shaking uncontrollably. 'Mum can't be dead. There must be some mistake.'

'Mum's friend Lisa said she was with Margaret,' Tommy repeated.

'Well, I'm afraid your mother's friend is a liar too, Tommy. It's your poor hard-working father I feel sorry for. His side of the bed wasn't even cold and that whore was out fornicating. It is not hard to obey when we love the one whom we obey, is it?' Noreen said, quoting a line from the Bible.

'That's enough now, Noreen. The children are clearly distraught. No matter what you thought of Valerie, they loved her. She's their mother.'

Noreen glared at Mrs Talbot. '*Was* their mother.'

CHAPTER FOUR

Valerie Boyle had been popular within the local community, therefore news of her untimely death, and the circumstances surrounding it, spread like wildfire.

'Where have all Mum's sympathy cards gone, Nan?' Linda made the mistake of asking.

'In the bin, where they belong. Your father will be home this afternoon and he won't be wanting to see those, will he? Not after what your mother did.'

Linda burst into tears. Hazel and Tommy had told her last night what lovely comments the neighbours had written and she'd yet to see them with her own eyes.

Tommy marched over to the bin and took the lid off.

'What do you think you're doing?' Nanny Noreen shouted, yanking Tommy away from the bin by his arm and smacking him across the backside.

'Linda hasn't seen those cards yet. I'm getting them out the bin.'

'No, you're not. I ripped them up into tiny pieces. Now make yourself useful. There's a shopping list on the kitchen top. I need items from the butcher's, the baker's, the greengrocer's and Mr Abbot's. The girls can go with you. You're getting no fresh air stuck in here.'

Lip quivering, Tommy picked up the shopping list and money. It was two days now since they'd heard the life-changing news and Nanny Noreen had not shown an ounce of compassion. Tommy hated living with her and could not wait until his dad got home. 'Come on, girls.'

'I don't want to go to the shops. We'll bump into our mates on their way to school and they will all know about Mum,' Hazel warned.

'You've got to face your friends at some point, love, so best to get that out of the way. It isn't your fault your mother was a whore,' hissed Nanny Noreen.

Tears streaming down both their faces, Linda and Hazel reluctantly followed their brother out the door.

It didn't take the children long to realize the gossip-mongers were out in force. People whispered on street corners, then stopped and looked in pity as they walked past. Some even crossed the road to avoid them. A few of their neighbours were kind. Mrs Young who lived opposite gave them a sixpence each to spend on sweets, and Mr Abbot wouldn't take the money for the baked beans, sugar or brown sauce. 'You put that towards some flowers for your lovely mum,' he said softly.

'We should have brought Rex with us,' Tommy said miserably, as they trudged towards the butcher's. Tommy was worried about his beloved dog. Nanny Noreen wouldn't allow him inside the house, and he could sense Rex was miserable in the kennel. His eyes were forlorn.

About to reply, Hazel heard a voice from behind her scream, 'Oi, I want words with you, Tommy Boyle.' Hazel recognized the voice immediately. It was Billy Fletcher, who was deemed to be the best fighter in her year at school.

His face as angry as hell, Billy ran towards Tommy and pushed him hard in the chest. Tommy stumbled backwards and fell on his arse. 'What did you do that for?'

Billy towered over Tommy. 'Your mother was a slag. If it weren't for her, my dad would still be alive.'

'Takes two to tango,' Tommy mumbled bravely. Billy was at least a foot taller than him and a stone heavier.

'My mum is in bits, thanks to your whore of a mother,' Billy shrieked. He then proceeded to kick Tommy in the head and stomach as though he were a football.

Linda burst into tears. 'Stop it! Leave our brother alone,' she yelled, trying to push Billy away. 'Do something, Hazel. Do something!'

Not knowing what else to do, Hazel picked up a nearby loose paving stone and cracked Billy over the head with it. He fell to the pavement, and unfortunately for him, smashed his skull against the edge of the kerb.

Cliff the butcher came running out of his shop. 'What's going on?'

Seeing copious amounts of blood oozing from Billy's head, Hazel dropped the paving stone in horror.

News of Billy Fletcher's untimely death and the circumstances surrounding it also spread like wildfire. So much so, Nanny Noreen heard about it minutes before the police knocked on the door. She was distraught, Hazel was her favourite grandchild.

Alexander Boyle arrived home during the mayhem. He was shocked to the core and immediately offered to accompany Hazel to the police station. It was said parents shouldn't have a favourite child, but Hazel was his, by miles. She looked like him and had all his mannerisms. There would never be any doubt over him being her father. None whatsoever.

Stony-faced, Alexander witnessed his daughter being questioned. 'Tell the policemen the truth, love. You need to tell them everything that happened,' he urged.

'I already told you: Billy pushed Tommy over then started to beat him up. Tommy is only small and he's younger than Billy. Billy is in my year at school and all the boys say he is the best fighter. I didn't mean to hurt Billy, I swear I didn't. I just wanted him to stop hurting my brother.'

'Did Tommy say or do anything to antagonize Billy?' asked one of the coppers.

'No. Not really,' Hazel replied truthfully. 'All Tommy said was "It takes two to tango," because Billy called our mum a slag. Since our dad started working away, Tommy is the man of the house.'

Alexander pursed his thin lips. Not any more Tommy wasn't, he thought. Not after all that had happened this week. Things needed to change. Like father, like son.

* * *

Tommy and Linda were huddled up together inside Rex's kennel. Both were scared that Hazel would get into big trouble. They were also discussing their future.

'I don't like Nanny Noreen,' Linda admitted for the first time. 'She has never been like a real nan to us. It's only Hazel she buys nice things for.'

Tommy sighed. Their father was the same, but over the years Tommy had got used to that and learned how to deal with it. 'I think it is because Hazel was the first-born child. I never used to think Dad liked me much, but once I started getting into football things got better. Perhaps we have to find more in common with Nanny Noreen.'

'Like what?' Linda asked. 'All she ever talks about is God. She doesn't even like the Osmonds. She told me Little Jimmy is spreading bad vibes amongst girls my age. What does that mean, Tommy?'

'I don't know. But I really hope Dad and Hazel come home soon. Hazel was only protecting me. It was an accident.'

'All that blood, Tommy. It was awful,' Linda mumbled.

Tommy shut his eyes. Witnessing Billy Fletcher die would haunt him for the rest of his life.

When their father arrived home alone later that evening, both Tommy and Linda were gobsmacked.

'Where's Hazel?' Linda panicked.

Alexander pointed at Tommy. 'Thanks to him, your sister isn't allowed to come home. Now, go to bed. Both of you. This very minute!'

* * *

The next time Tommy and Linda saw Hazel was the day of their mother's funeral. She was outside the chapel with a woman and man they'd never seen before.

Tommy ran over to her. She looked awful, had lost weight and had dark circles under her eyes. 'We've missed you, Hazel. Where you living? Dad hasn't told us anything.'

As her brother tried to hug her, Hazel showed little emotion. 'I'm in a bad girls' home.'

'But you're not a bad girl. You didn't mean to kill Billy Fletcher,' Linda replied bluntly.

Hazel shrugged. This time ten days ago, she had a loving mum and family. Now she was living in a horrible place, with horrible children. She hated it there, wished she was dead.

The chapel was packed to the rafters. Valerie had been a chatterbox who loved nothing more than a good old chinwag as she scrubbed her doorstep, cleaned her windows or walked to the shops. The rumours of how she'd died and who she had been with meant the nosy parkers were all in attendance. Some had barely known Valerie, but felt compelled to attend her funeral.

Tommy sobbed like a baby as he stared at the coffin. His mum had been so pretty and full of life. How could she now be dead and inside that wooden box?

Alexander leaned towards Tommy. 'Stop snivelling. You're showing yourself up,' he hissed.

Tommy bit his lip and pinched himself in the hope it would stop him from crying. He couldn't help being so upset. He had loved his mother dearly.

'I miss her so much, Tommy,' Linda wept.

Tommy squeezed Linda's hand and glanced at Hazel. She was showing no emotion, just staring into space. Uncle Ian locked eyes with him and smiled, so Tommy forced a smile back. The woman and man who had accompanied Hazel were standing at the back of the chapel by the door and Tommy wondered if they were staff from the bad girls' home. He doubted they were Old Bill, as very few women were capable of doing that job. That's what his dad said anyway.

Secretly pleased Nanny Noreen had refused to come, Tommy glanced at his father. His face was devoid of expression. He had been really nasty to him this past week, but Tommy guessed he was sad because of losing his wife and Hazel having to go away. They didn't even watch the football together at the weekend; his dad said he was too busy.

The vicar said some nice things about his mum, but not enough, Tommy thought sadly. She had been much more than just a mother of three. She had cooked delicious dinners, knitted him tank tops, run him up flares on her sewing machine, and taken him to the pictures regularly. She wasn't some average mum, she truly was the best.

When everyone stood up to sing 'The Lord Is My Shepherd', Tommy and Linda both heard shouting. They turned around. The door of the chapel was open and two policemen were struggling with some people.

'Where is she? Where's the evil child who killed my Billy?' Tommy heard a woman bellow. Nobody was singing any more, they were all fixated by the commotion. Tommy stood on the pew to get a better view.

'Murderers! First, my Terry and then Billy. My heart is broken in pieces. May you all rot in hell,' the woman screamed, before being carted off by the police.

'Was that Billy Fletcher's mum?' Linda asked Tommy. She hadn't seen the woman.

Tommy was about to reply when his father yanked him off the pew with such force he twisted his ankle.

Tommy woke up next morning with a throbbing ankle and broken heart. He and Linda had thought their mum would have a grave nearby that they could visit and lay flowers on. It had been a huge shock to find out her body had been burned and all that was left of her now was a pile of ashes.

'You awake, Tommy?'

'Yeah.'

Linda perched herself on the edge of her brother's bed. She had been so upset over the awful events of yesterday, she had wanted to stay with Tommy last night, but Nanny Noreen had forbidden her to. 'You're not a little girl any more, Linda. Brothers and sisters of a certain age shouldn't share the same bed,' she'd snapped.

'Dad wants to take me out for the day, but I don't really want to go,' Linda informed her brother.

'Is he taking me too?'

'No. That's why I don't want to go. Did you hear him come in drunk around midnight? He knocked the grandfather clock over and it smashed. He scares me when he drinks too much.'

'I heard him knock something over. Did he say where he's taking you?'

'No.'

'I ain't staying indoors with that old witch. But I'm too scared to go out in case I bump into any of Billy Fletcher's mates. They're bound to want to beat me up after everything that's happened and I can't even run properly 'cause my ankle hurts too much.'

'I wonder when we will see Hazel again? I don't 'arf miss her, Tom. And Mum.'

Tommy's eyes filled with tears. 'Me too.'

As the children clung together like two lost souls, neither had any idea there was far more upset to come.

'You need to pack a case, Tommy. Your Uncle Ian will be picking you up soon,' said Nanny Noreen.

Tommy dropped his *Shoot* magazine in shock. 'What! Why?'

'Because you're going to stay with him. Your dad can't look after you. He has to go back to work soon.'

'What about Linda? Is she coming too?'

'No. Linda will stay with me.'

Tommy felt his pulse quicken. This didn't sound short-term. 'What about Rex? Where will he live?'

'Rex is going to live on a farm. Be nice for him. He'll have lots of space there to run around,' Noreen lied.

Tommy's face crumpled. 'No. I'm not leaving Rex, or Linda. I can't. I won't.'

'There's no alternative, I'm afraid, Tommy. Your dad's going back to the oil rigs and I can't look after two of you.'

Stifling a sob, Tommy ran out into the garden and crawled inside Rex's kennel. He draped his arms around the dog's neck. 'I'm being sent away to live with my Uncle Ian. You're being sent away too, but not with me. You're going to live on a farm. You'll like it there. Be better than being stuck out here, boy. And I will visit you, I promise. I'm so gonna miss you, though. I love you, never forget that, Rex.'

Within the hour, Tommy's anguish had turned to acute anger. He barely knew his Uncle Ian, had only ever met him about four times. What right did his father have to palm him off like some unwanted rubbish? Any decent man wouldn't go back to the oil rigs. He would stay at home and care for his kids who'd lost their mother, Tommy fumed.

'I made you a fried-egg sandwich,' Nanny Noreen said as Tommy came into the kitchen. She didn't hate the boy, but could never love him either.

'I ain't leaving Linda and I ain't leaving Rex. What time will my dad be home?'

'Not until late. Now, go pack your case. Uncle Ian will be here soon.'

'You can't make me go. I won't,' Tommy yelled, knocking the plate and sandwich on to the lino.

Nanny Noreen sighed. 'You have to. Uncle Ian is your only known blood relative. It's either that or a children's home.'

'What? I don't understand.'

Nanny Noreen actually felt quite sorry for the child and wished Alexander would have told him. 'There is no easy way to say this, Tommy, so I shall just be blunt. Your father isn't your real father; so I'm not your real grandma either. I'm sorry, boy. But you have your mother to thank for that.'

Feeling nauseous and dizzy, Tommy bolted out of the front door.

It was the local bobby, PC Kendall, who found Tommy in a dishevelled state in Barking park. He had only recently joined the police force and Mrs Young had told him, while he was on the beat, that she'd seen young Tommy run from the house in his navy Parka, tartan flares and white trainers, looking extremely distressed.

PC Kendall sat on the bench next to the forlorn figure and ruffled his hair. Valerie Boyle had been a beautiful woman inside and out. A lot of his colleagues had fancied her. They reckoned she was the spitting image of the actress in the *Carry On* films.

'Go away. I want to be alone,' Tommy mumbled.

'I want to help you, Tommy. I'm a policeman and that's my job. I wasn't much older than you when I lost my mum, ya know. Fourteen, and it was tough. It's true what they say, though: time is a healer. I know it doesn't feel like it at the moment, but one day you'll be able to think about your lovely mum and smile again. Nobody can ever take the wonderful memories of her away from you. They last for ever.'

'But it's not just my mum, is it? It's everything.'

PC Kendall sighed. The Hazel incident had been a major talking point at the police station. It wasn't every day a fourteen-year-old girl clumped a lad of the same age over the head with a paving block, killing him stone dead. 'Why don't we get you home, eh? Your dad will be worried and it's cold out here. That wind is bitter today.'

'I ain't got a dad.'

'Course you have. Alexander's your dad.'

Tears streamed down Tommy's face as he looked the local bobby in the eyes. 'He ain't my real dad. My nan told me today. She ain't my real nan either. That's why Rex has to go to live on a farm and I gotta live with Uncle Ian,' he gabbled.

PC Kendall winced. He knew life could be cruel, but not this cruel. Poor little Tommy had lost everything in less than a fortnight. He hugged the freezing boy close to his chest. 'I'm so sorry, mate. I truly am. I know how much you love Rex. So, is Uncle Ian related to your mum?'

'Yeah. He's her weird brother.'

'Weird? What do you mean by that?'

Tommy shrugged. 'My dad – sorry, I mean Alexander – always called him a weirdo. Not to his face, like.'

Though he hadn't been a copper long, this triggered alarm bells in PC Kendall's mind. 'Is your uncle married?'

'Yeah. To a woman called Sandra. She's very fat.'

Kendall relaxed slightly. 'They got kids?'

'No. They got cats.'

'Where do they live?'

'South London, but I don't know the road name. It's a smaller house than ours and not very clean.'

PC Kendall took a notepad out of his pocket and wrote something down. He handed it to Tommy. 'This is the phone number of the police station I work at. Any problems, you call and ask for me, OK?'

Tommy nodded. 'Thank you.'

'Right, let's get you home. I thought we might stop at Mr Abbot's on the way and buy you some sweets. What's your favourite?'

'Sherbet lemons.'

PC Kendall smiled. 'Sherbet lemons it is then.'

CHAPTER FIVE

So, that's where it all began. Feels pretty good to get it off my chest, if I'm honest.

It makes me smile to think I once confided in the Old Bill. Having said that, he was all right was PC Kendall. Not like some of the sharks I've since met.

So many coppers are on the payroll of villains, you wouldn't believe it. No integrity or conscience. Always on the take. I know because I've dealt with the unscrupulous bastards. They are worse than most of the gangsters I've mixed with. Reason being, they couldn't give a shit who they trample on. Play ball or get nicked, that's the option for many.

I'm rambling now, so let's go back to my story. From the day my mother died, my life wasn't my own for a while. Saying it had its ups and downs wouldn't just be an understatement. I'd liken it to a Boeing 747 hitting a hurricane.

I was twelve, naïve, and honestly thought I had hit rock bottom. I hadn't. There was far worse to come.

You know the name: Tommy Boyle. Now read on and I'll explain what happened next . . .

Tommy was walking along the canal looking for the stray dog he'd made friends with, when he was unexpectedly jumped on and bundled to the ground.

'No. Give me that back. It's mine,' Tommy insisted as his duffel bag was ripped from his shoulder and the contents tipped on the grass.

'Shut it, ya little squirt,' said one of the lads, aiming a sharp kick at Tommy's head.

Another boy pinned Tommy to the ground.

'Oi! Whaddya think you're doing, Marshall? Leave him the fuck alone,' bellowed a voice in the distance.

When his attackers fled without his belongings, Tommy sat up and locked eyes with a dark-haired lad who looked slightly familiar. 'You all right?' the boy asked.

'Yeah. Thanks for that.'

'You're the new boy at school, ain't ya?'

Tommy nodded and stood up. The boy was a lot taller than him. 'You in my year?'

'Yeah. I'm Danny. Danny Darling.'

'I'm Tommy Boyle. Who were them boys, by the way? Do they go to our school?'

'Nah. They live on the Walworth Road side. Us Bermondsey boys don't like 'em. You won't get no more grief from that lot. I already did three of 'em over.'

Tommy's eyes widened. 'Are you a good fighter then?'

Danny grinned. 'Yeah. I'm a boxer. Gonna be a pro one day. You should try it, ya know. Look at my muscles,' Danny bragged, taking off his jacket.

Tommy felt Danny's biceps. 'Wow! I dunno if I'd be any good, mind. I'm too short.'

'No, you're not. A lot of the best boxers are short lads. There's all different weights in boxing. Come on, I'll show you the gym.'

And just like that a friendship that would last a life-time began.

Lynn's Boxing Club was off Albany Road, and as soon as Tommy walked inside he was filled with a sense of excitement.

The smell, talk and general atmosphere was electric and Tommy couldn't take his eyes off the lads sparring in the ring. Alexander had never been into boxing, therefore Tommy had little knowledge of it up until now.

'See that lad in the photo on the wall – the one in the blue shorts holding a trophy?'

'Yeah.'

'That's my elder brother, Ronnie. He's turned semi-pro now, but my trainer reckons I'm far better than he was at the same age.'

'Really! How old are you then? And how old's Ronnie?'

'I'm in your year at school, you numpty. Thirteen, I am. Ronnie's eighteen, and I got a younger brother Eugene who's ten. I also got a sister, Donna. She's fifteen. You got brothers and sisters?'

'Two sisters: Hazel and Linda. I don't live with 'em no more, though. I got sent to live with my uncle.'

'Why?'

''Cause my mum died in a car crash and I then found out my dad weren't my real dad.'

'That's well shit. Bet you miss your mum.'

'I do.'

'I miss my dad too. He's been in prison for the past ten years, but he'll be out soon.'

Tommy's eyes widened. 'Why has he been in prison?'

'Because he murdered someone. He shot them with a gun.'

'My sister Hazel murdered someone too, with a paving stone.'

'Really?'

'Yeah. The police took her away then sent her to a bad girls' home.'

'Wow! That's mental. Shall we spar in the ring? I won't hurt you, I promise. I wanna teach you how to protect yourself.'

Tommy grinned. 'Yeah, I'd like that.'

'There we are. All tucked in. Would you like me to bring you up a mug of cocoa and a couple of chocolate digestives, Tommy?' Uncle Ian asked.

Tommy faked a yawn. 'No, thank you. I'm very tired tonight.'

Uncle Ian kissed Tommy on the forehead. 'Night, night then. Don't let the bed bugs bite,' he grinned.

When his uncle left the room, Tommy smiled as he thought about his magical day. It was seven weeks now since his mum had died, and this was the first time he'd felt truly happy since.

Moving to South London hadn't been easy. Uncle Ian and Auntie Sandra lived in a two-bedroom house off the Old Kent Road. Tommy's mother's house had been spotlessly clean, but Auntie Sandra's wasn't. It was shabby, dusty, smelled of cat's piss and very often there were shit stains down the toilet for days on end. She didn't even have a toilet brush and bought the most awful toilet paper. It wasn't soft like his mother had used. It was like grease-paper, and Tommy struggled to clean his bottom properly with it.

Auntie Sandra was a short, fat woman who ate like a horse. She rarely bathed and her hair was long, grey and greasy. She stank too, of sweat and another odour Tommy could not quite distinguish. She was all right towards him, but he could sense she didn't really want him there.

Uncle Ian, on the other hand, had been very welcoming and generous. He bought Tommy all his football magazines, and as many sweets as he wanted. He'd recently surprised him with the best kite Tommy had ever seen. It looked like a big multicoloured eagle. Uncle Ian had even promised to buy him a portable TV for his thirteenth birthday, which he could watch alone in his bedroom. Tommy was elated by this news, as the small TV downstairs was rarely switched on. Auntie Sandra and Uncle Ian only ever watched the news and Tommy felt awkward asking if he could watch *Top of the Pops* or *The Big Match*. He would also feel a bit silly watching such programmes with them. Neither of them were into pop music or football. They listened to the radio and played board games such as chess or draughts.

Starting a new school hadn't been easy either. Tommy had felt invisible at times, like a lost sheep. Hopefully, now he'd met Danny all that would change. They were walking to school together tomorrow and going back to the boxing gym after their lessons.

For once, Tommy drifted off into a happy sleep. But at 4 a.m. he woke in a cold sweat. It was the usual kind of nightmare. In this particular one, Hazel had hit Rex over the head with a paving stone and killed him. Then his mother had told him she wasn't his real mother.

'I didn't know you lived at number forty-four. Nobody likes your aunt and uncle, ya know. My mum calls them oddballs,' Danny informed Tommy after school the following day. 'And your aunt well stinks,' he added.

Munching on a bag of chips dripping in vinegar, Tommy suddenly didn't feel hungry any more. He felt embarrassed.

Uncle Ian was a short, dumpy man who wore thick-rimmed glasses and old-fashioned clothes. Tommy thought he looked like the comedian Benny Hill, but he was far less cool. At least Benny Hill was funny. 'My mum was nothing like my uncle.' Tommy squirmed. 'Wanna see a photo of her?' He carried one around with him; it made him feel she was still with him.

Danny nodded, then studied the image. 'She is very pretty. She looks like Barbara Windsor. My brother Ronnie well fancies Barbara.'

Tommy handed Danny another photo. 'That's my sisters and my dog Rex.'

'Are you keeping in touch with your sisters?'

'No. I tried to, but the phone has been cut off where Linda is living and she hasn't replied to my letters. I don't even have an address for Hazel.'

'Where's your dog?'

'Alexander found him a farm to live on in Essex.'

Danny felt sorry for Tommy. It had been tough for him over the years because his dad was inside, but at least he had his brothers, mum and sister. 'Wanna come round mine for Sunday dinner? My mum cooks an ace roast.'

Tommy nodded. Auntie Sandra's roast was the worst he'd ever tasted. 'Yes, please. You sure that will be OK with your mum?'

'Yeah, course. Don't say where you're going, though. My family have got a bit of a reputation round 'ere. Your aunt and uncle might try and stop us being pals,' Danny warned.

'I won't. I promise.'

'Cool. You wanna go to the boxing gym now?'

Tommy grinned. 'Yeah. Race ya there.'

On the Saturday morning, Tommy was bored, so lay on his bed reading his football magazines. Danny wasn't around today. His elder brother had recently bought a car, so he'd driven Danny up north to watch Millwall play away.

Tommy much preferred spending time alone in his room than downstairs. He had very little in common with his aunt or uncle, which made it a struggle to find subjects to talk to them about. He had a portable radio in his room, so would rather listen to his favourite stations, alone.

A tap on his bedroom door made Tommy jump. 'Who is it?'

'Uncle Ian. OK to come in?'

'Yes. Of course.'

Tommy smiled as Uncle Ian sat on the edge of his bed. As usual, he was at a loss for what to say. If a person didn't like pop music, TV, or football, Tommy had come to the conclusion it was difficult to have a conversation with them. Those were the main topics of conversation in his old house.

'Sandra is going to visit her sister in the Isle of Sheppey today. She won't be back until tomorrow. So, I thought you and I might do something nice.'

Tommy's heart sank. Saturday afternoons were all about listening to the football results come in. 'Like what?'

'Well, the wind seems reasonably strong. How about we go to the park and fly your kite? I thought I would treat you too. I know how much you want a record player in your bedroom.'

Having missed his old record player almost as much as he missed Rex, Tommy flung his arms around his uncle's plump shoulders. 'Thank you. I would love that.'

Flying the kite was a bit of a let-down. The wind had dropped and the kite wouldn't stay up in the air for long.

'Cor, look at that, Uncle Ian!' Tommy was transfixed by the red and orange plane some boy was flying.

'Do you like aeroplanes, Tommy?'

'Never been in a real one, but I like that. It's ace.'

'Let's go and ask the boy's dad where he bought it from then.'

'Why?'

'So we can get you one.'

'No. You've been too kind to me already and I don't expect you to keep buying me things.'

'I can afford it. That's why I go to work in the factory.' Uncle Ian put an arm around Tommy's shoulders. 'I just want you to be happy.'

Tommy felt uncomfortable, but couldn't put his finger on why. 'I am happy. Thank you,' he mumbled.

Tommy was thrilled with the record player from Dixons, then even more elated when Uncle Ian handed him a fiver and suggested they stop at a record shop. 'You're going to need some vinyl to play on it, aren't you? Go on, take it,' his uncle urged.

Tommy excitedly leapt out of the rusty Morris Minor. Slade were currently topping the charts with 'Cum On Feel The Noize' and he couldn't wait to get his hands on that. 'How much can I spend?'

'All of it. Want me to come inside the shop with you?'

'No,' Tommy said, rather too abruptly. Record shops were for cool dudes and he would hate to be spotted inside one with his uncle. 'I shall be a while. I'll meet you back at home.'

Uncle Ian pointed towards a pub. 'I'll be in there. Just poke your head around the door when you're ready. I thought we'd stop and get fish and chips on the way home for our tea.'

'OK. See you soon.'

Tommy had never been inside a record shop in South London before and this one was buzzing. The Sweet's 'Blockbuster' blasted out of two giant speakers and the bloke and lady serving behind the counter both wore tartan flares, high shiny red platform boots and black leather jackets. They looked like twins.

Tommy was in his element as he sorted through the vinyl. Seven-inch singles weren't cheap any more, had gone up to fifty pence each, and this was the first time he'd ever had the luxury of buying ten all at once.

Tommy bought Slade, The Strawbs, The Faces, Gary Glitter plus six more, then left the store with a big smile on his face.

'Did you enjoy today, Tommy?' Uncle Ian asked, before stuffing a whole wally in his mouth.

'Yes. Thank you.'

'Best dish in the world this, you know.'

Tommy nodded in agreement. He'd already devoured his cod and chips.

'Fancy a game of chess?'

'I don't know how to play chess,' Tommy replied honestly.

Uncle Ian squeezed his nephew's hand. 'I will teach you.'

Tommy was dying to go upstairs and play his new records, but he didn't want to seem ungrateful or unsociable. 'OK, thank you.'

Uncle Ian set the board up. 'Have you made some new friends at school now? I noticed you've been coming home later.'

'Yes. I have actually. Is it all right if I go out with them tomorrow afternoon? We've organized a game of football over the park,' Tommy lied.

'Of course. You be good to me, Tommy, and I will be good to you, if you get my drift?'

Tommy didn't understand, but smiled and nodded nevertheless.

Tommy stared at the TV in silence. It had been Uncle Ian's idea they pack up the chessboard and watch *Match of the Day* together.

'Who's that who just scored?' asked Uncle Ian.

'Martin Chivers.'

'What team does he play for?'

Tommy glanced at his uncle as though he were an alien. Surely everyone knew who Martin Chivers played for? He had scored the two away goals in the 1972 UEFA Cup Final, for goodness' sake.

'I'm going to run a bath. Sandra doesn't like us to use too much water, but seeing as she isn't here, we'll make the most of it.'

Having missed the regular baths he was allowed to have at home, Tommy nodded in approval. He wanted to be clean and look his best to meet Danny's family tomorrow. 'OK, thanks.'

The first warning bell rang in Tommy's head when his uncle informed him they couldn't be using two lots of water and they had to share the same bath.

'Erm, can't I have a bath after you?'

'No. The water will be dirty and cold. Didn't you ever share a bath with your mother and sisters? Or your dad?'

'Well, yeah. But not for ages. I used to get in after my sisters.'

'We can't upset your Auntie Sandra. I had to fight tooth and nail to take you in and she always checks the water bill.'

Tommy breathed deeply. He could not think of anything worse than having to share a bath with Uncle Ian, but the man had been so kind to him recently, he could hardly refuse. 'OK then.'

Uncle Ian's body looked even more awful with no clothes on and Tommy averted his eyes from the rolls of fat. Thankfully, there were lots of bubbles in the bath and Tommy sat frozen against the end with the plug hurting his bum, while his uncle splashed about like a beached whale at the other, cracking unfunny jokes.

'Want me to scrub your back, Tommy?'

'No, thank you. Can I go to bed now, please?'

'Of course. Let me get you a towel to dry yourself.'

Having not gone through puberty himself, Tommy was shocked as his uncle struggled to get out of the bath. His willy looked huge and hard. Like a snake.

CHAPTER SIX

Suzie Darling was a funny, loud lady with auburn hair, dimples and a welcoming smile. She swore a lot and her house was clean, but not particularly tidy. Tommy immediately felt at home as he sat on the brown Dralon sofa.

'You OK, Tom? Not gone all shy, have ya?' Danny joked.

'I'm fine, thanks,' Tommy lied. He had lain awake most of the night thinking about Uncle Ian. Tommy was yet to get sexual urges himself, but he knew lads who had, and he couldn't help worrying his uncle had been sexually aroused when he'd got out of the bath. Was that why Alexander always called him a weirdo? Was Uncle Ian some kind of pervert?

'Whaddya think of me mum?'

'She's nice and very pretty. Where are your brothers and sister?'

'Eugene's playing football, Donna's gone down Petticoat Lane with her mate and Ronnie's a biker, so he could be anywhere. They'll all be home for dinner though. No one cooks a roast like my mum. She works in the Prince of Wales pub as a cleaner. Do you know it?'

Tommy shook his head.

'She don't earn much, but Ronnie does. He pays for most of our food, bills and rent as my dad's inside.'

'Does Ronnie work as a boxer? Is that his actual job?'

Danny chuckled. 'Nah. He earns some from the boxing, but he does other stuff too.'

'Like what?'

'Same as me dad. Ronnie's a ducker and diver.'

Knowing Danny's father was banged up for murder, Tommy decided not to ask any more questions.

Danny was right about one thing. Suzie Darling cooked an ace roast. Tommy had thought nothing could beat his mother's and felt disloyal even admitting as much to himself.

'Want some more pigs in blankets, Tommy?' Ronnie Darling asked. Danny had told them about the tough time Tommy had been through. They were all shocked who the lad lived with. Ian and Sandra Taylor kept themselves to themselves in this neck of the woods, but even so they weren't liked. Rumours had surfaced a few years back – about Ian in particular.

Tommy grinned and gratefully accepted the food. He liked Ronnie, who had arrived home dressed in black leathers. He was funny and extremely cool.

'Want some more parsnips?' asked Suzie, shoving a load on Tommy's plate. The poor little mite looked like he needed feeding up a bit.

'Thank you, Mrs Darling. This is like a Christmas dinner. It was very kind of you to invite me round.'

Tommy's mother had always told him 'Good manners cost nothing.'

'You're very welcome, my love. Our Danny speaks highly of you. Anytime you want to pop round, feel free. But please call me Suzie. Mrs Darling makes me sound like one of the blue-rinse brigade down East Street market,' Suzie chuckled.

'Do you really live at number forty-four, Tommy?' asked eleven-year-old Eugene. He was quite impressed with Danny's new friend, but he and his pals played knock-down ginger at Tommy's aunt and uncle's house. They called them 'The Stinkies'.

Kicking his youngest brother under the table, Ronnie quickly changed the subject. 'Danny says you like football, Tom. Who do you support?'

'I did support Celtic, but since finding out my dad ain't my dad, I don't want to support them any more. Spurs are my team now.'

Ronnie ruffled the boy's hair. Tommy was a good lad; he could sense that, with an air of vulnerability about him. 'Wanna come over Millwall with me and Danny next Saturday? I'll treat you.'

Tommy's eyes shone. He had yet to attend a proper football match. 'You bet I do. Thank you.'

'Here she is, the latecomer. Dinner's in the oven, burnt, young lady,' tutted Suzie. 'Serves you right for saying you'd be home by three and coming in at four.'

Tommy was rather taken aback when the stunning girl with big blue eyes and glossy long blonde hair sauntered into the kitchen. She was wearing a white catsuit and red platform shiny boots like those people serving in the record shop yesterday. He nudged Danny. 'Is that your sister?'

'Yeah. That's our Donna. Pain in the bloody arse, she is,' Danny laughed.

Eyes as big as organ stops, Tommy stared at the girl. At that moment, he had his first ever sexual feeling and it felt like heaven.

Life returned to normal back at Uncle Ian and Auntie Sandra's house. The dinners were bland, Auntie Sandra spoke to him only when she could be bothered and Tommy spent most of his time in the sanctuary of his bedroom, playing his records and listening to the radio.

On the Saturday he was due to attend the Millwall game, Tommy heard the tap-tap he'd come to dread on his bedroom door. The bath incident had not been mentioned again and Tommy was far too embarrassed to tell Danny about it. 'Who is it?'

'Uncle Ian. OK to come in?'

'Yes. Of course.'

Uncle Ian smiled as he plonked his fat self on the edge of Tommy's bed. 'Sandra is visiting her sister in the Isle of Sheppey again this weekend, so I thought we might do something together. I found a shop that sells those aeroplanes. I'll treat you to one, then we'll fly it over the park. Sound good to you?'

Uncle Ian stank, a mixture of stale sweat and smoke. Tommy had a strip wash every morning at the bathroom sink, but he'd never noticed his uncle or aunt do so. 'I'm sorry, but I'm going out with a friend today.'

'Can't you cancel seeing your friend? I thought you wanted one of those aeroplanes.'

'No. Thank you for offering, but I'm not bothered about having one now.'

Uncle Ian eyed Tommy suspiciously over his thick-rimmed glasses. 'You've been going out an awful lot recently. Where exactly are you going today?'

'Football. I'm going to watch Millwall.'

'You will do no such thing, lad. I am not having you mixing with hooligans. You are my responsibility now.'

'But I can't let my friend down and we are going with an adult. My friend's older brother is eighteen,' Tommy protested.

'Who is this friend of yours? Only you've been spending a lot of time with him recently. You're hardly ever at home.'

Fighting the urge to inform Uncle Ian that this wasn't his home and never would be, Tommy bit his tongue. He felt like crying. 'Johnny – he's in my class at school,' he lied. 'Please let me go, Uncle Ian. I've always wanted to go to a proper football match. I promise I won't be home late. We can spend the evening together and do whatever you want then. Please, I beg you.'

Uncle Ian softened and handed Tommy a pound note. 'Go on then. Enjoy yourself. But I want you home here by seven at the latest.'

Feeling a sense of relief wash over him, Tommy took the money and smiled. 'Thank you.'

Uncle Ian stood up. 'Your friend Johnny. What's his surname?'

There was a lad called Johnny in his class, so Tommy decided to play it safe. 'Rodgers.'

As he left the room, Uncle Ian frowned. He knew the Rodgerses and wasn't aware Johnny had an older brother. Tommy had better not be lying to him. He hated liars.

Tommy was buzzing as he walked towards Millwall's ground. Fans were already singing at the top of their voices and the delicious smell of fried onions wafting from the burger and hotdog stalls made him feel a bit emotional. His mum had cooked lots of meals with onions and that smell reminded him of happier times. He was genuinely happy today though, and was sure his mum would approve of his new friend and Danny's family. They were all very kind to him.

'You hungry, Tommy?' asked Ronnie Darling.

'I am. Get us a burger,' ordered Eugene.

Ronnie grabbed his younger brother in a playful headlock. 'Nobody asked you, ya little squirt. And you'll get sod all until you say the word please,' Ronnie chuckled.

When a group of men collared Ronnie for a chat, he handed Danny a fiver and told him to get them some food.

'Doesn't your brother know a lot of people,' Tommy said to his friend.

Danny grinned proudly. 'Yeah. My dad's even more well known, ya know. My whole family are really. Nobody messes with us. That's why them boys who picked on you ran off sharpish.'

Not wanting to pry, Tommy changed the subject. 'Isn't your brother a biker all the time?' Ronnie wasn't wearing black leathers today. He was dressed in faded flared jeans, trainers, and a black bomber jacket. He looked no different to any other football fan.

'Ronnie's a biker when he wants to be a biker,' Danny laughed. 'He's the master of disguise, my brother. The pigs hate him.'

Not understanding what Danny meant, Tommy decided the best thing to do was smile politely.

'Hello, Ian. How are you and Sandra keeping?' asked Mr Patel the newsagent.

'Yes, we're fine, thank you. Could you make me up an extra-large bag of penny sweets, the kind that twelve-year-old boys like. And I'll take a copy of every football magazine you have, please.'

'Ah, is this for young Tommy who is staying with you?'

'I'm actually Tommy's guardian now. His mother unfortunately died in a car crash.'

'Oh, I am very sorry to hear that. I see Tommy earlier with his friend, young Danny. They buy bubble gum to take to the match with them.'

'Danny who?'

Mr Patel handed Ian five magazines and a big bag of mixed sweets. 'Danny Darling. Everybody knows young Danny around here,' he chuckled.

With a face like thunder, Ian threw the money on the counter, snatched the magazines and sweets out of Mr Patel's hands and stormed out of the shop.

* * *

Tommy Boyle joined in with all the fans chanting 'We are Millwall, from the Den' as he left the ground. Everyone was buoyant and the atmosphere was awesome. Millwall had scored a late winner, but the funniest part of the day had been when the peanut seller had asked Ronnie to look after a sackful. Ronnie had started chucking handfuls in the air, then everybody nearby joined in, including Tommy. The crowd then started singing, 'We hate peanuts and we hate peanuts,' which Tommy thought was hilarious. He'd felt part of something for once, a tribal feeling.

'Wanna come back to ours?' Danny asked, when they made it back to the Old Kent Road.

Tommy's heart suddenly lurched. 'No. Erm . . . I better not.'

'There'll be lots of nice grub. Mum always lays out a big spread for us after we've been to football.'

'I can't. Uncle Ian said I got to be home by seven.' The thought of spending another evening alone with his uncle without Auntie Sandra being around filled Tommy with dread. Say he insisted they share another bath together? Tommy had already made his mind up. No way was he doing that again. It made him feel dirty, not clean.

'Right, I'm off to meet a bird, lads. Make sure you take Eugene straight home, Dan,' ordered Ronnie Darling.

'Thank you so much for taking me to the game today, Ronnie, and paying for me to get in,' said Tommy.

Ronnie ruffled the boy's head. 'You're very welcome,

pal. So, you still a Spurs fan? Or you gonna be a Millwall nutcase, like us?'

Tommy grinned. 'Millwall, definitely.'

'You're late,' Uncle Ian snapped.

Tommy stared at his feet. He'd literally salivated at the mouth when Danny informed him his mother was preparing chicken, ham, beef, pork pies, pickles and hot crusty bread, so had ended up having his tea at his pal's house after all. 'I'm sorry.'

'So, where have you been?'

'Erm, with Johnny,' Tommy lied. 'His mum invited me in and I didn't want to come across as rude. I won't be late again, I promise.'

Uncle Ian forced a smile. 'Come and say hello to our guest.'

Tommy followed his uncle into the small dining room that was adjoined to the lounge. The chessboard was out and there was a bottle of brandy on the table. The man grinning at him was fat, bald and looked older than Uncle Ian. 'Hello,' Tommy said awkwardly.

'This is my friend, PC Norman. He's off duty tonight and wants to have a word with you. I'll leave you to it,' Uncle Ian said, shutting the door.

Tommy eyed the policeman suspiciously. He looked nothing like PC Kendall or any of the other local bobbies in Barking. He wasn't wearing a uniform and Tommy could not but wonder if one would even fit him.

'Sit down, Tommy.' Norman patted the seat next to him.

Tommy did as he was told. 'Have I done something wrong?' he asked innocently.

Norman smiled. 'No. But you are knocking around with a bad crowd. I have said nothing to your uncle as I didn't want to get you into trouble, but those Darlings are bad news. I know you have been to the Millwall game today with Danny. I also know you went back to Danny's house. You must promise me you will have no more to do with that family. Your Uncle Ian has been very good to you, taking you in when nobody else wanted you, so you need to be a good boy for him.'

Tommy was a bit taken aback. 'OK,' he muttered.

'The Darlings are bad people, Tommy. The last lad Danny got friendly with was found floating in the River Thames.'

Tommy's eyes widened. 'No way! Really?'

Norman ruffled Tommy's hair. He was a handsome kid and he could see why Ian was so smitten with him. 'Yes. Really. Keep away from the whole family.'

'What did PC Norman want to talk to you about?' Uncle Ian enquired later that evening.

'Not much. Just told me to be a good boy. Can I go to my room and play some records, please?' Tommy was confused. He felt at ease with Danny and his family, much more at ease than he did with his uncle and aunt.

'Not so fast. I bought you some presents earlier. They're on the kitchen top.'

Instinct told Tommy he shouldn't accept any more big presents from Uncle Ian, so he was relieved to see only sweets and football magazines.

'Well?' Uncle Ian grinned.

Apart from flying saucers and blackjacks, Tommy wasn't a fan of penny sweets. Linda had loved them. She'd scoff bagfuls. But he was chuffed with the football magazines; he only had one out of the five. 'Thanks, Uncle Ian. Can I go to my room and read my mags, please?'

'Not until you've had some supper and a bath.'

Tommy froze. He was yet to get big stonkers himself (that's what the lads at school called them) but he was sure Uncle Ian had had one last time they shared a bath. 'I'm not hungry, I ate at Johnny's. And I'm not dirty, I had a strip wash at the sink this morning.'

'I won't force you to eat, but you have to have a bath, lad. Auntie Sandra doesn't like us to use too much water, so now's the time to have one.'

'No. I don't want one.'

Uncle Ian knocked back his drink and paced the room. 'You are starting to get on my nerves, Tommy. I have been very kind to you, and not only are you lying to me, you are also defying my orders. Do you see me as some kind of a fool? Do you? I know exactly where you have been today and who with, you lying little toerag. Now do as I say. Go run a bath.'

'OK. But I'm getting in it on my own, not with you.'

Uncle Ian grabbed Tommy by the shoulders and pushed him up against the wall. 'I make the rules in this house, not you.'

Tommy felt extremely uncomfortable. Uncle Ian reeked of alcohol, his eyes were glazed and he had a twisted, vicious look on his face that reminded Tommy of

Alexander when he'd come home drunk and lash out at his mother.

'Bullies come in all shapes and sizes. Always stand your ground, Tommy, even if there are four of 'em or a bloke is bigger than you. You'll survive if you get a good hiding. It's better to fight back than surrender,' Ronnie Darling had told him earlier today.

'Tommy, Tommy! Get back here,' Uncle Ian bellowed, when his nephew kicked him hard in the ankle and bolted up the stairs.

Gutted that his brilliant day had been spoiled, Tommy flung himself on his bed and wept. He so wished he could speak to his sisters or hold Rex in his arms once again. He missed his mum most of all though. Why did she have to die? He hated living here.

Ever since his mother had died, Tommy had taken to leaving the radio on low of a night. For some reason, the music comforted him and made him sleep better.

David Bowie's 'John, I'm Only Dancing' was playing when Uncle Ian crept into his room. Tommy decided to pretend he was asleep, as he usually did.

Normally, Uncle Ian would kiss him on the head and turn the radio off, but tonight he was lurking and breathing heavily.

'Leave me alone. What d'ya think you're doing?' Tommy squealed when his uncle put his hand under the blankets and started tugging at his pyjama bottoms.

'Shut it. You belong to me now.'

Tommy tried to scream, but Uncle Ian pinned him down and pushed his face against the pillow.

Wriggling like an eel, Tommy didn't stand a chance against a man who weighed seventeen stone.

Tears streaming down his face, Tommy wanted to die. He had thought losing his mother was the worst thing imaginable, but it wasn't. This was.

CHAPTER SEVEN

Tommy threw a stone into the canal and watched it skim across the muddy water. He'd spent the past few days hanging out here, could not face going to school.

Stroking the stray dog he'd nicknamed Lassie, Tommy pondered his predicament. He had debated whether to call PC Kendall and tell him what had happened, but not only did he feel too ashamed to do so, the pervert's words were still fresh in his mind: 'This has to be our little secret, Tommy. You mustn't tell Auntie Sandra or anyone else. Nobody would believe you anyway.'

The awful happenings of Saturday night had only lasted a few minutes, but to Tommy it had felt like an eternity. One thing he was sure about was it would never happen again. He couldn't and wouldn't allow it to. The pain had been indescribable and he was still struggling to walk properly and go to the toilet.

'There you are!'

Tommy jumped at the sound of his friend's voice.

Danny Darling plonked himself next to Tommy. 'Why ain't you been at school? I was gonna knock on your door yesterday, but I didn't want to get you into trouble.'

'Not been well.'

'What's up with you then?'

'Just a bug.'

Danny eyed Tommy with suspicion. He hadn't known him that long, but Tommy's sparkling eyes and big grin had disappeared completely. 'Has something happened? That Walworth mob ain't picked on you again, have they?'

'No. Not seen 'em.'

'Well, you were fine over Millwall last Saturday and I can tell you're not now. What's wrong? I might be able to help.'

Tommy angrily threw another stone into the canal. 'You won't.'

'Has something happened to one of your sisters?'

'Dunno. Don't hear from 'em.'

'You ain't had agg with those weirdos you're living with, have you?'

Tommy wanted to cry, but instead kept a stiff upper lip. No way could he tell Danny the truth, but he desperately needed some advice. 'If I tell ya something, you got to promise me that you will never breathe a word to anybody.'

'I won't.'

'Swear on your mum's life.'

Danny did as Tommy asked.

'I think my uncle's a pervert. He made me share a bath with him and I noticed he had a big stonker when he got out. I'm scared of what might happen next, Danny. Say he comes into my room of a night or something? Say he touches me?'

'The dirty shitbag. Ronnie was right then. He always

said he was a nonce. Why don't you let me tell Ronnie? He'll sort the bastard out for you.'

'No. You can't tell anybody. You promised you wouldn't.'

'OK. I won't. What about your aunt? Was she at home when he got in the bath with you?'

'No. She stays at her sister's sometimes. If he comes into my room, Dan, what should I do? What would you do?'

'I'd hide a big dagger under my mattress and stab the dirty fucker.'

'Where can I get a big dagger from?'

'Come with me. I'll show you.'

'So, how was school today, Tommy?'

'Fine,' Tommy lied, without looking up. He shoved a whole sausage in his mouth. Mealtimes were the only time he spent in his aunt and uncle's company now and he couldn't bolt his food down quick enough. How could that perve act like nothing had happened? Tommy couldn't even look the bastard in the eye, let alone have a normal conversation with him. The most upsetting thing for Tommy though was that Ian was his mother's brother. His mum had been such a kind, funny, gentle woman. How could they even be remotely related?

'I thought we might go to Battersea Dogs' Home this weekend, Tommy. I know how much you miss Rex and your mum and sisters. Perhaps a new furry companion is the tonic you need to perk you up a bit?'

'The cats won't be happy,' Sandra hissed.

Ian smiled at the woman he'd married out of

convenience. He worked long hours at the factory, was the breadwinner, so she would have no say in the matter. 'I was thinking of a small dog, dear. What do you reckon, Tommy? Would a dog make you happy?'

Tommy pushed his plate away, his face distorted with anger. 'I don't want a dog. I don't want nothing off you.'

When Tommy bolted up the stairs, Sandra scraped the remains of his dinner into the bin, then silently washed the plates. They'd had to move out of their last address as a local lad had accused Ian of inappropriate behaviour. The case had never gone to court, the boy had withdrawn his allegations, and Ian had sworn blind to her he was innocent.

'You OK, love?' Ian asked. 'Tommy will be fine. He's missing his family and dog, that's all.'

Sandra nodded. She had an awful feeling in the pit of her stomach. Perhaps she should cancel stopping over at her sister's next weekend. Only, if history were to repeat itself, she couldn't bear the thought of vigilantes throwing eggs and bricks at the window again. She actually liked living round here.

'I'm sorry, David, but . . .' Tommy said, as he snapped each Bowie record he owned into tiny pieces and chucked them in the bin. No way could he listen to his favourite artist's music ever again. 'John, I'm Only Dancing' had been playing when the pervert had done what he'd done.

Tommy felt incredibly melancholy as the DJ on Radio Caroline played 'Long-Haired Lover from Liverpool'.

He missed his sisters immensely and hoped they were faring better than he was. Nanny Noreen had definitely had her landline cut off or changed. Tommy's guess was she had altered her phone number so he could not contact Linda. He reckoned she had intercepted the post too, as no way would Linda ignore his letters. As for Hazel, Tommy could only pray she was holding her own in the home. She'd always had a fiery temper, so could look after herself.

Picking up his duffel bag, Tommy took out the dagger. He ran his hand gently across the blade and was surprised to see blood spurting out of two of his fingers. Danny had said it was sharp, which was a good thing. Because, if that pervert ever tried to touch him again, Tommy would do what Hazel had done to Billy Fletcher. He would kill him, stone dead.

*

> 'Happy birthday to you,
> Happy birthday to you,
> Happy birthday, dear Mum,
> Happy birthday to you.'

Wishing he could sing 'Happy Birthday' to his own mother once more, Tommy plastered a smile on his face. He had become good at doing that recently, especially in front of the Darlings.

'I bought you these, Suzie,' Tommy announced, handing Danny's mother a box of Milk Tray.

Suzie thanked and hugged the little boy she had become so very fond of. There was a sadness about him and she guessed it was due to all that he had been through. His mother must have been a wonderful woman, Suzie thought. Tommy's manners were impeccable.

'I got you this, Mum,' Danny announced, thrusting a Carpenters album into his mother's hands. It was easy to thieve down that record shop in the Old Kent Road. So simple, he'd also helped himself to three seven-inch singles.

'Here's my present, Mum,' said Donna. She winked at Danny. Woolworths was also a doddle to thieve out of and she had presented her mother with far more than him.

'And last but not least . . .' Ronnie Darling chuckled, dragging a massive square thing into the lounge.

With an arm still around Danny and Donna's shoulders, Suzie looked bemused. 'What the bleedin' hell is that, Ron? Only, I ain't got room for ornaments of that size in my front room.'

Ronnie grinned. 'No more scrubbing the whites and soaking our underwear in a tin bucket for you, Muvver. This does it all for you. It's a washing machine.'

Suzie put her hand over her mouth. 'What! Like the ones they have at the laundrette?'

Ronnie kissed his mother on the forehead. 'Even better, angel. This one has a built-in tumble dryer.'

When Eugene handed her some Mary Quant eyelashes and a bright red lipstick, Suzie hugged each member of her family. 'How lucky am I to have such thoughtful children?'

Suzie turned to Tommy and gave him a second hug. 'And you can be my adopted son. You are welcome here any time, day or night, and I truly mean that, Tom.'

'Thank you.' Seeing Donna smile at him, Tommy quickly averted his eyes. She made his tummy flutter, a feeling he'd never experienced before. She also made him tongue-tied.

Over the next few weeks, Tommy spent more and more time with the Darlings. He was now totally converted to Millwall Football Club, having been to a couple more games, and he couldn't get enough of the boxing gym.

'Tom, enough please. Tommy! What the hell you doing? You're meant to be sparring, lad,' yelled the trainer as he yanked Tommy away from the kid he had pinned to the rope in the corner.

Tommy apologized to the boy and the trainer. He could not help the red mist that seemed to descend upon him the second he stepped inside the ring. All he had to do was think of what life had thrown at him recently, and before he knew it, he was knocking seven bells out of whoever.

'What the fuck is wrong with you lately? Has that nonce done something else to you?' Danny Darling asked, as he and Tommy walked home together.

Luckily for Tommy, 'The Perve' – as he now referred to Uncle Ian – had been giving him a wide berth. Auntie Sandra had not been to visit her sister again and, bar mealtimes, Tommy either hung out with the Darlings or listened to music and read in his room.

Spotting PC Norman, the perve's mate, walking towards him, Tommy ducked behind a nearby wall.

'What you doing now? Ya nutter.'

'That fat geezer, he's Old Bill. Ian is friends with him and if he spots us together, I'm dead.'

Danny burst out laughing. 'Who? Noncey Norm? He ain't the filth, you div. He's the local perve. Stand up. Don't be a wimp.'

Tommy did as he was told and was surprised when Norman crossed over the road and pretended not to see him. 'You sure he ain't Old Bill?'

'Positive. He's another oddball, like your uncle. Why are you dead if he spots us together? What's been said?'

Briefly explaining, Tommy was horrified when Danny chased after the man bellowing, 'Oi, nonce-case, I want a word with you.' Danny was totally fearless.

Tommy chased after his pal and grabbed his arm. 'Leave it, Dan,' he pleaded.

Refusing to look at Tommy, Norman cowered in the bus shelter. He was scared of the Darlings. Jack was a lunatic, which was why he was banged up, and Ronnie wasn't far behind his father. They were like a pack of dogs – if you touched one, the others would be on you. 'Leave me alone. I'll call the police if you touch me.'

'But you are the police, ain't ya? Only that's what you told Tommy, you fucking weirdo. You say one more bad word about me and my family and I will personally make sure Ronnie sorts you out good and proper. Why you lying? Pretending you're something you ain't. Ian put you up to it, did he?'

Norman Jenkins could feel the beads of sweat dripping down his face. He always perspired when cornered or frightened. 'Yes. Ian asked me to say it. I don't know why, I didn't ask. But I'm sorry and I can assure you, nothing of the kind will ever happen again.'

'It had better not, 'cause if it does, Ronnie will break both your fucking legs. You haven't seen me and Tommy together. Understand?'

Norman could barely breathe. He might be forty-two years old, while Danny was only thirteen, but he'd been a coward for as long as he could remember. He hated confrontation, had been picked on at school, and he was annoyed with himself for allowing Ian to talk him into a lie that might land him in trouble with the Darlings. 'I understand. Fully.'

When Norman scuttled away, Tommy slapped his pal on the back. 'That was well ace. He's petrified of you. How comes?'

''Cause I'm a Darling, Tom. Everyone round here is wary of my mob. We ain't a family to be messed with.'

'Do you think I could come and live with you? I would be ever so good and do lots of chores. I hate living with Ian and Sandra.'

'Dunno. I can ask my mum, see what she says.'

'Would ya?'

'Yeah. I'll ask her tonight.'

CHAPTER EIGHT

'Hello. I'm Mrs Ebdon from the children's Social Services department. May I come in, please?'

Ian immediately felt panicky. Surely Tommy hadn't told his teacher or friends what had happened? The boy had been acting strangely, keeping out of his way a lot, but Ian supposed that was to be expected. He remembered the first time the same had happened to him. His mother had been a brass, used to leave himself and Valerie alone of an evening while she earned a few bob on street corners. He was only nine years old when a neighbour whom he'd called 'Uncle Ted' had forced himself upon him while his mother was out grafting. 'How can I help you?' Ian asked, desperately trying to sound composed.

'It's about Tommy. I had a visit from a Mrs Darling asking if Tommy could live with her family. She seems to think it is not working out, Tommy living with you, and he would be happier living with her.'

Ian was livid. 'I have forbidden Tommy to go anywhere near that family. Murderers and scoundrels, the lot of them. I am quite capable of taking care of my own nephew, thanks all the same.'

'Well, this is the thing, you see. We can't just hand children over to families who have no blood ties to the child. They would have to apply to adopt Tommy and, as you say, the family do not have the best of reputations. Mrs Darling was insistent Tommy was unhappy living with you though, which is why I felt the need to pay you a visit. Tommy's welfare has to be top priority. Can I have a little chat with him?'

Having popped to the shops to get a loaf and some corned beef, Sandra returned home. 'Who are you?' she asked, eyeing the woman with suspicion. Sandra knew her house was filthy, and somehow visitors made her even more aware of it. Especially posh-looking ones like the stuck-up cow who was currently standing in her hallway.

Ian gave his wife a warning glance. 'This is Mrs Ebdon from children's Social Services. It seems that Tommy has been knocking around with that awful Darling boy and the mother wishes to adopt him. Tommy's been fine here, hasn't he, love? He's fed and clothed well. That music you can hear is coming from Tommy's bedroom. He's thirteen next week and we've bought him his own portable TV for his bedroom, haven't we, Sandra?'

'Yes. Ian has bought the lad lots of gifts. He wants for nothing.'

'Could I speak with Tommy, please?' Mrs Ebdon asked again.

'Yes, of course. You make Mrs Ebdon a cup of tea, Sandra, while I get Tommy. He's probably not even dressed yet.'

'No tea for me, thank you. I've not long had one,' Mrs Ebdon fibbed. It was one of those dirty homes that smelled of cat's piss, therefore no way would she drink out of a cup.

Lying on his bed singing along to 'Metal Guru', Tommy jumped as his uncle burst into the room. 'What d'ya want?' he asked fearfully. His uncle always knocked first and Tommy could see he didn't look too happy.

Ian turned the music up a touch and grabbed Tommy by the arm. 'There is a woman downstairs from Social Services. She wants to ask you some questions. You are to tell her you are very happy living here, got that? Only, if you tell her any different, I will find out and I won't be best pleased. You know what happened last time you upset me, don't you?'

Feeling nauseous, Tommy gabbled, 'I'll tell her I'm happy. I swear I will.'

'Thank you for your visit,' Ian said curtly as he shut the front door. Mrs Ebdon had spoken to Tommy alone in his room and the devious little scrote had then announced he was off out. Ian hadn't wanted to argue with the lad, not in front of that nosy cow, so had wished Tommy a nice time. He would wait until the ungrateful little shit came home later, then give him what for.

'Why are you drinking?' Sandra asked, as Ian poured himself a large port and brandy. Even he knew that he turned nasty when inebriated, which was why he rarely touched alcohol.

'None of your business. I want you to go and stay

at your sister's tonight. You haven't visited her for a while.'

Sandra felt uneasy. 'Why?'

'Because I bloody said so, woman. Go pack some things. Stay two nights. Off you go.'

As Sandra trudged upstairs, she could not help but feel sorry for Tommy. If Ian was drunk, he was bound to batter the lad when he came home, like he'd battered her in the past. All she could do was hope he did nothing worse than that.

'You should have told the woman the truth. Why didn't you say your uncle got in the bath with you and he had a big stonker? She would have let you live with us then,' Danny Darling stated.

'Because he threatened me, then I heard him come up the stairs. He was earwigging outside my room, I know he was.'

'How did he threaten you? What did he say exactly?'

'Nothing much,' Tommy muttered. 'He just sort of said I'd be in trouble if I didn't say I was happy living there.'

'He needs a clump. You should tell Ronnie everything you've told me.'

'No. I can't. Please don't say anything to Ronnie.'

'I won't. I promised ya and I never break a promise.' Danny took his penknife out of his pocket and made a small cut on the palm of his hand. 'Do the same,' he ordered, handing the knife to Tommy.

'Why?'

'You'll see.'

When Tommy did as asked, Danny clasped his hand so their blood mixed together. 'Don't matter if you don't live with us. This means we're brothers anyway. Blood brothers.'

Tommy's eyes shone with delight. He had always wanted a brother. 'Really?'

'Yeah, really. Now where shall we go? Record shop or boxing gym?'

'Boxing gym.'

Danny leapt up and playfully punched Tommy on the chin. 'Come on then, Henry Cooper. Race ya there.'

'Hello, Norman. I have been ringing you for the past few hours. Have you only just got home?' Ian enquired.

'Yes,' Norman lied. He hadn't been answering his phone since his altercation with the Darling boy.

Ian produced a bottle of port and a bottle of brandy from a carrier bag. 'Sandra is visiting her sister, so I thought you and I might have a bit of fun with the boy later at mine.'

Norman shook his head. 'I can't. I've already made plans.'

'You! Plans! Don't make me laugh. You never go out, only to the shops or mine.'

'I'm visiting my aunt. She hasn't been too well.'

'Be a devil and let's have some fun. Tommy has been a naughty boy, roaming the streets with that Darling lad again. Bad boys deserve to be punished,' Ian chuckled.

'No can do. Sorry, Ian.'

'But you said you liked the lad.'

'Yeah, I do. But I really need to see my aunt. She sounds as though she's on her last legs.'

'Oh well, your loss is my gain,' Ian smirked.

'Certainly is. Enjoy,' Norman shut his front door, ran to the bathroom and doused his sweaty face in cold water. If Tommy squealed to those Darlings, Ian was a dead man walking. Literally.

'You're late,' Ian snapped when Tommy walked through the front door.

Tommy glanced at his watch. He hadn't wanted to come home tonight, but knew he had little choice. His only consolation was that Auntie Sandra would be here, as he'd asked her yesterday if she would be visiting her sister this weekend and she'd said no.

'It's ten past nine. You are taking liberties lately, Tommy. Massive liberties. I thought I told you to stay away from those Darlings. They're no good, do you hear me? No bloody good at all.'

'But I like Danny and he's the only real mate I've met round 'ere. If I stop knocking about with him, then I got no one and I'll be lonely.'

Ian smiled. 'You've got me, but you don't seem to want to spend any time in my company these days. I'll do you a deal. You be nicer to me, and I'll allow you to be friends with Danny. How does that sound?'

Suddenly aware the perve had been drinking, Tommy froze. 'Where's Auntie Sandra?'

'Answer my question first, then I'll answer yours.'

'I don't know what you mean.'

'Oh, I think you do, Tommy.'

Tommy's eyes burned with fire. 'You come anywhere near me again, and I swear I will tell Ronnie Darling. I mean it. I will, and he will do you over.'

When Tommy ran up to his room, Ian paced up and down the lounge. Ronnie Darling would most certainly do him over, as his nephew had so politely put it, but Ian doubted the lad would ever have the balls to tell Ronnie anything. Bar his sister, he had never told anyone what had happened between himself and Uncle Ted. Especially once he'd got used to all the wonderful gifts Uncle Ted bought him and the great days out they had together. Surely, given time, once the initial shock had worn off, Tommy would feel the same way about him?

Brain fuddled by the amount of alcohol he'd supped, Ian paced up and down the threadbare filthy carpet. He had to think very carefully about his next move. Very carefully indeed.

Tommy lay on his bed thinking about his mum, sister and Rex. He never thought about Alexander or that old witch Nanny Noreen. They had put him in this situation so, to him, they were both dead.

Feeling nauseous, Tommy put his hand under the right-hand side of the pillow to check the handle of the dagger was in the right spot, if push came to shove. No way would he tell Ronnie or Danny if his uncle were to violate him again. He never wanted anybody to know. It would make him feel abnormal. He was a Millwall fan now and wanted to be a boxer when he grew up. He refused to be known as some poor molested orphan. He'd die of shame.

Deciding to turn his music off so he could hear Ian approaching, Tommy picked up his *Shoot* magazine. He couldn't concentrate on reading it though. He had no idea where that fat cow he was forced to call Auntie Sandra was, but he prayed she would come home soon.

It was past midnight when Ian made his way up the stairs. He had decided at one point not to touch the boy again, but then he'd had a few more drinks and his mind had drifted back to the past . . .

Valerie had always been the popular one. Like him, she had no idea who her father was, but it was obviously a different man to the one who'd fathered him. Valerie was pretty, vibrant and confident, whereas he had always been the total opposite. He'd been a chubby boy with few friends and no one to confide in. It had taken him weeks to pluck up the courage to tell his sister what Uncle Ted had been doing to him, but she'd been going out with pals that day and was too busy tarting herself up to even listen.

And now her precious son was going to be well and truly initiated into the world Uncle Ted had introduced him to all those years ago.

Unable to sleep, Tommy could feel his heart beating at an incredibly rapid pace. He hadn't got undressed, was too scared to in case he needed to run out of the house. He'd even debated whether to sleep down by the canal, but that was no long-term solution. Danny was right. Killing the perve was the only way out and he didn't even care if he was sent to a bad boys' home. Hazel might not have been happy in the home she'd been sent to, but at least she was safe from perverts like Uncle Ian. Anything had to be better than living like this.

'Tommy, you awake?'

Having switched his lamp off, Tommy did not reply. He could smell the stench of alcohol mixed with cigarettes. He could also hear the perve's laboured breathing.

'Tommy, Tommy, wake up. Look, I am sorry if I shouted at you when you came home. But I miss what we had. I want us to be close again,' Ian slurred.

When the perve began to stroke his face, Tommy wasn't taking any chances. He pulled the dagger from under his pillow and plunged it straight in the left-hand side of Ian's neck.

Stunned, Ian fell backwards on the bed.

'You dirty bastard,' Tommy bellowed.

Having guessed it would come to this, Tommy had already packed the treasured photos of his mum, Hazel, Linda and Rex in his duffel bag, along with PC Kendall's phone number, his Millwall programmes and records.

'Tommy, help me. Call an ambulance,' Ian rasped, holding the neck wound.

Tommy took one last look at the fat bastard. 'I hate you, ya nonce. I hope you die.'

'Please. Please help me.'

Aware that his once grey-looking sheets were rapidly turning to claret, Tommy grabbed his belongings, ran down the stairs and legged it along the street as fast as his little legs would take him.

CHAPTER NINE

The nearest phone box was only a couple of minutes away, but it was out of service, so Tommy ran towards the Old Kent Road.

It was gone midnight and there were drunks staggering about the streets, but Tommy wasn't scared. After living with that perve, nothing and nobody would ever scare him again.

There was a lad already in the phone box and Tommy silently willed him to hurry up. PC Kendall was the only person he could think of turning to for help in this particular situation. He was too young to run away and was bound to meet other perverts like Ian if he was forced to live on the streets.

When the phone box became free, Tommy darted inside and with trembling hands dialled the number. 'Can I speak to PC Kendall, please?'

'PC Kendall isn't on duty at the moment. Is there anything I can help you with?' came the reply.

'No. I only want to speak to PC Kendall. He's my friend. It's important. I think I might have killed someone.'

The officer on night duty could tell Tommy was a

kid. Instinct told him this was no crank call though. 'What is the number you're calling from, lad? Have a look and read it out to me.'

'Will PC Kendall call me back? I'm not telling anyone else what happened, only him.'

'Yes. I will call him at home. What's your full name?'

Tommy reeled off his name and number, put the phone down and it rang within a couple of minutes, the shrill tone making him jump. 'Can you help me, please? Uncle Ian turned out to be a pervert and I think I might have killed him.'

PC Kendall was alarmed. 'Where are you, Tommy?'

'Along the Old Kent Road. I'm not sure exactly where, but there's a club over the road playing Ska music with lots of black people going in and out.'

'Where is your uncle?'

'At his house. In my bedroom.'

'What's the address, Tommy? I need to call an ambulance. It's for the best, trust me.'

Tommy reeled off the address.

'Right, stay where you are and I'll find you. Stay close to or inside the phone box. I'm on my way.'

A man turned up, wanting to make a call, so Tommy had to leave the phone box. He was huddled inside a shop doorway, clutching his duffel bag to his chest, when he spotted Ronnie Darling walking towards him. Ronnie had his dark hair slicked back, was dressed in a smart suit with a pretty woman on his arm. Tommy had to look twice to make sure it really was him.

'Shit,' Tommy mumbled, looking at his feet, but it

was too late. Ronnie had already clocked him. 'What's happening, Tommy lad? What the hell you doing sat there this time of night?'

'I'm waiting for someone.'

Highly suspicious, Ronnie crouched next to the lad. He looked frozen. 'Who? Only it's nearly one and that club over the road kicks out in a bit. Full of Samboes, that is. No way am I leaving you here, it ain't safe. Come on. You're coming home with me.'

Tommy shook his head while praying PC Kendall would hurry up. It seemed ages since they'd spoken. 'No. I must stay here. I'm waiting for a friend.'

'Danny?'

'No. Not Danny. Look, I'm fine, honest. You go.'

'I'm freezing, Ronnie. What we standing here for?' asked the pretty blonde.

Ronnie glared at his current bit of fluff. ''Cause this kid is a close family friend and he's out here on his own. Jump in a sherbet if you're cold.'

Clocking a car crawling along the kerb, Tommy leapt up. Thankfully, it wasn't a marked police car. It was a Volkswagen Beetle.

As Tommy ran towards the vehicle, Ronnie grabbed hold of his arm. 'No you don't, lad. Who is this pal of yours?'

PC Kendall stepped out of the car and flashed his badge. 'I'm here to help, Tommy. He called me. He's in trouble.'

Ronnie looked at Tommy in disbelief. He'd thought the lad was one of their own. Had he been planted by the Old Bill to befriend his brother? Was he some miniature grass? 'You little shitbag,' Ronnie mumbled.

Tears stinging his eyes, Tommy shoved Ronnie in the chest. He felt so upset Ronnie had turned against him. His heart told him to blurt out the truth to Ronnie. But how could he? Tommy didn't feel like a little boy any more. No way did he want the Darlings finding out what his uncle had done to him. That was shameful. 'It ain't what you think. Tell Danny and your mum thanks for everything. I will never forget you all. You're like family to me.'

When Tommy leapt in the car and it sped off, for the first time in his life, Ronnie Darling was speechless.

Instead of handing Tommy over to the authorities in South London, PC Kendall took him back to Barking police station and gently questioned him there. He had already heard that Ian Taylor had been alive when found, but was in a critical condition and it was touch and go whether he would survive. Apparently, he had lost a lot of blood and had the police not broken the door down when they did, to allow the ambulance men entry, Ian would have been dead within minutes.

'Can you tell us what happened, Tommy?' asked the blonde female officer. She smelled nice and was quite pretty, like his mum, but no way could Tommy open up to her. 'Can I talk to Peter alone?' Tommy asked. PC Kendall had insisted earlier he was to refer to him by his first name. He could tell the lad had experienced a torrid time and wanted him to feel comfortable enough to tell him. He could kind of guess what had happened and his heart went out to the lad. Tommy had always been a good kid.

'Let me speak to Tommy alone,' Kendall urged his colleague.

When DS Bright left the room, Kendall repeated the question.

'Uncle Ian did something bad to me. Really bad.'

'Tonight?'

'No. A few weeks ago, but tonight he was going to do it again. I know he was. He came into my bedroom and Auntie Sandra was visiting her sister again. That's when it happened the last time.'

Though it was only a few months since Kendall had last seen Tommy Boyle, his once bubbly nature had all but disappeared. The boy was still as polite as ever, but his once sparkling eyes were dull and lifeless – hardly surprising, in the circumstances. Kendall softly asked some more questions, then made a decision. 'I need you to be brave, Tommy. I want a doctor to examine you. It might prove to be a bit embarrassing and uncomfortable. You OK with that?'

Tommy shrugged. 'I suppose so. Will I get sent to a bad boys' home, d'ya think? Ya know, like Hazel got sent away?'

Tommy hadn't explained what had happened to him in explicit detail, but it was crystal clear to Kendall. 'I'm still in pain when I do number twos and there's blood on the toilet paper,' Tommy admitted, staring at his hands in shame.

Kendall wanted to hug the boy but knew that, after what had happened to him, it might only upset him all the more. He leaned across the desk. 'I promise you, I will do everything in my power to put that evil bastard away, Tommy. Not you. You were acting in self-defence.'

'I hope he dies,' Tommy said bluntly.

'I don't, boy, for your sake. Better if he lives, then gets his just deserts in prison. But that's between me and you, OK?'

For the first time since PC Kendall had picked him up, Tommy managed a smile. 'Yeah. I'd like him to be beaten up badly. Thanks for helping me, Peter. I didn't know who else to call.'

The next twenty-four hours passed in a blur for Tommy. He was subjected to an examination, more interviewing and told his uncle was still alive.

He was then taken to stay with a woman called Maureen who had a clean home in Dagenham. She was kind to him. His bedding smelled fresh and the room was spotless.

It was on 17 March, his thirteenth birthday, that Tommy was told by a magistrate he would be sent to live at a children's home in Dagenham.

PC Kendall, and Maureen whom he'd stayed with the past few nights, accompanied him. Tommy had been told to speak only when spoken to by the magistrate, but was full of questions when they left the hearing. 'So, is this a bad boys' home? Will I have to go back to school? Why can't I live with the Darlings? Will my uncle be sent to prison?'

Urging Tommy to calm down, PC Kendall answered each question in turn. 'The home you are going to is the one Maureen thought you would be most suited to.

It's not for children who have been in trouble and it's mixed, boys and girls. One of Maureen's friends runs it and Maureen had to pull a lot of strings to get you in there, so you mustn't let her down, Tommy.'

'I won't. I remember my mum going to Dagenham once. I think she took my sisters with her too, but I ain't never been there.'

'At a guess, I'd say Dagenham's only about four miles from where you used to live. Maureen thought it best you didn't return to Barking because of the Fletchers and what happened with your mum and sister. You need a fresh start.'

'But I ain't scared of anyone now. My mate Danny taught me how to box. Why can't I live with his mum? She wanted me to move in.'

'I'm afraid that's not possible, lovey. Danny's father has been in too much trouble with the police,' Maureen explained.

Kendall ruffled the lad's hair and urged him to get in the car. 'You mustn't forget what the magistrate told you, Tommy. He gave you a stern warning that if you were to get into any more trouble, things wouldn't be so simple next time. I know what happened wasn't your fault, but you can't go around plunging knives in people. You need to work hard at school and pass your exams, so you can get yourself a decent job when you leave. Your mum, Valerie, was a wonderful lady and that is what she would want you to do.'

'OK.'

'As for Ian Taylor, the police questioned him yesterday and he denied the accusations. But, because your medical examination proved certain things, the police will be charging him anyway. He's been accused of a similar offence in the past, but the charges were dropped and the case never made it to court.'

'I won't have to go to court, will I?'

'You'll have to give some form of evidence. But hopefully you won't have to stand in the dock or see your uncle.'

'I can't tell strangers what happened. I won't.'

'Look, don't worry about that now. We'll cross that bridge when we come to it, and you will have my support and Maureen's every step of the way.'

Tommy spent the rest of the journey deep in thought. Just three months ago, he had a loving mum, two sisters who constantly squabbled over the record player, a beautiful dog, a man he called Dad and a woman he called Nan.

Now he had none of those things. They were all gone, in the blink of an eye.

Tommy had expected the children's home to be a stark-looking property set in its own grounds. 'Is this it?' he asked, as the car stopped outside a big house on the corner of a street with lots of other houses.

'Yes. You see those three properties?' Maureen pointed. 'Well, the council knocked them all into one to create this home. There are a few others in Dagenham, but this has a pleasant feel to it, Tommy. It's more laid-back and the staff are nice too. I thought a mixed environment would be better for you than to be surrounded by all boys.'

Tommy was ushered inside the house by Maureen. PC Kendall, who had visited Tommy's uncle's home to pack up his clothes and belongings, fetched the suitcase out of the boot.

A plump, short lady and a tall, dark-haired man with a kind face greeted them. The man grinned. 'Welcome to Maylands, Tommy. A little birdy told us it's your thirteenth birthday today, so we thought we'd throw you a party later to mark the occasion. Not every day you become a teenager, is it? I'm Ray, by the way, and this here is Connie. We manage Maylands, so any problems – you come straight to one of us.'

A little lad wandered over. 'I'm Kevin. What's your name?' he pried, tugging at Tommy's sleeve.

Tommy spied a spotty-looking thin girl peering at him from around a doorframe, but she disappeared when he made eye contact with her. 'Thanks for the offer, but I don't want no birthday party this year.' Tommy's mum had always made a big fuss of his birthday and the thought of celebrating one without her did not appeal to him at all.

'It's nothing major, Tommy. We bought a couple of cakes and thought it might be a nice way of introducing you to the other residents. Most of them are at school at present and they all love cake,' Connie chuckled.

'I'd rather no one knew it's my birthday,' Tommy insisted.

'No worries, lad. We understand,' Ray replied. 'Make our guests a cup of tea, Connie, while I show Tommy around.'

Maylands looked after children between eleven and

sixteen years old, and Tommy was told he would be sharing a bedroom with another newcomer. 'Benny only arrived here last week himself, so we thought it might be nice if you two shared. He's half-caste. You OK with that?'

'Yeah. Why wouldn't I be?'

'I was just checking, as Benny had a tough time in the previous home he lived in. He was bullied because of his colour.'

'How many lads actually live here?' Tommy enquired.

'Eleven at present, and nine girls. We like to think of ourselves as one big happy family here, Tommy. We are easy-going to a degree, but have a strict no-bullying policy. You are allowed to come and go as you please, provided you arrive home in time for dinner. That is served at 6 p.m. every day, including Sundays.'

'So, can I go out on my own at weekends?' A plan was already forming in Tommy's mind. He'd find a local boxing gym and join it. He had money saved, mostly what the perve had given him.

'Seeing as you are now officially classed as a teenager, yes, you can. We have a separate set of rules for the under-thirteens. But we don't advise you going out alone. Most of the lads stick together, as do the girls.'

'OK.'

Ray smiled. 'Want to take a look at the games room?'

Tommy nodded politely. He couldn't think straight. His head was all over the place.

When PC Kendall and Maureen left, Tommy unpacked his belongings and lay on his new bed. It was rock hard and when he inspected it further, the mattress had a plastic cover over it, which Tommy assumed was in case he pissed himself in the night.

He looked around the room. It was small with two single beds, two tiny chests of drawers, but he was drawn to the posters on the left wall. One was of the West Ham football team, but the others were sketches. One in particular caught his eye. It was a close-up of a dog's face.

All of a sudden, the door burst open and a lad with a big Afro appeared. 'You must be Tommy.'

Tommy sat up. 'And you must be Benny.'

'Yeah. I am. And believe me, you give me any shit, like my last roommate did, I will punch your fucking lights out.'

'Why would I give you shit? I don't even know you.'

'Because I'm black.'

'One of my best mates at my old school was black.'

Benny softened and held out his right hand. 'Nice to meet ya, Tommy.'

'Likewise.'

'So, what's your story?'

'Whaddya mean?'

'How did you end up here?'

'My mum died and then I found out my dad weren't me real dad. You?' Tommy asked. Ray had reassured him that all his details would remain confidential and he was only to tell the others what he was comfortable with.

'My mum didn't want me living with her no more. She got a new bloke and me and him didn't get on.'

'That's well bad.'

'So is my mother, the dirty stinking whore.'

'So, what's it like in here? Ray and Connie seem all right.'

'They're OK. But don't believe all that bullshit Ray told you on arrival. Did he mention the no-bullying policy?'

'Yeah.'

'Well, that's bollocks. One of the lads tried to set fire to my hair on the way home from school last week. He is one nasty fucker.'

'What's his name?'

'I ain't no grass. You'll find out for yourself soon enough. I've only been here a week and I know the rules already. Act sweet in front of Connie and Ray, and what happens outside of the home stays outside of the home. Got that?'

Tommy nodded, then pointed at the sketches on the wall. 'They yours? I like the dog.'

'That was my dog, Spike. I drew him myself.'

'No way! That's well ace. My dog has gone to live on a farm in Essex, but I'm gonna find out where and visit him soon. If I give you a picture of Rex, would you draw him too?'

'There ain't no such thing as a dog going to live on a farm in Essex, Tommy. Not in our world. That's what we're told when they kill 'em off.'

Tommy suddenly felt sick. 'What?'

'A farm in Essex means your dog was taken to the vet and put down. I know 'cause the same thing happened to my Spike.'

A lone tear rolled down Tommy's cheek. He couldn't believe what he was hearing.

Tommy spent the rest of his birthday with his head under the blankets. He couldn't get Rex's trusting face out of his head. He'd loved his smell, his big slobbery kisses, and throwing sticks for him in the park. They'd been mates, best mates, and now he would never see Rex again. He was gone, like everyone else Tommy cared about.

'You OK, Tommy?' Ray tapped on the door. 'I brought you a sandwich and a drink.'

'I don't want anything, thanks. But I'm sure I'll feel better tomorrow,' Tommy lied. He'd had to get out of meeting the other lads and having dinner tonight. Could not face food or company, so had feigned illness.

'OK, lad. Give Connie or me a shout if you need anything.'

When Ray's footsteps drifted away, Tommy propped his pillow up against the wall and punched it repeatedly.

He was no longer that innocent young boy he'd been before his mother died. He was now a streetwise, angry young man.

PART TWO

The course of true love never did run smooth.
William Shakespeare

CHAPTER TEN

Life in a children's home ain't no bed of roses let me tell you, but thankfully I managed to settle in fairly quickly.

The staff were OK, so were most of the lads, and I bonded with three in particular.

I also made an enemy. Wayne Bradley was a real pain in the butt. A nasty, vindictive, violent bully.

By this point, I was no normal teenager, mind. I had issues, plenty of them, and I wasn't prepared to take shit from any bastard. I'd already nearly killed one wrong'un and I'd do it again if pushed too far. I had no fear. Reason being, I had nothing left to lose.

I often thought of my dear friends, the Darlings. But I had made my mind up that I never wanted to see them again. Their kindness would stay with me forever and I would never forget them, Danny in particular. But I needed no reminders of my short time spent in South London, thanks very much. I had new friends now and was determined to start afresh.

Sometimes in life though, all your plans go to pot and fate can be a fucker.

If only I'd known then what I know now.

You'll see where I'm coming from soon enough . . .

Summer 1975

'Behave yourself, lads. No scrapping or drinking alcohol. You're to be back here by ten on the dot. Don't let me down now, will you?' warned Ray.

Tommy Boyle smiled sweetly. 'We won't mess up, and thanks again for giving us permission to go. We truly appreciate it, don't we, lads?'

Standing behind Ray, Benny Crooks did a fingers-down-his-throat gesture.

'Yeah. Cheers, Ray,' said Martin Smith (a.k.a. Smiffy).

Knowing the first thing they would do was drink the cider they'd hidden earlier, Dumbo couldn't help but giggle.

Tommy shook his head in despair as the four of them bowled outside. The monthly teenage disco at the local Catholic club was an extremely important event.

'What's that for?' Dumbo winced, when Tommy slapped him around the head.

Luckily for Benny, his big Afro saved him from any pain Tommy's right hand might have caused. 'You're such an arse licker,' Benny chuckled.

'And you two need to grow the fuck up,' Tommy spat.

When his pal stormed off, Smiffy caught up with him and slung a friendly arm around Tommy's neck. 'You know what they're like. They don't mean no harm. They're just immature.'

No way would Tommy ever hurt Benny, Dumbo or Smiffy. The four of them were good buddies, watched one another's backs. But ever since what had happened to him, Tommy struggled to control his temper at times. He was no little squirt any more either. Since arriving at the children's home two and a half years ago, Tommy no longer worried he would live the rest of his life as a dwarf. Not only had he shot up in height, his regular boxing training meant he could more than handle himself these days. He was strong, lean and the most feared lad at the home. That hadn't always been the case, mind. That arsehole Wayne Bradley had led him a dog's life once upon a time.

'Here we go,' Smiffy grinned, lifting the bottles of cider out of the bush. There was a no-alcohol policy at the youth disco. Only soft drinks were sold, but anyone even remotely cool would have a skinful before they arrived.

'You got the hump with me, Tommy?'

Tommy glugged at the cider, then handed the bottle to Dumbo (a.k.a. Darren Prattley). Dumbo had earned his nickname because his ears were so bloody massive. He was also as thick as two short planks. 'Nah. I ain't got the hump, but you need to be more savvy in front of Ray. You and Benny acting like divs will only enlighten him to the fact we'll be boozing.'

Smiffy lit up a cigarette. The monthly disco had only been going since May but was already a big hit. 'Tommy's right. You two need to act more sensible, otherwise you'll balls this special privilege up for us.'

Benny nodded. 'Understood.'

Dumbo grinned. 'Yeah, sorry.'

* * *

By the time the lads arrived at the Catholic club, they were in high spirits. Lots of their schoolmates were already there, but the four lads always made a pact to stick together. Most of the kids at Eastbrook Comprehensive were cool towards them. Tommy had carved out a reputation as one of the hardest boys in his year, but because of their upbringing and the stigma attached to living in a children's home, the boys always felt far more comfortable in one another's company.

'You look like one of the Jackson Five with that clobber on,' Smiffy laughed.

Dressed in a silky orange shirt with a huge collar and beige flared trousers, Benny grinned. 'Fuck you. I is the bee's knees. You watch the girls flock my way. I got the moves.'

The lads chuckled as Benny danced to the sultry sound of George McCrae's 'Rock Your Baby'. Benny's dad was from Jamaica and Benny had never met him. Tommy reckoned he must have been a cool dude though. Benny's mother was an ugly fat cow, so the lad must have inherited his looks, charm and slick moves from elsewhere. He was popular with the girls too. At the last couple of discos he'd ended up snogging at least four.

Seeing Laura Higgins, one of the best-looking girls in his year, staring at him, Tommy turned his back on her. He knew he wasn't a bad-looking lad because he'd been asked out by loads of girls, but he always declined. He had never even kissed a girl, not properly anyway. The thought of getting close to anyone after what that perve had done to him, literally filled him with dread.

So he chose to concentrate instead on his boxing and football, and having a laugh with his mates.

Dumbo nudged Tommy. 'Laura Higgins keeps looking at me.'

Rather than inform his pal he had more chance of flying to the moon than copping off with Laura Higgins, Tommy smiled. 'Yep. I think you're in there, pal.'

The rest of the evening passed in a happy blur. Benny stole the show by limbo-dancing to Typically Tropical's 'Barbados', which earned him a snog with two girls. Smiffy pulled a munter who gave him a wank outside. Dumbo got a slap around the face when he pinched Laura Higgins' bum, and Tommy spent most of the evening trying to avoid Laura Higgins and another girl with ginger hair who kept following him around.

'I got that chick's phone number,' Benny grinned as they ambled back towards the home.

'Which one?' Smiffy asked.

'The blonde with the big knockers. Her dad hates blacks, apparently, so I can't pick her up from her house. I'm gonna take her to the pictures next weekend, though. We'll sit in the back row, obviously,' Benny chuckled.

Tommy took the packet of mints out of his pocket and ordered the lads to suck them. The effects of the alcohol had now worn off, but it was better to be safe than sorry. Ray would be waiting for them to arrive home. He always was.

'Shit! Look, I got come all down me strides,' Smiffy announced.

'I'm surprised you even got a hard-on with that monster, let alone managed to come,' Benny chuckled.

'Yeah. She weren't a looker, was she?' Dumbo said. 'But I wish I could have got a wank. All I got was a smack round the clock.'

The jovial banter continued for the rest of the short journey back to Shitlands. They rarely referred to their home as Maylands any more. It was their own private joke.

'I can't believe you didn't ask Laura Higgins to dance at the end. I'd have been in there like a rat up a drain-pipe if she'd been drooling over me all night. She's hotter than a fucking gas cooker,' Smiffy announced, playfully grabbing his best pal in a headlock. He and Tommy had been inseparable ever since Tommy had arrived at Maylands. Nobody beforehand had had the balls to stand up to that arsehole Wayne Bradley, but Tommy had. Smiffy had been extremely impressed by Tommy's bravery. Though he'd only been tiny at the time, and as a result he'd lost the fight, Tommy had still given Bradley a run for his money and a shiner of a black eye.

'Well? Why didn't you ask her to dance?' Smiffy repeated.

''Cause he's a bum boy,' Benny joked.

Unable to stop himself, Tommy grabbed hold of Benny by the throat and rammed him up against a nearby wall. None of his pals knew his story. All Tommy had disclosed was that his mum had died, his sister had been sent away and he'd then found out his dad wasn't his real dad and his nan wasn't his real nan, therefore he wasn't wanted.

'What the fuck, Tom. I'm only messing with you,' Benny exclaimed, his eyes bulging.

Dumbo's eyes welled up. His pals were his world and he hated them fighting. Both his mother and father had been violent alcoholics and junkies, and seeing Tommy grabbing Benny by the throat and pinning him against the wall brought back awful memories of his terrible childhood.

Smiffy grabbed Tommy by the arm. 'Let's not argue, mate. We've all had a great night. It'd be such a shame to spoil it.'

Instead of punching Benny, Tommy punched the wall. 'Don't ever say shit like that to me again, OK? I ain't no bum boy, I just don't like slags, and that's what Laura Higgins is – I can tell. My mum was a slag and that's why she died.' Tommy often had dreams of his mother and in those dreams he still loved her. But, in the cold light of day, he found her death easier to cope with if he told himself he hated her. If she hadn't been out whoring with Terry Fletcher, he'd never have been separated from his sisters, sent to live with that disgusting nonce-case, and Rex would still be alive.

What angered Tommy also was the memory of that awful Christmas when he'd asked his mother outright whether there was any truth in the accusations he'd heard his father throw her way. She'd looked him straight in the eye, insisting she had no idea who Terry Fletcher was. As a child, his mother had always drummed it into him: 'a liar is worse than a thief'. She was a fucking hypocrite as well as a slag.

'Well? Did you have a good night?' Ray grinned, as

he opened the front door. None of the residents were allowed their own keys. Both he and Connie lived at the home, so one of them was always there to greet the residents. They also employed part-time staff who helped out with the cooking and cleaning during the day.

'Yeah. Great night,' Tommy muttered. He had to get up early tomorrow for boxing, and wanted to go to bed now.

'It was blinding. Thanks again for allowing us the special privilege, Ray,' said Smiffy.

'Can we go again next month?' Dumbo asked bluntly.

'Provided you behave yourselves in the meantime, I don't see why not,' Ray winked. 'Some letters arrived for you earlier, Tommy. Connie forgot to give them to you,' he added.

'Some! How many?' Every month, Tommy would receive a lengthy letter from Danny Darling with a ten-pound note enclosed from Ronnie. Other than that, PC Kendall was the only person to write to him. That month's letter from the Darlings had arrived only last week, so it couldn't be Danny writing.

'Two.'

The hairs stood up on the back of Tommy's neck. Had one or both of his sisters finally found him? He had no idea how Hazel or Linda were. Their old house had been sold and new people were living in that old cow Nanny Noreen's house, as Tommy had visited it last year in the hope of seeing Linda.

Ray handed Tommy the letters. 'Oh, and while you were all out enjoying yourselves, we had a familiar face return to Maylands.'

'Who?' Benny asked, hoping it was Carly Macintosh, who'd left only last week to live with her mother again. He'd fancied Carly something rotten.

'Me,' boomed a familiar voice.

Benny, Smiffy and Dumbo all looked at one another in horror as Wayne Bradley's grinning face appeared around the doorframe of the games room.

Tommy didn't flinch. He stared straight into the eyes of the bully who'd once terrorized them, yet acted like butter wouldn't melt in front of Ray and Connie. 'All right, Wayne? What a lovely surprise. It's great to see you again, sunshine.'

'I can't believe you said that to him, Tommy. He knew you were taking the piss. Now he's gonna make all our lives a misery again. His old cronies still all live locally, ya know,' Smiffy warned, strutting up and down the room he and Tommy shared. There were only fifteen of them living at the home at present, ten lads and five girls. It had been a great place to live since that arsehole Bradley had left around eighteen months ago. The atmosphere had changed almost instantly the day that nasty bastard had walked out the door.

Remembering the incident with Patch, Tommy's lip curled. When he'd first arrived at the home, there'd been a stray dog that used to hang around. He was a little Jack Russell and Tommy and Dumbo both took a particular shine to him. They'd wrap scraps of food in tissue and take it outside to feed Patch regularly.

One sunny day, for no reason whatsoever, that evil tosser Wayne Bradley decided to pick Patch up and wring his neck right in front of them. Both Tommy and Dumbo had been distraught. That's why, the following day, Tommy had attacked Wayne on the way home from school.

'What you thinking, Tommy? Did you see the state of Dumbo? He pissed himself as we came up the stairs, poor bastard. He's petrified of that psycho.'

'You leave the fucking psycho to me. I ain't a little boy no more, Smiffy. Now do me a favour. Pop next door and make sure Dumbo and Benny are all right. Tell 'em not to worry, OK. Give me ten minutes or so alone. I want to read my letters, in private.'

'OK, mate.'

When Smiffy left the room, Tommy studied the handwriting on both envelopes. His heart beat wildly as he recognized neither. Tommy studied the postmarks. One was from Clapham, the other Barking. Deciding to open the one from Barking first, Tommy stared at the letter with his mouth wide open. It was from his mum's friend Lisa Clayton explaining she had some information for him regarding his father and asking him to call her on the enclosed telephone number.

Tommy read the letter again. Memories flooded back of his mum going missing and him traipsing round to Lisa's house in the snow with his loyal buddy Rex by his side.

A lone tear ran down Tommy's cheek and he angrily wiped it away. He knew Lisa had moved home because he'd gone to her old house to confront her a year or so ago over who his real father was. Did she know where his dad lived? Taking deep breaths to calm

114

himself, Tommy ripped open the letter posted from Clapham. When he realized who it was from, he was unable to stop the tears any longer.

Dear Tommy,

I do hope this letter gets to you.

I miss you so much, and Mum, Hazel and Rex.

I am living in Clapham now with Nanny Noreen and I am so unhappy. Dad has a new girlfriend called Brenda, and she is horrible. She has a young son of her own who I hate too. His name is Daniel and they live a few streets away. Dad is still working on the oil rigs and we are never allowed to mention your name any more indoors. I barely see Dad, to be honest. I am stuck with Nanny Noreen most of the time and have to attend this awful Catholic school where I am made to do Hail Marys and confess my sins every five minutes.

I have made one good friend here though, Alice Piper. She and her lovely mum Catherine live a few doors away from us and have sort of become my saviours.

I have been very upset these past few weeks. This would have been Mum's 35th birthday and it was Catherine who helped me track you down. I thought you were still living with Mum's weird brother, Uncle Ian. I had no idea you were now in a children's home. What happened with Uncle Ian? Are you happy where you are? And have you heard from Hazel? I haven't. I know Dad goes to visit her regularly, and Nanny Noreen does too, but they never allow me to go.

Sorry to ask so many questions, Tommy. But I am writing this letter in my friend Alice's house and she is helping me to word it. Alice's mum Catherine reminds me of our wonderful mum. She is so pretty and kind and bakes lovely cakes.

Please write back to me at the below address. It's Alice's address and she and Catherine do not like Nanny Noreen much either. They pretend to for my sake, but on the quiet we all call her a silly religious old cow.

Love you, Tommy, even more than Little Jimmy Osmond these days (haha).

Miss you and our old life so much.

Your little sister,

Linda xxx

Smiffy walked back in the room. 'Whatever's wrong, mate?' he asked, his face full of genuine concern. He'd only ever witnessed Tommy upset once before. He'd heard muffled sobs coming from under his blankets on the night after that evil bastard Wayne Bradley had strangled Patch.

Shoving both letters under his mattress, Tommy lifted his T-shirt and dried his eyes. 'Nothing. Leave me alone. I'm fine.'

'No you ain't. Talk to me, Tom. I'm your mate. Don't keep things clammed up. My nan used to say that ain't no good for ya.'

Tommy puffed his cheeks out. 'My mum's best friend

wrote to me and so did my little sister. I think my mum's mate knows who my real dad is.'

'Well, that's great, ain't it?'

Tommy shrugged. 'All depends what he's like, don't it? He could be dead for all I know. Or some fucking arsehole.'

CHAPTER ELEVEN

'No good stood square on, Tommy,' yelled Ted the boxing trainer.

Tommy Boyle ducked, then danced around the ring.

'That's it, lad. Good footwork. You've got a minute left to go.'

Tommy upped his game as he always did near the end of a bout.

'Decent jabs, Tommy. Keep your guard up. There's a good lad.'

Smiffy cheered loudly as Tommy was declared the official winner.

Tommy shook the other lad's hand, then stepped out of the ring. He trained three times a week after school at a boxing club in Dagenham, then on a Saturday would take part in bouts against lads from rival clubs. They were only three rounds, but Tommy loved the buzz of being declared the winner on a regular basis. It gave him a sense of achievement and importance.

Ted Barrett had a soft spot for Tommy Boyle. He was aware the lad had been through a tough time, as he knew the Darlings out of South London. Ted ruffled

Tommy's hair. 'Have a good weekend and I'll see you on Monday. You did good today.'

'Cheers, Ted.'

'Oh, and while I think of it, I saw your pal the other day – Danny Darling. He asked after you and I told him you were doing well, like. I know you write to one another, but why don't you pay him and his family a visit one day? I know they'd love to see you again.'

Wondering exactly how much Ted knew, Tommy averted his eyes. 'Yeah, I'll drop Danny a line and sort something. Gotta dash, else I'll be late to meet me pals.'

On the bus journey back to Maylands, Tommy was deep in thought. He loved the Darlings. They were a kind, warm family and had been so good to him. Tommy had no wish to ever see them again though. The reason being, he knew they knew what that perve had done to him and he felt far too embarrassed to look them in the eyes, Danny especially.

The case against his Uncle Ian had never got to court. Tommy was relieved about that, as he just wanted to try to forget the whole thing and move on with his life the best he could. All Tommy had been told by PC Kendall was Ian had been given bail and, shortly afterwards, someone had set fire to his house in the middle of the night. He had managed to escape, along with that fat cow Auntie Sandra, but had then left the area, never to be heard of or seen since.

Tommy wasn't stupid. A downstairs window had been broken into, petrol doused all over the carpet and he guessed the Darlings had something to do with it.

PC Kendall had sworn that what had happened to him wasn't common knowledge, but Tommy was certain Ronnie knew as he'd been the one who'd spotted him sitting in the doorway that night, trembling with fear. Tommy could not remember exactly what he'd said to Ronnie before PC Kendall had picked him up, but he knew he'd said something. He'd also told Danny about the bath incident and guessed Danny would have since told his family.

'You all right, Tom? You're ever so quiet,' Smiffy remarked. 'You thinking about your dad? When are you going to phone that lady?'

'Dunno. Probably later. And no, not thinking about my dad. Why would I? I don't even know him. Look, I fancy a bit of time on me own this afternoon. You head on out choring with the others.'

'What! But why? Oh, come on, Tom. It won't be the same without you. It never is,' Smiffy insisted. The clothes allowance and pocket money they received was a pittance, so pilfering wasn't a crime, it was a necessity.

'My mum would've been thirty-five today, ya know.'

'Oh shit, mate. I'm sorry. Why didn't you say something earlier?'

'No point. Not gonna fucking bring her back to life, is it?'

Benny and Dumbo were sitting on the kerb outside Maylands. Both looked glum.

'What's up?' Smiffy asked.

'Wayne Bradley. He's started again already. After you

two left earlier, me and Benny decided to play some records. He followed us,' Dumbo said.

'And?' Tommy snapped.

'He started name-calling, all the usual insults. But then he took a penknife out of his pocket and started scratching me records. I can take being called a nig-nog, Tom, but not me vinyl being damaged. They were me Ska records too. I flew at the bastard, but you know what a lump he is. He got me in a headlock and laughed in my face,' Benny explained.

'Where was Ray and Connie?' Smiffy asked. The record player was downstairs.

Tommy cracked his knuckles. He had a habit of doing that when riled. 'Where's Bradley now?'

'Gone out. He said I looked like a character out of that film *Freaks* we watched that time. I ain't that ugly, am I, Tommy?' Dumbo asked in earnest.

'No, mate. Course you ain't. Not being funny, but Ray and Connie are fucking useless. Look how they reacted on the day that bastard killed Patch.'

On the day Patch had been throttled, Dumbo had screamed blue murder and Ray and Connie had come running outside. Being a grass was not cool, but for once, they'd all been so disgusted by what they'd witnessed, every single one of them had blurted out the truth.

Wayne Bradley had been sent to his room, then that afternoon, Connie had sat the rest of them down for what she described as a 'little chat'.

Tommy could remember that little chat as though it were yesterday. 'I've spoken with Wayne and he knows what he did was wrong. Apparently, he was bitten by a dog as a young child and has been petrified of them ever since. I am not condoning what he did, but Wayne says he feared Patch was about to attack him. He's very sorry for his actions.'

Tommy hit the roof, insisting that Wayne's version of events was utter bullshit. It was then Connie explained that Wayne's childhood had been very difficult and he'd been subjected to extreme violence himself.

Tommy had wanted to remind Connie he hadn't had it easy either, had been the victim of a nonce-case, but instead he'd kept his trap shut in front of the others. That secret he would rather take to his grave with him.

'What you thinking, Tommy?' Dumbo asked.

Tommy cracked his knuckles again. 'I'm thinking I'm gonna get hold of Bradley away from this gaff, and hurt him so bad, he'll wish he'd never been fucking born.'

Tommy put his pen down and studied his words.

Dear Linda,

I can't tell you how overjoyed I was to hear from you. I have missed you so much, and Hazel, Rex and Mum.

Sorry to hear you're not happy living with the religious old witch, but it doesn't surprise me. Bit of luck, one day she will get lost and Saint Anthony won't be able to find her!

On a serious note, really chuffed your new mate and her mum are looking out for you. I met a family when I lived in South London and they looked out for me too. They still write to me now and send me money.

The home I am living in is OK. Uncle Ian and Auntie Sandra were oddballs, so I'm much happier here than I was with them. I have three good mates and the four of us go everywhere together. Smiffy is my best pal, but Benny and Dumbo are great lads too. We watch one another's backs, so to speak.

You wouldn't recognize me now, sis. I am 5 foot 8 inches tall and I've filled right out. I'm into boxing, train regularly at a local gym. My trainer Ted reckons I got the makings of a top boxer, if I put my mind to it and keep out of mischief.

I have never heard anything from Hazel either. I wrote to PC Kendall (our old bobby) a while back to see if he could arrange a visit for me. He wrote back saying he tried, but couldn't.

I would love to visit you though, or you visit me. Obviously, I won't come anywhere near the old crow's house. Let me know what you think and whatever you do, don't take this letter indoors in case the witch finds it. Leave it at your mate's house.

Your loving brother,
Tommy xxx

Tommy wrote the address on the envelope, Lisa's phone number on his arm, bolted down the stairs and came face to face with Maureen. 'Er, hello. How are you?' Tommy asked awkwardly. Maureen was the lady whose house he'd been taken to after being questioned at the police station for stabbing his uncle. Maureen was a nice lady, but Tommy always felt tense when he saw her these days. He knew PC Kendall must have told her what had happened to him, and the older Tommy got, the more humiliated he felt that others knew of his plight.

At that moment a girl stepped out of the downstairs bathroom. Tommy's jaw dropped open. He remembered skinheads being all the rage when he was growing up, but fashion had changed since then.

'I'm fine, thank you, Tommy,' Maureen replied. 'This is Scratch. She's spent the past week or so living at mine and is now moving into Maylands.'

The girl had blonde shaved hair with a long fringe and bit at the back, and was dressed in light Sta-prest trousers, a button-down collared shirt and what looked like steel- toe-capped Dr Marten boots. Tommy couldn't help but stare at her. She also had lots of earrings and was wearing a navy Fred Perry cardigan. Not knowing what else to say, Tommy said, 'Ain't you hot in all that clobber?'

'Who are you? The local weatherman?' the girl snapped.

Taken aback, Tommy immediately apologized. 'No offence, I just meant it's sweltering outside and in 'ere.'

'So?'

'Right, I'll be off then. Got a letter to post,' Tommy said, edging past Miss Attitude. 'Nice to see you again, Maureen.'

Having already been forewarned that the newcomer hated her real name and insisted on only her nickname being used, Connie said, 'Come with me, Scratch, and I'll show you around. The girls' bedrooms are in a different part of the building to the boys'. Girls and boys aren't allowed in one another's rooms, but other than that you'll eat together and can freely mix together. Would you like to see your bedroom first? Or the rest of the rooms?'

'Don't care.'

'Hang on a minute, Tommy,' Maureen shouted. 'Scratch, you go with Connie, love.'

'What's up?' Tommy asked, as Maureen caught up with him outside.

'Nothing, lovey. Ray's been telling me how well you've been doing with your boxing and in general. I'm so pleased. You have come on leaps and bounds, haven't you?'

'Cheers,' Tommy mumbled, feeling awkward.

'I was wondering if you could do me a small favour.'

'What?'

'Could you please keep an eye on Scratch for me? You know, just look out for her in general. She's been through an extremely tough time recently and I know you know what that's like.'

Guessing what Maureen was referring to, Tommy stared at his feet. 'OK.'

'Thanks, Tommy. And please, can we keep this little conversation between ourselves. Don't mention it to Scratch or your friends. I know I can trust you.'

'Yeah, no worries.'

* * *

Tommy walked to the nearest phone box, only to discover it was out of order, so he trudged towards the one on Oxlow Lane.

It was a baking hot day and Tommy wondered how the lads were getting on in Romford. Some of the clothes they chored they kept for themselves. Anything else, they sold to Bob the Fence who drank in the Beacon.

Usually, Tommy and his pals would spend their ill-gotten gains on records, booze and cigarettes. But these past few weeks they'd been saving every penny. Next weekend was the Dagenham Town Show, the biggest local event of the year. The fairground was awesome and it had been Tommy's idea they club all their money together so they could go on as many rides as possible. The fair stayed for a couple of weeks after the actual Town Show and it was a cool place to hang out. Tommy loved the atmosphere of the fairground. An air of excitement surrounded it and he couldn't wait until next weekend.

The next phone box was free, worked, and Tommy felt the first stirring of nerves as he dialled his mother's friend's number. The phone was answered on the third ring. 'Hello. Is that you, Lisa? It's Tommy, Valerie's son.'

Tommy felt anxious as he made his way to Dagenham Heathway. He and his pals would often come here to thieve. Dewhurst's was an easy target to steal meat from, and Mr Byrites and the Jean Joint were a doddle to try items on in the changing room, then walk out with some under their own clothes.

Lisa had said very little on the phone. All she'd said was she'd meet him at the Wimpy on Heathway hill at 2 p.m.

Tommy was early, so had a browse through the records in Woolworths. He was desperate to get a copy of the current number one, 'Tears On My Pillow', but he and the lads had made a pact to one another not to buy another record until after the fair had gone. Tommy was not a person to go back on his word, so after picking up the record, he reluctantly put it back on the shelf.

At 1.55 p.m., Tommy walked over to the Wimpy. He peered through the window, but didn't spot Lisa until she waved at him. She'd once had long brown hair, but now it was short, wispy and blonde.

Lisa stood up and tried to hug Tommy, but he was no longer a touchy-feely person, so he dodged the embrace and sat down at the table.

'Are you hungry? Would you like a burger?' Lisa asked.

'No, thanks. I just wanna know who my dad is.'

'We need to order something, Tommy, else we won't be allowed to sit in here.'

'OK. Get me a Coke and a cheeseburger then. Please.' Tommy felt sick, rather than hungry.

Lisa called a waiter over, then turned back to Tommy. 'Wow! Look at you. The last time I saw you, you were this tiny little whippet. When did you grow so tall and where did all those muscles come from?' Lisa smiled. Tommy looked sullen, not the happy little boy she remembered.

'Got the muscles from boxing and I grew taller

when I took up smoking. Me mum used to say to me, "You must never smoke. It'll stunt your growth." Another lie. Then again, me mum lied to me a lot, didn't she, Lisa?'

Lisa sighed. It was clear Tommy had turned into an angry young man and in a way she couldn't blame him. 'Your mother worshipped the ground you walked on, and if she did lie to you it was only to protect you, Tommy.'

'Really?' Tommy replied, his voice laden with sarcasm.

'Yes, really,' Lisa insisted.

'So, who's me real dad then?'

Lisa took a deep breath. There was no harm telling the truth now, she supposed. 'One of the pubs your mum worked in as a barmaid, she met a man who put a smile on her face once again. She was having it extremely hard with your dad at the time. He was a very handsome man, could charm the birds off the trees. He most certainly charmed your mother, as she began an affair with him. It wasn't a fling, Tommy. Your mum was truly in love with this man. He was wild, looked up to by many, a bare-knuckle fighter, by all accounts.'

Tommy's eyes widened with excitement. 'My dad was a bare-knuckle fighter!'

'Alexander found out about your mum's affair. He was spying on her outside the pub one night, by God he beat her black and blue when she arrived home. Shortly afterwards, your mum learned she was pregnant with you. She didn't know who the father was at first, but as you turned from a baby into a toddler, it became obvious you wasn't Alexander's. Your hair was the same colour as Patrick's, so were your eyes. You even had his freckles. Patrick had freckles on his nose too.'

'Patrick. That's a cool name. Did he know about me? Why didn't my mum leave Alexander and run away with my dad? Surely, if he was a prizefighting champ, he could have handled Alexander?'

'The situation was complicated, Tommy. Patrick was also married with kids.'

'Kids! So I have half-brothers or -sisters. Were they boys or girls?'

'I think he had two boys and a girl, but it might have been the other way round. Your dad did meet you, but only the once. I went with your mum to a pub in Canning Town to take you to see him.'

Tommy's heart was racing. 'What happened? Did he like me?'

'Yes. Patrick held you in his arms. He was besotted with you, if only briefly,' Lisa lied. She had to try and soften the blow somehow.

'Why didn't he see me again?'

'Because he was afraid of losing his wife and family, Tommy. By this time the affair with your mum was over. He told her to go back to Alexander, that it would be best all round if Alexander brought you up as his own son.'

'What's my dad's surname? Do you know where he lives now?'

Lisa fished inside her purse and handed Tommy a piece of paper. 'Flanagan is his surname. A year or so after you were born, he got sentenced to twelve years in prison for an armed robbery that went wrong. I really don't want to build your hopes up, Tommy, because chances are there will be no happy ending. But you have every right to know who he is now your mum's not here to tell you. You're not to mention where you got this information or the address from, though. I don't want any grief.'

'I won't. I promise,' Tommy said, staring at the piece of paper. The address was a pub in Stratford. 'So does my dad own this boozer? Or just work there?'

'Neither, my love. But that's where he drinks. You will be able to find him there most evenings in the week, or Saturday and Sunday lunchtimes. Whatever you do, don't go bowling inside the pub though, announcing who you are. You will need to speak to him outside, alone.'

'OK. Is my dad's house in Stratford too?'

'He doesn't live in a house, Tommy. Patrick lives in a caravan. Your father is an Irish gypsy.'

Stunned beyond belief, Tommy dropped his Coke all over his favourite pair of strides.

CHAPTER TWELVE

'Oi! Whaddya think you're doing? Leave her be,' Tommy ordered.

Yvonne Purdy was the female equivalent of Wayne Bradley. Not quite as evil, but certainly on a par when it came to bullying girls.

Yvonne stepped away from the new girl. Over the past six months, she'd developed an enormous crush on Tommy Boyle. His big brown eyes, long eyelashes and cheeky grin made her heart skip a beat. 'I weren't hurting her, Tom. I was only teaching her some manners. She's a stroppy little mare,' Yvonne explained.

'We were all stroppy when we first arrived 'ere. It's called survival,' Tommy retorted.

Wayne Bradley, who'd followed Tommy into the hall, was an interested spectator to this exchange. Since returning to Maylands, he couldn't help but notice the change in Tommy Boyle and he didn't like it, not one little bit.

Having already taken a shine to the new girl himself, Wayne let out a false chuckle. 'And there was me thinking you was a poofta, Tommy lad. You're out of your league with that one, sunshine. She'll take your little cock off with one swipe of those hobnail boots of hers.'

Tommy swung around, grabbed Wayne by the throat and shoved him against the wall. 'You can shut your fucking cakehole an' all.'

Connie appeared in the hallway. 'Whatever's going on? Your breakfast is getting cold.' Monday to Saturday the kids were only given cereal or porridge for breakfast. But on a Sunday, Ray would rustle them up a fry-up as a treat.

'Sorry. This is my fault. I started it off. We're only mucking around though,' Scratch piped up.

'Well, I'm glad to see you're settling in, Scratch,' Connie smiled. 'Now, chop-chop, into the dining room, all of you.'

'Cheers for not grassing. Wanna sit with me?' Yvonne Purdy asked Scratch. She was desperate to get in Tommy's good books. At least he'd noticed her today and no way would he fancy Scratch. She wasn't ugly, but dressed and sounded like a boy.

As Tommy followed the girls into the dining room, Wayne Bradley poked him in the back. 'You're dead, you wanker.'

Smiffy, Benny and Dumbo looked quizzically at Tommy. Sunday was the one day they never went thieving as all the shops were shut, but whether it be Matchstick Island, Parsloes or Ponfield Park, they always hung out together.

'Where you gotta go then?' Smiffy enquired.

Tommy hadn't let on to anybody, not even Smiffy,

about his father. He'd faked a headache last night, had needed to lie in a darkened room to get his head around the information Lisa had given him. Never in a million years would Tommy have dreamed his father was an Irish gypsy, but then certain memories from his childhood had come back to him. 'Been out with your pikey boyfriend again, have you?' he remembered Alexander shouting on a few occasions. It all made sense now. 'I'm going to see my mum's mate,' Tommy fibbed.

'Well, how long you gonna be? Where does she live?' Benny asked. 'We was thinking of going swimming over Leys for a change.'

'Lisa lives near the Heathway. Look, you lot go over Leys and I'll try to meet you there later.'

'I might ask that skinhead bird if she wants to come. I'd love to see her in a skimpy bikini,' Dumbo laughed.

'You leave her be,' Tommy ordered.

'Got the hots for her yourself, have ya, Tommy? Only I reckon she likes a bit of black meself,' Benny goaded.

Tommy waved a warning finger at all three of his pals. 'I mean it, lads. You disrespect that girl in any way, shape or form and you'll have me to deal with. Understood?'

Tommy got a District Line train to Mile End, then hopped on the Central Line to Stratford. He'd never been to Stratford before, so didn't have a clue where he was going. 'Excuse me, do you know where the Railway Tavern is, please?' Tommy asked an elderly lady.

'Yes, son. It's in Angel Lane.'

'Is that far?'

'No.' The lady gave Tommy directions.

As he approached the pub, Tommy could feel his heart pounding wildly. He was very impressed his dad was a bare-knuckle fighter. Should he mention he was a good boxer too? Would that help them bond?, Tommy pondered.

Lisa had warned him not to build his hopes up, but Tommy couldn't help but feel optimistic and excited. It wasn't every day a lad met his real father, was it? And surely Patrick was nicer than that shitbag Alexander? He must be, if his mum had truly loved him.

Mouth drying up, Tommy reached the pub. He hadn't known what to wear, so had kept it simple. His favourite faded flared jeans, black-and-white Gola trainers and white-and-black Adidas T-shirt.

Debating whether to just bowl inside the boozer, Tommy decided against it. His half-brother or -brothers must be older than him and they might be in the pub with his dad.

After what seemed like an eternity, an old man in a tweed cap came out. 'Excuse me, do you know if Patrick Flanagan is in there?'

'Yes, lad. On the table in the left corner playing cards with his muckers.'

'Could you get him for me, please?'

'Erm, yeah, I suppose so. Who should I say wants him?'

'Tell him Tommy Boyle. Valerie Boyle's son.'

'OK.'

The elderly man quickly reappeared. 'Patrick said not to go inside. He'll be out in a couple of minutes.'

'Thanks,' Tommy mumbled.

The couple of minutes seemed like an hour to Tommy. Lisa said she didn't know if his dad knew his mum had died. He couldn't know. Otherwise his dad would have tracked him down by now, surely?

As the man walked out of the pub with two pints in his hand, Tommy immediately knew it was his father. He locked eyes with him. They had the same colour eyes and hair, but his dad's was wavy and Tommy's straight. The man smiled and handed him a pint. 'All right, mush? Can't talk here, let's sit in my car,' he said in a thick Irish accent.

The car was a 1974 pale green Mercedes and as Tommy got in the passenger side, he'd already decided his father was far cooler than Alexander. He'd driven a crappy old Ford Cortina.

'Sorry to hear about your mum. A special lady, was Valerie.'

Tommy couldn't hide his shock. 'You knew she'd died!'

'Yeah. I heard through the grapevine. Made me very sad.'

Tommy stared deeply into Patrick's eyes. 'So, why didn't you come and see me? You know I'm your son, right?'

'Well, your mum thought you might be mine, but she was never totally sure. There was equally as much chance you were her husband's.'

Tommy took a gulp of his pint. This wasn't going

how he'd hoped it would. 'I'm definitely your son. We look alike. I look nothing like Alexander.'

Patrick ruffled Tommy's hair. 'You ain't got a flat hooter like mine, eh?' he chuckled.

Tommy studied his dad's nose. It was flattened. A boxer's nose, they called it down the gym. 'How many brothers and sisters have I got?'

'Half-brothers and -sisters. Four. That's if you are mine, of course. I honestly don't think you are, lad. You look nothing like my kids.'

'I know I am definitely yours because my mum told me not long before she died,' Tommy fibbed. He felt desperate to belong. He wanted Patrick to be his father.

'Drink up. You do like beer, don'tcha?'

Tommy's eyes welled up. Was that all his dad had to say to him? 'You could pick me up from where I live. We could go out for the day, get to know one another better. I won't tell anyone.'

Patrick sighed. 'Look, Tommy, I wish you well, but I can't be a part of your life. Neither can you be part of your brothers' and sisters' lives. You got two sisters of your own. Concentrate on them. My Mary would cut my cory off, she ever got wind I had another son. My kids wouldn't be none too happy either.'

Tommy felt deflated. He'd had no idea what to expect, but he hadn't expected to be rebuffed like this. 'Did you love my mum?'

'Love's a strong word. I was certainly very fond of Valerie. She was good fun and very beautiful,' Patrick replied honestly.

'My mum was in love with you, she would have run away with you.'

'Where you getting your information from?'

Not wanting to get Lisa into trouble, Tommy said, 'My mum told me you were a bare-knuckle fighter and you'd met me as a baby. Is that true? Only I'm a good boxer myself, ya know.'

'It was an affair, Tommy. Nothing more, nothing less. Yes, me and your mum had some laughs. But, I would never have left my wife and kids for Valerie and she knew that. I only ever saw you the once as a baby. Your mum turned up in a pub I was drinking in with you in her arms and a mate in tow. I told her there and then I could never be a father to you, and I still can't. One day when you have a family of your own, you'll understand.'

Near to tears, Tommy sank the rest of his pint, put the empty glass on the rubber mat and opened the passenger door. His dad hadn't even bothered asking him about his boxing, where he lived, school, his aspirations in life, nothing. It was clear he was an arsehole who was totally disinterested in him.

When Tommy got out of the car and slammed the door, Patrick felt a twinge of guilt. He leapt out himself. 'Hang on, lad. Not so fast.'

Tommy turned around, his face contorted with anger. 'What? Gonna ask about my wonderful fucking life in a children's home, are ya?'

Patrick pulled a wad of notes out of his pocket and peeled off five twenties. He hadn't known the boy lived in a children's home. 'Treat yourself to something nice, lad. Sorry I can't be any more help, but you're a survivor. I can see it in your eyes.'

Tommy wanted to tell him where to shove his money, but a hundred quid was a fortune to him and he'd been desperate for ages to get a decent record player for his room. The communal one was crap.

'Bye, Tommy. Be lucky in life,' Patrick said, as the money was literally snatched out of his hand.

Tommy pocketed the dosh and took one long last look at his father. He said nothing as he walked away. There was sod all left to say.

Feeling as deflated as a burst balloon, Tommy got off the train at Dagenham Heathway and trudged dejectedly down the hill. No way was he going to Leys to meet the others. He wasn't in the mood for Benny's pranks, Smiffy's endless questions or Dumbo's thickness today. He wanted to be alone. Not long before she died, his mum had said to him, 'Tommy, life is full of obstacles. We have to learn how to overcome them.'

Tommy had no idea what he'd done in life that was so terrible to make him deserve it, but he'd literally had an assault course load to deal with. Would his luck ever change? Last night he'd lain in bed imagining this bare-knuckle-fighting hero of a father who would actually want to be a part of his life. Instead, he'd learned not only had his dad never really loved his mother, he had seen his son as some nuisance he could rid himself of with a pint and a hundred quid.

As he reached Oxlow Lane, Tommy heard his name called. He turned and was surprised to see Scratch running towards him. 'All right? What you up to?' she asked.

'Nothing much.'

'Fancy getting some cider and chilling over the park? I got some money and I know an offie that'll serve me.'

Tommy shrugged. He knew from past experience that wallowing in self-pity wasn't the answer. 'Yeah, sod it. Why not? But I'll pay for the cider.'

'Nah. I don't take nothing from no one, me. We'll go halves.'

It had been a hot summer so far and today seemed even warmer than usual. Tommy took his T-shirt off. They'd come to Central Park and had found some shade under a tree.

'What's your real name?' Tommy asked.

'Rosie. I hate it. It's an old lady's name. I hate my surname too. It's Peacock.'

'What you done to your arm?' Tommy asked, when Scratch finally took off her Fred Perry cardigan.

'Arms,' Scratch replied, showing him the inside of the other. 'I cut meself. That's how I got my nickname.'

'Why?'

Scratch shrugged. 'It's a habit, that's all. Makes me feel good at the time. So, tell me about Maylands. How long you been there? What's it really like?'

Scratch was surprisingly easy to talk to and the more cider he sank, the more Tommy found himself opening up to her. He spoke openly about his mum, sisters, Rex, and even told her about his meeting with his real father.

'My real dad got murdered when I was four. He was stabbed outside a pub in East Ham,' Scratch said without a hint of emotion. 'I don't really remember him, but I've been told he was a good bloke.'

'Your mum alive?' Tommy enquired.

'Yes, unfortunately. She went off the rails after my dad died, not that I remember her ever being on the rails. She's a smackhead. Will sell anything for her next hit, me included.'

'Whaddya mean by that?'

'Long story. Can't be arsed talking about it, if I'm honest. I hate my mother. If she dropped dead tomorrow I would fucking celebrate.'

'Sorry you've had such a shit time of it.'

Scratch shrugged. 'That's life, innit. I was taken away from her when I was twelve. I've spent the past few years living with different foster carers. I had grief at my last placement though. The eldest son was a nonce, so I ended up stabbing him in the eye with a screwdriver.'

'Wow!' Tommy was impressed. 'Did you get arrested?'

'I got questioned, but not charged. Then I was taken to stay with Maureen for eight days before I turned up at Maylands.'

'How old was he?'

'Who?'

'The nonce you stabbed?'

'Twenty. Horrible bastard. Blind in one eye now. Shame I never stabbed him in both.'

Tommy chuckled. 'I like you. You're cool.'

Scratch grinned. 'Is it all right if I hang out with you

and your mates? I ain't a girlie girl. I'm a tomboy. I won't cramp your style. Promise.'

Tommy wasn't too sure if Smiffy, Benny and Dumbo would want a girl knocking around with them, but tough shit if they didn't. He was the one who called the shots.

He returned the grin. 'I don't see why not,' he said.

The rest of the afternoon flew by. Bumping into Scratch had been fate, Tommy reckoned. She was the tonic he needed after the knock-back his father had given him.

Tommy had never met a girl like Scratch. Not only did she love Ska music, Westerns and football, she was also partial to a spot of pilfering.

Scratch turned on her front, dug her elbows into the grass and rested her chin in her hands. 'So, what's your long-term plan, then?'

'Whaddya mean?'

'I mean, where do you see yourself in, say, five years' time?'

'Already told ya. I wanna be a pro boxer.'

'But what if you don't cut the mustard? Not saying you won't, but you need to have a back-up plan, just in case.'

Tommy shrugged. 'Probably have a bash at the building game, or roofing. What about you?'

'I want to join the army.'

Tommy burst out laughing. 'And do what? Women can't fight in wars.'

'There's other jobs women can do in the army.'

'Yeah, cook.'

'Piss off.'

Tommy grinned. 'I'm only messing with ya. I can see you in combat gear, as it goes.'

'So can I. Be guaranteed a roof over me head an' all. Where you gonna live when you leave Maylands? When do you turn sixteen?'

'Next March. Smiffy'll be the first to leave and he's gonna find us a gaff to share.'

'How's he gonna afford it?'

'I dunno. He'll get a job, I suppose. He's no idiot, Smiffy. He's a good lad.'

'What's the time, Tommy? The park looks empty all of a sudden.'

Tommy glanced at his watch. 'Shit! Time we made a move; else we'll miss out on getting fed.'

Scratch put on her cardigan and stood up. 'All that stuff I told you earlier about my mum, and me being in foster care, d'ya think we can keep it between ourselves?'

Tommy grabbed Scratch in a gentle headlock. 'Yeah, course we can. Same goes for me meeting me dad today. I never told the lads where I was going, pretended I was visiting me mum's mate. I might tell 'em she gave me the money to get a record player. I don't really fancy explaining the whole sorry saga to anyone else. No point, is there?'

'Not really. Worst ways, you can always say I chored the record player when you get one.'

Tommy chuckled. 'That actually ain't a bad idea, ya nutter. The boys'll be well impressed with that one.'

As the pair of merry misfits left Central Park the one

thing both were sure of at that point was they'd probably be pals for life.

What they didn't know back then was that they would actually prove to be one another's downfall.

CHAPTER THIRTEEN

It's funny the things you remember when you've got a gun pointed at your head.

For me, it seems it all begins – and ends – with Scratch. When we first met, it soon became apparent she had a crush on me. The lads at Shitlands used to rib me over it something chronic. I used to laugh along with them, but inside I felt a bit embarrassed if I'm honest.

I only saw Scratch as a mate. She had a pretty face, but with her skinhead and Dr Martens she was the ultimate tomboy. She fitted in well with our little gang. Like the rest of us, she didn't give a shit and was good fun to be around. She was also fearless, an unusual quality in a girl.

One evening that sticks in my mind in particular is when Scratch and I watched *The Godfather* together. I can't remember where the other lads were, but I know it was just the two of us. Neither of us had seen the film before and were that glued to the TV that Ray allowed us to stay up past our bedtime to watch the end. Scratch quickly became engrossed by the character that Al Pacino played, Michael Corleone. 'I'd like to marry a man like him one day and live that kind of life,' she announced.

I can't remember the exact wording of the rest of our conversation, but it went something like this.

'No. You bloody wouldn't,' I retorted. 'You'd be looking over your shoulder every minute of every day waiting to get shot or arrested.' I then had to cover my eyes at that now-infamous horse head scene in the bedroom.

'I bloody well would,' Scratch insisted. 'Better than leading a boring life like my junkie mother and her scumbag pals. I love power, guns and excitement.'

I honestly thought Scratch was winding me up, but when I uncovered my eyes and clocked the defiant look on her face, I realized she was serious.

'Well, rather you than me,' I laughed. 'Sod that for a game of soldiers.' She laughed too and then made me feel awkward by resting her head on my shoulder.

Of course I had no inkling at that point that I would be leading a similar kind of life in the not-too-distant future. Not quite Mafia level. But I'd be involved in organized crime, and looking over my shoulder would become a necessity . . .

Tommy Boyle studied himself in the communal mirror. They weren't allowed mirrors in their rooms any more. Ray and Connie deemed them too dangerous, ever since Trish Johnson had topped herself by slitting her wrists with one.

'Looking as gay as ever, Tommy lad. Going to the Town Show with your new bird, are ya? I know your type. You're only knocking around with her to hide your natural queerness,' taunted Wayne Bradley.

'Do one, prick!' Tommy hissed.

'You wanna start showing me some respect, Tommy lad. Otherwise your little girlfriend might suffer the same fate as Patch did.'

When Tommy flew at Wayne, Smiffy grabbed hold of his pal. 'Leave it, mate. He's goading you on purpose.

He wants you to clump him so you ain't allowed to go to the Town Show. I overheard him telling Fat Brian his plan.'

Fat Brian poked his head around the door of the games room. 'Who you calling fucking fat?'

'You, ya tub of lard,' Smiffy retaliated.

'Nobody likes a snitch, do they, Brian?' Wayne sneered. 'See you later at the fairground, bum boys. I'd watch me back, if I were you.'

'Behave yourselves. No drinking alcohol and make sure you have something to eat. I don't mean candyfloss either,' Connie smiled. She knew how important attending the Town Show was to the kids, therefore the older ones were allowed to skip dinner today, providing they spent the extra pocket money they'd been given on food.

'Have fun, guys. Make sure you look after Scratch, and you're to be back here no later than ten,' Ray added. Aware of what a difficult life Scratch had endured, both Ray and Connie were thrilled with how she'd settled in. Tommy had well and truly taken her under his wing. So much so, he'd pretended his new record player was her old one to increase her popularity with the other lads.

'Candyfloss,' Benny chuckled as soon as they were out of earshot. 'I ain't eaten that shit since I was about ten.'

'What we got in the kitty?' Smiffy asked.

'Thirty-nine pound, twenty-two pence,' Scratch grinned. She'd known Smiffy in particular wasn't keen on her knocking about with them at first, but he'd changed his tune since Tommy had pretended she'd chored that record player.

'Let's get some marijuana, eh?' Benny suggested.

'Sounds good to me,' Smiffy replied.

'Yeah, man,' Dumbo grinned.

'No,' Tommy snapped. 'If we bump into Bradley and his cronies later, we'll need to have our wits about us.'

'I've got me penknife on me,' Smiffy announced.

'Me too,' Benny replied.

Tommy said nothing. Most of the lads he knew carried a penknife, but he never did. He'd got away with stabbing the perve, but knew he'd never get away with such a crime twice.

'Is it too early for alcohol?' Scratch asked.

Tommy smirked. 'Nah. Never too early for a cider.'

'No way! Look at 'em spinning around. I'd be sick if I was inside that,' Dumbo said, his eyes transfixed by the Red Devils flying display.

'Look, one's jumped out. Imagine if his parachute didn't open. He'd land in the crowd and splatter 'em,' Benny pointed out.

'If that were to happen, let's hope Wayne Bradley and Fat Brian are standing directly beneath,' Tommy retorted.

Everybody creased up, bar Dumbo. Even the mention of Wayne's name sent shivers down his spine. He wished he was brave like Tommy and not scared, but he couldn't help the way he was. He'd been beaten senseless by his alcoholic parents on a regular basis as a child. That's where his fear of violence originated from.

Another baking hot day, lots of families were leaving the Town Show as Tommy and his pals arrived. Some carrying coconuts, others goldfishes in plastic see-through bags. Tommy had no interest in any of the tents. It was all about the fairground for him and that only came alive of an evening.

'Mmm, I love the smell of fried onions. Who fancies a hot dog?' Smiffy asked.

As they made their way towards the hot-dog stall, Dumbo grasped Tommy's arm. 'Please don't look round, but Wayne Bradley is standing by the bumper cars and he's spotted us.'

Scratch whooped with joy as the guy spun their car around on the Waltzer. Tommy grinned. At least she was enjoying herself. The lads were all ill at ease, he could tell. Ever since Wayne Bradley had laid eyes on them earlier, he, Fat Brian and another lad had been following them around the fairground. There was no sign of the little gang Bradley usually knocked around with. Tommy had ordered his pals to stay calm and act normal, but it had most definitely spoiled their day. Nobody could relax, himself included.

Scratch and Tommy got off the ride and walked over to where the others were. 'Right, where are they?'

'Opposite. They've been dossing us out,' Benny informed Tommy. Benny was a lover not a fighter. He didn't like the sight of blood, especially his own.

'How we gonna get out of here, Tommy? They'll follow us across the park, I know they will,' Dumbo warned.

Tommy glanced around. The fair was still quite busy,

but it was dark now. 'Right, this is the plan. You know them caravans we walked round earlier, the furthest away?'

Smiffy nodded.

'We're heading back there, OK? I'll take on Bradley. If Fat Brian joins in, you clump him, Smiffy. Same goes for the other bloke, Benny. If he starts, smack him one. You stay 'ere with Scratch, Dumbo, and look after her,' Tommy ordered.

'I don't need looking after. I want to see this. I'm coming with you,' Scratch replied obstinately.

'Can't we just walk out the park with a load of other people?' Dumbo pleaded. He was shitting himself.

'No. We fucking can't. Months we've been looking forward to today and those pricks have ruined it. I ain't scared of Bradley or the other two. Confronting 'em is the only way to end this.'

Smiffy shrugged. 'OK. Let's do it.'

'You in?' Tommy asked Benny.

'Yeah. Course.'

'No knives though, lads. Give those to Dumbo to look after,' Tommy instructed.

'Say they pull knives on us though?' Benny asked.

'Bradley's too clever to use a blade. He's sixteen in a few months, and then he'll be let loose into the big wide world. He ain't gonna get himself banged up and jeopardize that. As for Fat Brian, he ain't got the bottle to use his fucking fist, let alone a blade. Dunno about the other fella, obviously, but hopefully yous won't get involved anyway. If I take out Bradley, that should be the end of it.'

Benny and Smiffy discreetly handed Dumbo their penknives.

Tommy looked across the Waltzer and locked eyes with Wayne. He held his stare for about five seconds, then turned back to his pals. 'OK. Let's start walking.'

Dumbo hadn't felt as terrified in years as Tommy led them away from the bright lights of the fair. He could still hear the music; the Bay City Rollers were playing in the distance.

'This way,' Tommy hissed, darting between a couple of caravans. He then broke into a run, to the furthest. Tommy leaned his back against the caravan and put his finger to his lips. The element of surprise was always the best tactic.

Scratch squeezed Tommy's hand as a sign of moral support. She then squeezed Dumbo's hand, he was shaking like a leaf.

Hearing the enemy approach, Tommy psyched himself up by thinking of Patch. 'Where the fuck they gone?' he heard Fat Brian ask.

Tommy waited a few seconds, then leapt out. 'Looking for me, are ya?' he bellowed, punching Wayne hard in the back of the head.

Stunned, Wayne turned around and threw a punch at Tommy. He missed, but Tommy didn't. His fist connected with Wayne's ugly mug and he fell backwards, landing on the grass.

Seizing the opportunity, Tommy repeatedly booted Wayne as hard as he could in the side of his head.

When Fat Brian and the other lads tried to pull Tommy away, Smiffy and Benny intervened. 'This is between them two, not you. It's a one-on-one,' Smiffy hissed.

'Yeah. None of your business. Leave 'em to it,' Benny added.

Wayne Bradley staggered to his feet and threw another wild punch. This time it did connect, but such adrenaline ran through Tommy, he barely felt it. 'You no-good animal-torturing scumbag. This is for Patch,' Tommy shrieked, raining blow after blow on Wayne's putrid face.

Scratch watched on in awe as Tommy literally smashed seven bells out of Wayne Bradley. She'd had no idea when he'd told her he wanted to be a pro boxer that he was this bloody good.

Everybody was in a state of shock at the ferociousness of the attack – bar Dumbo, who was jumping up and down clapping his hands with glee.

'Me teeth. Me fucking teeth,' Wayne mumbled, blood pouring from his mouth.

Tommy didn't stop. He carried on punching until Wayne finally fell to the ground, motionless.

Turning to Fat Brian, Tommy grabbed him by the throat and pushed him against the caravan. 'Grass and I'll beat you twice as hard,' he warned. He glared at the other lad. 'What's your name?'

'Darren. I think he's dead. You've killed him,' the lad said. He was the one visibly shaking now, not Dumbo.

'Darren who?'

The lad held his hands up. 'Oliver. Darren Oliver. Look, I don't want any trouble with you, Tommy. This was Wayne's beef, not mine.'

'Grass and you're dead,' Tommy spat.

'I won't grass. I swear I won't,' Darren promised.

Smiffy, Benny and Dumbo all stood over Wayne, laughing. He'd made their lives at the home such a misery in the past; this was the best payback ever.

'You're fucking awesome!' Scratch said, playfully punching Tommy on the arm. 'But you're covered in claret. What you gonna say to Ray and Connie?'

Tommy was that fired up, his hands were trembling as he took the cigarette Dumbo offered him. 'You're a hero, Tommy. A true hero. I wish I was more like you,' Dumbo gushed.

Fat Brian crouched and tried helping Wayne to his feet. He was still dazed, had lost his two upper front teeth. 'How am I gonna get him back to Maylands?'

Tommy glanced down at his clothes and cursed himself for wearing his favourite white Adidas T-shirt and Levi jeans. Even though it was dark, he could see he was splashed in blood.

'Shall we make a move?' Smiffy suggested.

Tommy paced up and down, furiously puffing on his fag. 'Right, this is what we're gonna do. We're gonna get him outside Central Park, then one of yous run to the phone box and ring a cab. Or Ray? Ring Ray. He's always said if anything bad were to happen, then we were to call him first.'

'And what we gonna say when Ray turns up?' Benny asked.

'That Wayne got mugged by the gypsies and we all helped him out. Got that, Brian?'

Fat Brian stared at his feet rather than look at Wayne,

who was now standing up. He hung out with Wayne at Maylands, but knew he'd only been invited to the Town Show as Wayne's other mates were on holiday. 'Yeah. The gypsies did it,' Brian mumbled.

'Wayne wandered off with a girl. We searched for him and found him like this. Got that, all of ya?' Tommy reiterated.

Smiffy chuckled. 'Yep. Ya gotta love the gypsies.'

Ray was horrified when he arrived outside Central Park in his Morris Marina. 'Whatever happened?' he gasped.

'In ya get, mate,' Tommy said, putting an arm around Wayne's waist.

'Fuck off,' Wayne whispered in Tommy's ear.

Tommy couldn't help but smirk. He could still hear the music in the distance from the fairground. Van McCoy's 'The Hustle' was playing. He would have to buy that next week, to remind him of this victorious moment.

'Is it all right if I go now? I live at Dagenham East,' Darren Oliver asked, shuffling from foot to foot.

Tommy patted Darren on the back. 'Yeah, you get off, mate. Thanks for your help.'

Wayne got in the passenger's side and Tommy urged Scratch, Smiffy and Benny to get in the back. 'Me, Dumbo and Brian can walk back,' Tommy told Ray.

'OK. But come straight home,' Ray insisted. 'Connie will make you some sweet tea with plenty of sugar to help with the shock. I will drop the others off, then take Wayne to Casualty. He needs to be seen by a doctor.'

Having unwound his window, Wayne shook his sore head. He felt sick, stupid, tired, and all he wanted was to go to bed. 'I don't need to go to the hospital, Ray. Just give me some painkillers and let me sleep it off.'

'I'm afraid I can't do that, Wayne. It's against Maylands' rules. You've been attacked. We need to get you checked over and report the incident to the police.'

When Ray pulled away from the kerb, Wayne Bradley stared straight ahead. The schools had shut yesterday for the six-week summer holidays. That's why his usual pals hadn't been around today. Philip and Mark – the twins – had gone to their parents' caravan in Clacton, and Tony had gone to Spain with his mum and dad.

'You all right, Wayne? How you feeling, mate?' Smiffy goaded, nudging Benny and Scratch.

Already planning his revenge, Wayne took a deep breath. Tommy Boyle was no Joe Bugner; the only reason he'd won the fight was because he'd caught him unawares and that first lucky blow he'd landed had left Wayne stunned.

As for Smiffy, Benny and Dumbo, they couldn't fight their way out of a paper bag. Wayne had already decided to make their lives a misery as soon as he felt well enough. Especially Smiffy, after taking the piss like he had tonight. He was top of Wayne's hit-list. Fat Brian and Darren Oliver were close seconds. What kind of so-called pals were they? Any true mate would have waded in and helped him.

Sitting next to Smiffy, Scratch nudged him. 'Are you still in pain, Wayne?'

Wayne was no snitch. Besides, he was confident he'd

get retribution somehow. 'No. I'm fine now, thanks. I will hunt down who did this to me though, and get my own back. I always do.'

'None of that silly talk, please, Wayne,' Ray ordered. He and Connie were not a couple. But for different reasons, both were childless. They loved their job. The kids they cared for were their family.

Scratch nudged Smiffy again. 'Did you get a good look at the gypsy, Wayne?'

Benny put his hand over his mouth to stop himself laughing.

Wayne took another deep breath. That skinhead bitch was really irritating him now. He tilted Ray's interior mirror and stared her in the eyes. She would pay big time for disrespecting him.

CHAPTER FOURTEEN

Tommy parted his hair on the left, then flattened the top with a blob of Brylcreem so it didn't stick up. Long hair was all the rage at present. Smiffy and Dumbo had both grown theirs, but Tommy preferred his neat and tidy because of his boxing. It got in his eyes otherwise.

Poking her head around the door, Scratch wolf-whistled. 'Blimey! You look smart,' she chuckled. 'Never seen you go out in anything but jeans and trainers before. You excited?'

'Very,' Tommy grinned. His mum had always insisted he dress up for special occasions and today was most certainly one of those. He hadn't seen his little sister Linda in over two and a half years and he could not wait to see her again.

Sitting on a corner table with a couple of the younger lads, Wayne Bradley planned and plotted as he ate his cornflakes. It was six days now since he'd taken a bloody good hiding and he was ready to rise from the ashes.

When questioned by the police, all Wayne had said was he'd been led across the park by a girl, then jumped on from behind by three lads. 'They didn't have a Dagenham accent, but I can't be sure they were gypsies. It all happened so fast, was dark. I haven't a clue who they were,' he'd lied.

'Morning, Wayne. I called the dentist. Your new teeth will be arriving next Friday, so I booked you an appointment for the following Monday. That OK with you?' Ray asked.

'Yeah, thanks, Ray.' Wayne smiled. He knew how to play the game, was extremely polite and well behaved whenever Ray and Connie were around. 'It's OK for me to go out today, isn't it? My mates are all back from holiday now. I could really do with seeing 'em. It'll cheer me up no end.'

'Are you sure you feel up to it?'

'Yeah. I feel fine now,' Wayne replied.

'OK. I know how stir-crazy you must be going stuck in here. No going anywhere near that fairground though, do you hear me?'

'Yes.'

'I mean it, Wayne. Same goes for all the others. After what happened to you, the fair is off limits and if anybody disobeys that, they'll lose every privilege they have for a whole month,' Ray warned.

Wayne nodded and glanced across the room. He knew Tommy was spending the day with his sister. He also knew that the three stooges – Smiffy, Dumbo and Benny – had arranged to go to the fair later. It was amazing what you could hear through the grapevine if you paid the younger kids ten pence to do a bit of earwigging. They'd do anything for a packet of sweets.

Aware that he was the butt of yet another joke, Wayne averted his eyes instead of reacting. Those arseholes would pay for disrespecting him. He would make damn sure of it.

Dressed in his beige Levi corduroy flares, a short-sleeve brown shirt and his Hush Puppy desert boots, Tommy paced up and down the pavement, puffing on a cigarette. He'd received another letter earlier this week from Linda asking if he was free on Friday. He'd called the number she'd asked him to, and spoken to Linda's friend's mum.

Having been told to keep an eye out for a light brown Ford Zephyr, Tommy's heart raced as one rounded the corner. Seconds later, his sister leapt out of the back and ran towards him. 'Linda! You've got so big – I mean tall.'

Linda looked up at Tommy. 'Not as tall as you. But what are you doing smoking?'

Tommy chuckled, dotted his fag out, then held Linda close to his chest. 'I ain't 'arf missed you, ya know.'

Linda looked up at him, her eyes glistening with a mixture of tears and joy. 'Not as much as I've missed you. It's so good to see you again, Tommy.'

The journey to Southend took around an hour. Tommy could remember his mum and Alexander bringing himself and his sisters here once, but they must have been young, as Linda had no recollection of it.

Linda's friend Alice seemed nice, as did her parents, Catherine and Roger. 'We'll go for a wander, Linda, so you can spend some time alone with your brother. Let's meet back here in say two hours. That OK? And then we'll all go for something to eat,' suggested Catherine.

'That's fine and thank you so much again for arranging this. It truly means the world to me,' Linda replied squeezing her brother's hand.

'Bye, Linda. Have fun,' Alice waved.

'So where does Nanny Noreen think you are?' Tommy enquired, steering Linda towards the beach.

'Here. Catherine told her she was taking Alice to Southend for the day and asked her if I could come too. I was surprised Nan said yes, if I'm honest. She's ever so strict. But I'm thirteen next week, aren't I? So Catherine told Nan it was a birthday treat.'

'Thirteen, eh. What will you be doing on your actual birthday? Will Alexander and the old witch make a fuss of you?'

Linda shrugged. 'Dad's away on the rigs and Nan's breathing is bad now, so probably not. I'd rather spend time with Alice and her family anyway. It's so much nicer in their house than ours. I keep all my books and magazines there. Nan nearly had a cardiac when I brought a copy of *Pink* magazine home. She flicked through it and said it was immoral and gave young girls bad ideas. I'm only allowed to read the Bible and Enid Blyton. Not allowed posters on my bedroom wall or a record player. Nan reckons pop stars and their lyrics send out the wrong signals. She is such a religious nutjob. And I hate the clothes she buys me, I'm not allowed to choose anything. I've put on too much weight to be able to fit into Alice's. I'm just thankful I have to wear a uniform at the school I go to. That's the only time I don't feel different to the other girls.'

Tommy had been shocked by Linda's weight gain and drab appearance, but would never say so. He put a comforting arm around her shoulders. 'It won't always be like this, ya know. By the time you reach sixteen, I'll be sorted with me own gaff and you can come and live with me. I'll make sure you've got your own bedroom and you can have nice clothes, posters on the wall, and play records all day long. How does that grab ya?'

Linda's eyes shone. 'I would love that, Tommy. I really would.'

'As for your weight, don't worry about it. It's only puppy fat. You'll lose that as you get older.'

'I eat lots of sweets and crisps because I get so bored when I'm indoors, Tommy. I'm not even allowed to watch TV much. There's sod all else to do but eat. So tell me everything. What's the home like? And why did you leave Uncle Ian's?'

Knowing the question was bound to arise, Tommy had already thought of a plausible explanation. He told his sister Ian used to beat him and he'd contacted their old bobby for help.

Linda squeezed her brother's arm. 'Oh, Tommy, that's terrible. Did PC Kendall arrest Uncle Ian? I can't believe he beat you up.'

'Nah. But I wouldn't have wanted to go to court anyway. Best thing I ever did was ring PC Kendall. I'm happy at Maylands, got some great pals there.'

'Well, they must treat you well. You look ever so smart. Do they buy all the lads Levis?'

'Nah. We're given a clothes allowance, but me and the lads have got a little racket going where we earn a few bob on the side. Ray and Connie who run the home are ever so nice, but a bit dense. If they spot us wearing new clobber, we just say we got it from the local jumble sale,' Tommy chuckled.

'Make sure you don't get yourself into any trouble, Tommy.'

'Don't worry. I'm too wise for that. Fancy an ice-cream? You still addicted to screwballs?'

'I prefer a ninety-nine now.'

Tommy stood up. 'Race ya to the ice-cream van.'

'What's the plan then?' asked Philip and Mark Timms in unison. Identical fifteen-year-old twins with cruel eyes and sadistic tendencies, they often thought alike and spoke simultaneously.

Having already explained what had happened last weekend, Wayne grinned like a Cheshire cat as he pulled the see-through bag from his pocket and waved it in the air. It contained LSD tabs. 'We're gonna catch one of 'em, ram these down the back of their throat. Then take 'em on the ride of a lifetime.'

'What sort of ride?' Tony Carrington enquired. He had a nasty streak himself, but felt the others took their little escapades a tad too far at times.

Tapping the side of his nose, Wayne chuckled. 'You'll soon see.'

'You've changed, Tommy,' Linda announced.

Tommy propped himself up on his elbow. 'In what way?'

'I don't know how to explain it. You just seem different, I suppose. Your voice sounds deeper and instead of being chatty like you once was, you don't say much. You've told me nothing about your life now, only that you got some racket going on. You haven't even mentioned your friends. It's me that's been doing all the talking. And you look different. More like a man than the brother I remember.'

'I can't help the fact I've grown up, Linda. Ask me some questions then. What do ya want to know?'

'Have you got a girlfriend? You're very handsome now. I bet you have to fight the girls off.'

'I haven't got a girlfriend as such, but I've got a good girl mate. She only moved to the home recently.'

'Do you think you'll end up asking her out?'

'We do go out, but not like boyfriend and girlfriend. I'm only interested in making it as a pro boxer, Lin. I got plenty of time for girls once I've achieved my dream. What do you want to do when you leave school?'

'I don't know. I like typing, so I wouldn't mind working in an office. If Nan had her way, I'd probably become a nun.'

'I won't let that happen, I promise,' Tommy chuckled. 'You still loved up with little Jimmy Osmond?'

Linda screwed her nose up. 'No. I'm a Bay City Rollers fan now. I love Les McKeown. "Bye Bye Baby" is my favourite song,' Linda said dreamily. 'What about you? You still into David Bowie?'

'No.' Tommy's face clouded over.

'What's the matter?' Linda was getting worried now.

Tommy smiled. 'Nothing. I'm just into other kinds of music these days. I like Ska and Soul.'

Linda's expression suddenly turned serious. 'I know we're only half-brother and -sister. Nan told me. Have you ever tried to find out who your real dad is?'

Wanting to wipe the short meeting with his real father from his memory, Tommy shook his head. 'Perhaps when I'm older. Whoever he is, he's never bothered looking for me.'

'Well Nan reckons my real dad was the bloody window cleaner now.'

Aware that his sister was on the verge of tears, Tommy put both arms around her and held her close to his chest. His mum's pal had actually told him that day in the Wimpy that his mother had also had an affair with their window cleaner Robin around the time Linda was conceived and Alexander had doubts she was his. 'That's why Hazel has always been Alexander's favourite. She's a ringer for him and the only one he's positive is his child,' Lisa had explained.

Unlike himself, who'd had no option but to toughen up, Linda was young and fragile, therefore Tommy wasn't about to admit his findings. 'Take no notice of idle gossip. Your dad was always paranoid, accusing our mum of all sorts. If you weren't his daughter, you wouldn't be living with Nanny Noreen.'

Linda burst into tears. 'I wish I wasn't his daughter, Tommy. I hate him.'

'Yeah, man. I is well stoned,' Benny grinned, flopping flat on his back and staring at the clear blue sky.

'Why wouldn't Scratch come out with us? I still

fancy her, even though Tommy says I mustn't,' Dumbo admitted, snatching the joint out of Benny's hand.

'You got no chance with her, Dumbo. She fancies Tommy. I've seen the way she looks at him. Anyway, good job she ain't here. She'd only grass us up to Tommy for getting stoned, then going to the fair,' Smiffy said.

'True. Tommy acts like our dad at times,' Benny chuckled.

Smiffy took a big lug on the joint. As much as he idolized Tommy, his pal could be a bit of a killjoy at times. Tommy wasn't a fan of marijuana and was forever telling them off if they got too stoned or sloshed.

'You sure Wayne won't go to the fair?' Dumbo asked.

'Positive,' Smiffy laughed. 'The ugly bastard ain't got no teeth. Would you go to the fair looking like that? He ain't been out all week.'

'How much in the kitty?' Benny asked. They still had money in the kitty from last weekend, but Tommy was looking after that. They'd had a good little earner with their thieving this week though, always did when it was the school holidays.

'Eighteen-pound-odd. What I suggest is we get something from the chippy, rather than eat at the fair. They stripe you up for grub over there. I would rather spend our dosh on cider and the rides,' Smiffy said. When Tommy wasn't around, he tended to take charge.

Benny stood up. 'I'm gasping and ravenous. Let's make a move, shall we?'

As the lads jovially made their way out of Ponfield Park, they had no idea of what lay ahead. If they had, they'd have run a mile.

* * *

As they approached the fairground, Tony Carrington was having serious doubts. 'You sure we'll get away with this, lads? I mean, how we gonna capture one of 'em?'

'Easy. We chase the others off. We'll follow 'em around, wait until it's getting dark, then pounce. I dunno if the bird'll be with 'em, but if she is, we'll have to chase her too,' Wayne replied.

Tony looked alarmed. 'What bird?'

'Oh, just some skinhead tart they knock about with now. Don't worry about her; she's like a geezer anyway. Trappy little bitch, she is.'

'Any preference to which one we grab?' Philip asked Wayne.

'Erm, not really. They're all cunts.'

'Drop us at this shop on the left, please. I need to get some cigarettes,' Tommy said. 'And thank you so much for looking after Linda, bringing her to see me and taking us both out. It's been a lovely day,' Tommy added.

Turning around in the passenger seat, Catherine Piper smiled. Considering he lived in a children's home and had lost his mother, Tommy was a lovely lad with impeccable manners. 'You're very welcome. We'll try to bring Linda to see you again before Christmas.'

'Thanks,' Tommy said.

'Linda, why don't you get out of the car and say a proper goodbye to your brother? Take your time. We're in no rush,' Catherine smiled.

Linda leapt out, threw her arms around Tommy's waist, and clung to him like a leech. 'Do you mean what you said earlier? Can I really come and live with you when I turn sixteen?'

'Of course. I'd never let you down. I promise.'

Linda smiled. 'Write to me soon at Alice's, won't you?'

'You try stopping me. And don't forget to have a snoop, see if you can find out an address for Hazel.'

'I will. But as I already told you, no letters come to ours any more. I reckon Hazel stopped writing to Dad, or he has them sent to his girlfriend's house.'

'Just keep your eyes peeled and your ear to the ground.'

'OK. I love you, Tommy.'

'Love you more, Sis.'

'I reckon the Octopus is our best bet. Bound to land on the ride itself rather than any innocent bystander if he freaks out and leaps off,' Wayne mused.

'The big wheel is a definite no-go. Too many people underneath. What about the Dive Bomber?' Mark suggested.

Philip chuckled. 'Whoever falls out the Dive Bomber will get splattered all over the place.'

'Including me, probably. Not the Dive Bomber. Fuck that,' Wayne laughed.

Tony was worried. 'What you gonna say to people afterwards? That he just jumped?'

'Yeah. Let's get on there, do a trial run. I need to make sure I can stand up on the thing. I've gotta pretend I tried to save him,' Wayne grinned. 'You'll be on the ride behind me, so all you got to do is back the story up. Even if I do end up giving him a gentle push.'

Philip and Mark smirked at each other. 'Come on then. What we waiting for?' Mark chuckled.

'All right. What records you bought?' Tommy asked Scratch. It was dinner time at Maylands and the dining room was half empty. Even some of the younger kids were absent.

'Linda Lewis' "It's In His Kiss". Oh, and I treated you to "The Hustle".'

'Really! Ah, cheers. That's nice of ya,' Tommy grinned. 'So where are the others?' he asked.

Scratch shrugged and sat next to Tommy. 'They were acting odd earlier, a bit shifty. I heard Dumbo say something about getting the drugs first, so I decided to do my own thing. I got the impression Smiffy didn't want me hanging around today anyway.'

'Stay there. I'll be back in a tick.' Tommy found Ray tidying up some rubbish in the garden.

'Hello, Tommy. Did you have a nice day with your sister? Dinner won't be long. Corned beef, chips and beans.'

'I had a great day, thanks. Where is everybody, Ray? The dining room's empty.'

'A couple of the younger lads have spent the day with family members. They'll be back by seven, and young Ricky Dawson is spending the weekend with a lovely foster couple who are interested in offering him a permanent home.'

'Where's Smiffy and the lads?'

'Gone to the pictures. They asked if it was OK to skip tea and eat out, so I gave them permission. Didn't they tell you?'

'No. Where's Wayne and Brian?'

'Brian's in bed. He had an unfortunate accident. He fell down the stairs earlier, poor lad. Wayne's gone out with his friends. The ones that have been on holiday.'

'Shit,' Tommy mumbled as he darted back to the dining room.

'What's up?' Scratch asked. It was obvious by Tommy's expression something was wrong.

'I think the lads have gone to the fair and I think Wayne might be over there too,' Tommy whispered.

'Shit!'

'Exactly! Fucking idiots.'

'Pick it up. Go on, quick,' Smiffy urged Dumbo. A woman had dropped a red purse on the grass.

Dumbo edged closer to the purse, pretended to tie the lace on his trainer and expertly slipped the purse down the back of his trousers.

'She's looking for it. Come on, let's go,' Benny urged.

The lads darted behind the coconut shy. 'Open it then,' Smiffy demanded.

'Well?' Benny asked.

Dumbo's eyes lit up. 'There's over twenty-five quid!'

'Yeah, man,' Benny chuckled.

'Touch! Dump the purse, Dumbo,' ordered Smiffy.

'We can have loads more goes on everything and get some more munch. I'm starving,' Dumbo replied.

'How many joints we got left?' Smiffy enquired.

Benny looked inside the silver tin. 'Two. Shall we have one now?'

'Nah. Shooting Gallery first, then we'll sneak off for a joint,' Smiffy replied.

'What about me hot dog?' Dumbo enquired.

'Have that after a joint. You'll be even more hungry then.'

As the lads made their way to the Shooting Gallery, they didn't have an inkling that for the past hour, their every move had been watched.

'I ain't standing here no longer. It'll be quicker to walk,' Tommy said, kicking out at the bus stop in frustration. He had that horrible churning feeling in his gut, a feeling of impending doom.

'I'm sure they'll be all right, Tommy. The fairground is probably packed. There isn't much Wayne and his mates can do in front of all those people, is there?'

'Go back to Maylands, Scratch, and wait for me there. I got a bad feeling it's gonna kick off and I don't want you getting caught up in it.'

'No. I'm coming with you,' Scratch insisted, her face etched with determination.

Having walked away from the fairground, Smiffy, Benny and Dumbo were sitting on the grass, stoned, backs against a caravan.

'What was that?' Dumbo leapt up. 'I heard something.'

'Sit down, you tart. It's the gear, innit. Strong shit, this is. You were paranoid earlier, thought we were being followed by the woman whose purse you stole,' Smiffy chuckled.

'I didn't steal it. It fell out of her bag,' Dumbo protested.

Benny nudged Smiffy. 'You could've handed it back though, couldn't ya? You only had to tap her on the shoulder,' he chuckled.

'Sit down, for fuck's sake,' Smiffy ordered Dumbo. 'You look like Bert out of *Sesame Street* stood there.'

Holding his balls, Benny rolled around on the grass. 'He does look like Bert. It's the ears that does it.'

All of a sudden, Dumbo let out a deafening scream. 'Run. Fucking run,' he shrieked.

Scrambling to their feet, Smiffy and Benny did as they were told. Unfortunately though, one of them glanced around, stumbled and fell.

Having run through Central Park at a pace Roger Bannister would be proud of, an out-of-breath Dumbo leaned against the railings in Rainham Road North. He had no idea where Benny and Smiffy were, or what he should do now. He didn't even have any money on him. Benny was holding the kitty.

'If you're ever in any kind of trouble and do not have any money on you, call Maylands and reverse the charges,' Ray and Connie always reiterated. But how could he? They weren't even meant to be at the fair and he'd hate to get the others into trouble. He'd seen the scary twins, that's why he'd legged it. Perhaps Wayne wasn't even with them and the twins had just chased them for a laugh, he hoped.

Dumbo broke into another run. The only thing he could do was head back to Maylands and pray the others were safe and did the same.

* * *

'Open your mouth again. There's a good boy,' Wayne Bradley chuckled, as he rammed another tab of LSD inside.

'Don't give him no more, for fuck's sake,' Tony warned. 'He looks out of his trolley as it is. How many did you give him in the first place?'

'Three.'

Mark Timms grabbed Wayne's arm. 'Tone's right. He looks a proper victim. You give him any more, they won't let him on a ride.'

Wayne stared at his prey. 'Stand up,' he ordered.

As their victim unsteadily rose to his feet, Philip Timms roared with laughter. 'State of that. We're gonna have to pretend he's a flid or something.'

'I don't feel well. I want to go home. Please don't hurt me.'

Wayne smirked. 'We ain't gonna hurt you. We're just going on a little ride together. Now walk.'

Having never been so relieved to see someone in his lifetime, Dumbo hugged Tommy like he was a long-lost relative. 'I was so scared. I thought I was gonna die,' he gabbled.

Tommy shook his pal by the shoulders. 'I can't understand you. Calm down and speak slowly. Where are the others?'

'I don't know. We were over by that caravan where you beat Wayne up and they just appeared and started chasing us,' Dumbo wept.

'Who?' Tommy bellowed.

'Wayne's friends. The scary twins.'

Tommy's heart lurched. 'Scratch, go back to Shitlands with Dumbo. I'll sort this.'

As Tommy ran towards the bright lights of the fairground, Scratch grabbed Dumbo's hand. 'No. Wait for us. We're not leaving you alone,' she shouted.

'I don't feel well. I can't breathe properly. Please, let me go home. Everyone's staring at me.'

'I will take you home. But let's go on the Octopus first. You can sit next to me. I'll look after ya, I promise,' Wayne replied reassuringly.

Smiffy's eyes darted about like ping-pong balls. The Bee Gees' 'Jive Talkin' was playing and for a second he thought he saw the Bee Gees in the crowd. Couldn't people see he was about to be murdered? Why wasn't anybody helping him?

'Ah, missed out. Our turn next,' Mark laughed, as the fairground worker held his arm out to suggest the ride was full.

'You all right, Smiffy lad?' Philip grinned.

Smiffy cowered. He was sweating like a pig and the music was hurting his ears. He'd just seen a monster in the crowd too, and his head was pulsating as if his brain were about to burst. People were looking at him, laughing. Were they all in on his murder too?

Feeling more paranoid than ever, Smiffy decided it was shit or bust. He couldn't turn around and run as there was now a big queue behind him and he was sure he had seen Tommy standing the opposite side of the ride. The only way he could escape was to run across the actual ride, duck the spinning cars, then Tommy would save him.

'Look, he's keen,' Wayne sniggered as Smiffy edged in front of him.

The Octopus had eight arms attached to it. Cars at the end of each arm would spin while moving up and down. Smiffy took a deep breath, then bolted.

'Oi! Stop! Come back,' yelled the fairground worker.

'Tommy,' screamed Smiffy.

'What the fuck!' exclaimed Wayne.

Onlookers looked on in horror as two cars narrowly missed the lad. They then screamed as a third hit him full on, sending his body flying through the air as if catapulted.

'Wow!' mumbled the twins, as Smiffy's body landed in the queue behind them.

'My baby, my baby,' a woman shrieked. 'Help! My baby is trapped.'

As chaos enveloped them, a crowd gathered around the injured. Wayne and his pals barged their way to the front.

'Fuck, no,' Tony put his hand over his mouth. Smiffy was lying motionless in a skew-whiff position. The bones on his right shoulder were jutting out of his skin and his neck was at such an unusual angle, it had to be broken.

There were a dozen or so people either lying injured or sitting on the grass in a daze. But worst of all, as some men moved Smiffy, a young girl appeared underneath him. She looked about three, had blood seeping out of her nose and her ears and didn't seem to be breathing. Her mother was hysterical, understandably screaming blue murder.

Tony punched Wayne in the arm. 'I knew this was a bad idea, you dumb fucking bastard.'

'Let's go,' said Mark Timms.

As the twins and Tony broke into a run, Wayne was grabbed by the fairground worker. 'Who is he?'

'Who?'

'The silly fucker who ran across my ride and caused this mayhem.'

Wayne was out of his depth now. He'd wanted to terrorize Smiffy, pay him back for tormenting him all week, but he wasn't sure he'd meant to break his neck. Neither had he expected a child to be killed. 'I don't know him. Honest, I don't. He was in the queue in front of us.'

'Liar,' the man spat. 'Paddy, Arthur, Bill, keep hold of this one until the police arrive. He was with the lad. The mates have run off.'

There was an eerie silence at Central Park by the time Tommy arrived. People were leaving in droves, no music was playing and all the rides had stopped. 'What's happened?' Tommy asked a random lad.

'There's been an accident. Some lad flew off a ride or summink and crushed a little girl.'

'Where? What ride?' Tommy had this awful feeling in the pit of his stomach.

'The Octopus. The police and ambulance men are there now. I didn't see it meself, but they've shut the bloody fair because of it.'

With Dumbo and Scratch in hot pursuit, Tommy ran towards the Octopus. Please God it wasn't Smiffy or Benny, he silently prayed.

'You can't go any further, lad,' a copper said, holding out his arm. The area had now been cordoned off and everyone except the witnesses had been told to go home.

'What's happened?' Tommy asked the copper.

'A lad and kid are dead. That's all you need to know. Now scarper.'

'But our mates are missing. We can't find 'em. Who is the lad? What does he look like?' Dumbo asked.

'He looks dead. Now stop wasting my time and do one.'

Tommy pushed the copper. 'He ain't lying. Our mates are missing, you arsehole.'

'Leave it, Tommy,' Scratch warned, grabbing her pal's arm.

Realizing the lads were serious, the copper scolded Tommy for pushing him, before asking for descriptions.

'Benny's black and has a big Afro. He's wearing—'

'Nope. Not him. This lad's English,' the copper interrupted.

'Smiffy's got shoulder-length wavy blond hair. He's wearing faded jeans and a white T-shirt,' Dumbo said.

'Wait 'ere a sec,' the policeman ordered, before walking away and bellowing 'Guv.'

In that precise second, Tommy knew. He ducked under the tape and ran towards the covered-up body.

Scratch grabbed hold of Dumbo to stop him following Tommy. No way would Dumbo be able to handle seeing a dead body. It would freak him out.

Tommy's worst fears were confirmed when he saw the black Gola trainers poking out from beneath the sheet. Smiffy had exceptionally big feet, was forever joking to any girls he met that his cock was even bigger.

Tommy sank to his knees. DI Aycott crouched next to him and lifted back the sheet to reveal Smiffy's face. 'Is this your pal?'

Tommy nodded.

'What's his full name and address, lad?'

'He ain't got no proper address. None of us have. We live at Maylands, the children's home. His name is Martin Smith and this weren't no accident. Smiffy was murdered and I know who killed him.'

'Who?'

'Wayne Bradley.'

CHAPTER FIFTEEN

Smiffy's funeral. How I dreaded that. I couldn't get my head around the fact he was dead. Not just dead. Murdered.

Only a few days before he'd died we'd been planning the future. We turned sixteen within a few weeks of one another, had already made a pact to share a gaff.

Obviously, my dream back then was to make it as a pro boxer, but I wasn't delusional. I knew that was a long-shot. Smiffy had a cousin who was in the roofing game. He reckoned his cousin would give us both a job. I was so looking forward to us working and sharing a place together. But it wasn't to be. The Grim fucking Reaper made sure of that.

So, back to square one, I was. No plans for my future. No light at the end of the tunnel. I couldn't even be arsed with my boxing any more. Everything was an effort, even getting out of bed in the mornings.

But my real old man was right about one thing. 'You're a survivor. I can see it in your eyes,' he'd told me. Not that I've given him a second thought since. He's history. Can rot in hell with the likes of Wayne Bradley, my pervy uncle and that arsehole Alexander, for all I care.

Nevertheless, he was spot on. Only the strong survive in care. When you've had as many kicks in the teeth as I have in life, setbacks are no more than water off a duck's back.

Having said that, if somebody would have told me on the day of Smiffy's funeral that my luck was about to change for the better, I doubt I'd have believed them. Let alone being told this time next year I'd be married with a kiddie and earning more money than I could ever have dreamed of. I'd have laughed in whoever's face.

But that's exactly what happened. A whole new chapter in my life was about to unfold.

It's a bit of a rollercoaster what happened next. I, Tommy Boyle, was on my way up in the world.

So sit back and enjoy the ride . . .

'Today, we are gathered here to commemorate the life of Martin Cyril Smith . . .'

As the vicar droned on, Tommy Boyle stared into space, a stony expression on his face. There were only about twenty people present. Connie, Ray, some of the kids from the home and a few adults Tommy had never seen before.

Knowing how Tommy had been struggling since Smiffy's untimely death, Scratch squeezed his hand. Tommy immediately snatched it away. He didn't want sympathy. He wanted revenge.

Wayne Bradley had never returned to Maylands after Smiffy's death. They kept his whereabouts a secret but Tommy planned to find the bastard one day and torture him. His missed Smiffy badly. His best mate, gone just like that, in the blink of an eye.

He, Benny and Dumbo had given statements about the day/evening in question and after the post-mortem, the police had returned to the home to ask about Smiffy's use of drugs. Tommy had told them the truth, that Smiffy liked a puff, but would never dabble with LSD. 'Wayne must have forced it down his throat, I swear to ya,' he'd told DI Aycott.

Unfortunately, Benny and Dumbo had been questioned separately and their statements had conflicted his. Not only had they both denied smoking marijuana with Smiffy on the day he died, but Dumbo, the thick bastard, admitted that he, Benny and Smiffy had once tried an LSD tab and didn't like it.

Tommy had been livid when he'd learned what the other two had said. As if it wasn't bad enough that they had run off and left Smiffy in the clutches of Bradley and his evil cronies, they'd more than likely ballsed up the investigation as well. If Smiffy had been pushed off that ride – and Tommy had no doubt that was the intention – at least there'd have been eye-witnesses. The fact Smiffy had run bang into the ride left the police with very little evidence, Tommy guessed.

'You OK, love?' Connie whispered to Tommy. She was worried about him, as was Ray. Since Smiffy's death, he'd regularly come home stinking of alcohol and he'd given up his boxing. He'd also fallen out with Benny and Dumbo, and in Connie's eyes, was in a dreadfully bad place, the poor lad.

Tommy snarled at her, then at Ray when he passed by on his way up to the lectern to give a eulogy.

Ray cleared his throat. 'It is with great sadness I find myself here today. Martin, or should I say Smiffy, was such a wonderful young man, with a bright future ahead of him. When he first arrived at Maylands, Smiffy was no more than a slip of a lad. But he soon fitted in, became a valued member of our little community and always had a smile on his face. Never more so than when he was with his best mates, Tommy, Benny and Dumbo. The three of them were inseparable and—'

Tommy leapt off the bench. 'Inseparable!' He pointed at Benny and Dumbo. 'That pair of shitbags ran off and left him. As for you and her' – Tommy pointed at Connie – 'you two should never be running a home for kids. Thick as two short fucking planks, the pair of ya. I knew the day I met Wayne Bradley he was pure evil, but you two lapped up his fake niceness, you thick bastards. He terrorized me, all of us in fact, right under your stupid noses and you either chose to ignore it, or you seriously are that backward, you never saw it. Well, you all have blood on your hands now. Smiffy's.'

As Tommy ran from the chapel, the vicar, Ray and Connie looked totally shell-shocked.

Knowing where her loyalties lay, Scratch stuck a middle finger up, then chased after Tommy.

Tommy handed Scratch the bottle of cider. Instead of going over Ponfield Park, or Parsloes, their usual haunts, it had been Tommy's idea they hang out over what they referred to as 'The Castle'. It was an area of wasteland opposite Dagenham East station and Tommy was certain nobody would think of searching for them there.

'That was so funny when you swore at 'em all, Tommy. The vicar nearly had a heart attack,' Scratch chuckled.

'True what I said though, ain't it? I put money on it; Bradley has just been removed from the area and shoved to another cushty home. I bet he's terrorizing all the kids in there an' all. Life is so unfair, ya know.'

'Tell me about it. My mother was the devil in disguise. She sold me, ya know, in exchange for gear.'

Tommy propped himself up on his elbow. Up until Smiffy had died, he'd never drunk much alcohol. He'd share a bottle of cider with the lads if they were going somewhere special, but other than that he never craved booze like the others seemed to. But things had changed recently. Alcohol made him feel better, dulled the pain of losing Smiffy. 'What do ya mean, sold you?'

'What I say. She used to let this man look after me in exchange for drugs. He'd do things to me, horrible things. You can guess what I mean, can't you?'

Tommy put his arms around Scratch and held her tightly to his chest. 'I know exactly what you mean.'

'Well?' Connie asked hopefully, as Ray arrived home.

'No sign of them.'

'Do you think we should call the police?'

Ray shook his head. 'It's only eight p.m., Connie. They aren't even due home yet, we can't send out a search party just yet. It will look bad on us too if we do. We know Scratch is with Tommy, so at least he's not alone.'

'That boy is going off the rails, Ray, and it's breaking my heart watching it happen. He has so much potential to make something of his life, especially with his boxing talent. Do you think we should ring his trainer? Perhaps if Ted had another word with him, he might see sense. I would hate him to throw his life away.'

Ray squeezed Connie's hand. 'Me too, sweetheart. But Ted has already spoken to Tommy twice and that hasn't done much good. I have a better idea. I am going to call his friends in South London, the Darlings. They're the ones who write to Tommy every month and send him money. Perhaps they can get through to him? If they can't I dread to think what's going to happen to the boy.'

Scratch's story was harsh. From the age of nine, her mother had let a local drug dealer, a man in his forties called Alan, look after her. He lived in a tower block on the Gascoigne Estate in Barking and that's where the attacks had happened.

'I'll never forget his breath, Tommy. It stank of booze and stale smoke. He used to roll his own cigarettes, Golden Virginia. His fingers were yellow.'

'Did you tell your mum what was happening?'

'Yeah. But she said I was making it up, told me not to be so daft. She also warned if I told anyone else, the police would arrest me for lying and take me away. She knew I was telling the truth, the bitch. But she didn't want her little arrangement to stop – I was her meal ticket. Alan sold heroin and my mum couldn't get enough of the poxy stuff.'

'How did it stop?'

'I told my school teacher, Miss Simmonds. She was a kind lady and kept asking if everything was OK at home. I don't remember much about my time at Barking Abbey, but I remember telling Miss Simmonds what was happening with Alan. She instantly believed me and contacted a lady called Vera. Vera had a great big hooter and wore glasses, but she was nice to me too.'

'Did Alan get arrested?'

'Yes. But he died not long afterwards from an overdose. I was in foster care by then and Vera came to tell me in person. It's weird how it's the small things you remember. I know Alan had long greasy hair, like a hippy, but I can't picture his face any more. Sometimes though, I'll hear a record on the radio and it brings it all back to me. He'd play Canned Heat and Janis Joplin albums.'

Tommy nodded. He understood totally. 'What about the other lad you mentioned, the one you stabbed?'

'Stephen. Horrible bastard, he was. He cut the shell off the neighbours' tortoise.'

'Shit. That's rank. You have to be a right twisted bastard to hurt animals, I hate anyone that does.'

'Me too. I knew Stephen was, ya know, a wrong 'un all along. Caught him standing on a chair a couple of times, spying on me while I was taking a bath. There was a panel of glass at the top of the door. He's the reason I became a skinhead. My hair was long. He kept telling me how pretty I was and how he found my hair a turn-on. So I had it all cut off and bought some bovver boots. It didn't put him off though, unfortunately. It only made him even more fucking keen.'

'I can't imagine you with long hair,' Tommy smiled.

'I've not always been a tomboy. Shit happened in life to make me this way,' Scratch snapped.

'Sorry. I didn't mean to be rude. Did Stephen . . . ya know?'

'No. But I knew he was going to. I tried never to be left alone in the house with him, always used to go out if his parents went out. But one night his dad got rushed to hospital and his mum went with him. I was in bed, didn't even know an ambulance had been called until Stephen came into my room. He tried to kiss me and touched me up. I begged him to stop, but he wouldn't. He pinned me down, ripped my pyjama bottoms off and tried to, well you know. Luckily for me, I always slept with the screwdriver under my pillow. So I grabbed it and stabbed him straight through the eye. There was blood everywhere.'

'Good for you, girl. I admire ya. I stabbed someone once too, ya know. Someone who did something bad to me.'

'I know.'

'Who told you I stabbed somebody?'

'Nobody. But I know something similar happened to you that happened to me.'

For a moment Tommy felt sick to his stomach. 'How? What's been said?'

'I can just tell. I'm a good listener, ya know, if you ever want to talk about it.'

Tommy clammed up. 'Nothing really bad happened to me. Shall we go and get some more cider? There's an offie down the bottom of the hill.'

'Yeah, sod it. Why not?'

Connie handed Ray a cup of tea and brought up the inevitable. 'We're going to have to call the police, love. It's gone midnight now and in the eyes of the law they're still classed as children. I'm sure they're both fine, but if something were to happen to them, we'd be in trouble for not alerting the authorities.'

Ray sighed. He and Connie were regular church-goers and today's little outburst from Tommy had hurt them both deeply. They always tried to see the best in the children in their care. But had they been too lenient with Wayne? 'Could you call the police and explain the situation please, Connie? I've got a thumping head-ache. It's been a long day.'

Two hours and another bottle of cider later, Tommy finally began to spill his guts. 'You know what you said earlier, about not remembering some things, but music bringing stuff back to ya? Well, I used to be a massive David Bowie fan as a kid. Now I can't listen to him any more. If a record of his comes on the radio, I have to turn it off. And if he comes on the TV, I have to leave the room. Same goes for Benny Hill. He really freaks me out, reminds me of someone.'

Scratch squeezed Tommy's hand. 'Anything you tell me will never be repeated. Apart from Miss Simmonds, Vera and a policeman, you're the only person I've ever spoken to about Alan. I told a few people about Stephen, mind. Probably because I hoped they'd see me as some psycho and leave me alone.'

Tommy's eyes welled up. 'It makes me feel ashamed. Perhaps it's different for you, 'cause you're a girl.'

'Don't you think it makes me feel fucking ashamed too, Tommy? I feel violated and I very much doubt I'll ever get married and have kids like normal people do.'

'That's how I feel too.'

'Who was he? A family friend? Neighbour? It wasn't Wayne, was it?'

Tommy bowed his head. 'It was my mum's brother. I got sent to live with him after my mum died. But as I said earlier, nothing really bad happened.'

'Bastard. Did you tell someone?'

Tommy explained about the bath incident, his friendship with the Darlings and how he'd confided in Danny about that. He never went into any detail regarding his rape. He never wanted to talk about that again.

'Did he get arrested?' Scratch enquired.

'Yeah, but then someone set fire to his house while him and my aunt were sleeping. They got out alive, then disappeared.'

'People don't just disappear. Someone must know where the arsehole is.'

'I'll find him one day, don't you worry about that. Same goes for Wayne and a few others. I have a list of people I intend to get even with.'

'Can you add my mum to your list?'

'What's her full name and where does she live?'

Scratch reeled off a name and address. Tommy squeezed her hand. 'Consider it done.'

'What's the time, Tommy?'

'Nearly half one. We've still got half a bottle of cider left.'

'I bet Connie and Ray are having kittens. They've probably called the police already,' Scratch laughed.

'Serves 'em right. Perhaps my little outburst might help 'em see the error of their ways. Fat Brian told Ray that Wayne pushed him down the stairs on the morning Smiffy died, but Ray never told the filth that.'

'How do you know?'

'Because I told 'em and it was the first they'd heard of it.'

'I know you're still angry with Benny and Dumbo, but none of this is their fault. You should make up with them.'

'They fucked off and left Smiffy,' Tommy reminded Scratch.

'No. They ran because they were scared, Tommy. They feared for their own safety. Not everyone is brave and can fight like you. Speaking of which, you should go back to your boxing. Smiffy's death should make you even more determined to be able to handle yourself.'

'You're beginning to sound like my mother.'

'Do you still miss her?'

'Sometimes.'

'You thought any more about your real dad?'

'Nope. He's another on my get-even list.'

Scratch chuckled. 'You make me laugh. I am so glad we met. This is the happiest I've ever been since going into care, and I got you to thank for that.'

'You ain't so bad yourself.'

Scratch put her arms around Tommy's neck. 'You ever kissed a girl or had a girlfriend since what happened to you?'

'No.'

'Neither have I, kissed or had a boyfriend, I mean. Kiss me.'

'What!'

'You heard. Kiss me.'

'Why?'

'Because it might help us both move on.'

Tommy took a swig of cider for Dutch courage, then leaned towards Scratch.

Having arrived back at Maylands in the middle of the night, when Tommy was awoken less than six hours later, he was expecting a huge telling off.

Instead, Ray smiled at him. 'Get dressed and come downstairs. You've got visitors.'

Tommy sat up and scratched his head. 'Who?'

'They told me not to tell you. It's a surprise.'

Tommy threw some clothes on, his head all over the place. The kiss with Scratch had turned into more of a fumble and he didn't know if it was a good or bad thing that he'd become sexually aroused. It sort of made him feel normal, but it felt wrong at the same time. Scratch was his mate.

Hoping the unexpected visitors were his sister and the Piper family, Tommy bounded down the stairs. He was led into the back garden by Ray, and his jaw dropped as he laid eyes on Danny and Ronnie Darling for the first time in years. 'What you doing 'ere?'

Danny grinned. 'If the mountain won't come to Muhammad, or whatever the poxy saying is. Good to see you, pal. Fuck me, you ain't 'arf grown.'

'So have you,' Tommy said, as Danny hugged him.

He felt awkward, silly, but elated to see his pal at the same time.

Ronnie shook Tommy's hand. 'We heard what happened to your pal. I got a mate who lives round 'ere and he showed me the article in the *Dagenham Post*. So sorry, Tommy lad. That's why we're here.' Ray had asked Ronnie not to tell Tommy he had called him yesterday.

'Tommy, your friends have asked if you can spend the day with them and I've given my permission,' Ray said.

'I don't fancy going out,' Tommy retorted.

'Oh, come on, Tom. It's Mum's birthday and we're going to a steak restaurant. She'd be proper made up to see you. She's always asking after ya and if we turn up with you, it'll be the best surprise ever.'

'I dunno. I've not been wanting to do much lately.'

'All the more reason you should come out with us then. My old man'll be there, and Donna,' Danny grinned. He knew his pal had once had a crush on his sister.

'You can't blow us out, Tom. It took us over an hour to get here. Traffic was diabolical,' Ronnie added.

Even though Tommy had little interest in girls, he had never forgotten how pretty Donna Darling was.

'I'll leave yous to it,' Ray said diplomatically, before disappearing back inside the house.

'Come on, Tom. It'll be a laugh. We're gonna pop in the Lord Nelson first, have a couple of beers. That's my dad's local. What's not to enjoy, eh?'

'Where's the Lord Nelson?' Tommy enquired.

'Bermondsey.'

'I really don't fancy going back there. Say I'm recognized?'

'By who? For what?' Ronnie asked.

Tommy bowed his head. 'Ya know,' he mumbled, feeling ashamed.

'Oh Tommy. Hand on heart, nobody knows nothing,' Ronnie insisted, finally realizing and instantly forgiving young Tommy for turning his back on the family. 'After what happened, Danny told me what you'd told him. We agreed to keep it between us. Apart from us, nobody even knows your uncle was arrested, do they, Dan?'

'Nope. Scout's honour.'

'What about your family?' Tommy asked.

'Not said a word to 'em,' Ronnie lied. He had actually told his parents, but no way would they ever betray his trust.

'Nothing that happened was your fault, Tom. You were only a kid back then. Why don't we all agree never to mention that perve again and start afresh? You can't be blanking me any more. I won't let ya. We're blood brothers, don't forget,' Danny grinned.

Remembering the time they'd cut themselves on purpose, Tommy couldn't help but smile. 'OK. I'll come.'

Having stopped at a greasy spoon along the A13 for a fry-up, by the time they reached Bermondsey, Tommy felt more at ease.

Apart from looking a bit older and his hair being shorter, Danny had not changed at all. It was over two years since Tommy had last seen his one-time best pal and it felt like only yesterday.

'You ready to meet the old man? He's a scary-looking bastard, but don't worry, he won't bite,' Ronnie laughed, opening the pub door.

The first thing Tommy noticed about Jack Darling was his presence. He was standing with a group of men, a few were taller than him, but for some reason Tommy couldn't put his finger on, Jack stood out from the crowd.

Jack held out his right hand. 'Hello, Tommy. It's a pleasure to finally meet you, son. What can I get you to drink?'

'Erm, can I have a Coke, please?'

'Ignore that, Dad. He'll have a lager, same as me,' Danny said. 'We're gonna sit at that table in the corner.'

'That's well cool your dad lets you drink,' Tommy said, as Ronnie placed two halves of lager in front of him and Danny.

'I came home pissed from a party a few months back and my dad went mental,' Danny admitted. 'He said he didn't want me to drink behind his back any more and I was to only touch alcohol in front of him. He don't let me have much. Two or three halves at the most.'

Feeling grown-up, Tommy sipped his beer and studied Jack Darling. His features were chiselled, his dark hair wavy and he was dressed in a smart navy suit. Tommy knew he'd served ten years for shooting and killing a man and felt a bit in awe of him.

Ronnie stayed at the bar with his father, which

enabled Tommy and Danny to have a proper heart to heart. Tommy spoke openly about Smiffy's death and how he'd turned to booze since to ease the pain. 'The fairground worker said in his statement he heard Smiffy call my name, Dan. He must have thought he'd spotted me, but I weren't even there at the time he died. If only I was.' He also told Danny about going to the Railway in Stratford to meet his real dad and beating up Wayne Bradley.

'I can't believe you're half Irish pikey,' Danny laughed.

'Don't say that. It ain't funny.'

'I'm only messing with ya. Your father sounds like a right arsehole, though, so you'll have to share mine. I know the authorities wouldn't let you live with us 'cause of me dad's record, but they can't stop you moving in with us when you're sixteen, Tom. Ronnie's moved out now, ya know. He's got this bachelor pad with his pal and they're forever taking birds back there,' Danny chuckled. 'You can have his old room. My mum wouldn't mind. I know it's sad Smiffy's dead, but he wouldn't want you to fuck your future up. You need to get back to your boxing and look forward, not backwards.'

About to reply, Tommy's jaw dropped. Dressed in bright green hot-pants and white patent high-heeled boots, Donna Darling looked like a glamour model. She walked over to where they were sitting. 'All right? Where's Dad?' she asked Danny.

'Dunno. Probably in the khazi. You ain't planning on going to the restaurant looking like that, are ya? Dad'll go fucking mental if you are.'

Donna blew and burst a bubble with her gum, then grinned at Tommy. 'I know you from somewhere, don't I?'

Donna looked about five foot ten in her high platform boots and Tommy had never seen anybody with such long, perfect legs. He could barely take his eyes off them, let alone reply.

'You remember Tommy. He lived in South London for a while and I knocked about with him. He used to come round ours for tea.'

Not knowing what else to do, Tommy stood up and held out his right hand. Instead of shaking it, Donna laughed. 'Yeah, I remember. Blimey, you've grown. You used to be a little squirt. You're quite easy on the eye now an' all.'

'Donna,' a voice boomed.

Blowing Tommy a kiss, Donna strutted over to her father and was promptly told to 'Get yourself home and put something decent on.'

'Don't be having any designs on her. She's trouble with a capital T,' Danny warned his pal.

'I'm not. I wouldn't,' Tommy stammered. 'She's way out of my league and too old for me anyway.'

Danny put his hand over his mouth and leaned towards Tommy. 'She's knocking about with some fucking Turk. Ronnie caught 'em in a clinch outside a boozer and gave the bloke a dig. If my dad finds out, there'll be murders, trust me.'

When his mum was alive, Tommy had been taken to a couple of restaurants, but never one as posh as this. It was in the West End of London and not only had

Tommy never been to the West End before, but the juicy steak, giant mushrooms, sautéed potatoes and peas dripping in butter tasted simply divine.

Jack ordered the waiter to pour a drop of bubbly into Tommy and Danny's flutes. 'Not too much, mind. Half a glass, that's all,' he added.

'What about me?' asked thirteen-year-old Eugene.

'Just a sip for him,' Jack said, before standing up and holding his glass aloft. 'Happy Birthday to the best wife and mother in the world. Not only did you stand by me, Suzie, when many women would have walked, you have done a wonderful job raising our children. Well, apart from Donna that is,' Jack chuckled.

Everybody laughed, including Donna, therefore Tommy felt at ease joining in too. There was only the seven of them, the Darling family and himself. All of them had made him feel so welcome.

Tommy hated the taste of champagne, but pretended to like it.

'I've got a little speech too,' Suzie Darling announced.

'Go, Mum,' Ronnie clapped.

Sitting next to Tommy, Donna put her hand on his leg. 'This'll be good,' she whispered in his ear.

Tommy felt his face blush as her hand moved towards his thigh. For the second time in forty-eight hours he had an erection.

'I just want to say, I've had the best birthday ever. My presents are all wonderful, but there is one more thing I'd like.'

His wife had spoken to him earlier, so Jack knew exactly what she was going to say. 'What, dear?' he asked, playing along with the moment. His Suzie had a heart of gold and that boy had been through a lot.

'Tommy, will you do us the honour of moving into our spare room when you leave Maylands? Not only would Jack and I welcome you with open arms, we could do with some extra help around the house now Ronnie has moved out,' Suzie grinned.

Tommy was flabbergasted. 'Erm, I dunno what to say.'

'Say yes, ya div,' laughed Danny.

'There'll also be a job waiting for you, Tommy. A proper job, working for me,' Jack said. 'I have a legitimate business now. I supply gaming machines to pubs and clubs. Ronnie is already working for me and so will Danny and Eugene when they leave school. Not only will you be on a decent wage, you'll be part of our family,' Jack said proudly.

'He ain't having my room,' Eugene piped up.

'He wouldn't want your filthy room,' Suzie chortled.

Ronnie held his hands out. 'Surely that's an offer you can't refuse, Tommy?'

Donna put her hand on Tommy's leg again. 'Just say yes,' she urged.

Six pairs of eyes keenly awaiting his decision, Tommy felt a bit choked up. Smiffy had been his future. They were going to share a flat and make something of their lives together, but now he'd gone, what else did he have?

Relieved that his erection had deflated, Tommy stood up and held his glass aloft. 'Thank you so much. I'd love to take you up on your extremely kind offer.'

Jack ordered another bottle of bubbly before walking around the table and clenching Tommy's right hand. 'Welcome to the family, son.'

Little did Tommy know at that point what 'Welcome to the family' actually meant.

CHAPTER SIXTEEN

Spring 1976

'Where we going then?' Scratch asked. She was happy to be spending the whole day alone with Tommy, but was dreading him walking out that door on Monday morning. He was her soulmate and even though she'd never tell him that, Scratch worshipped the ground Tommy walked on.

'Well, seeing as it's such a nice day, I thought we'd go to Southend. I don't wanna go to the fairground, but there's the amusement arcades and the beach. I got plenty of dosh on me. We can have a nice bit of fish and chips washed down with a few ciders. How's that sound?'

Scratch linked arms with Tommy. Apart from a few drunken fumbles, nothing had happened between them. Scratch wished it would though. She wanted Tommy to be her first consensual lover, and hopefully her last.

On the train, Tommy stared out of the window deep in thought. He couldn't believe how quickly the months had flown by since it had been decided he would move in with the Darlings.

It had been Ray's idea that he stay at the Darlings' beforehand to make sure he'd be happy there. Tommy had spent two weekends there per month and enjoyed his visits every time. He and Danny were more like brothers than pals and if they weren't down the boxing gym, they'd be with Jack earning some extra pocket money or having a couple of beers in the pub with him and Ronnie. Suzie was a true diamond. Nobody would ever replace his real mum, but Tommy knew he was blessed as Suzie was truly the next best thing. She even fussed over him like a mother.

'What you thinking?' Scratch asked.

'That part of me will be sad to leave Shitlands. I'm gonna miss you big time. I know I've had flare-ups in the past with Ray and Connie, but they can't help being naïve. Their hearts are in the right place. I think I'll miss them too, a bit, and Benny.'

Knowing he had a decent home and job awaiting him was all Tommy had needed to get his life back on track. He'd made peace with Benny and Dumbo, got back into his boxing, cut down on the booze and had even given up thieving. Going out on the rob wasn't the same without Smiffy, and besides, Jack Darling had warned him to keep his nose clean.

Scratch squeezed Tommy's hand. 'You'll be fine. What's the betting you forget about all of us once you start work? You probably won't even remember our names by Christmas,' she chuckled.

Tommy threw a casual arm around Scratch's shoulders.

'No way will I ever forget about you. You're a one-off, ya nutter.'

The sun was blazing and it was exceedingly warm for the time of year. The beach was mobbed, but Tommy still managed to bag himself and Scratch a spot next to a group of teenage lads who had a radio playing at full blast.

'I hate this poxy song. Why is it every radio station insists on playing it every five bloody minutes?' Tommy complained. He was referring to Brotherhood of Man's 'Save Your Kisses for Me'.

'Probably 'cause it won the Eurovision, Tommy,' Scratch replied, before singing along with the lyrics to wind Tommy up.

Tommy cracked open two cans and handed Scratch a cider. 'Stop warbling and get that down your 'atch.'

'I'm so pleased you've got a nice family to move in with. Dumbo hates it in his bedsit, I overheard Connie telling Ray. It scares me a bit that in July it'll be me leaving. Say they stick me in some shitty bedsit and I can't get a job either?'

'You'll be fine. You're a much stronger person than Dumbo. I'll be working, so I'll be able to help you out. If they put you in a dump, I'll put a deposit down for somewhere decent for ya.'

'You still gonna write to me?' Scratch asked.

'Yeah, course.'

'And visit?'

Tommy nodded. 'I promise.'

'You better – or else, Tommy Boyle,' Scratch laughed.

* * *

'I'm burnt. Look at my arms,' Scratch announced. She had thankfully stopped self-harming, but still had scars on her arms from where she'd cut herself in the past.

'Ray reckons the weatherman said this is gonna be our hottest summer in years. I've burned myself too. Look,' Tommy urged, lowering the waistband on his jeans to show Scratch how red his stomach was.

'And your freckles have sprouted,' Scratch laughed. 'What time we heading back?'

Tommy glanced at his watch. 'It's only just gone four. We ain't due back until ten. What else do you fancy doing?'

'Let's head back to Dagenham, get some more booze and sit over the Castle.'

Tommy stood up and held out his hand. 'Your wish is my command, ya pisshead.'

'I'm getting a bit chilly now. Let's sit inside the Castle,' Scratch suggested.

Tommy climbed through the window, then held his hand out for Scratch. 'Be careful, there's broken glass on the floor.'

'Do you reckon this really was a castle in the past?'

'Dunno. I suppose it must have been if that's what everyone calls it. Looks more like an old war bunker to me though.'

Scratch put her arms around Tommy's neck. 'Gissa kiss, then.'

Tommy placed his arms around Scratch's waist. Ever since he'd seen Donna Darling again, he kept feeling horny. So much so, he'd recently taken up masturbating.

'Scratch, stop it,' Tommy groaned, as she began stroking his erection.

'Why?' Scratch whispered, as she tugged at the zip of Tommy's jeans.

As his penis hit the fresh air, it leapt into action like a cobra rearing its ugly head.

Hoping this would happen, Scratch had purposely worn her black miniskirt with her Dr Martens today. She lifted it up, pulled down her knickers and kicked them off.

Grabbing her by the buttocks, Tommy lifted Scratch up and placed her back against the wall. 'We really shouldn't be doing this,' he gasped, as she wrapped her legs around his waist.

'Oh, Tommy,' Scratch moaned.

Not really knowing what he was doing, Tommy pumped away like there was no tomorrow. He could hear cats fighting nearby, making awful noises.

'I love you, Tommy,' Scratch whispered.

Tommy didn't reply. Instead he made a weird noise similar to the fighting cats and for the next few seconds, thought he had died and gone to heaven.

Tommy woke up the following morning with a smile on his face. He'd really enjoyed what had happened; it kind of made him feel normal. Masturbation was nothing in comparison to actually doing it, he'd decided. But he still couldn't help feeling a bit confused and guilty. He did love Scratch, in his own way, but he didn't look at her in the same way he looked at Donna Darling. Scratch was a skinhead, a tomboy. Whereas Donna looked like a female should.

A tap on the door disturbed Tommy's thoughts. 'Come in,' he shouted.

'You OK?' Ray asked.

'Yeah. Sorry we were a bit late last night. It was my fault, not Scratch's.'

'No problem. You wasn't that late and, if Connie asks, I didn't notice you were slightly inebriated either,' Ray smiled.

'Thanks, Ray. You're a good man. Thank you for all you have done for me.'

Ray's eyes welled up. 'Get yourself washed and dressed, Tommy. Today is all about you, son.'

As expected, Ray and Connie's surprise was a party held in his honour. They'd made so much effort, decorating the games room with balloons and a banner wishing him good luck, that Tommy didn't have the heart to tell them he'd gone past the jelly and ice-cream stage.

Connie brought in trays of sausage rolls, chicken drumsticks and sandwiches. 'Who's hungry?' she chuckled.

While the younger kids made a grab for the food, Tommy gestured for Scratch to follow him into the garden. They hadn't had a chance to talk yet, not properly anyway.

Tommy sat on the bench. 'You OK?'

Scratch smiled. She felt awkward, not because they'd had sex, but because of what she'd blurted out. 'Yeah, I'm fine.'

'Look, about last night. I'm—'

'I know what you're gonna say and I'm sorry,' Scratch interrupted. 'It was a spur-of-the-moment thing and I didn't really mean it. Well, not in the way it came out anyway.'

Tommy was more confused than ever now. 'What you talking about?'

Scratch rolled her eyes, before putting her hands over her face. 'I didn't mean to tell you I loved you. It was the booze talking. Speaking of booze, this party is well boring. Shall I pop to the offie and get us some vodka to pour in the orange juice?'

Laughing, Tommy slung his arm around Scratch's shoulder. 'Great idea. And even though you might not love me, I'll always love you, girl.'

Scratch grinned like a Cheshire cat. Those were the words she'd been longing to hear.

The rest of the day turned out far better than Tommy could have envisaged. It had been a wonderful moment when his sister Linda had turned up out of the blue with the Piper family. They'd only been able to stay for an hour. Apparently, Nanny Noreen wasn't well and Alice Piper had told the old witch they were taking Linda to Petticoat Lane and wouldn't be long.

Dumbo turning up was another welcome surprise. He'd lost weight, looked like a beanpole, so no wonder he'd scoffed most of the cake. He clearly wasn't coping well living alone and Tommy felt blessed yet again to be moving in with the Darlings.

At 8 p.m. the younger children were told to go to bed and Connie ordered Benny to turn the music down.

'Can I stay here tonight please, Connie?' Dumbo asked. 'I really miss you all.'

'I'm afraid you can't, my love. It's against Maylands' rules. You can visit us again soon though.'

When Dumbo's lip started trembling, Benny gave him a hug. Tommy walked over and put an arm around both his pals' shoulders. He realized now it wasn't their fault that Smiffy had died. There was only one person to blame and that was Wayne Bradley. 'Keep your chin up, Dumbo. You'll have me on the outside soon to look after ya. We can meet up and do stuff together.'

'Really?' Dumbo asked hopefully. 'Do you promise?'

'Yeah, course. I'll visit you in the next couple of weeks. I'll take you up the council, see if they'll give you your own flat. I'll do the talking. Leave it with me and I'll get you out of that bedsit.'

'Thank you, Tommy. You're a true friend,' Dumbo grinned.

When Dumbo left, Benny offered to walk him back to the bus stop. Apart from Ginger Lorraine and Backward Paul, there was no one else present. Ray and Connie were in the kitchen tidying up.

'Fancy a walk?' Scratch asked. 'We can meet Benny on his way back.'

Tommy nodded and followed Scratch outside.

There was an alleyway around the corner and as they approached it, Scratch grabbed Tommy's hand and dragged him down it.

Tommy was like a lamb to the slaughter once Scratch

put her hand on his penis again. Within seconds, he'd
rammed her against the wall and was up her like a rat
up a drainpipe.

The following morning, Tommy felt emotional as he
put his bags next to the front door. Danny had been
allowed to take the day off school. He and Ronnie were
picking him up around noon.

'Do you want some breakfast, Tommy?' Connie
asked.

'No. I don't feel very hungry, thanks.'

Sensing the lad was having second thoughts about
stepping out into the big wide world, Connie walked
over to Tommy and gave him one of her special hugs.

'Thanks for everything, Connie. You and Ray have
been brilliant to me.'

'You're very welcome, my love. Scratch isn't going
to school today. She was ever so upset earlier, bless her.
She's really going to miss you. You will write to her,
won't you?'

'Yeah. Course. I'll write to Scratch every week and
you and Ray. I swear I will. I'm gonna visit as often as
possible too. I'll never forget what you've done for me.'

Connie smiled. 'Lovely. Don't you let me down.'

'Never. I always keep to my word, Connie. Where is
Scratch?'

'In her room. Pop up and see her, Tommy.'

Tommy made his way over the other side of the house
and tapped on Scratch's door. 'It's only me.'

'Come in.'

Scratch was sat on her bed, a forlorn figure, she'd

clearly been crying her heart out. Tommy sat next to her. 'Please don't be sad. I want you to be happy for me.'

'I am. But I can't help feeling sad an' all. I'm gonna miss you so much, Tommy.'

Tommy held Scratch in his arms and kissed her forehead. 'I'll write, I'll visit, and I'll be waiting outside for you on your sixteenth birthday.'

'I bet you don't even remember when my birthday is.'

'Yes, I do. July the fifth.'

'Is that a promise?'

Tommy did the sign of a crucifix. 'Cross my heart and hope to die.'

Scratch put her arms around Tommy's neck. 'Shall we be naughty and do it one more time in my bed?'

'Do what?' Tommy chuckled.

'Ya know. It.'

Tommy put Scratch's hand on his penis. 'As always, your wish is my command.'

'Ray, let's give Tommy his present now,' Connie bellowed.

'I got you a present an' all. Two in fact,' Scratch grinned.

Tommy chatting privately with Scratch in her room had worked wonders. Connie had been worried about the girl this morning, especially when she noticed fresh cuts on her arms, but she seemed in a much better frame of mind now, thankfully.

'You give him yours first,' Scratch urged.

Tommy opened the small box Ray handed him. 'I dunno what to say,' Tommy stared at the cufflinks. 'Erm, thanks ever so much. But you really shouldn't have.

You've done enough for me as it is.' Tommy had never worn cufflinks in his life and doubted he ever would, but it was a nice gesture nevertheless.

'Now open mine,' Scratch urged. 'Open the smaller one first.'

Johnny Nash's 'Tears on My Pillow' had been a massive hit last summer and Scratch had loved the record so much, Tommy had given her his copy. 'Every time you play it, I want you to think of me and I'll think of you when I play mine.'

'Ahh, bless 'em,' Connie whispered to Ray.

'Open the other one now,' Scratch ordered.

Tommy felt choked up as he did so. It was a framed photo of himself, Smiffy, Scratch, Benny and Dumbo. They were sunbathing in the back garden and all looked so happy. Smiffy had two fingers stuck up behind Dumbo's head and Benny was pulling one of his retarded faces. 'This is ace. I love it.'

'I took that,' Connie chuckled.

'Why is there black tape across the bottom?' Tommy asked.

Snatch grabbed hold of the frame and ripped the tape off to reveal the wording.

Tommy's eyes welled up as he read the print.

FOREVER FRIENDS
RIP SMIFFY
SHITLANDS 1975

Connie and Ray knew Tommy and his pals jokingly referred to Maylands as Shitlands and they didn't mind.

'That's beautiful, Scratch. Can you get me a tissue, please Ray?' Connie wept.

Near to tears himself, Ray was glad of an excuse to leave the room.

'I dunno what to say, apart from it's beautiful. I will treasure it, I promise.'

'All set, Tommy lad?' Ronnie grinned. 'Mother's rolled out the red carpet for your arrival. Your room's been decorated and she's cooking some fancy meal tonight. Chicken something or other.'

'Chasseur,' Danny said.

Tommy looked at him blankly. 'What?'

'Chicken Chasseur, that's what muvver's cooking. None of us have tasted it before.'

Tommy laughed. 'Come inside for a minute. There's only Scratch, Ray and Connie in, all the other kids are at school.'

Ronnie and Danny followed Tommy inside Maylands. 'Nice to see you again, Ray, Connie. And I take it you're the famous Scratch. Tommy speaks ever so highly of you,' Danny smiled.

Scratch linked arms with Tommy, much to his embarrassment. 'Erm, I need to start loading me stuff in the car now,' Tommy mumbled. As much as he adored Scratch, he didn't want his pals to know he'd had sex with her. She was a skinhead, after all.

'I'm really going to miss him,' Scratch announced.

Danny smiled. 'He talks about you all the time to me.'

'We'll look after him for ya, don't you worry. Right,

have all these bin bags gotta go in the car, Tom?' asked Ronnie.

'Yes, please.'

'Danny, help me with these while Tommy says goodbye to his friends,' Ronnie said.

Tommy gave both Ray and Connie a final hug, then turned to Scratch. 'I'll write to you in the next few days.'

When Scratch draped her arms around Tommy's neck, Ray and Connie glanced at one another, a worried expression on their faces. They'd been positive the children were just good friends and both silently prayed nothing untoward had happened between them.

Tommy pecked Scratch on the lips, then tapped the left-hand side of his head. 'Fifth of July. It's imprinted in me brain.'

Scratch smiled. 'And so it should be. You better turn up; else you'll be on my get-even list, Tommy Boyle.'

PART THREE

It is not in the stars to hold our destiny but in ourselves.
William Shakespeare

CHAPTER SEVENTEEN

5 July 1976. What a pivotal date that is in the whole story of my life.

Scratch's sixteenth birthday. The day I'd promised to return to Maylands. I'd sworn to collect her, having sorted her out somewhere decent to live.

It was also the day I got hitched. I realize now I should have handled things differently. To cease all contact with Scratch, the lads, Connie and Ray without any explanation at all was a coward's way out. But I was sixteen for Christ's sake. A wet-behind-the-ears teenager, not a man.

I recall my head being in the clouds during that long, hot summer. I'd made a new life for myself, felt part of a family once again. I was earning far more wonga than I could ever have dreamed of and I was also earning respect by the bucketload. Some days I had to pinch myself. Me, Tommy Boyle, hopelessly in love with a beautiful woman and a kiddie on the way. It was kind of surreal, one of the happiest times of my life.

But happiness doesn't always last and rash decision-making can backfire in an explosive manner. I know that now.

5 July 1976. The date that would come back to haunt me . . .

Tommy Boyle walked into the pub alongside Danny and was immediately taken aback by the massive cheer. 'What's going on, Dan?' he asked innocently.

Seconds later, all was revealed as Jack Darling fondly grabbed Tommy around the neck. ''Ere he is. The doomed one,' Jack chuckled. 'DJ – music,' he bellowed.

When the song 'I'm Getting Married in the Morning' blasted out of the DJ's speakers, Tommy was gobsmacked.

Ronnie put an arm around his shoulders and pointed to the banner on the wall.

GOOD LUCK, TOMMY LAD –
YOU'RE GONNA NEED IT!

Tommy laughed and blushed at the same time. The boozer was packed with blokes and all eyes were on him. He'd told Jack he didn't want a stag do, but now he'd got one, he felt a warmth inside. Like he belonged. The last proper party he had was when his mum held one indoors for his tenth birthday.

'How you feeling about tomorrow? You bricking it?' Ronnie asked, shoving a glass of bubbly in Tommy's hand.

'No. I feel good. Excited,' Tommy grinned.

'Well, you're a braver bloke than I am. I'd be crapping meself,' Ronnie joked.

The stag bash was a great success, the DJ brilliant. But as the evening wore on, an inebriated Tommy couldn't help feeling melancholy. Tomorrow, he would be marrying the girl of his dreams. How he wished his mum was still alive. She'd loved a wedding. Even Linda was unable to attend. She had to go to school and he still hadn't heard a word from Hazel.

'What you sitting alone in the corner for? You OK?' Jack enquired.

'Yeah. I just wish I had some family and friends coming tomorrow. I know you said not to invite anyone from Maylands, but can't I invite Benny and Dumbo to the reception? I know it's short notice, but I'm sure they'd love to come.'

'You've moved on from your days at Maylands now, Tommy. You're not damaged goods like them other lads. You've got everything going for you, including a nipper on the way. You need to forget about the past, concentrate on your future, lad.' Jack grinned and took an envelope out of the inside pocket of his jacket. 'Open it. Go on,' he winked.

Tommy could not believe his eyes. Inside the envelope was a birth certificate with the name Tommy Darling on it. 'What's this? I don't understand.'

Jack ruffled Tommy's hair. 'I got your name changed by deed poll as a surprise for you.'

'What! But why?'

'Because you're family now, ain't ya? One of us. You hated that bastard Alexander, so you don't want to go through life with his surname, do you? He wasn't even your real father.'

For the second time that day, Tommy was completely taken aback. 'I dunno what to say.'

Jack smiled. 'How about "thanks". You'll be amazed at how much more people respect you when you tell 'em you're a Darling. You wait and see.'

Tommy forced a smile. He didn't want to come across as ungrateful. 'Thanks, Jack. Means a lot.'

Connie peered out of the games room window. Scratch was still sitting out front with only her radio for company, bless her.

Connie sighed. She'd tried her best to warn the girl, let her down gently, but Scratch was still adamant Tommy would turn up today as he'd promised.

After leaving Maylands in March Tommy had initially kept to his word. He'd written to herself, Ray and Scratch every week, and he'd turned up unexpectedly one Saturday to visit Scratch. Then, about six weeks ago, all contact had ceased. Scratch's letters weren't answered, neither were hers. Dumbo hadn't heard from him either.

At first Connie thought perhaps Tommy had met a new girl. Scratch had since admitted to her that she and Tommy were actually boyfriend and girlfriend. But having raised Tommy these past few years, Connie knew he was a decent lad with good morals. Now she was worried something bad had happened to him. Had he fallen out with the Darlings and was no longer living there? That would explain why he wasn't replying to his mail. Or even worse, had he had an accident or got himself arrested? She'd tried to call the Darlings, but the number she had for them was now disconnected.

Connie marched into the kitchen. 'Ray, you need to drive over to the Darlings' house, find out what is going on.'

'I don't know South London, Connie. I'll never find where they live. Tommy's sixteen years old. He's probably just doing his own thing, love. I've already told you that.'

'No. The more I think about it, the more I am concerned something is wrong. Scratch needs answers and so do I. Tommy could be in trouble for all we know.'

'Benny hasn't kept in touch like he promised either, Connie. It's what young lads do. We nurture them, do our best. Then they venture into the big wide world and get on with their own lives.'

'Tommy has a good heart, Ray. Even if he had met another girl, I'm positive he'd have called or written to me or you on the quiet to ask us to break the news to Scratch gently. That poor little mite is going to be heartbroken by this evening and I can't allow her to move into a bedsit if she's not in the right state of mind. Her arms are full of fresh cuts. I'm frightened she might do something stupid.'

Ray sighed. When Connie got a bee in her bonnet, she always got her own way. 'All right. Give me the Darlings' address and I'll see if I can find their bleedin' house.'

Confident she would get her own way, Connie had already written down the address. She handed it to Ray. 'Please God, Tommy is OK.'

'Happy birthday, Scratch. I got you a present.' Dumbo handed Scratch a small box and then plonked himself next to her. 'Has Tommy been in touch?'

'No.' Scratch opened the box. It contained a silver

cross on a chain. 'Thanks, Dumbo. I love it. Can you put it on for me?'

'Course. I nicked it, like. But it's the thought that counts, isn't it?'

Scratch smiled. 'Sure is. You gonna hang around a bit? Wait for Tommy?'

'I don't think Tommy's gonna turn up.'

'He will. He promised me.'

'He promised me he would take me up the council, try and sort me a flat so I can get out of that shitty bedsit. Tommy's a liar.' Dumbo's disappointment only made hers worse.

As a car screeched around the corner, Scratch leapt up, her heart pounding.

'Well?' Dumbo asked.

Deflated, Scratch sat back down. 'No. It's not Tommy.'

Standing at the front of the aisle, Tommy's nerves were kicking in. His bride was late but he wasn't unduly worried about that. It took her hours to get ready, even on a normal day. He was more on edge about giving his speech later. He'd written one out and lost the piece of paper.

Danny put his arm around Tommy's shoulders. It was an honour to be his best pal's best man. 'You all right, mate?'

'Yeah,' Tommy lied. The church was mobbed and, apart from Jack's pals from the Lord Nelson, he barely recognized a soul.

'The bride's arrived,' Eugene bellowed, seconds later.

Tommy's mouth dried up as the organist sprang into action. Apparently, some Catholic churches refused to play 'Here Comes the Bride', but Father Michael was a personal friend of the Darlings and he'd fallen over backwards to help them arrange the wedding at such short notice.

Tommy glanced around and was temporarily left breathless. The dress was low-cut, sleeveless with a tight bodice and a massive silk train. Never had he seen anybody look so beautiful. She looked like a model out of one of the glossy magazines.

As his bride walked towards him holding her father's arm, she smiled at him. Tommy truly felt like the luckiest lad in the world. Donna Darling was about to become his wife, his life was surely made.

Connie was hopping about like a cat on a hot tin roof. Ray had been gone ages. The silly old sod had no sense of direction. She always sat in the passenger seat with the *A to Z* when they had to travel out of the area to pick up a child, so chances were he'd got himself lost. She had told him to stop at a phone box and call her as soon as he had any news. So why hadn't he done so?

Connie glanced out of the window again. She'd been so pleased when Dumbo turned up to keep Scratch company. She'd rung him yesterday and pleaded with him to come. 'Scratch is positive Tommy will turn up, Dumbo, and I don't think he's going to. That girl is going to need company and a friend tomorrow,' were Connie's exact words. She'd then bribed him by offering to cook him a roast on Sunday.

She lifted her mug of tea for a sip and nearly dropped it when Ray's car pulled up outside. She hadn't told

Scratch where Ray was going, didn't want to build her hopes up.

Connie ran into the hallway. 'Well?' she said, as Ray stepped through the front door.

'It's not good news, Connie.'

'He's been arrested, hasn't he? I knew it.'

'No, love. Tommy's fine. It's not good news for Scratch, mind. There was nobody home at the Darlings', so I knocked at the neighbour's. Tommy's getting married today.'

Connie put her hand over her mouth. 'Getting married! To who?'

'Donna Darling. Jack's daughter. Tommy's got her in the family way.'

Connie was gobsmacked. Poor Scratch. Today was her sixteenth birthday. How the hell was she meant to explain something like this? As for Tommy Boyle, Connie was furious with him. She and Ray had been bloody good to that boy. How could he get hitched without even telling them? The lad was a coward.

The hall where the reception was held had been transformed into a stunning sea of white. Drapes hung from the ceilings and walls, and a white flashing dance floor had been laid especially for the occasion. Suzie planned most of it. She had an eye for interior design.

The meal was fabulous. Rib of beef and chicken for main course, served with sautéed potatoes in the nicest sauce Tommy had ever tasted. There was free booze on the tables for everyone. Jack had really pushed the boat out.

Danny was the first to give a speech. After getting them all laughing with a few stories about when he first met the groom, he told the guests, 'Tommy's always been more like a brother to me than a friend.'

Jack was next up. He cleared his throat and laid his hand on Donna's shoulder. 'Like any good father, I love my daughter dearly. You do worry about girls more though and believe me when I say my Donna has given me many a sleepless night over the years. Every father wants their daughter to marry a good lad – one of your own, so to speak. So when romance blossomed between these two, Suzie and I were over-joyed. Tommy had a tough time of it growing up. His mother died when he was only twelve, then he was pushed from pillar to post. But he's a lad to be proud of, which is why I changed his name to Darling. He's one of us now, part of the family. Myself and Suzie couldn't be bloody happier that he is marrying our Donna.'

When everybody cheered and Jack tapped him on the back, Tommy guessed it was his turn to say some-thing. He'd never had to get up and speak in front of so many people before. 'Erm, I'd like to thank Jack, Suzie, Ronnie, Danny and Eugene for welcoming me into the family like they have. But most of all, I would like to thank Donna for making me so happy. I know I'm only young, but I'm mature for my age and I cannot wait to be a husband and a father to our child. Oh, and thank you all for coming and sharing our special day with us. Means a lot.'

Relieved he got a big round of applause and could

now sit down again, Tommy squeezed Donna's hand. 'I love you,' he whispered.

'I know you do,' Donna smiled.

After spending ages planning the correct words in her head, Connie went out the front. Scratch hadn't eaten all day, neither had she moved from that spot. 'I need to talk to you, Scratch. Come inside please, love.'

'Has Tommy been in touch?' Scratch asked.

'Can I come inside too please, Connie? I'm starving. You got any food?' Dumbo enquired.

'Ray's in the kitchen. He'll make you a sandwich. Come into my office, Scratch. I need to talk to you about Tommy, in private.'

Scratch leapt up and followed Connie into the house. Lots of reasons why Tommy had stopped contacting her had been drifting through her mind lately. The two of them were soulmates, and she knew he would never let her down, so her guess was he'd got into trouble and had perhaps got sent to borstal. Tommy always said he was going to get his own back on Wayne Bradley for what he'd done to Smiffy. So maybe he'd found out where Wayne was, and then got nicked.

Connie shut her office door. 'Sit down, love.'

'Have you heard from him? Has he called you?' Scratch gabbled. She had butterflies in her stomach, big bloody butterflies.

Connie leaned across her desk and squeezed Scratch's hand. 'Tommy isn't coming to meet you today. I am so sorry Scratch, I really am.'

'Why? Is he in borstal?'

'No. He's not in borstal. He's moved on, my love.'

'Moved on where? Doesn't he live with the Darlings no more? Dumbo said if he doesn't turn up, me and him will go to the Darlings' house tomorrow. We've got the address because of his letters.'

'No. You don't want to do that. Ray went to the address today to find out what was going on.'

'And?'

'And it's best you forget about Tommy. He isn't the brave lad any of us thought he was.'

'Why? What do you mean? What's Tommy done?'

'I'm going to get in touch with Maureen, see if we can get you your own flat rather than a bedsit. But in the meantime I want you to stay here. Against Maylands' usual rules, I know, but Ray is in agreement and—'

Scratch stood up and smashed her fist against the desk. 'Tell me what Tommy has done, Connie. Because if you don't, I swear I will visit him tomorrow and find out for my fucking self.'

Knowing Scratch would do exactly that, Connie took a deep breath. 'I'm so sorry to have to tell you this, but today Tommy got married to Donna Darling. He got her in the family way.'

Scratch's face drained of colour. So much so, she looked like a ghost. 'No. There must be some mistake. Tommy wouldn't do that to me.'

'It's true, Scratch. The Darlings' neighbours told Ray.'

Spotting a fountain pen on Connie's desk, Scratch snatched at it and repeatedly stabbed herself in the left arm. 'No, noooo. Fucking nooooo.'

Hearing a commotion, Ray ran into Connie's office and Dumbo followed. Ray snatched the pen out of Scratch's hand and held her tightly.

Dumbo was bemused. 'What's going on?'

Scratch slumped to the floor, clutched her knees with her hands and rocked to and fro. 'You were right about Tommy, Dumbo – he's a liar. He's gone and married Donna Darling. He got her pregnant.'

Dumbo was appalled. He paced up and down the office and punched the wall. 'I will never forgive him for this. Not only has he let me down, Scratch, he's let you down too. I hate his guts. Tommy Boyle can rot in hell for all I care. I wish him dead.'

CHAPTER EIGHTEEN

Autumn 1978

'Did you pack your toiletries?' asked Caroline Birch.

'Yes. I don't think I've forgotten anything.'

'How you feeling?'

'A bit nervous. I just hope there are some nice girls there and it's not all blokes.'

Caroline smiled and hugged the girl she had become so very fond of. 'You'll be fine. Just be yourself.'

'Me and Mikey don't want you to go away, Scratch,' said ten-year-old Fiona.

'You mustn't call her Scratch any more, Fi, I've told you that a hundred times. Her name is now Kim.'

Kim a.k.a. Scratch felt close to tears as she said her goodbyes to the children. She would miss both immensely.

Caroline looked out of the window. 'Your cab's just pulled up.'

Kim walked into the hallway and picked up her case. 'Thanks, Caroline – for everything.'

'You're very welcome, sweetheart. Don't forget to ring me, and Connie. We're both so proud of the wonderful young lady you've become.'

Kim waved as the cab pulled away. It was time to start her new life.

Tommy Darling shivered as he stepped out of Danny's Ford Capri. The autumn air was sharp, the wind gale-force.

'You not got your Crombie with ya?' Danny enquired, slipping his over his metallic blue suit.

'Nah. Me and Don were rowing before I left and I forgot to grab it.'

'Oh well. You ready?'

'As always.'

'You OK, Eugene?' Danny asked.

'Cushty.'

The three lads looked a formidable sight as they sauntered inside the rundown back-street boozer. All wore smart suits, expensive shirts, shoes and ties.

The film *Grease* had taken the country by storm this year and 'Summer Nights' was playing on the jukebox. The punters fell silent.

The landlord's face drained of colour. He'd been expecting another visit, but not this soon.

'We'll talk out the back.' Danny strolled behind the bar without waiting for a reply.

'Please don't involve my wife and daughter,' Bruce gabbled. 'They're upstairs,' he lied.

Danny pushed Bruce into the hallway. 'Got our dosh yet?'

'Not all of it, but you can take whatever's in the till and I promise I'll square up with you next weekend in full.'

Grabbing Bruce by the back of his neck, Danny marched him down to the cellar. The man was a borderline alcoholic, chain-smoking piss-taker.

'Don't hurt me. I'll get you your wonga, I swear,' Bruce pleaded.

Danny shoved Bruce down the last few stairs and he landed in a crumpled, cowering heap. 'You were spotted in the bookies today placing a bullseye on some nag you had a tip on. Still running round Fontwell, is it?'

Teeth chattering, Bruce tried to explain. 'My mate said it was a dead cert. I was only gambling to try and get you your money on time.'

'Don't insult our intelligence by fucking lying, Bruce,' Tommy bellowed, crushing the man's right knee with the sole of his shiny black loafer.

Eugene whipped out the baseball bat from inside his Crombie. 'One or both?' he asked.

'One – for now,' Danny replied.

'No. Please God no. I've got a pub to run. If I can't work, I can't pay you.'

Eugene lifted the bat and repeatedly smashed it against Bruce's right knee. The pain was immense and Bruce could not help but squeal like a pig.

'We'll take what's in the till and be back on Friday for the rest. There's a oner on top of the original debt now, for wasting our fucking time,' Danny hissed. 'And if you haven't got it by then, you'll be dealing with my father and our Ronnie in future. Understand?'

Wishing he had never got involved with the Darlings, Bruce nodded dumbly.

* * *

On the train journey, Kim thought up a story. She didn't want people knowing her past. Being a care home kid, the daughter of a drug-riddled prostitute wasn't exactly the impression she wanted to give out. She'd hated her birth name Rosie Peacock. The kids at school used to call her Rosie Posey. She hated her nickname now too. Scratch was in her past. Dead and buried. Kim Regan was her future. She'd chosen Regan after Jack in *The Sweeney*. It seemed fitting, seeing as she was embarking on a career in the police force herself.

After Tommy had left her high and dry, it was Connie's idea she move to Kent to live with her niece and her husband. Caroline and Keith had fostered children in the past and even though Kim was sixteen by then, they happily took her in.

Caroline and Keith were strict, but kind. Their home was spacious, spotless, and Kim quickly settled in. Keith worked in the police force and Kim loved hearing his stories of past and present crimes. The Yorkshire Ripper was still on the loose, had killed numerous women in the past year alone, and the more Kim learned about police procedure, the more she thought about not joining the army after all.

Kim had loved her role as housekeeper, and spending time with Fiona and Mikey, but she was eighteen now and knew she wanted more out of life. Since leaving Maylands she'd worked hard to pass her exams; under the influence of Caroline and Keith, she'd acquired a burning ambition to succeed.

Seeing a skinhead girl jump on the train, Kim smirked.

Skinheads were back in fashion now and the girl looked exactly how she used to.

'You'll need to change your image if you want to get somewhere in life. Very few employers will offer a job to a skinhead,' Keith had warned her.

Kim still wore her blonde hair short, but in a more feathered, feminine style. She didn't dress up much, felt far more comfortable in casual clothes, but enjoyed experimenting with make-up and painting her nails. That was the one part of her new job she was dreading. She had to wear a skirt. Kim hated skirts, hadn't worn one since having sex with that lying, waste-of-space, Tommy Boyle.

Aware that the two lads who'd just got on the train were ogling her, Kim ignored them. She had no interest in lads, would never trust another.

'You going Hendon?' asked the ginger lad.

'Yes.'

The dark-haired one slapped his pal on the back. 'See, I told you there'd be some fit Dorises there, didn't I?'

Kim glared at the pair of laughing idiots. 'Who you calling a Doris, ya wanker?'

'Oops. Cheer up, love. She's a fiery one, Paul. Probably got one of them chastity belts on.'

As the lads continued to mock her, Kim ignored them and stared out of the window. Keith had warned her what to expect and, by the looks of it, he'd been spot on. All she could do was pray she wasn't the only girl there.

* * *

'Where to now?' Tommy asked, as they pulled away from the pub.

'The Globe. Machines need emptying.'

'I'm surprised Bruce's wife never showed her ugly mug, racket he was making,' Eugene chuckled. He was sixteen now and inflicting pain on people was part of his everyday life.

'His old woman's never in. The gran looks after the daughter while that fat cow spunks her money down the bingo. Or our money, should I say,' Danny spat.

'D'ya reckon he'll pay up?' Tommy asked.

'Be a very silly move if he doesn't, won't it?'

Tommy grinned. He liked his job, got off on being feared and respected in equal measures. Jack Darling wasn't a man to be messed with, everyone knew that, and even though Jack rarely got his hands dirty any more, the threat of having him in the background was enough to scare the living daylights out of most. And Tommy loved being a Darling, the day he was given that name changed his life.

'I seriously can't wait until Saturday. We gonna bet big?' Tommy asked.

'Too right,' Danny replied. He hadn't been good enough to make it as a pro boxer himself, but he was immensely proud of his older brother. Saturday would be Ronnie's sixth professional fight and he was currently unbeaten. The last bloke he'd fought, a Glaswegian, had been knocked spark out in round one, such was the power of his brother's right fist.

'Is your mum gonna come?' Tommy asked.

'Nah. Ronnie begged her to, but she won't. After

what happened to me, her nerves can't take it.' Danny had been fighting at amateur level when he'd lowered his guard and got knocked out cold. He was fine once the smelling salts were shoved under his nostrils, but his mother wasn't. Suzie had been hysterical, and since then she'd refused to watch her boys fight. 'You coming round ours for a bite to eat before the party tonight, Tom? Or you popping home?'

Not fancying the third-degree off Suzie or another argument with her indoors, Tommy replied, 'Neither. I'm gonna grab some fish and chips, then I'll meet you in the Prince of Wales.'

This was the life, he thought, boxing and booze and giving his trouble and strife the swerve, a perfect night.

'All right? God that geezer went on, didn't he? Can't wait to start the proper training, can you?'

Kim smiled at the girl. They'd spent the afternoon being shown around, then were taken into the auditorium for a long speech about what joining the police force actually meant. Kim shook the girl's outstretched hand. She had short dark hair with a quiff, striking green eyes and was very pretty even though she walked and spoke like a bloke. 'It's Samantha, isn't it?'

'Sam, I prefer. What's your name again? I'm shit with names.'

'Kim. I'm starving. Are you?'

'Yeah. Let's go get some grub. Dunno where the other two girls have gone. Both spent most of their time in there eyeing up the lads. Did you clock 'em? Can't be dealing with silly tarts, me. I'm here to make something of my life.'

'Me too,' Kim chuckled. 'And yes, I did clock 'em and thought exactly the same as you.'

As the girls walked off towards the canteen area, little did they know a strong friendship had already been formed.

Excusing himself from a few lads he knew at the bar, Tommy put some records on the jukebox and sat alone at a corner table. He'd felt a tad melancholy all week, kept thinking back to the past.

He hadn't kept in touch with anybody from Maylands, but that didn't stop him remembering his old pals from time to time. He'd let them all down, he knew that – Scratch especially. But sometimes life took you in strange directions and he could never have predicted back then the way his would pan out.

Within a week of moving in with the Darlings, Tommy was working full-time. It had soon become apparent that his job wasn't exactly above board. Part of it was to force publicans to install Jack's gaming machines, rather than politely ask them. Then there was the protection money to collect. Publicans would pay a monthly rate for their boozers to be kept trouble-free.

A fortnight later, Tommy had been stabbed in the shoulder. He, Danny, Ronnie and Ronnie's best pal Dean Griffiths (a.k.a. Griff) had been sent to Balham to eject some troublemakers from a boozer. A brawl had taken place with a gang of bikers and Tommy had ended up on the floor, covered in claret. Jack didn't like the lads going to hospital as that meant the police would get involved, so Tommy was taken back to the Darlings' house and stitched up by a private doctor who was on Jack's payroll.

It was while Tommy was off work recuperating that Donna Darling started to make a play for him. She was like his very own Florence Nightingale, tending to his every need. When she started offering him extras, Tommy was flattered – bowled over, in fact – but he'd politely declined, even though his penis was urging him otherwise. The Darlings had been good to him and under no circumstances would he betray their trust in that way.

Then, approximately a month after he'd moved in, Jack had taken him to one side. 'Donna has asked my permission for you and her to start courting, Tommy. Now I know you're only young, but you're very mature for your age. I've spoken to Suzie and she's in agreement. You have our blessing.'

Tommy had been a bit taken aback, and scared. Donna was a couple of years older than him and was no wallflower. He'd felt even more daunted when Ronnie had rented a pal's caravan and he and Donna were sent to Clacton on holiday for a week to get to know one another better.

The inevitable happened. Tommy had fallen hopelessly in love and Donna was soon pregnant. On 5 July 1976, the day Tommy was meant to meet Scratch, he'd actually been getting hitched to Donna. Everything had happened so fast. Too fast, he knew that now.

'Hello, Tommy. How you doing, son?'

Thoughts snapping back to the present, Tommy stood up and shook the man's hand. Peter Hiller was a nice bloke, a pal of Jack's. 'All good my end. How about yourself?'

'Plodding on, as you do. How's that lovely wife and son of yours?'

Tommy smiled and spoke glowingly of both. He'd become an expert at pretending everything was hunky-dory. Case of having to, really.

'I've pulled,' Danny announced. 'That bit of totty who looks like Charlene out of *Dallas* keeps looking at me.'

Eugene burst out laughing. 'She looks more like Fat Anne who works behind the bar in the Nelson.'

Danny asked what bird his brother was looking at.

'The one with the spare tyre round her gut, standing by the door.'

'Not her, you plonker. The one wearing the Olivia Newton-John strides. She's stood by the stereo system.'

'Oh, yeah. She ain't bad. In fact, she's proper.'

As Danny and Eugene both joked about what they'd like to do to the girl in question, Tommy grinned politely. He could never join in with such conversations or laddish behaviour. Reason being, he'd made the mistake of marrying their sister.

The recruits were housed in three tower blocks. Each had their own room, which was pretty basic: a single bed, stainless steel basin, a small wardrobe and chest of drawers. The women were allocated the top floors of Block B and Kim was pleased her room was next to Sam's. There was a strict policy: males were not allowed in females' rooms and vice versa.

Kim cleaned her teeth, put her pyjamas on and climbed into bed. It had been a long day, quite scary in parts, but she'd survived it.

She stared at the photo of Keith, Caroline, Fiona and Mikey she'd placed next to her bed. Her eyes welled up. She missed them dreadfully already.

'All right, Tommy? Fancy seeing you here. You're looking well. How's life been treating you?'

Recognizing the voice, Tommy swung around. It was Yvonne Purdy. 'Jesus! You've changed. How long you been a skinhead?'

'About six months. And to think I used to take the piss out of your mate Scratch,' Yvonne chuckled.

'You seen Scratch?' Tommy asked hopefully.

'No. Nobody's seen her since she left Maylands. She disappeared one day without anyone knowing. Did you hear what happened to Wayne Bradley? I read about it in the *News of the World*.'

'Yeah. Didn't surprise me. I always knew he was a fucking monster.' Wayne had been given a fifteen stretch in 1977 for raping a mother and daughter and holding them hostage. Apparently he'd been dating the thirty-three-year-old mother and things had gone wonky when she'd tried to end their relationship. He had broken into the house, raped the mother, then tied her up and forced her to watch him repeatedly rape her fourteen-year-old daughter, who was, by all accounts, a virgin.

Wayne's defence claimed that he was off his head on drink and drugs, had no memory of the attack and was dreadfully sorry for his actions. He'd been sent to Feltham. Thanks to Ronnie having a couple of pals in Feltham, Wayne had already had a taste of what was to come. He'd been slashed with a razor and had sugared boiling water thrown over him.

Tommy couldn't wait for the day the bastard was released. It had always rankled that he'd got away scot-free for what he'd done to Smiffy and Patch, and retribution was long overdue. The Feltham welcome was just a little taster.

'Did you hear about Ray?' Yvonne asked.

'No.'

'He's got cancer.'

'Jesus! Is he gonna be OK?'

Yvonne shrugged. 'You should visit Maylands. I usually go at least twice a year. We can drop in together next time, if you like?'

'I'm married,' Tommy said bluntly. Yvonne had always shown out to him in the past.

'I ain't trying to crack on to you,' Yvonne chuckled. She grabbed Tommy's arm. 'You see that skinhead over there? The tall one with the swallow tattoo on the side of his neck? That's my boyfriend, Vincent. He's from Clapham. That's where I live now. We share a council flat with another couple.'

'Sweet. So how d'ya know Colin?'

'Colin who?'

Tommy rolled his eyes. 'The geezer whose house we're stood in, celebrating his eighteenth.'

'Oh, I don't really know him. Vincent's brother does. Weird night to hold a party, on a Monday though, ain't it?'

'Colin works on a fruit and veg stall, has to be up early at weekends. Most of his pals are market traders an' all, and today is his actual birthday. So, who is your boyfriend's brother?'

About to explain, Yvonne was stunned when a glamorous blonde bowled up behind Tommy and punched him hard in the back of the head. 'Why is it every time I show up unexpected you're chatting up some slapper?' hissed the blonde.

Tommy turned around. His wife was with her trappy sidekick, Kerry Cummins. 'What the hell you doing 'ere? Yvonne's an old pal, we go back years. Where's Robbie?'

'I've never heard you mention an Yvonne before. Who is she? The famous Scratch?'

'Who you calling a slapper?' Yvonne bellowed. She'd been the hardest girl at Maylands, didn't take shit off nobody.

Donna looked Yvonne up and down. 'As if you would stand a chance with my Tommy anyway. I've seen better-dressed dustmen.'

When Yvonne grabbed Donna's hair, both lost their balance and ended up rolling around the floor like fishwives.

Danny and Eugene waded in and dragged their sister outside to calm her down. Not for the first time in his life, Tommy wished the ground would open up and swallow him as he scrambled around the carpet picking up the contents of his wife's handbag. One item in particular caught his eye.

With a face like thunder, Tommy marched outside. 'Wanna tell me what you need these for?' Tommy grabbed Donna by the throat and waved the packet of condoms in front of her eyes.

'Calm down, mate,' Danny urged, trying to get in the middle of the warring couple.

'Calm down! Calm fucking down! Ask her who she's shagging, Dan, go on. Only I ain't never worn a condom in my life. She's a dirty whore, that's what she is.'

Feeling the colour drain from her face, Donna pleaded her innocence. 'They're not mine, honest. They're Kerry's. Ask her, if you don't believe me.'

Kerry, who'd been earwigging, stepped forward. 'They're mine, I swear. I didn't bring a bag out with me tonight. Don's got my lipstick and keys an' all.'

Unable to control his fury, Tommy told Kerry to fuck off then glared at his wife. 'Liar!' he hissed. 'Don't take me for a cunt, Don, else I'll swing for ya.'

When Danny grabbed his arm, Tommy shoved his pal in the chest. 'I want you to tell your parents every-thing – and I do mean everything. Only I ain't putting up with this no more. She's out most nights with that slut of a mate of hers, shagging Christ knows who. Yet I ain't allowed a night out on me own without her turning up, making a scene. Have I got "mug" stamped on me forehead, or what? Tell your parents I want a fucking divorce.'

CHAPTER NINETEEN

Time is a funny old thing. You never know how much time you've got left, or what sort of legacy you'll leave behind.

I remember the day Donna and I told Jack and Suzie we were expecting a baby very well indeed. I'd literally been crapping myself all morning, had expected them to be furious and scold me for not being more careful.

Instead of being angry, Jack and Suzie couldn't have been more jubilant. Both hugged me close to their chests, gushing how wonderful the unexpected news was. It seemed as though they could not wait to be grandparents, took it literally in their stride. Jack then took me and the lads over to Catford dog track that evening for a proper celebration.

Ronnie, Danny and Eugene were equally thrilled by the news and we all ended up getting hammered. Jack had been given a couple of tips. Both dogs romped home at decent odds and between the five of us we won just over ten grand.

Eugene was sick in the cab, so Danny offered to take him home. I was ready for my bed at that point, asked to go with them, but Jack was having none of it. 'This evening is all about you, son. Me, you and Ronnie shall pop in my pal's club for a nightcap,' he insisted.

The club was a strip joint. Naked girls were cavorting in front of leering, pervy-looking old blokes and I immediately felt uncomfortable.

Jack ushered me into a booth and ordered a bottle of champagne. He made a toast to me and his unborn grandchild, but not to Donna. Ronnie went off into another booth to pay some blonde to dance for him.

'I don't want you to be worrying about the wedding, Tommy. Suzie and I will sort out all the details and I'll be footing the bill, of course.'

Because I was inebriated, I couldn't quite comprehend what Jack was saying. 'What wedding?' I asked dumbly.

'Your wedding, you numpty,' Jack chuckled.

I was horrified and it must have showed on my face. 'Donna and I haven't discussed getting married, Jack. I'm only sixteen.'

Jack's expression quickly turned from jovial to serious. 'I don't fucking care if you're twelve, lad. If you're old enough to put my daughter in the family way, then you're old enough to marry her.'

'But we're only—' I began to protest but Jack butted in. He was glaring at me now.

'No buts, Tommy. You will do the right thing and propose to Donna. Now, do you fucking understand me?'

That was the first time I remember being scared of Jack Darling. I nodded my head repeatedly.

So that was it. Like it or not, I was getting married. I had no bastard choice in the matter. But looking back, that wasn't the worst thing that happened. There was treachery going on that night. The real game is as old as the Bible. It ain't your enemy that will bring you down, just ask Cain and Abel . . .

'Dadda,' Robbie smiled.

Tommy lifted his son out of the bath, wrapped him in a towel and kissed him on the forehead. 'Shall we go to the park this morning? Just me and you?'

As per usual, Robbie merely stared at him blankly.

He was nineteen months old now and, unlike other kids of his age, hadn't quite picked up the art of talking and walking. He was a happy child though, rarely cried, but smiled a lot.

Feeling extremely sorry for herself, Donna appeared in the doorway. 'We need to talk, Tommy.'

Tommy treated her to a look of disdain. Even in a towelling dressing gown, with last night's make-up on and mascara plastered around her eyes which made her look like a panda, Donna still had the ability to look beautiful. His mother had been the same, but unlike Donna, his mother had been beautiful on the inside too. 'I got nothing to say to you,' Tommy spat.

'Well, I've got something to say to you. I'm sorry for turning up at the party and kicking off, but I swear on Robbie's life those dunkies were Kerry's, not mine. I know you think I have, but I've never cheated on you, Tommy, and I never would. I want you to call Danny and Eugene and tell 'em to keep schtum. Only, if they say something to my dad and he storms round 'ere and clocks the handmark you kindly left on my face, it'll be you in big trouble, not me.'

Tommy sat on a roundabout with his son on his lap. He often came to the park alone with Robbie. It was one of those places that helped him think straight.

Last night wasn't the first time he'd put his hands around Donna's throat or given her a slap. It was the first time he'd let his guard down in front of the Darlings though. His marriage was volatile. If he had a pound for every time Donna had punched him, he'd be rich. She was always flying off the handle, accusing him of something or other. Most days he dreaded going home.

Tommy knew he had issues. When Robbie was born early, with a mop of dark hair, he'd been convinced that the child wasn't his. Thankfully, the Darlings had managed to convince him otherwise and Robbie was his world now. Intimacy was another problem. He loathed foreplay or oral sex. Whenever he and Donna argued she would inform him how crap he was in bed. The truth hurt, but Tommy couldn't help the way he was. He still regularly saw his uncle looming towards him in his nightmares and would wake up in a trembling cold sweat.

When his pager bleeped, Tommy scooped his son in his arms and headed towards the nearest telephone box. Usually, his pager going off meant there was some trouble in a pub that needed dealing with.

Tommy called Jack at home first. Nobody answered, so he rang the Lord Nelson. Jack wasn't there either. 'Shit,' Tommy mumbled. He'd been unable to get hold of Danny or Eugene earlier as Donna had requested. So chances were, they'd already opened their traps and Jack was round at his gaff.

Tommy's worst fears were confirmed when he clocked Jack's gold Mercedes. He and Donna lived in a three-bedroom house in South Lambeth, a wedding present from Jack and Suzie.

Having hurriedly stopped at a florist, Tommy awkwardly handed Donna the bunch of flowers. He smiled at Jack and Suzie. 'All right? This is a nice surprise.' Jack and Suzie rarely visited his gaff, it was usually vice versa.

'I think we need to have a little chat, son, don't you?' Jack said.

Suzie picked up her grandson and turned to Tommy. 'The boys told us what happened last night, hence our visit. We're here to help though, not point the finger. Donna has already admitted she was in the wrong turning up as she did.'

Tommy sat on the edge of the armchair next to his wife. Her eyes were red raw and so was the right-hand side of her face where he'd slapped her. She'd called him a 'weirdo' and 'freak of nature' when they'd got home last night, that's why he'd clumped her. She was forever insulting him and her insults hurt.

'What have you got to say for yourself, Tommy?' Jack asked.

Deciding it was better to be honest than continue living a lie, Tommy took a deep breath. 'I don't think our marriage is working. We want different things in life. I reckon we got hitched too young.'

'How can you say that?' Donna gasped. 'Don't you love me?'

'Yeah, course I do,' Tommy lied. 'But all we seem to do lately is argue. Perhaps I should move out for a while, give us some space?' Tommy wasn't sure he'd ever been in love with Donna in the first place. He'd been a sixteen-year-old lad with raging hormones. It wasn't as though they had anything in common.

Totally oblivious to what was being said, Robbie was

cradled against his gran's bosom, sucking his thumb. Suzie looked at Jack in horror. She certainly hadn't expected this.

'Marriage is all about commitment, Tommy. "I promise to be true to you in good times and bad" – don't you remember your vows, lad?' Jack snapped.

Tommy had learned over the years, attack was the best form of defence. 'Of course I do. But put yourself in my shoes, Jack. How would you feel if every time you went out, Suzie turned up uninvited and created a scene? Everyone last night clocked those rubbers fall out of Donna's bag. I've never felt so humiliated in my whole life,' Tommy exaggerated.

Jack glared at Tommy. 'I wouldn't be happy, but neither would I ever raise a hand to my wife. Real men don't do that.'

'I told Mum and Dad it was the first time that had happened,' Donna gabbled. 'And how sorry you were this morning,' she fibbed. Donna was gobsmacked Tommy wanted to move out. Men lusted after her whenever she went out with Kerry, so why didn't her own husband? They still had sex regularly, but it was always a quick shag rather than proper love-making, which frustrated Donna no end. She'd always orgasmed with her previous boyfriends, but never with Tommy.

Tommy held his hands up. 'You're right, Jack. I should never have raised my hand to Donna and I can assure you I never will again. I lost my temper, it was a spur-of-the-moment reaction and I'm very sorry. But this is why I think Donna and I need some time apart. Our relationship seems toxic at present.'

When Donna burst into tears, Jack's steely eyes blazed. 'You married into a Catholic family, Tommy. You were raised a Catholic yourself, weren't you? I'm afraid separation is totally out of the question. Donna has been given a stern talking to. She won't be going out gallivanting with her friend Kerry any more. Neither will she be spoiling any evenings out that you have. Will you, Donna?'

'No,' Donna mumbled. She was slightly lost for words. For all Tommy's faults, she didn't want to divorce him.

Suzie forced a grin. 'What you two need is another child. Wouldn't it be lovely for Robbie to have a little brother or sister?'

'Great idea,' Jack replied.

'Erm, Donna don't want another kid yet, do you, Don?' Tommy informed his in-laws.

Donna shrugged. She didn't want to lose her husband, so if another child was the answer, then so be it. 'Perhaps Mum and Dad are right?'

When Jack asked Donna where her contraceptive pills were, Tommy opened his mouth, but no words came out. Did his wife tell her parents everything about their sex life? He hoped not.

Donna ran upstairs, then reappeared with a packet.

'Go flush them down the toilet then, love. You go with her, Tommy,' Jack ordered.

Tommy felt like a rabbit caught in a trap as he watched the pills pop out of the packet and disappear down the toilet one by one. Was he meant to be happy about this latest development?

'I'm sorry, Tommy,' Donna whispered.

Jack grinned as his son-in-law and daughter re-appeared. 'Put the kettle on, love,' he ordered Suzie. 'I need to discuss a bit of business with Tommy in private.'

Tommy followed Jack up the stairs and was stunned as he was grabbed around the throat and shoved into his son's bedroom. 'Is this how you grabbed my daughter last night? Or was it more like this?' Jack hissed, tightening his grip.

'I'm sorry, Jack. Truly sorry,' Tommy spluttered.

Jack let go of Tommy. 'And so you fucking well should be. Look, I don't want to fall out with you. You're a good lad deep down. But neither do I want my wife or daughter upset – and currently both are. My family has been good to you, Tommy, never forget that. I put a roof over your head, took you in like one of me own. I even gave you my name.'

'I know, Jack, and I'm eternally grateful.'

'Good. Glad we're singing from the same hymn sheet. So what I want you to do now is trot down those stairs, give it half an hour or so, and then tell my wife and daughter how sorry you are and how determined you are to make your marriage work. Thanks to me, you have a good job, a nice home, a beautiful wife and you're earning decent wonga. Therefore, you will make your marriage work, Tommy. You will put every inch of your heart and soul into doing so. Understand me?'

Knowing he had no other option but to nod, Tommy

nodded so profusely, it reminded him of the plastic duck his mother had once bought him that dunked its head in water. It had looked like it was about to drown. Exactly how he felt right now.

CHAPTER TWENTY

Any animosity between myself and Jack was soon forgotten. The following day he took me and Danny to a posh car showroom.

'You need to upgrade your image, lads. People judge a man on what car he drives. Capris are for boy racers, not businessmen like yourselves. I want you to pick out something classy, both of you.'

I looked around the showroom, my eyes like organ stops. There was nothing over three years old and the prices were extortionate.

I stopped to admire a gleaming mustard-coloured Mercedes Benz 280e. 'Do you like that one, Tommy?' Jack asked.

'Yes. But it's a '77 plate, way out of my league.'

Jack put an arm around my shoulders. Danny was over the other side of the showroom looking at a BMW. 'Did you give any more thought to our chat last night?'

I had lain awake most of the night and thought of little else. I would never be allowed to divorce Donna, I knew that now. 'Yes, Jack,' I replied. 'I want my marriage to work and am determined to make that happen. For all Donna's faults, she has given me the best gift in life I could wish for: a beautiful son.'

Jack grinned. 'Good lad. Now get in the car and take it for a test drive. Don't worry about the cost — my little treat, son.'

I shook my head. 'I can't let you shell out all that money, Jack. I'd be taking liberties.'

Jack chuckled. 'I got more money than I know what to do with, son. Now get in the car.'

What I didn't realize back then was that this gift, along with all the others, was Jack's way of owning me . . .

'All right, bird? Stick the radio on then,' Sam ordered, flopping backwards on to Kim's bed.

Kim did as asked. Boney M's 'Rasputin' was playing on Radio One. It had been a gruelling week, mentally rather than physically. There was lots to learn, A and B reports, and they'd had it drummed into them time after time what becoming a police officer actually meant.

'So what's the plan?' Sam asked. There were only three other females at Hendon – Tina and Lucy, the two slappers, who spent most of their time flirting with any male with a pulse, and an older woman called Wendy who had arrived a day late. Wendy had gone home for the weekend, as had some of the lads.

'Let's go for a walk, get to know the area better. Then later we'll check out that pub, the Leather Bottle, if you like?'

'Sounds good to me. I wouldn't mind trying that Chinese an' all. The slappers went there last night.'

Kim smiled. 'What you wearing?'

Sam rolled her eyes. 'Clothes.'

Tommy met up with the lads in the Thomas A Beckett down the Old Kent Road. It was a well-known boozer, popular in the boxing community because of the gym upstairs. Muhammad Ali, Joe Frazier and even Henry Cooper had trained there, as did Ronnie.

Donna wasn't coming to the fight. Jack had insisted she stay indoors and look after her mother.

Danny slapped his pal on the back. 'You all right, Tommy lad? How's the new wheels? I'm loving mine.'

'Me too. Drives like a dream,' Tommy grinned. He was in a fairly good mood. The drinks were flowing freely and the atmosphere was jovial. Donna had been on her best behaviour since her parents' little visit. She wanted sex all the time though, which Tommy found tiresome. He was making an effort, mind. He'd even gone down on her this morning. There was no way out of his marriage, so he had chosen to make the most of it. For now, at least.

'Want another drink, Tommy?' asked Eugene. It had been Eugene who'd grassed him up to Jack for putting his hands around Donna's throat. 'You told us to tell our dad everything. I didn't mean to dob you in it. I never said you hurt Donna,' Eugene had explained.

Tommy looked at his watch. Ronnie was top-of-the-bill at York Hall; his fight was at 10 p.m. 'Let's make tracks, shall we? I want to see all the fights.'

'So, what's your story then? I've told you all about my dysfunctional family,' Sam laughed. She'd been telling Kim about her childhood, growing up in Walthamstow. Her dad had walked out one day and never come back.

'My mum's dead and I never really knew my dad,' Kim replied honestly. She'd been informed last year of her mother's demise. She'd been found in her flat, her corpse rotting. The police reckoned someone had been in the flat with her, then left. They weren't sure of the actual cause of death, but said it was probably a drug overdose.

'Sorry to hear that. How old was you when she died, your mum?'

'She only died last year. We wasn't close. I didn't live with her.'

'Who did you live with then?'

'My aunt and uncle,' Kim lied. She liked Sam, but couldn't be arsed opening up about her past. This was meant to be a fresh start for her.

'How ya feeling, bro?' asked Danny.

'Yeah, good. I feel sharp. Been training hard all week,' Ronnie replied. Whenever a fight was nearing, he stepped away from the family business to concentrate on his training.

'I've put five hundred quid on ya. Evens was the best price. He's six to one, the other geezer,' Danny informed his brother. The bloke Ronnie was fighting was relatively unknown. He was Algerian, but had been living and training in Tottenham. This was his third professional fight and he was yet to lose. His previous opponents were nothing special though and Ronnie was confident he'd beat him.

'Right, let's strap those wrists up,' said Ronnie's trainer.

Jack hugged his eldest. 'Good luck, son. We're all rooting for ya.'

'Cheers, Dad.'

When Danny and Eugene hugged Ronnie, Tommy

did the same. 'Go knock him dead. Not literally, like. But ya know what I mean.'

The Leather Bottle was in Edgware and was popular with the recruits. The two slappers were already in there, sitting at a table full of lads.

'Come and sit over 'ere, girls,' shouted the ginger idiot Kim had met on the train.

'Let's keep ourselves to ourselves, shall we?' Kim suggested. Most of the male recruits were brash and raucous and Kim could tell a few were already drunk.

'Sod ya then, you pair of dykes,' shouted Ginger.

'I'll knock that prick out in a minute, he keeps on,' Sam threatened.

'All right, ladies? Can I get you both a drink?'

Kim swung around. It was a guy she'd noticed clocking her in the restaurant and he was even better looking up close. His accent had taken her by surprise though. 'We're OK. But thanks anyway.'

'I'll have a pint, please. Lager. Where do you come from?' Sam asked.

The lad smiled, showing off a set of perfect white teeth. 'Liverpool. What about yourself?'

'Walthamstow. You can get my mate a pint an' all.'

The lad turned to Kim and winked. 'I'm Jay, by the way.'

The cheer as Ronnie stepped inside the ring was immense. A popular bloke, all his pals were there to support him.

Tommy loved boxing, preferred it to football these days. He and Danny rarely went over Millwall any more, but would attend plenty of boxing events. He even got a buzz out of watching the kids fight. 'Go, Ronnie,' Tommy bellowed.

Jack clapped wildly as his son landed an early couple of punches. He'd been a decent boxer himself back in the day; only long spells in prison had stopped him from making the grade.

Ronnie danced around the ring in his trademark blue shiny shorts. He was having a decent first round and he knew it.

'Go, Ronnie,' Eugene bellowed, his heart beating wildly.

'He won that round, hands down,' Tommy grinned as the bell sounded.

Back at the Leather Bottle, Kim was feeling flushed and wasn't sure if it was the alcohol or Jay's penetrating eyes having an adverse effect on her. He was incredibly striking, had dark skin, black hair and the most beautiful brown eyes. His parents were apparently Irish.

'Shall we put some music on the jukebox, then get these lads a drink?' Sam suggested. John seemed OK too. He came from Newcastle.

'I'll get another round in. My mother would kill me if I let a woman buy me a drink. She's old school,' Jay laughed.

Kim followed Sam over to the jukebox. 'They're all right, aren't they? At least you can have a sensible conversation with 'em,' Sam said.

'Yeah. They seem OK.'

'He's well got the hots for you, that Jay. I can tell.'

'As I told you earlier, I'm not interested in blokes.'

'I don't blame you. My brothers treat girls like shit. Women are a far better species.'

Not realizing that Sam also had the hots for her, Kim linked arms with her pal. 'You can say that again.'

'Put your guard up, Ronnie. What ya doing, bro?' Danny shouted.

'Come on, Ronnie. You can do this, son,' Jack yelled. After winning the first few rounds, Ronnie had been caught by a right hook. He'd hit the canvas and had since looked out of his depth.

'Fucking hell, Ronnie. What you doing, mate?' Tommy winced. The Algerian was giving Ronnie a pasting, literally.

'He's done for, Dad. He's had it,' Eugene said, stating the obvious.

All of a sudden, it was like everything went into slow motion. The Algerian hit Ronnie so hard he seemed to fly through the air before landing flat on his back. His whole body then went into spasms.

'Shit, Dad. What's wrong with him?' Danny shrieked.

Jack leapt out of his front-row seat and into the ring. Ronnie was twitching, having some kind of fit.

When the doctor stepped into the ring, Tommy and Danny looked at each other in despair. Ronnie was in a bad way. A very bad way indeed.

Throwing her arms about like Tina and Lucy had been in the pub earlier, Kim sang along to the Jacksons' 'Blame It on the Boogie'.

Sam grinned. 'What about when Tina fell over? Those lads were laughing at her you know, not with her.'

Imitating Tina stacking it, Kim threw herself on the floor.

'Get up, you nutter,' Sam chuckled.

Feeling inebriated, Kim flopped on to her bed next to Sam. Jay and John had wanted them to go on to another pub, but Kim had flatly refused. It had been ages since she'd drunk copious amounts of alcohol, hadn't done so since leaving Maylands. Today had been great, but Kim was determined not to make a fool of herself here. She'd done that with Tommy, and look where it had got her.

When Sam placed her hand on her left boob and tried to snog her, Kim recoiled in horror. She jumped off the bed. 'What the fuck d'ya think you're doing?'

'Sorry. But I thought . . . ya know. You said you didn't like blokes, preferred women.'

'Not in that way. I hate lads because I had my heart broken once, OK. Doesn't mean to say I fancy bloody women.'

Sam burst out laughing. 'I actually thought you were coming on to me earlier. Especially when you held my arm all the way home.'

'Well, I weren't, OK. Look, you ain't ugly, mate, and if I were that way inclined, I might've snogged you back. But I'm not. So get over yourself, geezer bird. You got more chance of copping off with those slappers Tina and Lucy, than me.'

Currently in the charts was the Rose Royce smoochie 'Love Don't Live Here Anymore'. Chuckling away like a drunken sailor, Sam grabbed Kim's hand. 'Dance with me, bird. Then I promise I'll leave you alone and forget all about me knock-back, for good.'

As Sam swung her around the room like a ballroom dancer, shrieking the words 'You abandoned me', Kim could not help but laugh herself.

Today had been a funny old day. It was the first time she hadn't missed the only family she'd ever truly felt part of.

Suzie Darling was in bits when she arrived at the hospital with Donna. It had been Jack who'd encouraged their sons to box. She hated the sport and something like this had always been her biggest fear. 'Where is he? What happened?' Jack had told her very little on the phone; all she knew was that Ronnie had lost the fight and was at the London Hospital in Whitechapel.

Jack held his wife in his arms. 'We're waiting for an update. He had some kind of fit, I think.'

'A fit! What, like an epileptic fit?' Suzie burst into tears and pummelled her fists against Jack's chest. 'Why didn't you listen to me, eh? I always told you the sport was bloody dangerous.'

'It's not Dad's fault, Mum,' Danny said. 'We all wanted to box.'

'Not any more you don't. None of yous will ever step in a ring again, d'ya hear me? And that includes you, Tommy. You're a married man with a child.'

Not knowing what else to do, Tommy nodded. That was his boxing career over with then. What Jack and Suzie said had to be obeyed.

'Dad, Dad. You all right?' Danny asked. They all looked over, Jack was holding his head in his hands, a strange expression on his face.

Suzie screamed as her husband fell to the floor in front of her very eyes. So did Donna. 'Do something, Tommy,' Donna shrieked.

Tommy legged it down the corridor and grabbed hold of a nurse. 'We're here with the boxer who got rushed in. But my father-in-law's just collapsed now an' all.'

'Well?' Danny asked as Suzie reappeared.

'How is he, Mum?' asked Eugene.

'Conscious and talking. His speech is a bit slurred. The doctor reckons he might have had a stroke. They want him to rest tonight and will give him a scan in the morning,' Suzie explained.

'Did you see Ronnie as well?' Tommy enquired.

'No. They won't let me see him yet. What a night, eh? I meant what I said earlier. No way are you three ever stepping into a ring again. Boxing should be banned. Dad wants to see you, Danny, and you, Tommy.'

'Can't I see him too?' Eugene asked.

'You can see him afterwards. He's only allowed a couple of visitors at a time.'

It was a shock for both Danny and Tommy to see Jack lying in a hospital bed with a drip in his arm. His skin was a greyish colour and his speech sounded like that of a drunk.

'I'm tired now, but I wanted a quick word,' Jack slurred. 'With everything that's happened tonight, you two need to take over the reins for a while. People might try to take liberties if they know Ronnie and I are out of action. Don't fucking let 'em. I've taught you everything I know. Now it's time for you to step up to the mark. Understand?'

Tommy and Danny both nodded. 'Yes,' they said in unison.

CHAPTER TWENTY-ONE

'Sorry, lads. No can do. There's another little firm taken over this patch now and I can't be paying both of you,' the landlord explained.

Danny Darling leapt over the bar like a kangaroo and grabbed Bill Edwards by the throat in front of his small crew of lunchtime regulars. This was the third time today a landlord had refused to pay what they owed and Danny was pissed off with it. 'Who is this other firm, Bill? I want names – fucking now.'

'The Archers, out of Deptford. Not being funny, Danny, but with everything that's happened, I can't rely on you any more. Nobody came the last two times I had grief in 'ere. The Archers have more manpower.'

When Eugene lunged forward to give Bill a clump, Tommy intervened. 'This ain't getting us nowhere. We need to talk to your dad and brother.' Tommy liked Bill, didn't want to see him get hurt. It was hardly his fault another firm had put the squeeze on him.

Cursing, Danny stormed out of the pub. It was five weeks now since Ronnie had lost his fight and his father had suffered a stroke, and things seemed to be going from bad to worse. They were short on manpower.

Ronnie was wary though, didn't trust outsiders. Neither did his father.

'What we gonna do?' Eugene asked. It was clear that with his father, Ronnie and Griff out of the picture, publicans viewed himself, Danny and Tommy as nothing more than three silly teenagers. Ronnie had upset his pal Griff when he'd blurted out on a hospital visit he'd shagged Griff's wife before they'd met, and Griff had quit working for Jack the very next day.

Danny started the engine of his BMW. The Barron Knights' 'A Taste of Aggro' belted out of the stereo, which seemed rather apt. Danny sighed and turned the music down. Both his father and Ronnie seemed changed men since *that* night. His dad was only forty-six, had been told to take it easy, change his lifestyle and diet. As for Ronnie, all he'd done since coming out of hospital three weeks ago, was doss in his old bedroom and knock back the booze while being waited on hand and foot by his mother. Danny felt sorry for his mum. She tried to put on a brave face, but caring for two disgruntled patients wasn't easy. He'd caught her crying in the kitchen the other day, poor cow.

'What exactly do we know about these Archers?' Tommy asked.

'Not much. Only that Dad had some beef with Alfie Archer once upon a time. They were in the nick together, I think. Ronnie knows more about the family than me,' Danny replied. 'We need to tell Ronnie what's happened. Perhaps this is the news he needs to stop wallowing in self-pity and get his arse back into gear. We can't tell me dad. He's gonna think we've failed him.'

Ronnie Darling was at home, sulking in his old bedroom. He'd put on a bit of timber, didn't bathe regularly any more and hadn't had a shave in weeks. Boxing had been the most important thing in his life and now it was gone, finito.

Ronnie knew it was his fault his father had keeled over. It must have been the shock of realizing his eldest son was nothing more than a fucking loser. His dad had been as fit as a fiddle until he'd hit the canvas. Nobody had been able to explain why he'd had a fit. He'd also suffered a slight bleed on the brain. It made him feel like a dickhead. He wasn't even allowed to drive.

'You all right, boys? Hungry?' asked Suzie Darling. 'I was about to sit down and watch *Pebble Mill*, but I can make you some lunch, if you like?'

'We're fine, thanks, Mum. We ate at the café earlier. Where's Dad?' Danny asked.

'Gone for a walk, so he says. Personally, I'd put money on it he's in the bloody pub. I smelt whisky and cigar smoke on his breath after he returned from his walk yesterday. I wish he'd do like the doctors told him.'

'Dad's his own person, Mum. You ain't gonna change him. He'll be fine. He's not silly. He won't go overboard,' said Danny. He'd hated the sight of his father shuffling about like an old man when he'd first come out of hospital, was relieved he felt well enough to go to the pub again.

'Ronnie in his room?' Eugene asked. Silly question really, seeing as his brother only came out of it to use the toilet these days.

'Yes. Not been downstairs all day. I'm worried sick about him. He looks like a bleedin' tramp – and smells like one an' all.'

'He'll be fine, Mum. Ron needs time to adjust, that's all,' Danny insisted. 'Right, we're popping upstairs. Got a bit of business to discuss.'

'OK. Give me a shout if you need any refreshments. And try and get your brother to have a bleedin' shower.'

Ronnie leapt off his bed like a raving lunatic and punched the wall. 'Bill Edwards said what?'

'That the Archers have taken over our patch. Well, some of it,' Eugene replied bluntly.

For the first time since the night of his fight, Ronnie had fire in his eyes and belly. His father hated that old tosspot Alfie Archer, and Glenn, the nephew he was in partnership with, was no better.

Tommy leapt back in shock as a plate was thrown across the room, narrowly missing his head. It smashed against the wall behind him. He was used to seeing Ronnie strutting about like cock-of-the-walk, not re-enacting a Greek wedding in a pair of Y-fronts and a filthy rotten T-shirt.

'I can't believe yous three useless fuckers did nothing,' Ronnie bellowed. 'You should have smashed up Edwards' boozer, and the other two. It'll be the gaming machines next, ya know, if we don't nip this in the bud,' Ronnie snarled.

'We didn't know what to do for the best,' Eugene argued.

Ronnie wanted to smash his youngest brother in the face and tell him that's what he should have done, but he somehow restrained himself.

Eugene was sixteen, still a kid. He didn't really understand how their world worked. Neither, in fairness, did Danny and Tommy. All three were good to throw a punch or smash a kneecap, but now the Archers had taken a liberty, a big statement had to be made.

'Where you going, Ron?' Danny asked worriedly.

'To a phone box. Drive me, will ya. I need to call in a couple of favours.'

'But you ain't got no clothes on,' Eugene reminded his brother.

'Yes, I fucking know that. I'm gonna have a shower and get dressed first. That Alfie Archer will rue the day he decided to cross the Darlings. Trust me on that one.'

Bill Edwards looked up in horror as a deranged-looking Ronnie Darling stormed behind the bar with Danny, Tommy and Eugene in tow. Ronnie had a baseball bat in his hand and Bill's life flashed before his very eyes.

Ronnie lifted the bat and began smashing it against the optics one by one. The sound of splintering glass sent a few punters running out of the door. The others, frozen with shock, stayed put.

'Please, Ronnie. Stop. Look, I'm sorry,' Bill pleaded.

'This is what you do, lads, when somebody refuses

to pay you what they owe,' Ronnie shrieked, continuing his rampage.

'Leave Bill alone or I'll call the police,' demanded one brave elderly man.

Ronnie marched over to the bloke and stared him in the eyes. 'No, you fucking won't. Cos if you do, I'll not only kill you, I'll burn your whole family alive. Now get out,' Ronnie bellowed. 'Same goes for the rest of ya. Pub's closed.'

As his regulars scuttled off, Bill tried to reason with Ronnie. 'I will pay you, every penny. Just give me a week or so. But I can't be paying the Archers too. Their prices are dearer than yours,' Bill said, near to tears.

Ronnie clumped Bill around the side of the face with the bat.

Tommy winced. Bill didn't deserve this. He'd always paid up on time in the past.

Ronnie kneeled on the floor next to his prey. He picked up a shard of glass and pressed it against Bill's right cheek. 'Right, I wanna know exactly who paid you a visit and every single word they fucking said. Got me?'

When Bill started blabbing, Tommy, Danny and Eugene glanced at each other. All were thinking the same thing. They should have left Ronnie in his bedroom.

Rather than going home, Tommy decided to take a drive around Barking, the area he'd been raised in. He'd passed his driving test earlier that year and loved driving about in his new Mercedes Benz. He'd come a long way in life since leaving Maylands and had Jack to thank for that.

Tommy had a lump inside his throat as he sat opposite the house he'd grown up in. It looked exactly the same as when he'd lived there, apart from the porch that had been added. The curtains were closed, but when Tommy shut his eyes, he could picture himself, his mum and sisters laughing and singing in the lounge while watching *Top of the Pops*. He looked up to where his old bedroom used to be. He could remember that clearly too. All his football posters, proudly plastered across the wall next to his bed. He'd been a Celtic and Spurs supporter back then.

When a vision of Rex, his beloved Alsatian, popped into Tommy's head, tears ran down his cheeks. It had been a bad idea coming back here; stupid, in fact.

Taking one last look at the house he knew he would never visit again, Tommy put his foot on the accelerator. He needed a brandy. In fact he needed a bottle.

Blurry-eyed, Tommy drove for about five minutes before stopping at a random back-street pub. He wasn't in the mood for socializing around his own neck of the woods. Too many people knew him there and he wanted to be alone to think. Company was the last thing he needed today of all bloody days.

The boozer was tiny, but had a homely feel to it. There was an open fire, a Christmas tree, lots of decorations and tinsel draped around the bar.

Tommy ordered a large brandy and a pint off the pretty Irish barmaid, then sat at a table near the jukebox. Today had been a crap day all round. Ronnie had trashed three boozers and walloped each landlord who'd refused to pay up – unjustly, in Tommy's opinion. What had happened was the Archers' fault, nobody else's. Giving a piss-taker such as Bruce a dig was one thing, but Tommy's heart had gone out to poor Bill earlier. Ronnie had sliced the poor bastard's right cheek in half. Deep down he knew Ronnie had a screw loose and would never be the same. Ronnie had seemed untouchable, maybe that's why he was feeling so bloody maudlin.

Hearing Slade's 'Merry Christmas Everybody' play on the jukebox, Tommy sighed. He'd once loved Christmas, but ever since his mum had died he'd loathed this time of year. He could remember that last Christmas they'd spent together as a family as though it were yesterday. That bastard Alexander had come late on Christmas Eve and clumped his mum, giving her a real shiner.

Picturing his sisters, Tommy managed a smile. 'Long-Haired Lover from Liverpool' had been number one in the charts and Linda had been obsessed with Little Jimmy Osmond. He thought of Hazel and wondered how she was and what she was doing now. He doubted she was still locked up after all this time, but neither he nor Linda had had any contact with her in years. Perhaps one day their paths would cross again. All he could do was hope Hazel was happy and hadn't forgotten him.

Linda was doing well. She was living in Clacton with the Piper family, had a typing job and her first boyfriend. Nanny Noreen had been furious when Linda had walked out on her. The old witch had died a few months later. Tommy hadn't attended her funeral and had been surprised to learn shortly afterwards she'd left him a thousand pounds in her will. She'd left the same to Linda. Tommy hadn't wanted what he saw as guilt money, so had insisted Linda have his inheritance too. He wasn't a forgiver or forgetter.

Alexander had remarried and moved back to Scotland, by all accounts. He had another baby now, a son. Tommy felt sorry for the boy and the woman he was married to. He wondered if he hit and raped her like he had his own mother. Chances were, if Hazel had been released, she had moved to Scotland too. Linda didn't hear from Alexander any more. He'd called her an 'ungrateful little mare' the day she'd left Nanny Noreen's and they hadn't spoken since.

Debating whether he should contact his old pal, PC Kendall, to see if he could somehow trace Hazel, Tommy quickly decided against it. Jack had a couple of bent coppers on the payroll, but otherwise wasn't keen on the boys in blue. PC Kendall would probably know what he was doing for a living now and, if he started asking questions, it might open up a can of worms. Tommy owed Jack big time. That man had been the nearest thing to a father figure he'd ever had and he would never betray him.

The music having stopped, Tommy was about to put another record on when a familiar voice made him freeze. The colour drained from his face and his hands began to tremble. It couldn't be, could it? Surely it couldn't be him?

'Your usual, Tom?' asked the barmaid.

'Yes, please, pet. You know me, a creature of habit.'

All those terrible memories came flooding back in an instant. The kite, the bath, the night he'd come into Tommy's room and . . . The things he'd spent years trying to forget.

Tommy knew he had to get out of this pub, but wasn't sure his legs would be able to carry him.

Feeling as though his head was about to explode, Tommy took the plunge, but as he did so took a brief glance at the man being served. There was no doubt about it; it was him – the perverted bastard who had all but ruined his life. He looked fatter, balder, but the resemblance to Benny Hill was still there.

Tommy darted outside and round the side of the pub, then leaned against a wall to steady himself. He felt faint. Seconds later, he spewed his guts up.

'Charming,' an elderly lady said, voice laden with sarcasm.

Tommy didn't bother replying. If only she fucking knew.

His mind completely blown, Tommy drove to an off-licence, bought a half-bottle of brandy and knocked it back to calm his frayed nerves. 'Tom, my fucking arse! You lying, treacherous, perverted cunt,' Tommy hissed, throwing the empty bottle into the footwell.

To say he was shaken to the core was putting it mildly. How dare that filthy bastard name himself after him and move to the area where he'd grown up. The area where his beautiful mum had lived, before she'd died. The pervert's own sister!

Repeatedly clicking his knuckles, Tommy banged his head against the steering wheel. Did his animal of an uncle still have the hots for him? Was that why he'd called himself Tom and moved to the area he was raised in? That boozer was obviously his local. That Irish barmaid knew what he drank. No wonder Ronnie had no joy when trying to trace the arsehole a couple of years ago.

Wondering whether to go back to the pub and follow the disgusting shitbag home, Tommy knew he couldn't, not tonight anyway. It had been a long day, a stressful one. He could barely see straight, let alone think straight.

'Where the bloody hell you been?' Donna Darling shrieked.

'Out,' Tommy spat.

'Out where? I spoke to Danny. He said you finished work hours ago.'

'No Spanish inquisition tonight, Don, please. I really don't fucking need it.'

Donna stood up. 'Oh my God! You're drunk.' She stared out of the window. 'And you drove your new car home in that state! Do you not care at all about me and Robbie? You could have killed yourself.'

Tommy stared at his wife. She was a fine one to start acting virtuous. Talk about the pot calling the kettle black. He could never open up to her, about anything, let alone his past. He briefly thought of Scratch. She might not have been as beautiful as Donna, but she'd been his best bloody friend. He could talk to her about anything and everything. She understood him, whereas Donna never would.

'Well? What you got to say for yourself?' Donna screamed, hands on hips.

Tommy sighed. 'You know you said I could have killed myself tonight, Don? Well, if you want to know the truth, I wish I fucking had.'

CHAPTER TWENTY-TWO

Life at Hendon was tough, but both Kim and Sam were thriving on it. They were the only two females left now. The older lady had only lasted a week and now the two slappers were history. Tina had been caught with a bloke in her bed, drinking wine. She'd been dismissed the next day. Lucy had then left of her own accord, much to Kim and Sam's amusement.

Lots of lads had dropped out too. The training was anything but bloody easy. Recruits had to get up at 6.30 a.m. and by the time she got to bed in the evening, Kim was totally exhausted.

The academic side of the training Kim had found the hardest. The endless tutorials in the classroom learning about the law. So instead of frequenting the bar of an evening like the slappers had, Kim and Sam had swotted together, trying to absorb every piece of information they'd learned each day. They'd then quiz one another on the answers until they were imprinted in their brains.

Spotting a mark on her uniform, Kim wetted a flannel and frantically began rubbing it. Her uniform consisted of a jacket, knee-length skirt, white shirt, a soft hat, horrid thick tights and a pair of drab-looking flat black shoes.

Even a speck of dust would warrant a telling off, let alone a crease. Kim and Sam had spent many hours in the ironing room of an evening, trying to perfect the art.

The physical side of her training Kim had found much more enjoyable. Some mornings her muscles would ache so much she could barely get out of bed, but on the plus side she had never felt so fit in her whole life. She'd learned judo, spent hours in the pool swimming laps, trained hard in the gym and could now run like a whippet. She loved the role-acting too, learning how to restrain, arrest and handcuff a suspect, and how to use a truncheon.

Satisfied she'd got the mark off, Kim picked up the photo of Caroline, Keith, Fiona and Mikey. After being pushed from pillar to post all her life, they were the nearest she'd ever had to a proper family. Most of the recruits who lived in or around London had travelled home at weekends, but Kim hadn't. She'd wanted to cut the apron strings, felt it was time to branch out on her own.

Kim planted a kiss on the photo then put it back on the chest of drawers. She phoned Caroline once a week, and Connie. They were extremely proud of her and that gave Kim a huge buzz. She wanted to make them proud, give them something back in return for their support and kindness. It wasn't every day a child from Maylands became a police officer. Both herself and Connie had been horrified to read what Wayne Bradley had done to that poor child.

Kim's thoughts were disturbed by a tap on the door. It was Sam. 'How you feeling? I didn't sleep too well.'

'Me neither. I'm so nervous.' There were three exams to pass at Hendon and today they would find out the results of the final one.

Sam plonked herself on Kim's bed. 'It's my birthday today. Passing would be the best present ever.'

'No way! Why didn't you say something before-hand? I would've got you a card and a present.' Sam making a pass at her hadn't ruined their friendship. If anything, it had strengthened it. That was their very own private joke and they'd often mock one another about it when alone.

'I'm not really into birthdays. I didn't even do anything special for my eighteenth last year. What about you? When is yours?'

Kim rolled her eyes. 'Don't ask.'

'Why?'

'Because I have two, like the queen. My mother always told me my birthday was July the fifth. But after she died, my aunt and uncle applied for a birth certificate for me and it turned out I was actually born on April the fifth.' Kim still referred to Caroline and Keith as her aunt and uncle. It wasn't that she didn't trust her friend enough to come clean about the past; she just didn't want to talk about it. Her months at Hendon had been the happiest time of her life. She still had nightmares though, mostly about Tommy Boyle. That July the fifth in 1976 had almost done her in. To think she'd sat outside Maylands like an idiot, thinking Tommy would turn up, when all the while her knight in shining armour was busy marrying Donna Darling. How naïve she must have been back then. Not any more though. Tommy might still haunt her in her sleep, but never again would she trust a man. She was totally focused on her career, determined to make it in this world off her own bat. There was only one person in the world you could really trust and that was yourself.

Sam was perplexed. 'I thought you said you lived with your mum's sister? Surely she must have known when you were born?'

'It's a long story, my mum was a bit of a drunk. I don't really like to talk about it.'

Sam put an arm around Kim's shoulders. 'I get that. My mum's a pisshead an' all. But I want you to know, if you ever need to chat to anyone, I'm here for ya.'

Kim put her arms around Sam and hugged her tight.

''Ere, you ain't trying it on with me, are ya, bird? Only, you had your chance and blew it – big time.'

Kim laughed. 'You should be so bleedin' lucky.'

Donna Darling moved her head rhythmically, trying to get a response from her husband's flaccid penis. There was none. It was as limp as a giant worm. 'I'm getting sick of this. How we gonna have another baby if you can't even get it up?'

Tommy sat up, swung his legs over the side of the bed and put his head in his hands. Five days had passed since he'd laid eyes on his nonce-case of an uncle, and he still couldn't get the image of the bastard out of his mind.

'Don't you fancy me no more? Is that it?' Donna shrieked.

'No. It's not that. I've not been sleeping properly. I feel stressed.'

'Well, best you go to the fucking doctor and get something to de-stress yourself then.'

'I will,' Tommy lied.

'I mean it, Tommy. It's bad enough you won't let me suck your cock, let alone this. I've said it before and I'll say it again, there's something wrong with you. You're a freak of fucking nature.'

When Donna stormed down the stairs, Tommy picked up the radio/alarm clock and aimed it at the wall. Donna was spot on. He was a freak of nature. But it wasn't his fault.

In a classroom in Hendon, Kim and Sam sat anxiously next to one another. Five names had been called out and told to leave the classroom.

Glancing to her left, Kim smiled at Jay. He crossed his fore and middle fingers together and winked at her.

Kim's heart skipped a beat. Jay had that effect on her. Nothing had happened between them, but he was a lovely guy, genuine. She and Sam had spent most weekends hanging out with Jay, John and Leroy. Racism was rife at Hendon, and Kim admired the way Jay and John had taken Leroy under their wing. Leroy was the son of West Indian parents and Kim thought he was great. He had a brilliant sense of humour, reminded her in some ways of Benny.

When the remaining recruits were told they had all passed their final exam, there were whoops of delight, hugs and handshakes all round.

Clinging on to each other, Kim and Sam jumped up and down, brimming with excitement. They were officially

WPCs now, and could barely believe it. 'We did it, bird. We fucking did it!' Sam chuckled.

Tears streamed down Kim's face. 'I can't believe it. I must ring Caroline and Connie.'

'Why you crying, ya nutter?' Sam grinned.

'I dunno,' Kim laughed. But she did. She had come so far from that self-harming, shop-lifting little skinhead she'd once been; she could barely believe she'd actually achieved something so brilliant in life. Finally Scratch was dead, it was WPC Regan from here on in.

'What's up, Tom? You're definitely not yourself. Is it Donna? She been playing you up again?' asked Danny Darling. He, Tommy and Eugene had stopped at a café for a full English, but Tommy had barely touched his.

Tommy pushed his plate away and picked up the *Sun* newspaper. 'I'm fine. Me and Donna are OK. I ain't been sleeping well, that's all,' he replied, before pretending to read an article about unemployment being at a post-war high.

Last night, Tommy had gone back to the pub he'd seen his uncle in and sat outside in his car. His plan had been to follow the evil bastard, find out where he now lived. But not only had his uncle not showed, all it had done was remind him of more terrible memories. Then Donna had let fly at him for arriving home late and he'd ended up having one of his excruciating nightmares.

Tommy sipped his mug of tea. He knew if he involved the Darlings they would help him, but he couldn't.

Obviously, Ronnie and Danny knew a bit about his plight. But the only person who he'd even remotely opened up to was Scratch. He wanted to kill his uncle, throttle him with his bare hands, but even the thought of touching him or being in close proximity made Tommy want to vomit.

Eugene talking about Ronnie snapped Tommy's mind back to the present. 'I still don't understand why Ronnie had to tell Griff that he'd screwed his missus. Griff was reliable, an asset to the firm. Do you reckon if Dad had a word with Griff, he might come back to work?' Eugene asked.

Danny shook his head slowly. 'No chance.' Even though Griff hadn't been married to her at the time, he was livid – understandably so.

'Ronnie weren't thinking straight. It's not his fault,' Tommy said. 'Life's a bitch, unfortunately.'

'You're ever so cheerful at times, Tommy. Anyone ever told you that?' Eugene chuckled.

Ignoring Eugene's little dig, Tommy glanced at his watch. 'What time we gotta meet your old man?'

Danny studied his pal. There was definitely something wrong with him. 'Noon. You sure you're OK, mate?'

'Yes, Dan. How many more times you gonna ask me the same fucking question?'

Danny and Eugene glanced at each other. They knew when to shut up.

Jack Darling had the spring back in his step. His speech had returned to normal and he felt on top of the world. He'd been for a check-up yesterday and his cholesterol was significantly lower. He'd taken the doctor's advice and eaten more fruit and veg. He'd also cut down on salt, reduced his alcohol intake and knocked the cigarettes on the head. He still enjoyed a few whiskies and cigars, mind. A man had to have some pleasures in life.

'Well, what do you reckon?' Jack grinned at his eldest son. They'd had no more grief from publicans since Ronnie's little rampage. He was slightly disappointed Danny and Tommy hadn't sorted it alone, but he hadn't coated them off. The Archers were a handful. All the publicans had coughed up what they owed, and the rest had paid up on time. Jack felt they now needed their own base though. A place where they could operate from properly. He had registered the gaming machines as a legitimate business, but it wouldn't hurt to register another. He only declared a small percentage of his earnings to the taxman and his recent illness had given Jack food for thought. He had plenty of money stashed away, and Suzie's dream was to own a little cottage in the countryside where they could spend weekends and holidays. By setting up another business, Jack could not only cover his arse with the taxman, he could grant his wife her wish.

The premises, formerly a furniture showroom, were just off the Old Kent Road. 'Yeah, I like it. It's got potential,' Ronnie grinned.

Jack knew his eldest wasn't quite the same man he'd been before that fight. His defeat had knocked the stuffing out of him in more ways than one. Desperate to boost Ronnie's confidence again, Jack put an arm around his shoulders. 'Glad you like it. Only, I want you to manage the gaff.'

Ronnie's eyes lit up. He'd hated disappointing his father, was well chuffed his dad still had such faith in him. 'I won't let you down. I promise.'

'I know you won't, son. No more smashing the fuck out of the likes of Bill Edwards though, eh? I got a lot of stick over that one.'

Before Ronnie had a chance to reply, Danny, Eugene and Tommy arrived. Danny glanced around the empty, musty-smelling property. All his father had told him was to get the lads there by noon as he had something exciting to show them. 'What we meant to be looking at?' Danny enquired.

Jack chuckled. He wasn't one for champagne, didn't even like the taste, if he was honest. But today he'd purchased a couple of bottles, and some paper cups to pour it in.

'What's going on, Dad?' Eugene asked.

Tommy said nothing. All he could think of was his nonce of an uncle and his penis no longer working.

Ordering his boys to raise their cups, Jack bellowed, 'Welcome to our very own headquarters. We're turning this gaff into a bar. It'll be opening early Feb. The licence is already sorted, thanks to one of my bent mates,' Jack winked.

'It ain't very big, is it?' Eugene pointed out. 'The Butlers' club in Whitechapel is much bigger than this.'

'It's no smaller than Tin Pan Alley, and that's worked out all right for the Frasers. Anyway, we don't need a bigger gaff. I don't want any old Tom, Dick and Harry in 'ere. We want our own kind, punters we can trust. I'm gonna hire a couple of doormen, separate the wheat from the chaff.'

Danny grinned. 'Our very own bar. I love it. What we gonna call it?'

Jack lit up a fat cigar. Dressed in a beige roll-neck, slacks, a brown sheepskin coat, with his thick signature gold chain around his neck, he didn't look like a man who'd recently had a minor stroke. 'Well, we can't call it Darlings – that sounds like a pooftas' hang-out. So, I thought we'd call it Churchill's. That's your mother's maiden name. A tribute to her and good old Winston,' Jack chuckled.

Ronnie grinned. 'That's a brilliant name. Got a bold ring to it.'

'You like the name, Tom?' Danny enquired. His pal was yet to utter a word.

Tommy forced a smile. 'Yeah. I do.'

Jack's expression turned serious. 'Before we can concentrate on this gaff, we got a problem that needs sorting, lads. The Archers paid a gang of bikers to go on the rampage late last night. Trashed six of our boozers and our gaming machines. Been inundated with phone calls this morning from distraught landlords, and I'm fucking fuming. Without Alfie and Glenn, the Archers wouldn't even have a firm. We need to take 'em out ASAP.'

His mind on other matters, Tommy only caught the back end of the conversation. 'Take 'em out where?'

Ronnie chuckled and slid his right forefinger across his throat. 'Take 'em out, out. Rid the universe of the fucking scum.'

Tommy's eyes widened. Smashing a few kneecaps and faces in was one thing. But actual murder! That wasn't part of his job description. Or was it?

The atmosphere at Hendon was one of jubilation. Kim had phoned Caroline and Connie. As expected, they were over the moon with her news. Connie had even burst into tears, bless her.

'I wonder where we'll be posted to? Wouldn't it be great if we were together,' Sam said, knowing that was highly unlikely.

'It sure would. But it isn't gonna happen. I only hope we're near each other. Perhaps we can save up, share a flat together. I'd love that.'

'Me too. As long as you don't try it on with me though,' Sam winked.

Kim laughed and pushed her lunch to one side. They were in the canteen, but she was far too excited to eat at present. 'What are your aspirations? You know, in the long run?'

'Undercover. Imagine how exciting that would be, infiltrating gangs and pretending you're somebody else. What about you?'

'Child protection. I want to help kids, lock up the scum who abuse 'em. Especially the nonces.'

'Wow! Heavy shit. Not sure I could stomach it. What made you choose that?'

Not wanting to give anything away about herself, a fleeting image of Tommy flashed through Kim's mind. 'I knew a lad who was abused by his uncle. We were close, once.'

'Is that the lad who broke your heart?'

Jay's arrival saved Kim from answering any more awkward questions. 'How's my two favourite ladies?' he grinned.

'We're good. But please stop calling me a lady, 'cause I so ain't one,' Sam laughed.

'We celebrating tonight or what? John and Leroy are up for it. How about we have a couple in the bar here, then head off to the Chinese? I feel like getting bladdered, but I won't enjoy it as much if you two don't join us,' Jay winked, his gaze fixed on Kim.

Feeling those butterflies somersault in her stomach, Kim did her best to remain cool. Jay had the same effect on her as Tommy once had and she knew from past experience that was a recipe for disaster. 'We might do. We'll let you know later,' she said rather abruptly.

When Jay walked up to the counter to get some food, Sam shook her head. 'Why are you horrible to him at times? Not only is he one of the nicest blokes I have ever met, it's clear to a blind person he's in love with you.'

Kim glared at her pal. 'Don't talk such crap. All he wants is his leg over. That's all they ever want. You said the same about your brothers.'

Sam leaned across the table and squeezed Kim's hand. 'I don't know much about this lad who broke your heart. But, fuck me, he did a good job of it. Don't let him ruin the rest of your life, mate. Everybody deserves a chance of happiness and Jay's a good 'un, I'm telling ya.'

* * *

Tommy Darling leapt in his car and drove. He had no idea where he was driving to, not at first anyway. His head was mashed. The events of this past week had truly taken a toll on him.

Cranking the stereo up, Tommy sang along with Bob to 'No Woman No Cry'. It reminded him of happier times. Training at the boxing gym in Dagenham, idle afternoons chilling over Parsloes Park or Matchstick Island. Life at Maylands hadn't been that bad. So he did a U-turn. Finding out Ray had cancer had been preying on his mind. Ray had been good to him over the years and the least he could do was pay him a visit.

Tommy stared at Maylands for what seemed like ages. He felt nervous. Would Ray and Connie welcome him with open arms? He'd been out of order not keeping in touch, he knew that much. Thinking of Smiffy, Tommy sighed. He still missed his pal terribly and if he wasn't having nightmares about his uncle, he'd be having them about that fateful evening at the fairground. The image of Smiffy's distorted dead body would never truly leave him.

Taking a deep breath, Tommy grabbed the gifts off the back seat and marched boldly up to the door.

Ray answered, clearly shocked. So much so, he put his hand over his mouth and said nothing for what seemed like ages.

'You OK, Ray? I bumped into Yvonne Purdy recently and she said you'd been ill. I had to come and see you. I brought you this,' Tommy said, handing Ray a bottle of Jack Daniels.

'Tommy! Jesus! What a lovely surprise this is. And don't you look smart, all suited and booted.'

'Is Connie around? I brought her these,' Tommy said, brandishing a huge bouquet from behind his back. 'Can I come in?'

'Of course you can, lad. But beware, Connie was very upset you lost touch with us and your friends. She might be a bit off with you. She's in the office.'

'I'm sorry. I know I should've kept in touch with everyone.'

Remembering what Tommy had been through before arriving at Maylands, Ray put a comforting arm around his shoulders. He'd worked in the care system long enough to fathom Tommy was still a troubled soul, even now. He had *that* look in his eyes.

Gesticulating for Tommy to follow him, Ray tapped on the office door. 'We've a visitor, Connie. A blast from the past.'

'Come in.' Connie's expression darkened as she locked eyes with Tommy. He looked every inch the little gangster she'd heard he'd become. 'What do you want?' she asked, her tone unfriendly.

'I heard Ray was ill and wanted to come and see you both. I brought you these.' Tommy awkwardly put the flowers on the desktop.

Ray shuffled from foot to foot, as he always did when anxious. 'I'll leave you to it. I'll be in the kitchen, Tommy.'

'So, what is it you want exactly?' Connie spat.

Tommy bowed his head. He hadn't exactly expected the red carpet treatment, but neither had he prepared himself for this kind of rebuff. 'Look, I'm sorry for not keeping in touch with anyone, Connie. But as you well know, shit happens in life. I was a wet-behind-the-ears sixteen-year-old when I left 'ere. I'm married with a son of my own now and can clearly see the error of my ways.' Tommy placed an envelope on Connie's desk. 'There's a grand in there. Take the kids on a nice trip and buy them some new toys.'

'Well, I hope you're happy in life, Tommy, and I wish you well for the future.' Connie's tone was cold, harsh in fact. 'But I don't want your money, thank you very much. I know where it's come from and that sort of money isn't welcome here.'

Tommy stared at the photos on the wall of past residents. Smiffy's was there, Dumbo's and Benny's, but there wasn't one of him. That hurt. Clocking the framed photo on Connie's desk, Tommy picked it up.

'Put that down,' Connie screeched.

Ignoring Connie's order, Tommy stared at the image. Scratch was in the photo with an older couple, a girl and a little boy. 'She looks happy. Is she?' Tommy asked.

Connie snatched the photo out of Tommy's hands and put it inside a drawer. 'She went to live with a family after she left here. Became a nanny to their two children. She's doing fine. No thanks to you, mind. I never had you down as a coward, Tommy. All you had to do was ring me or Ray and we could have let that poor girl down gently. All day she sat out the front waiting for you. She was adamant you wouldn't let her down.'

Tommy felt choked. He still had the photo hidden

away that Scratch had given him before he'd left, but he could never bring himself to look at it. Neither could he play the record she'd given him: 'Tears on My Pillow'. 'I'm truly sorry and am so pleased she's happy now. What about Benny and Dumbo? Do they keep in touch?'

'Dumbo does. Benny doesn't. Now, if you don't mind, I have lots of paperwork to plough through. Take care of yourself, Tommy, and don't forget to take your money with you.'

Realizing he was being dismissed, Tommy picked up the envelope and without uttering another word left the room. He had always thought Connie was a kind, forgiving soul, not a bitter old bat. He'd only been a kid back then, for goodness' sake.

'All right?' Ray asked, when Tommy walked into the kitchen.

'Not really. What did I ever do that bad for Connie to hate me so much?'

'Take no notice. She's been in a foul mood all week,' Ray lied. 'You in a rush to get home?'

'No. But I ain't staying here any longer. I know when I'm not wanted.'

'Meet me at the Farmhouse Tavern,' Ray whispered. 'I've got to pop out in a bit. I'll buy you a pint.'

Tommy smiled. 'OK.'

Tommy bought himself a large brandy and stared out of the window. He had never been inside the Farmhouse Tavern before, but the surroundings brought back plenty of memories. There was a gypsy site nearby and he could remember traipsing through the fields where the gypsies kept their horses. Smiffy had leapt on the back of one once. It had bucked, sending Smiffy sprawling. How he, Dumbo and Benny had laughed over that. Another time Dumbo had got chased by one. His long legs trying to sprint and the expression of fear on his face had been priceless.

When Ray arrived, Tommy insisted on buying the drinks. 'Please don't insult me, Ray. It's the least I can do after all you did for me.'

'OK, Tommy. I'll have a Guinness then, please.'

Tommy placed the drinks on the table. 'So, how you doing? Yvonne said you had cancer.'

'Yes. Testicular. They had to remove one of my balls. I'm OK now though, touch wood.' Ray tapped the table. 'They gave me the all-clear on my last appointment. I haven't got to go back for another six months.'

'That's great news, Ray. I'm pleased for you.'

'So, how's life treating you? I like your car. Very posh.'

'I'm doing OK. I work for Jack Darling. We supply gaming machines to pubs. It pays well. I got hitched a bit too young, mind. But I've got a cracking son, Robbie.' Tommy took a photo out of his pocket and handed it to Ray.

'He's a belter, Tommy. Handsome little chap.'

'Thanks. He's my reason for getting up in the morning.'

Thinking that was an odd thing to say, Ray gently questioned Tommy about his marriage and life in general. The lad didn't open up to him. Ray knew there was more to Tommy's job than he was letting on. PC

Kendall still visited Maylands from time to time and had told himself and Connie that Tommy was involved in some kind of pub protection racket.

'So, why does Connie hate me so much? Is it because I let Scratch down on her birthday?'

'I honestly don't know, Tommy,' Ray lied. 'I haven't seen or heard from Scratch since she left Maylands,' he added in earnest.

'I saw the photo of her in the office. Connie said she lived with a family and worked as their nanny.'

'Yes. And that is all I know.'

'You got an address for her?'

'No. I haven't. But I do know where you can find Benny and Dumbo. The info never came from me though, OK?'

'Mum's the word.' Tommy tapped the side of his nose twice.

'Benny works in a tyre shop along the A13, not far from the Princess Bowling Alley. It's on the opposite side of the road. He's got a kiddie now too.'

'Has he!'

'Yes. A little girl. He lives with the mother in Barking somewhere.'

'What about Dumbo?'

'The Cross Keys pub. He does odd jobs in there for the guvnor. If he's not working, you'll find him drinking in there.'

'Thanks, Ray.' Tommy handed him the envelope. 'Connie wouldn't take this off me, so I want you to take it. Treat all the kids to something nice. There's a grand in there.'

Ray smiled. 'That's ever so kind of you, Tommy. We had our budget cut earlier this year so money is a bit tight at present. I suppose I'd better make a move now before Connie gets suspicious. I need to get to the Post Office before it shuts too.' Ray handed Tommy a piece of paper. 'If you ever need anyone to talk to or confide in, call me on this number instead of Maylands. It's my friend Stan's. Leave a message and I'll get straight back to you.'

'OK. Will do.' Tommy scribbled something on the back of a cigarette packet. 'That's my phone number. If you find out an address for Scratch, let me know. Don't mention Scratch if my old woman answers though. She's a possessive one, is Donna.'

Ray put the cigarette box in his pocket. 'You take care, Tommy. It's been a joy seeing you again. Be happy, lad.'

Tommy drove to the tyre fitters first. It had an open front. Reggae music blared out of a huge speaker.

'What can I do for you?' asked a bloke with dreadlocks.

'Erm, I'm looking for an old pal of mine, Benny. I was told he worked here.'

Dexter Evans eyed Tommy with suspicion. The tyre fitters was a cover for the more lucrative business of selling hashish. 'What's your name?'

'Tommy Boyle.' Benny wouldn't know him as Tommy Darling.

'Wait there.'

It seemed fitting that as Benny strolled towards him

Bob Marley's 'I Shot the Sheriff' was playing. It was another song that reminded Tommy of their days at Maylands. Tommy grinned. Gone was Benny's huge Afro. He had short dreadlocks with bright beads. The look suited him, even with his navy overalls on. 'How you doing, mate?'

'Yeah, good. What d'ya want?'

Benny wasn't smiling, didn't look remotely pleased to see him. 'I fancied a catch-up. What time d'ya finish? I'll buy you a drink.'

'No can do. Sorry.'

'Another time?'

'Not being funny, Tom. But you turn up out of the blue after blanking your pals for years. You can fuck right off, man.'

'Oh, come on, Ben. Give me a break. I just got the cold shoulder from Connie.'

'She tell you where I worked, did she?'

'No. Somebody else did. I hear you've got a little girl. Congratulations. My son Robbie'll be two soon. Christmas Day he was born.'

'I couldn't give a fuck about you or your son, Tommy. I've moved on in life, just like you did. I got proper friends these days, not fake ones.'

'Look, I'm sorry for not keeping in touch. You still see Dumbo?'

'No. I gotta get back to work now. Don't come 'ere again, will you? My boss is a bit funny. He don't like strangers sniffing around.'

'But I ain't a fucking stranger, am I? We were good mates once, Benny.'

'Were, yeah, once. Now we ain't mates any more. Laters, Tommy.'

Nobody had dared speak to him like that in years. He'd clumped blokes for far less. But this was Benny and Tommy couldn't bring himself to wallop him, so he swallowed it, walking away without looking back.

Six foot three and built like a beanpole, Dumbo was easy to spot propping up the bar in the Cross Keys. 'Tommy!' Dumbo shrieked, his eyes welling up.

'How you doing?' Tommy asked.

'Pissed,' Dumbo chuckled, introducing Tommy to his equally inebriated friends.

'What d'ya want to drink?' Tommy asked.

'Snakebite. Why didn't you invite me to your wedding? I thought we were mates.'

'We are mates. I'm sorry. Everything happened so fast.'

'But you left us all. You promised you would look after me when I left Shitlands and you fucking let me down,' Dumbo slurred, when they finally sat down at a table. 'You were gonna help me get a council flat.'

'I know and I'm sorry.' Tommy had had enough of apologizing for one day, was sick of saying the sorry word. 'You seen Benny lately?' Tommy asked.

'Yeah. He sells drugs now. Always out with his new friends. He's forgotten his old friends too.'

'You heard from Scratch?'

'Nope. Last time I saw her was on the day you were meant to be picking her up. She was so upset when Connie told her you were getting married that day. We all were.'

'Shit,' Tommy mumbled. No wonder Connie had the arse with him earlier. 'Who told Connie I was getting married?'

'I think Ray drove over to where you lived and the neighbour told him you got the girl pregnant and was getting hitched that day. You were bang out of order, Tommy. Scratch was in bits.'

Tommy listened to Dumbo rambling on for another ten minutes or so before losing the will to live. Dumbo was that drunk, he could barely understand him. He felt bad enough over the way he'd treated Scratch, didn't need to keep being reminded what an arsehole he was.

'Where you going?' Dumbo asked.

'Home.' Tommy pulled out a wad of money and handed Dumbo a hundred pounds. 'Treat yourself to something nice for Christmas.'

Dumbo's eyes lit up. 'Thank you, Tommy. When you coming here to see me again? It's my birthday Friday week. Let's go clubbing. Meet me in 'ere at eight o'clock.'

'All right,' Tommy lied. He would never return to Dagenham or Maylands. All those memories he'd held close to his heart had suddenly vanished. Dumbo was a drunk, Benny an arrogant prick and Connie a bitter bitch.

His life belonged in South London now and if he was to be involved in the murders of Alfie and Glenn Archer, then so be it. The Darlings were the only true friends he had left. He was a Darling and his shit trip down memory lane made him want to never forget it.

CHAPTER TWENTY-THREE

'Someone's coming out,' hissed Ronnie Darling. He stared into the side mirror. The nearby streetlight illuminated the two shadows. 'Hold your horses . . . Nope. It ain't them.'

It was 4 a.m. and still there was no sign of Alfie and Glenn Archer. Every Thursday evening they attended an illegal card school above a greengrocer's in Peckham and Jack had decided that was where they should be snatched.

'You OK, Tommy?' Danny asked. They were parked right in front of Alfie Archer's silver Jaguar XJ6. The plan was for the lads to jump out of the back of the hooky gas van and bundle the Archers inside.

Tommy was shivering, a blanket wrapped around his shoulders. It was freezing and he just wished the Archers would hurry up. He couldn't feel his fingers, or his toes. 'Yeah,' he mumbled.

Five minutes later, Ronnie said the words everyone had been waiting for: 'It's them. Ready. Go. Now!'

Incredibly excited about the day ahead, Kim got up at 5 a.m. She knew where she was being posted to now.

Islington wasn't an area she was even remotely familiar with, but that was where she would be working, in N Division.

Sam was also N Division. She'd been posted to Hornsey. Both girls were thrilled about this as they'd wanted to work near one another. Caroline and Keith had kindly offered to give Kim the deposit money to rent a flat, so that was the plan. She and Sam would share a flat together.

Jay's posting was to Limehouse. He was H Division. Leroy and John wouldn't be too far away either. They'd both been posted to stations in East London.

Having no family of her own, Kim had invited Caroline, Keith and the kids to her passing-out parade. They were the ones who'd helped mend her broken heart after leaving Maylands and had encouraged her to pursue her dream of becoming a WPC. Connie was coming too and Kim couldn't wait to see them, show them what she'd achieved. She had missed them, but not as much as she thought she might. Hendon had certainly taught her how to stand on her own two feet.

Kim picked up her warrant card and smiled. Any doubts she might have had were long gone. She'd made the right decision, without a doubt.

In a disused building on the outskirts of Kent, Alfie and Glenn Archer were tied to two wooden chairs with thick rope.

A stout, short balding man in his early fifties, Alfie Archer was the first to have the duct tape ripped from his mouth. 'Well, well, well. Who's a dirty boy then? Pissing in your strides is never a good look, is it, Alfie?' Jack Darling chuckled.

'Jack, let me explain, mate. None of what has happened is Glenn's or my fault,' Alfie gabbled. He and Glenn had expected some kind of retribution, but not a bloody ambush. The fact they were three sheets to the wind hadn't helped matters. They'd been slung inside that van like lambs heading to the slaughter. Alfie was sober now, mind. In fact, he had never sobered up so quickly in his lifetime.

Jack crouched in front of the trembling wreck. Alfie's moustache didn't suit him, it never had. 'Whose fault is it then, Alfie? Ya know, that you tried to take over my boozers and trashed my gaming machines.'

'Gerry Colloff. We owe him money – fifty grand, to be exact. We ain't got the dosh to pay him. So, he made us work for him. It's him who wants your pubs, not us.'

'Who is Gerry Colloff?' asked Ronnie.

'Shut up,' Jack hissed. He was shocked, stunned in fact. He and Suzie had never mentioned Colloff to their children.

Gerry Colloff was the bloke his Suzie had been engaged to when he'd first met her. She'd called the engagement off shortly afterwards and Gerry had always vowed to have his revenge. He was no man's fool, had done a fifteen stretch in Parkhurst for murder and had been behind a fair few riots in there. He'd palled up with Frankie Fraser before Frank had been released.

Jack ripped the duct tape off Glenn. 'This true, is it?'

Glenn took a minute to catch his breath. He had a cold and was struggling to breathe through his nose. 'Alf's telling the truth, Jack,' he wheezed. 'I swear he is.'

'So, where can I find Gerry?'

'We don't know. He's based in the Costa del Sol,' Glenn replied honestly.

Picking up a wrench, Jack hit the side of Glenn's head with such force both he and the chair went flying. 'I want answers. Proper fucking answers. Now, I'm gonna ask you again, where can I find Gerry Colloff?'

Aware that Jack had over-exerted himself and was currently out of breath, Tommy took the wrench off him and gave Glenn another clump, this time on the shoulder. 'Answer the man,' he bellowed.

Blood was flowing from a gash above Glenn's eye. He tried to lift his arm to wipe it away, but both arms were still secured to the chair. He looked up at them from the floor, terrified. 'In the Costa del Sol, I swear. He was over in England about six weeks ago. We met up with him then.'

'Glenn's telling you the truth, Jack,' Alfie said.

'Shut up, you. You've always been a fucking old liar,' Jack spat. He turned to his sons and Tommy. 'See if removing a few teeth gets us some answers, lads. There's a hammer in that bag and some pliers.'

Spotting her adopted family among the crowd, Kim ran towards them, her arms outstretched. 'I did it,' she shrieked.

Connie had tears in her eyes as she hugged the girl

she'd nurtured and grown to love so very much. 'Look at her in her uniform, Caroline. Doesn't she look smart?'

'Very smart. Well done, darling.' Caroline flung her arms around Kim. 'Keith and I are so proud of you. You're a credit to us all.'

'Over the bloody moon for you,' Keith grinned.

Desperate to get Kim's attention, ten-year-old Fiona poked her in the arm. 'Look what I made you.'

The homemade card was a lovely gesture. Fiona had drawn a policewoman on the front, who looked just a teeny bit like her. 'Thank you, sweetheart. I love it.'

'Kim,' said a little voice.

Kim bent down and lifted Mikey out of his pushchair. 'He's got so big.' She put her free arm around Fiona. 'I've missed you both so much.'

'They've missed you too,' Caroline replied. 'Fiona is so excited you're coming home with us today and spending Christmas with us. Mikey's learned lots of new words. He can't quite say your name properly yet, but he's getting there. All we've heard on the journey here is Kim this and Kim that,' Caroline chuckled. 'Fiona is so in awe of you, she has now decided she wants to be a policewoman herself.'

'Brilliant,' Kim laughed. 'Come and meet my friends. You'll love them.'

'Can I have a quick word with you? In private,' Connie whispered in Kim's ear. She had been debating whether to tell her, especially today of all days. But Kim had always been adamant that if Tommy did rear his ugly head she wanted to be told, immediately.

Kim linked arms with Connie and excused herself from the others. 'What's up? Is Ray OK?'

'Yes, Ray's fine, love. The latest scan he had came back clear. Look, I didn't know whether to tell you this today, but I'm going to. Tommy showed up at Maylands earlier this week.'

Kim felt the colour drain from her complexion. 'Why? What did he want?'

'It was a social visit. He'd heard via the grapevine Ray had cancer. He turned up with a bottle of booze for Ray and an enormous bouquet for me. He then tried to give me a thousand pounds to treat the kids. I told him where to shove it, in my own polite manner.'

'A thousand pounds!'

Connie rolled her eyes. 'He looks every inch of the little gangster I'd heard he'd become. Expensive suit, shoes, driving a big flash Mercedes. You had a lucky escape, my girl. I'm telling you.'

There was silence for a long time.

'Did he mention me?'

'Yes. He asked after you. I told him what we agreed. I gave him short shrift, don't you worry about that. He was in my office for no more than two minutes before I booted him out. I can tell Ray still has a soft spot for him, mind. The silly old sod.'

'Oh, well. I doubt you'll be seeing him again.'

'Most definitely not! Now you go and enjoy your day. I am so very proud of you. Look how far you've come.'

Kim hugged Connie. 'Thank you, Connie. For everything.'

* * *

At the exact same time Kim's passing-out parade was taking place, Tommy Darling was handed a gun. 'Shoot him,' Jack Darling ordered.

Tommy was startled. 'What! Why me?'

'Why not?' Jack snapped. Tommy's weird behaviour had been bothering him for a while. The lad was part of the family now, so best he started pulling his socks up.

Tommy glanced at Danny, Ronnie and Eugene. All eyes were on him, their expressions blank.

Knowing he had no choice, Tommy stepped over the dead body of Glenn Archer and walked up to Alfie, who was still tied to a chair.

'No, lad. Please God no. I'll work for you, Jack. I'll set the Colloffs up for you. On my dear old mum's life I will,' begged Alfie.

Tommy glanced at Jack. 'Do it,' barked Jack.

Tommy's hands trembled as he placed the barrel against Alfie's right temple. He owed Jack big time. Thanks to him he had a lovely gaff, a top-of-the-range motor and was earning more cash than he'd ever dreamed of. But most of all he had a family. He wasn't a Boyle any more. He was a Darling. Tommy shut his eyes and pictured his perverted uncle's fat face.

Seconds later, he pulled the trigger . . .

PART FOUR

Hell is empty
and all the devils are here.
William Shakespeare

CHAPTER TWENTY-FOUR

So that's how I became a murderer, was easier than I thought to be honest. I wasn't exactly proud of myself afterwards, but I felt no guilt neither. If the Archers hadn't tried to wrong us Darlings, they'd still be alive. It was as simple as that.

I've overheard firemen and coppers say, in the past, you get used to watching people die and it was no different in our world. Probably better if anything, as we were only witnessing wrong 'uns snuff it, not decent human beings, no women or kids.

The only part of it I wasn't fond of was the dismembering of the bodies. Neither was Danny. It was bloody hard work and it turned our stomachs. So much so, we couldn't even fancy a Big Mac and chips until the following day.

I didn't like it but it seemed I had a gift for it. I did what I had to do. Jack, Ronnie, Danny and Eugene were my family now. They were loyal to me, as was Suzie.

Or so I thought. How wrong can a man be?

1983

'What we doing today, Dad?' asked six-year-old Robbie Darling. Saturdays were his favourite day of the week. His mum always went out shopping, so he and his dad spent the day alone, doing laddish things.

Tommy grinned at his son. Robbie was the light of his life. His hair was dark, his eyes a chocolate brown and he had the cheekiest of grins. Jack reckoned he took after himself and his own father and, after seeing photos of them as kids, Tommy couldn't help but agree. He hoped his son didn't grow up like Jack though. He wanted Robbie to lead a normal life. 'Choice is yours, boyo. Millwall are at home, if you wanna go there? But it's such a nice day; we could take a trip to the seaside and see your Auntie Linda if you like?'

'Seaside.' Robbie clapped his hands excitedly. 'But can we go McDonald's first, please?'

'Yeah. Course we can.' Saturday daytime was Tommy's only official time off work. The rest of the week he always had to have his pager handy in case he was needed for something or other, even on a Sunday. Jack had slowed down now, spent a lot of weekends with Suzie at their cottage in the countryside. Ronnie still had a screw loose, so it was up to himself and Danny to ensure the business was run properly.

'I'm off out. Going down the Roman with Kerry,' announced Donna.

Tommy smirked. She wasn't going out with Kerry; neither was she heading to Roman Road market. She was meeting her boyfriend. She'd been at it for a while – at least six months, Tommy reckoned. He could smell the sex on her when she came home. He wasn't bothered, mind. As long as she kept it low key and he wasn't made to look a fool. Whoever she was seeing didn't live locally, as he'd checked the mileage on her Volkswagen Beetle.

Donna bent down to hug Robbie. 'Have a lovely day with Daddy.'

'We're going to the seaside, Mummy,' Robbie announced.

'Well, best you bring me back a stick of rock then,' Donna beamed.

Tommy smiled politely. With her permed blonde hair, sea-blue eyes and size-ten figure, Donna was still extremely attractive – but not to him. He hated the silly white leggings and turquoise blue jacket she was wearing with the massive shoulder pads. She thought she looked like something out of *Dallas*, but to Tommy she looked ridiculous. In fact, there wasn't much about Donna he did like, apart from the son she'd given him. 'Have a good shopping trip,' he said.

'Thanks. I will.'

'Dad,' Robbie said when his mother left the house. 'Why don't you and Mummy share a bedroom? You know my friend David? His mum and dad always sleep in the same bed.'

Tommy picked his son up and swung him in the air. 'Because your mother snores too bleedin' much. Next question?'

'Morning, bird. Lover boy not 'ere?' asked Sam.

'No. He had to work late again last night. Probably 'cause of that robbery. They still haven't caught anyone.' Earlier in the week gunmen had held up a Security Express van in Shoreditch and escaped with what was being described as the biggest cash haul in British history. It was the talk of the police force at present. Some were saying the sum involved was five million, but Kim had been told it was more like seven. 'You look happy. I take it you spent the night at Jenny's again?'

'Sure did,' Sam grinned. 'Nymphomaniac, she is. Seriously can't get enough of me.'

Kim held her hands up. 'That is way too much information while I'm eating my breakfast,' she chuckled. Kim was thrilled Sam had finally found the woman of her dreams and it amused her greatly that Jenny was ten years older than Sam, had an eight-year-old son and looked a bit like Dolly Parton. You would never put the two together, but both Sam and Jenny seemed smitten since meeting four months ago at a gay bar in Greenwich.

'I need a strong coffee. I had far too many Malibu and pineapples last night. My head's bloody pounding,' Sam sighed.

Kim laughed. That was another thing that amused her greatly. Sam had always sunk pints until she met Jenny. Now she was a Malibu drinker.

After leaving Hendon, Kim and Sam had rented a flat together in Seven Sisters. They'd since moved to Barnet. Barnet wasn't cheap, but it was better than living in an area where they might be easily recognized.

Sam was based at Islington police station, which had been Kim's first posting, while Kim had moved over to Kings Cross. Both had been promoted to DS, so they wore plain clothes now rather than official uniforms. They were also trained SO10 officers, and as such would get called to New Scotland Yard to take part in undercover operations from time to time.

Kim handed Sam a coffee. 'That prostitute who was found in a bad way died early hours of this morning. Banksy called me to tell me.'

'Poor cow,' Sam replied. The woman in question had been in her early twenties. She'd been brutally raped, then beaten to a pulp. 'Do they reckon it's the same bloke who attacked that other brass last month?'

'It's looking that way. Both very similar attacks.'

'Some twisted loony-tune, no doubt. I had some shit news yesterday an' all. That Griffiths bloke who was shot in the back of the head last week. The witnesses have gone cold all of a sudden. Obviously been got at. We're sure we know who did it – one of the Darlings out of South London. But proving it is gonna be difficult. The suspect has a water-tight alibi an' all, the tosser.'

Darling was an unusual surname. The only time Kim had heard it before was in relation to Tommy. He'd gone to live with a family in South London called Darling. 'What's the suspect's first name?'

Sam took the latest bulletins out of her bag. 'The suspect is Ronnie; he's the one at the top of the page. The others are family members. Proper little firm, they are. Darlings by name, but certainly not by nature. Jack, the father, did a long stretch for murder and they're suspected of other killings. They've terrorized publicans south of the water for years, by all accounts. The victim in this case used to work for 'em, so we've got a motive, though fat lot of good that'll do us with no bloody witnesses.'

Kim's complexion drained of colour as she stared at one photo in particular. He looked older, his face weather-beaten. His hair was cropped and he had a scar on his left cheek. There was no mistaking those eyes though. Kim shuddered. It was as if he was looking straight at her.

'What's the matter?' Sam asked.

Kim pointed at Tommy. 'I know him.'

'Really! How?'

Kim trusted Sam implicitly, but had never told her the full horror of her past. What was the point? Not only did she have no wish to think or speak about it, she'd thankfully moved on in life. 'You remember me telling you I once had my heart broken when I was young?'

'Yeah. Not by him, surely?'

Kim nodded. 'His surname was Boyle back then, not Darling. You can't say anything. Imagine the stick I would get off Banksy and the guv'nor if they found out I'd once been in a relationship with a felon on their wanted list!' Banksy was Kim's work partner. He was a chauvinistic piss-taking bastard, but on the whole they worked well together. He was a bloody good copper.

Sam's eyes lit up. 'Speak to the guv. You'd be perfect to go in undercover if you know Tommy. Would he be pleased to see you, do ya think? Where do you know him from? School?'

'Yeah. Sort of. There was five of us who used to knock around together. I don't want to go in undercover though, not on this case.'

'But why not? The geezer broke your heart. Perhaps we could work together on this one? Think what it would do for our careers if we were to bring a firm like the Darlings down.'

Kim shook her head. 'No way. I'm not getting involved.'

'You're not still in contact with him are you?'

Kim glared at her best friend. 'Don't talk shit. I haven't seen him since I was fifteen.'

'You're long overdue a catch-up with him then. You could organize a school reunion or something similar,' Sam grinned. 'Please, think about it, mate. If we did this together and pulled it off, we'd make detective inspector before you know it.'

In McDonald's, Tommy was having one of his funny turns. A man sitting on a nearby table looked like a kiddy-fiddler and he kept looking over at himself and Robbie, smiling.

'What you doing, Dad?' Robbie asked, when his father snatched his quarter pounder off the table and put it back inside the brown bag.

'Come on. We're going. You can eat your grub in the car.'

'But I want to eat it now. Why can't we eat it here, Dad?'

Aware that the man was still looking at them, Tommy leapt out of his seat, walked over to him and to the astonishment of the other diners, grabbed him by the throat. 'What ya looking at, eh?'

The startled man dropped his milkshake all over his

trousers. 'Your son. He reminds me of my own grandson, Toby,' he stammered.

'Liar! You're a fucking nonce-case,' Tommy hissed.

Robbie tugged his father's arm. 'Stop it, Dad. Please stop it. Everyone is looking at us,' he cried.

One of the staff appeared. 'Is there a problem?'

Tommy released his grip on the man's throat. 'Nah. My son and I are just leaving.'

'My food's still on the table, Dad,' Robbie sobbed, as his father dragged him out the door.

'Leave it. I'll get you another meal.'

Tommy was shaking as he put the key in the ignition of his new silver Mercedes. He'd had one of his nightmares last night, the first in ages.

'Why did you have a go at that man?'

Tommy hugged his visibly upset son. He knew where his uncle lived and loathed himself for not having the guts to seek retribution. Trouble was, he couldn't face the bastard. Neither could he face a long prison stretch for murder. 'Because I didn't like the way he kept looking at you. There are some bad men in this world, boy.'

'Like the bogey-man?'

'Yeah, similar. You don't ever talk to strangers or accept a lift in a car if anyone offers you one. Understand?'

'You've told me that loads of times.'

'And now I'm telling you again, so just you remember it. Right, shall we head straight to the seaside, get something to eat there?'

Robbie nodded.

Tommy took a deep breath to calm himself. Sometimes

it felt like his past was catching up with him and he had no idea how to stop it.

'What do you think?' Jay Delaney asked Kim. They were getting married this summer, had been saving like mad for their dream home. House-hunting wasn't easy as they both worked long hours. Jay had recently been promoted to DS, and was now based in Hackney.

'I think the kitchen is too small, and the garden.'

'Sorry to waste your time, mate. It's a lovely property but not quite what we're looking for,' Jay explained to the owners.

Kim sat in the car with her eyes shut. She couldn't get that image of Tommy out of her head; wished Sam had never shown it to her. She hated him. But did she hate him enough to put him inside? She'd moved on in life, was happy now. Visiting her past wasn't something she would enjoy. She just wanted to forget all about Scratch and enjoy her life as Kim.

New Order's 'Blue Monday' was on the radio. Jay turned it down. 'Right, what's up?'

'I thought the kitchen and garden were too small.'

'I'm not talking about the house. You've been acting strange since I picked you up. What's wrong?' He'd pursued Kim for months after leaving Hendon, until she had finally succumbed to his charms. They'd been together ever since. They were good together, trusted one another implicitly, but didn't live in one another's pockets. Jay often hung out with his work colleagues and Kim with hers. The only thing they seemed to disagree over was children. Jay wanted to start a family in the not-too-distant future, but Kim was adamant she didn't want kids. She was very career-minded and all Jay could do was hope she would change her mind one day. He loved her enough to marry her though, whatever the outcome.

Kim sighed deeply. She took the bulletin out of her handbag and placed it on Jay's lap. If she couldn't seek advice from the man she would soon be married to, then who could she seek advice from?

She would only tell him the parts she needed him to know though. The rest was nobody's business but hers.

'Can I sit over there, Dad, with Jessica? Her dad said we can have an ice-cream. Is that OK?' Robbie asked warily.

Tommy grinned at his son. He'd found himself a little girlfriend today, kept holding her hand. 'Yeah, course it is. Go on, off you trot.'

'He's a dear little soul, isn't he?' beamed Linda. She loved spending time with Tommy and her nephew, especially on days such as this when they could sit on the beach watching the world go by.

Tommy cracked open a beer and stared at the sea. He felt chilled now, that earlier incident forgotten. He liked Clacton. It had a serenity about it that didn't exist in South London. His dream was to one day live here alone with Robbie, but he couldn't see that happening anytime soon. 'How're the Pipers doing?' he asked.

'They're all good, thanks. Alice has a new boyfriend and seems quite loved up. How's things between you and Donna?'

'I haven't seen much of her lately, so that's good. She's been going out a lot, glammed up to the nines with a spring in her step. She's definitely got herself a fancy man, but I've no idea who he is.'

'Oh, Tommy. That's awful.'

'Nah. It's a good thing actually. I only wish she'd sod off with him – provided she left Robbie with me, of course. Over my dead body is she taking my boy to live with another bloke. Her dad wouldn't stand for that anyway. He's old school, is Jack.'

'I wish you could meet someone and be happy like I am. Paul is the best thing that's ever happened to me,' Linda gushed.

Tommy put an arm around his sister's shoulders. Paul was Mr Average. Nothing special to look at, or talk to; worked for his father, fitting carpets. He was perfect for Linda though and clearly adored her. Tommy would much rather his sister be with Mr Average than some bloody Jack-the-lad. 'Nobody is happier for you than me, Sis. You made any wedding plans yet?' Paul had surprised Linda last Christmas Day by getting down on one knee and popping the question.

'We've looked at some brochures and venues. Neither of us are in any rush. We'd rather save up first, so we'll have a deposit for our own home. We was thinking summer 1985. I definitely want a church wedding. Paul's parents are going to pay for the reception and our honeymoon. Not as if I have a dad to ask, is it?'

'Nah. But you got me. I want you to have the best wedding ever, Linda. How about I give you five grand towards it?'

'Don't be so silly. That's way too much. I wouldn't expect you to do that.'

'But I want to, and I can afford to. You're the only proper family I've got left.'

Linda's eyes welled up. 'That's so kind of you. You're the best brother a girl could wish for. There is another favour I need to ask you though.'

'What?'

'Would you walk me down the aisle, Tommy?'

Tommy breathed deeply and stared at the calmness of the sea. He and Linda had tried to track Hazel down a couple of years ago. He had even hired a private detective, but to no avail. They hadn't managed to track down that bastard Alexander either. It was obvious they'd changed their names, or possibly even emigrated. Whatever the explanation, it was clear Hazel wanted no more to do with him and Linda. Linda still had the same surname, so Hazel could easily have found her if she'd wanted to.

'Say something, Tommy. You don't have to do it if you don't want to,' Linda said.

Feeling emotional, Tommy pulled Linda close to him. 'I'd be honoured to give you away. I bet Mum is looking down on us with a smile on her face right now.'

'D'ya really believe that?'

'Yes. I honestly believe she'll be at your wedding. Unfortunately not in person, but in spirit.'

Tears streamed down Linda's face. 'I do hope she is.'

'What you doing home? I thought you were staying around Jenny's,' Kim said to Sam.

'I was. But then her nan and granddad turned up unexpectedly. They don't know she bats for the other side, so I pretended I was a plumber who'd come to fix a leak in her bathroom and swiftly left.' She paused, looking uncomfortable about what she had to say next. 'Listen, please don't have a go at me, but I think I might have dropped you in it.'

'You what! I haven't done anything wrong.'

'I went out for a few bevvies with the guv and some of the lads yesterday afternoon. The Griffiths murder was the main topic of conversation and I happened to let slip you knew Tommy. Looks like we might be going in undercover.'

'Whatever made you blurt that out, Sam? Your guv is best mates with Hunter, you know that.'

'I was on pints and I haven't drunk 'em for a while. I was a bit pissed and regretted saying anything as soon as I'd said it. I am sorry, mate. I truly am.'

'Not as sorry as I'm going to be when Hunter calls me into his office for a grilling. Thanks, Sam. Thanks a fucking bunch.'

Singing along at the top of her voice to the Eurythmics' 'Sweet Dreams', Donna Darling drove happily towards home.

Josh Palmer was thirty-five, nine years her senior. They'd met when she'd been searching for a new car. Josh was a second-hand car dealer with premises in Wanstead, and it truly had been a case of love at first sight. Josh was blond, handsome, charming and cheeky. He literally had it all, including lots of money.

He lived in Loughton, Essex, where Donna had spent today. His house was massive, even had its own swimming pool in the back garden.

Today, Donna had told Josh she was pregnant with his child. Josh had an eleven-year-old daughter from a previous relationship and Donna had been slightly worried how he might react. She needn't have been. Josh was thrilled by the news and had asked her to move in with him.

Now all she had to do was find a way to break the news to her father. She'd explained the situation to Josh and had decided to act normal and cover up her pregnancy for the time being. Her father adored Tommy, as did her mother and brothers.

Thinking of her and Josh's earlier love-making, Donna smiled. Unlike Tommy, who was a selfish flop in bed, Josh was the total opposite. He made her feel loved, and gave her multiple orgasms. Her marriage to Tommy was dead in the water, had been for years. She needed to make her family understand that before dropping her bombshell, even if it meant disclosing intimate details which she'd hidden from them until now. They couldn't force her to stay in a loveless, sexless marriage forever more, but she knew what her father and brothers were capable of so had to tread carefully. If Josh ended up with a bullet in his head, she would literally die of a broken heart.

Donna let herself indoors.

'Hello, Mummy. Daddy and I had a great time. I met a girlfriend. Her name is Jessica.'

Donna picked up her excited son. Josh was willing

to allow Robbie to move in too, even though he had yet to meet him. Tommy wasn't going to be happy, but no way was she leaving her son behind.

Worst ways, if Tommy went ballistic, the truth would have to come out.

CHAPTER TWENTY-FIVE

Kim loved her job, but totally loathed her boss. An insensitive, arrogant, bolshie bastard, if he wasn't at his desk, DI Hunter could be found propping up a bar somewhere, usually at the Sutton Arms. She respected him as a police officer, as he was very good at his job. But on a personal level, she couldn't stand the bloke.

'Regan,' a familiar voice boomed. 'Get that cute little arse of yours in my office. Now!'

'Somebody's been a naughty girl,' chuckled Banksy.

Ignoring her work partner, Kim followed Hunter inside his office and forced a smile. Her palms were already sweaty. 'Morning, Guv. How are you?'

'Well, the polite thing to say would be all the better for seeing you, but we both know that'd be a lie, don't we? So, let's cut the small talk. A little birdy tells me you know Tommy Darling. That correct, is it?' Hunter wasn't a lover of female police officers; saw them as a waste of space. In his opinion, women belonged at home, cooking, cleaning and raising kids.

Silently cursing Sam and her big mouth, Kim said the lines she'd rehearsed: 'No, not really. I mean, I did know him as a kid, when his surname was Boyle. But I've had no contact with him since, none whatsoever.'

'You either know him or you fucking don't, Juliet Bravo. So, give me a simple yes or no. Do you know this man?' Hunter spat, shoving a photo of Tommy across his desk towards her.

'Yes, Guv. I know him.'

'How well do you know him? And please don't fucking lie to me, because I have a habit of digging up the truth.'

'I did know him quite well. But I don't want to go undercover on this case, Guv. Tommy was part of my childhood. It wouldn't be right.'

'I say what's right, Regan, not you. When you did your training, it was drummed into you exactly what becoming a police officer meant.' Hunter pushed a folder towards her. 'My job is to put this nasty bunch of shitbags behind bars. Everything you need to know is there. I want you to spend the next hour or however long it takes reading up on 'em. When you're done, come back into my office with a different attitude. Only, I won't work with lightweight officers, Regan. You refuse to play ball, I'll have your sorry arse kicked out of this station in the blink of an eye. Understand what I'm saying, treacle?'

Kim picked up the folder. She felt near to tears. 'Yes, Guv,' she mumbled.

Banksy burst into laughter as Kim returned to her desk. 'You don't look too happy. Spill the beans then, you strumpet.'

Not in the mood for Banksy's jokes, Kim hissed 'Fuck

off, prick!' before opening the folder. It wasn't Tommy she was trying to protect. It was herself and her own sordid past . . .

'Well, this is a nice surprise,' Suzie Darling exclaimed. She saw lots of Robbie, often babysat. But Donna rarely popped in unexpectedly. Not unless she wanted something.

'I was passing and the weather is so nice for the time of year, I thought I would treat you to a pub lunch, Mum. We can sit outside.'

Suzie eyed her daughter with suspicion. Donna was after something, that was for sure. For some inexplicable reason, Suzie did not have the close relationship with her daughter that she had with her sons, and with Tommy, who was like a son to her. She loved Donna dearly. But they rarely did mother/daughter things together. As a rule, Donna only ever went out for lunch with her mate Kerry.

'Well?' Donna smiled.

Wondering what the catch was, Suzie smiled back. 'That would be lovely, but I must have a bath first. I've been spring-cleaning all morning.'

Now she found herself under the scrutiny spotlight, Kim knew how the people she arrested must feel. As expected, Hunter was interested in what she'd already told him, but he now wanted to know the ins and outs of a duck's arse. This was one of the reasons she'd been reluctant to involve herself in this case. Yes, if successful, it would do her career the power of good. But, on the other hand, she dreaded the can of worms it might open.

She'd spent the past hour or so reading up on the Darlings. They were big fish. Not only were they under suspicion for the murder of Dean Griffiths, they were also believed to be behind the point-blank shooting of small-time crook Bobby Tobyn and the disappearance of six other men, including a publican and rival criminals Alfie and Glenn Archer. It was big time stuff and Tommy's name was all over it.

'So, let me get this straight. What you're telling me is you and Tommy went to the same school, were good pals and knocked about together with three other lads,' Hunter smirked.

'Yes. That's correct. And as I have already explained, I could arrange that school reunion with a click of my finger.' After a lot of soul searching Kim had decided to play ball. She knew the guvnor would be like a dog without a bone and she hoped if she did it on her terms, she could hide what she wanted to.

'Yeah, I get that. But what I don't get is how you think, by organizing this school reunion, Tommy Darling is going to spill his guts to you and inform you where six dead bodies are buried. Come on, do you think I was born yesterday? What's the real story here, Regan?'

Kim sighed. She so wished now she'd asked Keith's advice and Jay's. 'Tommy had a best pal, Smiffy. He was one of our gang. Unfortunately, he got killed at a fairground. Tommy and I sort of witnessed that and afterwards began a teenage relationship. We were both mourning and in shock.'

321

Hunter's eyes lit up. He laughed. 'You were fucking Tommy Darling?'

Kim looked defiantly at her boss. He looked like a drinker, had a ruddy complexion and a red bulbous nose. There also seemed to be the remains of his lunch in his moustache. She could see breadcrumbs as well as snot. 'Did you not fuck anyone in your teenage years that you now regret fucking, Guv?'

'Yeah, many times,' Hunter chuckled. 'But most of 'em are probably dead by now. I had a thing for me pals' mums once upon a time.'

Kim stood up. 'Look, let's just forget this conversation happened. I can see you're not taking me seriously and I have other work I can be getting on with. My in-tray and out-tray are full.'

'You on the blob are ya, Regan?' Hunter asked. Women were always touchy around their periods. His old woman was murder. He could never do or say a thing without setting her off.

'No, Guv. I'm not.' Kim's tone was full of sarcasm.

'Well, sit your arse back down then. And for your information, I am taking you seriously. Always have done. For a plonk, you aren't a bad copper.'

'Plonk' was the derogatory term for female officers, but as Kim sat back down, she had a smile on her face. That was the biggest compliment Hunter had ever given her.

Overall, opening Churchill's had been a success. The clientele was select, only private members were allowed, and many a game of poker was played until the early hours of the morning. One of the coppers on Jack's payroll was pretty high up at Southwark police station, so the Old Bill tended to turn a blind eye to any after-hours activities.

On the downside, Ronnie was now a borderline alcoholic. And the booze only made his mood swings worse, his temper was off the Richter scale.

Ronnie worried Tommy. He could go on the turn for no reason whatsoever. That blow to the brain had definitely changed him as a person and Tommy was concerned that one day they'd all end up in prison because of Ronnie's stupidity. Tommy had developed a fear of confined spaces over the years and knew he would never get through a stretch. The very thought of being locked in a prison full of men filled him with dread. He and Danny spent more time clearing up the mayhem Ronnie caused, and dosh on keeping people quiet so Jack and Suzie didn't know the half of it.

Even though Churchill's was usually busy, it didn't take a fortune, so they still ran the protection racket and gaming machine business. Jack also employed bouncers to work the doors of various nightclubs.

'You all right, Tom? You seem a bit quiet,' Danny remarked.

'Yeah, I'm fine,' Tommy sighed. He seemed to spend half his life at Churchill's lately and it bored him rigid. 'Any news on the baby?'

'Nope. Any day now though,' Danny grinned.

Tommy envied his pal. Lucy, Danny's wife, was twenty-eight, four years older than Danny, and was due to drop their second child any moment. Their son Archie had not long turned two. Danny was a great dad and he and Lucy were incredibly happy together. Tommy was chuffed for his best mate, but sometimes when Danny rambled on about his perfect life, it brought it home to Tommy how he and Donna were living this complete and utter lie. They never went on holidays, or did anything together as a family. Either Donna would take Robbie out for the day or Tommy would. They had dinner with family members occasionally, but that was about it. Tommy loved kids, would have adored more, but he'd now accepted that would never happen. He hadn't been able to get it up for years, had no sexual urges whatsoever.

When Eugene began banging on about his incredible night of passion with his new glamour model girlfriend, Tommy had to get out of the bar.

'Where you going, mate?' Danny shouted after him.

'To get a newspaper. Want anything?'

'Yeah. Get us a Marathon.'

As Tommy trudged the short walk to the newsagents, not for the first time in his life, he felt like a freak of nature.

'I need to speak to you about something, Mum. Something important,' said Donna.

Suzie Darling sipped her glass of red wine. Here we go, she thought to herself. 'Go on.'

'Tommy and I aren't happy. We haven't been for ages.'

'All couples go through bad patches, love. How do you think I felt when your father got put away for all those years? It wasn't easy, that's for sure.'

'That's different. You and Dad still loved one another. Tommy and I don't. We haven't even slept in the same bedroom for years. I'm sick of feeling unloved and unwanted. Tommy has issues, Mum. He isn't normal. I don't want to be married to him any more. I'm only twenty-five and I deserve to be happy.'

Suzie Darling wasn't stupid. She'd noticed the change in Donna these past six months. 'You've met someone else, haven't you?'

Donna took a deep breath. She had to be careful what she disclosed here. 'Yes, and he's lovely. He's slightly older than me, rich, has his own business. He makes me happier than I can ever remember being.'

'Is he English?' Suzie snapped.

'Yes. Of course he's English,' Donna snapped back.

'Oh well, I suppose that's something,' Suzie said sarcastically. 'And have you given a thought to Robbie while you've been out gallivanting with your bit on the side?'

'I love Robbie. You know he's my world,' Donna said, waving at her son, who was chasing another little boy around the beer garden.

'Your dad isn't going to be happy, Donna. You knew the score when you married Tommy.'

'I was no more than a child when I married Tommy, Mum. And we all know the reason I did.'

'Don't make excuses. You were old enough to get yourself in the family way. Does Tommy know you're having an affair?'

'No. It's hardly something I'm going to discuss with him, is it? Tommy doesn't want me, Mum. He never has, not really. Don't you remember all those years ago when you and Dad came storming round to our house after Tommy and I had a fallout? Tommy said back then he didn't find the marriage was working and he wanted out. But you and Dad being you and Dad, forced us to stay together. I can't remember the last time we even kissed, let alone had sex. Tommy's penis doesn't fucking work, hasn't done for years. So there you have it.'

'Don't you dare talk about your husband like that. Tommy is a good man,' Suzie scolded. 'Has Robbie met this bit on the side of yours?'

Donna was finding it difficult to hold her tongue. 'He is not my bit on the side. He is the love of my life. No, of course I haven't introduced him to Robbie yet. But he is willing to take Robbie on. He has a beautiful four-bedroom house and lives in a lovely area. All I want is to be happy, Mum. Don't you understand that?'

'I do, Donna. But you can't just uproot Robbie. Tommy has always been a wonderful father to him and that boy adores the ground Tommy walks on. Your dad and brothers will go apeshit, too. You know what they're like.'

'Which is why I thought you might talk to Dad for me, explain the situation. If he accepts it, then Ronnie, Danny and Eugene will too.'

Suzie Darling shook her head vehemently. 'Don't be involving me in this one. You want out of your marriage, *you* speak to your father and brothers. How do you know your new beau isn't actually an undercover cop? He could even be a sodding paedophile!'

It was Donna's turn to shake her head in disbelief. 'You know what? You're a truly shit mother. You've always been ruled by Dad and the boys, and you always fucking will be!'

'In my office, now!' Hunter bellowed.

Banksy chuckled. So much so, his cigarette flew out of his gob and into his mug of tea. 'Someone's in big trouble, Regan. Good luck.'

Kim followed Hunter with a feeling of trepidation. Much as she hated her boss, she'd been secretly thrilled by his back-handed compliment earlier.

'Sit,' Hunter ordered, as though she were a dog.

Kim felt dryness in her throat. That can of worms she'd feared might be opened, obviously had been.

'Tell me again where you first met Tommy Darling, and think very carefully about your answer, Rosie Peacock.'

Kim stared at her hands. 'Maylands Children's Home, Guv.'

'Well, why didn't you tell me that in the fucking first place?'

Kim felt near to tears, but was determined not to show herself up. For the second time that day, she stared defiantly at Hunter. 'Because I am ashamed of my shitty past. Who wants to be known as the child of an alcoholic, drug-riddled mother who was shoved from pillar to post through the fucking care system? That's why I changed my name by deed poll before applying to become a WPC. I wanted a fresh start. I haven't even told Sam or Jay. But I take it the whole world'll know, now you do.'

Hunter snorted. 'What the hell do you take me for? And for your information, I didn't exactly have the greatest childhood myself. My mother drank gin for breakfast and was flat on her back by lunchtime.' Hunter took a bottle of whisky out of his drawer. He poured some into two mugs and pushed one towards Kim. 'Drink it,' he ordered.

The liquid stung as it hit the back of Kim's throat, but immediately made her feel better, calmer. 'I'm sorry I lied to you and if you don't think I'm up for this job, I totally understand.'

Hunter smiled. Kim rarely saw him smile. His teeth were reasonably white, considering he was a chain-smoker. 'Actually, I think you're perfect for this job. No more lies though. If SO10 give it the go-ahead, any problems or doubts you might have, you come straight to me. Comprende?'

'Yes, Guv.'

An hour later, a 728 form was on its way to New Scotland Yard with a big red stamp on the back that said DELIVER BY HAND.

If only Kim knew then what would happen, she would have snatched that form back and ripped it into a thousand tiny pieces.

CHAPTER TWENTY-SIX

Lunchtimes at Churchill's were usually quiet, but today was busy. Word had got around that Danny's wife Lucy had given birth to a daughter yesterday and many of the regulars had popped in to wet the baby's head. Probably because they knew the bubbly would be free, Tommy thought to himself.

Danny Darling was on cloud nine. 'She's so fucking beautiful. Look at her, mate,' he urged, showing Tommy yet another snap of the newborn.

The child was perfect and Tommy could not help but feel a sharp stab of envy. He would have loved a daughter himself. 'She's a little stunner, Dan. You decided on a name yet?'

'Annabel. Lucy chose it. I wasn't keen on it at first, but it's kind of grown on me. Archie and Annabel has a certain ring to it, don'tcha think?' Danny beamed. 'I want you to be her godfather, of course.'

'I'd be honoured,' Tommy smiled. He was already godfather to Archie and Danny was Robbie's godfather. 'Honestly, I'm proper chuffed for you, mate, and Lucy.'

'Who would have thought when we first met at the canal, when I chased off those lads who jumped you, that all these years later we'd be best mates, related, and have kids of our own. We were only kids ourselves back then. Mad when you think about it, ain't it?'

'Sure is,' Tommy grinned.

'You and Donna should have another baby. I know you and her aren't exactly Romeo and Juliet, but it would bring you closer together. You're a brilliant dad.'

Tommy was saved from answering by Eugene grabbing his arm. 'There's some geezer outside asking for you, Tom. He reckons you were once best mates. Can't see it meself, mind. The bloke's a ringer for Rodney Trotter,' Eugene laughed.

Tommy shot out the front. 'Dumbo! Fuck me, you look smart.' The suit was ill-fitting, but Dumbo looked far better than when Tommy had last seen him pissed in the Cross Keys in Dagenham.

Thrilled that Tommy seemed genuinely pleased to see him, Dumbo grinned. 'I been for an interview up town. I heard you worked here a while back, so thought I'd pay you a visit. I want to set up a Shitlands reunion. Scratch suggested it.'

'Scratch!' Tommy felt his heart beat wildly. 'You seen her?'

'Yeah. She turned up out of the blue the other day. She ain't a skinhead no more, Tommy. Her hair is long and she's ever so pretty now.'

'Is she married? Got kids?'

'No. She's single and lives with her friend.'

Back against the wall, Tommy sank to his haunches. This had knocked him for six, but for once it was a very welcome surprise indeed.

* * *

'Where the fuck you been all day?' Banksy asked, when his partner finally appeared at her desk.

'Mind your own bastard business,' Kim retorted. Her background had helped her fit in well in such a male-dominated environment. She gave as good as she got, always. 'Where's the guv?'

'Having one of his long liquid lunches, I should imagine. Why? Got the hots for him all of a sudden, have ya? Speaking of which, I shagged some bird who reminded me of you last night.'

'Lucky you. As long as you were thinking of her, not me, as you shot your load. That's if you were sober enough to raise a gallop in the first place, of course.'

Banksy chuckled. 'Something's going down. Enlighten me. Go on.'

'You'll find out soon enough,' Kim retorted. It had been a gruelling couple of days. Yesterday she'd been risk-assessed, and today it had felt like taking a trip back down memory lane. She needed to get into Scratch's head again. What would Scratch wear now? What hobbies would she have? What type of job would she be in? The music question had been by far the easiest to answer as Kim and Scratch would be into exactly the same bands: UB40, Madness, and the Jam.

'Regan, in my office,' Hunter ordered when he returned minutes later.

Wondering if there was a problem, Kim was relieved when Hunter smiled at her as she sat down. 'I've just spoken to SO10. It's all systems go. I'll be briefing the team later this afternoon. Don't let me down now, Regan. This is a biggie. I'm naming it Operation Sting.'

Donna Darling eyed her husband suspiciously. He seemed happier, had the swagger back in his step. 'You look smart and smell very nice. Where is it you're going again?' Donna asked, knowing full well where he was off to.

'I already told ya. Having a reunion with some old pals I grew up with.'

'Seeing as these pals of yours were in care, don't you think a suit is a bit formal? I also think you might have overdone it with the Kouros. Did you pour the whole bottle over yourself?' Donna taunted. She'd guessed by Tommy's change of mood and the effort he'd made to spruce himself up that he would be seeing the infamous Scratch this evening.

'Why do you always have to be so nasty?'

For a split second, Donna felt a tad guilty. Any love she'd had for Tommy had diminished the moment his penis had packed up. But she didn't hate him. She actually hoped Scratch might take him off her hands. That would make everything so much easier. After her mother's unhelpfulness, she was still searching for a way to break the news of her relationship with Josh to her father. As for her pregnancy, she had yet to tell anybody bar Josh about that. Not even her best pal was in on the secret. 'I'm sorry. I hope you have a good night, Tom.'

Ignoring the cheating bitch he'd married, Tommy picked up his son and planted a smacker on his forehead.

'Be a good boy for Mummy, and we'll go play football over the park in the morning.'

Robbie grinned and flung his arms around Tommy's neck. 'Can I be the goalkeeper, Dad? When I'm a big boy, I want to be like Pat Jennings.'

Donna suddenly felt slightly nauseous. For all Tommy's faults, he was and had always been a great father to Robbie. She didn't even know if Josh liked football, she thought guiltily.

The Darlings were surprisingly supportive when Tommy admitted it was Dumbo who'd turned up at Churchill's to organize a reunion.

'Go enjoy yourself, lad. Take your Merc, and show 'em how far you've come. If you get slaughtered, don't drive it home, mind. Take the following day off an' all, no worries,' Jack had said.

'Get a cab home and I'll take you to pick your car up whenever,' Danny had insisted.

What Tommy hadn't told the Darlings was there was only himself, Scratch and Dumbo meeting up. Benny was in prison, Smiffy dead. It had only ever been the five of them. Nobody else had mattered.

As he neared the Farmhouse Tavern, Tommy could sense his heartbeat increasing. He and Scratch once had a special bond. Something he had never had with Donna. Perhaps only two abused children, who'd gone on to lose their virginity to one another, could truly understand that. All he could do was pray she didn't hate him now. He'd felt far happier these past few days than he'd felt in bloody years.

* * *

Kim was feeling slightly unsure of herself. SO10 had insisted that someone from SO11 be present for this initial meet, and that alone had put her on edge.

'How do I look? Do you think I've overdone it with the make-up?' she asked Sam. These past few days they'd been at it non-stop, moving into their police-owned temporary accommodation, a two-bedroom flat in Rainham. Kim's hair had been permed and yesterday she'd spent most of the day shopping for clothes and accessories that Scratch would now wear. She could remember Tommy once liking her in a miniskirt, so that's what she'd opted for.

Sam wolf-whistled, then laughed. She barely recognized Kim. 'If I weren't so loved up, I'd definitely give you one with me strap-on. Does he like his women wearing lots of make-up?'

Having seen a photo of Tommy's wife, Kim shrugged. 'I suppose he must do. He married one.'

The flat was wired for sound, with a camera hidden in a plant pot in the lounge. Hunter had wanted her to wear a wire, but Kim had flatly refused. She didn't feel comfortable with the surveillance team being forced upon her, let alone wearing a wire, and she would certainly need to gain Tommy's trust before she could start asking him awkward questions anyway. 'You ready to drop me off?'

Dressed in a London Underground uniform, Sam stood up. That was her cover story. She was a ticket collector who'd met Scratch in a boozer in Barking in 1980, and they'd been best mates ever since.

* * *

'Tommy!' Dumbo shrieked. Dumbo was wearing jeans, T-shirt and Puma trainers and Tommy immediately felt over-dressed. Donna wasn't usually right, but he'd definitely gone overboard turning up in a crisp white shirt and tailored suit. He felt like a wanker.

'What you drinking, Dumbo?'

'Pint of Coke, please. I don't drink alcohol any more.'

'What, not at all?'

'No. My drinking got really bad at one point, so I knocked it on the head completely.'

Tommy sauntered up to the bar and ordered himself a large brandy and a pint. He felt so bloody nervous. Should he bring up his failure to show up at Maylands on Scratch's birthday as he'd once promised? Or should he let sleeping dogs lie and see if she mentioned his betrayal?

Tommy put the drinks on the table and sat down. 'So how did Scratch get back in touch with you? I meant to ask the other day.'

Dumbo looked out of the window and smiled. 'You can ask her yourself. Don't she look different now?'

Tommy gasped as she walked into the pub. She was wearing a faded short denim skirt, a baggy black top with pink lips on the front and black stiletto sandals. Her blonde hair was now past her shoulders, a shaggy perm, and her bright pink lipstick matched the motif on her top. She looked a bit like Debbie Harry, who was better known in the music world as Blondie. Tommy stood up. 'Wow! You look incredible. It's so good to see you again.'

Scratch grinned. She had to keep thinking of herself

as Scratch now, not Kim. 'You're not looking so bad yourself, Tommy Boyle.'

Tommy gave her an awkward hug. 'What can I get you to drink?'

'Half a lager and lime, please. I'm a cheap date, me,' Scratch chuckled.

'Shall we sit in the beer garden?' Dumbo suggested.

'Yeah, let's.' Tommy had so many questions he wanted to ask, but didn't know where to start, so he let Dumbo lead the conversation. 'Did you hear about Wayne Bradley?' Dumbo asked.

'No,' Scratch lied. 'What happened to him?'

Dumbo explained the story of him getting arrested for raping a mother and her daughter.

'Fucking arsehole. He was always a wrong 'un, wasn't he?' She could see the surveillance team a few tables away. If anything were to go wrong, she'd been told to empty her handbag upside down on the table and pretend to search for something. One of the team had a West Ham shirt on, the other cropped hair and an earring. No way would Tommy or Dumbo sense they were Old Bill.

'He sure was. Once a piece of shit, always a piece of shit,' Tommy added. 'So, where you living now, Scratch?' he asked, keen to change the subject.

'Rainham. I share a flat with my mate. We've only recently moved there from Ockendon. Our old landlord wanted to sell up. Rainham's a better place, to be honest. It's nearer to work for me.'

'What do you do?' Tommy enquired.

'Nothing glam. I work in an office as a typist. I like it though. The girls are nice and we have a good laugh.'

'Does your mate who you live with work there too?'
Tommy was wondering if Scratch's mate was a bloke.

'No. Lee works for the Underground. Her real
name's Leanne, but she hates being called that. She's
a lesbian,' Scratch explained. Sam's undercover name
was Leanne Jones.

'Are you and her an item then?' asked Dumbo.

'Goodness, no,' Scratch laughed. 'She has a girlfriend
and I'm happily single. What about you two? I heard
you got married and had a son, Tommy.'

'I'm happily single too. I do sometimes shag my next-
door neighbour though. She's thirty-five,' Dumbo
announced proudly.

Tommy and Scratch both chuckled. Dumbo had well
and truly broken the ice with that little nugget.

'My son Robbie's six now. Top little lad, he is. My
marriage is shite though. Donna and I are like ships that
pass in the night. We got wed far too young,' Tommy
admitted.

'Sorry to hear that, Tommy,' Dumbo said.

'Me too.' Scratch squeezed Tommy's arm as a gesture
of comfort. He didn't look happy. His cheeky grin was
still there, but he had a deadness behind his eyes. Serves
you fucking right for leaving me in the lurch, she thought
to herself.

Dumbo stood up. 'Who wants another drink?'

Tommy pulled out a wad of notes and handed Dumbo
a score. 'Here you go – I'll have a pint of lager.'

'Thanks, Tom. I am a bit skint, as it goes. I didn't
get that job I went for up town.'

'What job was that?' Scratch enquired.

'It was for assistant manager of a bar. That's what I do now, I'm a barman. That's why I don't drink any more either.'

'That's a shame, Dumbo. I'll keep my eyes and ears open for you,' Scratch said.

Desperate to impress the woman he could barely take his eyes off, Tommy grinned. 'I might be able to help you out, Dumbo. Danny and I kind of run the business these days and we sacked someone for thieving the other day. The bar's in South London, mind. The one you found me at. That too far for you to travel? Where you living now?'

'At the Fiddlers. No, Tommy, I drive – I got my own little van, so could easily get there.'

'Aww, that's so nice of you, Tommy,' Scratch said, touching his arm again. It actually made her feel quite cheap and nasty when she remembered how she'd once thrown herself at him. They'd done it over the Castle at Dagenham East and even in alleyways. She certainly wasn't that sordid person any more.

Tommy stood up. 'I'll phone Jack now. Run it past him. Jack's like the dad I never had. He even changed my surname by deed poll to his. I'm Tommy Darling now, not Boyle,' Tommy grinned.

'Really?' Scratch exclaimed.

Dumbo got the drinks in and when Tommy returned from the public phone inside the pub, he had some very good news. 'Can you start on Friday? You got a week's trial.'

Dumbo beamed at Scratch, then Tommy. 'You bet I bloody can.'

* * *

Within the hour, the conversation flowed like they'd never left Maylands.

'What about that time I chored those sweatshirts in Romford, and the stallholder saw me and chased me the length of the market. I sent the man on the fruit and veg stall sprawling and he dropped a whole crate of bananas,' Dumbo chuckled.

Tommy and Scratch both creased up. 'Then the bloke who was chasing you trod on the bananas and went flying. Me and Smiffy went back to see if he was OK and they'd called an ambulance. Poor sod had a broken leg,' Tommy laughed.

'The funniest thing ever was when that horse chased you in those fields opposite here, Dumbo. I laughed so much watching you try to get away from it, I literally wet myself a bit,' Scratch chuckled.

'Yeah, that day was a blast. You weren't no angel yourself, though, Scratch. Remember when the bird in the Jean Joint chased you up the Heathway? You ran into the station, spotted a train coming on the opposite side, ran across the tracks, got on it and got off at Dagenham East, and you still had all the chored gear,' Tommy laughed.

Scratch forced a chuckle. She so hoped SO11 couldn't hear the conversation. She was a bloody pillar of the community these days, not that skinhead tearaway she'd once been.

They reminisced for hours, howling over the lost memories and trying not to talk about the lost years.

By closing time, Tommy was feeling slightly inebriated. It had been a brilliant evening. The last time he'd laughed so much was when Jack took him and the lads to the races. What a day that had been. Jack had been given a tip on a 25–1 outsider. They'd all put a grand on it and the horse had romped home. Afterwards, they'd ended up in some dodgy nightclub and had a blast.

Tommy raised his brandy glass. 'To Smiffy,' he toasted. That fairground incident had understandably had a deep impact on their lives. None of them had ever visited a fairground since, all agreed they couldn't face it.

'I'm gonna make a move. My neighbour's waiting up for me,' Dumbo grinned. 'We must meet up again soon. I am so happy I got a job, Tommy. Thank you.'

'Yeah. See you at noon on Friday, mate. I'll make sure I'm there to show you the ropes. No letting me down though. Put it this way: if Jack hadn't known the father of the lad he just sacked, he would've chopped his thieving fucking hands off,' Tommy chuckled.

Scratch hugged Dumbo, then sat back down. 'It's been nice to catch up, hasn't it?'

Her eyes were beautiful, Tommy thought. Why hadn't he noticed that before? 'I'm sorry, ya know, for not turning up that time.'

'Shit happens, Tommy. We were no more than kids back then.'

Tommy reached out and squeezed Scratch's hand. 'But we had something special, didn't we? I've never had that connection with Donna that I had with you.'

'I am genuinely sorry your marriage isn't a happy one. But yes, what we had was very special.' She looked into his cold dead eyes as though she'd waited to say this every day for years, 'I've never felt it with anyone else either. I missed you Tommy Boyle.'

Tommy's eyes lit up. 'Really?'

'Yes. Really,' Scratch smiled. 'I don't care that you've changed your surname. You'll always be Tommy Boyle to me.'

CHAPTER TWENTY-SEVEN

I cannot tell you how happy I was after meeting up with Scratch again. She looked so different to the way she used to look. Beautiful inside and out, same as my mum. She sounded different, more eloquent, but I suppose I did too. We were adults now, not kids. Dumbo still sounded the same though. He will always be a big kid, bless his cotton socks.

I suppose, looking back, it was that night that sealed my fate because once I'd seen Scratch again I found a part of myself I thought was dead and buried, and I couldn't shut it down. I even got a hard-on in bed that night.

It wasn't long before I saw Scratch again, but the next time was a date. God I was excited, but ever so nervous. She seemed as interested in me as I was in her, and it felt fucking amazing.

At the back of my mind I suppose I did worry about what the Darlings would do. Robbie was my world. He was such a daddy's boy, my absolute life that little lad.

Looking back now, I should have realized I was playing with fire. But I didn't at the time. More fool me.

Tommy was the first to arrive at the Indian restaurant. He wasn't a big lover of Indian food, but Scratch obviously was as she'd suggested coming here, saying the food was great. She obviously knew the area far better than himself and Tommy, being a gentleman, would always let the lady choose.

While getting ready, Tommy had never felt so excited since he'd been a young lad waking up on Christmas morning. Since seeing Scratch again, she'd been on his mind constantly. He could think of little else all day.

When Scratch arrived, she did not disappoint. Dressed in a skin-tight peach dress and high-heeled brown wedges she looked incredible. Tommy kissed her on the cheek and moved the chair so she could sit down. 'You look beautiful.' He was absolutely blown away.

Scratch grinned. 'And you look more like the Tommy I remember. Not that I didn't like you in your suit. You looked very handsome in it. But I prefer you in this outfit. Reminds me of the old days.'

Tommy felt a warmth inside. He had felt a bit over-dressed last night, so had chosen to wear a navy Fred Perry polo shirt, faded Levi jeans and his desert boots this evening. He liked the Mod look, thought it suited him. 'Thanks. What would you like to drink? Shall I order a bottle of champagne, wine? Tonight is on me, by the way.'

'My, my, how sophisticated you've become, Tommy. I'll stick to half a lager and lime if that's OK. You can take the girl out of Maylands, but you can't take the Shitlands out of the girl.'

Tommy laughed out loud. 'You are so right.' He called the waiter over. 'A pint and a half of lager and lime please, mate.'

* * *

The restaurant was quite empty and as Scratch asked him question after question, Tommy began to feel slightly uneasy. He knew the Darlings had a reputation but he wanted to protect her from that, so quickly closed the conversation down. 'I've already told you babe, it's all kosher with the Darlings, I help run a bar and Danny and I are in charge of the gaming machine side of things. Brilliant family they are, wouldn't be where I am in the world without them.'

Realizing she was going too fast too soon, Scratch smiled. 'I'm so pleased you ended up with a decent family, Tommy.'

'Me too. When Jack first changed my surname by deed poll and gave it to me as a surprise, I must admit, I was a bit taken aback. But soon after, I realized why he did that. Tommy Darling is a far better name for me than Tommy Boyle. They're my adopted family, Scratch, and without them, I wouldn't be the man I've become. I hope you understand why I didn't come back, I wanted to but I owed it to them not to.'

'I understand. I felt like that when I moved in with the family whose children I looked after. They treated me like one of their own.'

'Same here. So, what music you into now? It's weird, you know. I have thought of you so much over the years. You were the first skinhead I really knew. Then the Specials and Madness came out. Then boom, there were skinheads everywhere.'

Scratch chuckled. She truly felt uncomfortable though, as there was virtually nobody in the restaurant and

SO11 were sitting two tables away. 'I love the Specials and Madness. But I'm a big fan of the Jam too.'

Tommy grinned. 'Me an' all. I actually think we might be soulmates, but I'm gonna leave it to you to order the food. I've not really been to many Indian restaurants in my time. I prefer Chinese.'

'Why didn't you say so beforehand? I know a nice Chinese in Rainham.'

Tommy held Scratch's gaze. 'Because I'm a gentleman and you are my first and only love.'

It was only then Scratch felt a flicker of guilt. Tommy was still Tommy and even though she loved Jay, and was now DS Regan, Tommy was and would always be her first love.

'You OK, Tommy? You enjoying the food?' Scratch asked. He seemed agitated.

'I would be if that prick opposite would stop staring at me.' Tommy stood up, then marched over to a table where two men were eating. 'You got a fucking problem, mate?'

'No. It's Tommy Boyle, isn't it? Do you remember me? Kirk Jenkins. I was in the year below you in Eastbrook.'

'No. I don't remember you and if you don't mind, I hate people watching me eat. Move chairs, eh, before I move 'em for you.'

Scratch glanced at SO11 who seemed totally engrossed in their own conversation. It had been a bad idea coming here. If it kicked off too badly they would surely have to step in and then the whole operation could be blown.

'Tommy, your pager's bleeping,' Scratch said, relieved when he strolled back to the table as though he'd asked to borrow the salt.

It was only then she realized she was truly in over her head.

Scratch once again checked the interior mirror of the blue Ford Fiesta to ensure she wasn't being followed. SO10 had registered the car in her childhood name, Rosie Peacock, but if her job had taught her anything, it was that you could never be too bloody careful.

Hunter was already waiting at the desolate spot he'd chosen to meet her. He stepped out of his car and into hers. 'So, what's the problem?'

Scratch sighed. 'The surveillance team. Knowing they're nearby is putting me off my stride. I told risk-assessment that Tommy isn't a threat, and he isn't. This has to be done my way, or not at all. It's not going to work otherwise.'

Hunter lit up a cigarette and took a deep drag. He'd been very impressed yesterday when Regan had updated him on the events of her and Tommy's first meeting. Tommy arranging to take her out for a meal alone had been music to his ears. But Regan's early morning call today had worried him, hence this meet in Essex. 'What do you think went wrong last night?'

'Nothing. I dunno. It was just awkward. The restaurant I was told to choose was dead quiet. There was only three other couples in there, plus the surveillance couple.' Scratch rolled her eyes. 'I can't connect with Tommy in that type of environment and I could sense his discomfort too. There was no music playing or anything. The conversation was stifled, to say the least.'

'Was that why he left early, d'ya reckon?'

'No. I don't think so. As I said to you earlier, his pager bleeped. He apologized profusely before dashing off. All he said was there was some problem at work that needed sorting.'

'Did he arrange another date with you?'

'No. But he offered to drop me home first. I told him I was fine, that my mate would pick me up. He seemed a bit agitated, in a rush.'

'Did he give an inkling of what might have happened?'

'I think he mumbled something about Ronnie, but that was it.'

'You sure he doesn't suspect anything?'

'No. But he soon fucking will if I can't convince him I'm still the Scratch he once knew. If I can't pull that off, he'll lose interest quickly. I need you to sort this for me, Guv. I really don't want SO11 following me around.'

'Fair enough. Will you reconsider wearing a wire though?'

'No way! That will make me even more paranoid. I can tell Tommy fancies me, if nothing else. Say he makes a pass at me and feels the bloody wire? We're all in shit street then.'

Hunter chucked the butt of his Marlboro out of the window and immediately lit up another. 'What worries me, Regan, is if you're jumpy over the surveillance and wearing a wire, what the fuck you gonna be like when you get Tommy back to the flat and you know we're all watching and listening?'

'I'll be fine, Guv. Honest I will. There are just certain conversations about our past that I need to get out of the way first. When Tommy rings later, I'm going to suggest a day trip to Southend. We used to go there, back in the day. That's the way forward. I know it is.' Scratch had decided to broach the subject of their child abuse while in Southend. She would then tell Tommy she never wished to speak about it again. No way did she want her work colleagues listening in on that particular conversation; chances were, if she didn't bring it up, then at some point Tommy would. The quicker she got that one out of the way, the better.

Hunter coughed, a phlegmy splutter. 'Well, for your sake, I hope you're right. Because if you're found floating in the bastard sea, I ain't taking the blame, Regan, that's for fucking sure.'

'Chop-chop, Tommy. Load those tools in the fucking van, will ya? Whassa matter with you this morning? You've been walking around in a dream, lad,' bellowed Jack Darling.

'Sorry,' Tommy mumbled, obeying orders. A pal of Jack's owned a piece of land in Kent that a mob of Irish travellers had moved on to. They were refusing to leave, hence him having to leave Scratch in the restaurant last night. It had been gone ten by the time he'd reached Churchill's, at which point Jack had decided they'd be best doing the job in the daylight. Jack's pal was a good payer. Ten grand he was offering to remove the unwanted tenants.

The drive took around fifty minutes and as they

pulled down a desolate lane, Danny urged everyone to put their balaclavas on. They had plenty of back-up. Six of his father's doormen were in the Ford Transit behind.

'Right. Go. Now!' Ronnie bellowed, leaping out the back of the van, machete in hand. His dad had stayed at Churchill's, so he was temporarily in charge. He knew his father put Danny and Tommy in control of parts of the business these days. But not when it came to violence. He was the only pro boxer in the family, albeit retired.

Women and kids screamed as the ten balaclava-wearing men ran towards them, tooled up.

There were only five caravans, but out of those soon appeared a dozen-plus men and lads all armed with tools.

Mayhem quickly ensued. Tommy clumped a teenage lad repeatedly with his baseball bat and the lad went down like a sack of potatoes. A man leapt on Tommy's back, dragged him to the ground and began kicking seven bells out of him. At first Tommy didn't see his face properly, but when he clocked it, he couldn't believe his eyes. 'Dad!'

Patrick Flanagan ripped Tommy's balaclava off. 'Stay there, keep schtum and I'll sort this,' he hissed before covering his son's face again.

'Stop this shit! All of you,' Patrick bellowed.

Patrick's family and friends reluctantly did so. Joey Boy was well pissed off as he'd got the better of at least three of the men, but there was no arguing with Patrick. He gave the orders.

'Who's in charge 'ere?' shouted Patrick.

Ronnie held his hand up. 'Me.'

'Let's call it quits before any real damage is done. Give us a few hours to pack up our stuff and we'll be off this land later today.'

'Fair enough. But if you're not, we'll be returning with guns,' Ronnie warned.

Eugene and Danny were helped to their feet. Both had taken a pasting before being clumped over the head with a piece of machinery.

Patrick walked over to where Tommy was sprawled on the ground. 'I'm very sorry, boy. For everything. You take care of yourself. Heard your name bandied about a lot recently and I am truly fucking proud you made it in life. Like father, like son, eh? Be lucky.'

Tommy nodded, then scrambled to his feet.

'You all right, Tom?' Ronnie asked as they pulled away from the land. 'Dad'll ring the doc, get him to take a look at Danny and Eugene. You need looking at as well?'

'No. I'm fine,' Tommy replied. He actually was. Not only did he have Scratch back in his life, his real dad had acknowledged him as his son for the first time and told him he was proud of him. Perhaps Patrick Flanagan wasn't such a bad bloke after all. It was a strange feeling but it was like a part of him was healing inside. Tommy shook his head, he was going bloody soft, that's what it was.

Scratch ended the call to Caroline. She was so busy with work that she didn't visit the family who had sort of adopted her half as much as she should, which made her feel a bit guilty at times. But she made time to speak to them all on the phone regularly. Keith had retired from the police force now, was working in security.

Fiona would be fifteen in August, so Scratch had treated her to an early birthday present. Duran Duran mad, Fiona was, and she'd been thrilled when Scratch had informed her she'd got two tickets to see them live at the Dominion Theatre in July.

As for Mikey, he was six going on sixteen, football bloody mad. There was a little park in the road Caroline and Keith lived in and whenever Scratch called in the afternoons or early evenings, if Mikey wasn't at school, he'd be over there kicking a ball about with the older lads who lived next door.

Sam entered the flat and immediately took off the bastard Underground uniform she kept having to change in and out of. She was sweating like a pig in this heat. 'Has Tommy rung you yet?' she shouted out.

'No. But there's something I need to tell you.'

Having put on a pair of Adidas shorts and a T-shirt, Sam plonked herself on Scratch's bed. 'What's up?'

'Nothing. But I thought you should know I spent part of my teenage years living in a children's home. That's where Tommy and I first met.'

'But I thought after your mum, your aunt and uncle took you in?'

'They're not my real aunt and uncle, they're relations of Connie, who ran the home. When I started at Hendon, I didn't want to own up to my background. Who wants to be known as the care home kid?'

Sam put an around her pal's shoulders. 'I would never have judged ya, you know.'

'I know that. Others would have though. All I wanted was to forget about my shitty past and concentrate on building a decent future.'

'Well, you've certainly done that. So why you telling me this now?'

'Because if Tommy comes round here, you're bound to find out anyway. Plus, I don't want you referring to Caroline and Keith as my aunt and uncle. Far as he's concerned, they're a couple who gave me a house-keeping/nanny job. Don't mention they're related to Connie, for goodness' sake.'

'Course not.'

The phone rang and Scratch snatched at the receiver. It was Tommy.

The following morning, Scratch was up with the larks. She'd had a crap night's sleep. She couldn't remember exactly what the nightmare was about, but she knew Tommy was in it and Jay. They were arguing, fighting over her, and Jay called off their engagement. That's all she could recall.

Scratch lay in the bath thinking about her fiancé. Jay had been extra busy at work since the Security Express van robbery and they'd hardly seen one another lately. She was looking forward to the weekend though. At long last he had some time off and they'd planned to view some more properties, then spend a romantic Saturday night in a hotel in Hertfordshire. She could not wait to spend some quality time with her man.

'Morning, bird. All ready for the seaside? Got your bucket and spade?'

'Very funny.'

'Good luck today.'

'Thanks. Why you up so early?'

Sam grinned. 'Spending the day with the missus. Taking her shopping.'

'You're a changed woman since meeting Dolly Parton, you are,' Scratch laughed.

''Ere, not so much of the woman. Geezer bird suits me just fine.'

Tommy didn't know Rainham too well, so had to stop twice and study his *A to Z* before finally finding the right address. He'd told Jack his sister had a bit of bother and he needed to sort it urgently to get the day off.

Tommy rang the buzzer of number 5. Scratch answered immediately and said she was on her way down.

Tommy opened the passenger door of his Mercedes.

'Wow! I love your posh car.'

'It had only done twelve thousand on the clock when I bought it. You look really nice, by the way.'

Scratch hadn't known what to wear, so had opted for denim pedal-pushers, a bright green vest top and jellies. She'd also brought a sweatshirt with her in case it got chilly later. 'You look nice too. Won't you be hot in those jeans though?'

'Nah. I'll be fine. Got me trunks on underneath in case we fancy a dip. My legs are as white as a sheet, so I didn't wanna scare off any holiday-makers.'

Scratch laughed. 'Well, I certainly won't be taking a

dip. I've been petrified of the sea since watching *Jaws*,' she lied.

'I got the stereo system in the boot. Thought we could chill on the beach with a couple of cans and listen to some tunes. I made a special cassette up last night. All the songs that remind me of Maylands. I thought you might like it.' Tommy had thought about his time at Maylands a lot since meeting up with Scratch again. They'd had some great laughs, running wild without a care in the world. He hadn't appreciated that kind of freedom at the time, but he bloody did now. He couldn't wait to take another trip down memory lane today with the girl who knew him better than anybody.

'Awww, that's so thoughtful. Can't wait to listen to it. What's that mark on your face, Tommy? You hurt yourself?'

'Long story that involves my real dad, believe it or not.'

'No way! What happened?'

As Tommy started to talk, Scratch was mentally making notes.

'Robbie, this is Mummy's friend, John,' lied Donna Darling. She didn't want to use Josh's real name yet, in case Robbie dropped her in it. She could just imagine her dad and psycho brothers making numerous phone calls to track Josh down, then making him disappear off the face of the earth.

'I like your car.' Robbie pointed at the gleaming red Ferrari.

'Thanks, Robbie, and it's nice to finally meet you. Your mum's told me lots about you.'

'What football team do you support?'

'West Ham.'

'Boooo,' Robbie chuckled. 'They're a rubbish team. Me and my dad support Millwall. They're the best.'

Josh grinned. 'Wanna see my garden? I got a big pool. Do you like swimming?'

'Yeah, but can we go for a ride in your car first, please?'

Donna and Josh shared a smile. So far so good, both thought.

Tommy cracked open two cans and handed one to Scratch. The beach was busy, but not too crowded, like school holidays were. 'The Who and the Kinks always remind me of Smiffy, ya know. He was old before his time. I bet now the Mods are back in fashion, Smiffy would've been one,' Tommy said sadly.

'Poor Smiffy. He was a good lad. Reminds me of Benny, this does. I haven't heard it for ages.' The song was George McCrae's 'Rock Your Baby'.

'Didn't you keep all your records then?' Tommy asked, surprised.

'Yes. They're still at the couple's house I used to work for. I must pick them up next time I visit,' Scratch fibbed. 'I can't believe Benny's in prison, can you? I wonder how he's doing?'

Tommy shrugged. Dumbo had informed them that Benny had got a five stretch for drug dealing. 'Benny's a survivor. He'll be all right.'

'Your job sounds dangerous. Don't you ever worry that you'll end up in prison too?'

Tommy unbuttoned his short-sleeve shirt. 'Yeah. I do, as it goes. Especially since Ronnie had his accident. He's never been the full shilling since. Shame really. Before that fight, I used to look up to him. Now, I just see him as a liability.'

Scratch took a sip of lager. 'What fight? And what exactly does a liability mean? You know I never went to school much.'

'He got hurt in a boxing match years ago. I dunno. He cocks up a lot and the rest of us have to clear up his mess. I sometimes wish I had a normal job and lived by the sea. But I earn bloody good money, so I shouldn't really complain.'

'What's stopping you? Money isn't the be-all and end-all.'

'You wouldn't understand. But to put it bluntly, Jack or Ronnie would never let me walk away from the firm. I suppose I know too much.'

Scratch's intense SO10 training had taught her never to overdo it with the questions for fear of raising suspicion. 'Fancy an ice-cream?' she asked, changing the subject, but knowing she was slowly but surely reeling Tommy in.

'Robbie, time to get out of the pool, love. We need to go home soon,' shouted Donna.

'Why do we? Can't we stay here a bit longer, Mum? Please,' Robbie begged.

'Another half an hour then.'

'Watch my dive, John,' Robbie yelled, performing yet another belly-flop.

Donna squeezed Josh's hand. Today had been a brilliant success. Josh had cooked a lovely lunch and they'd eaten it on the terrace while sipping champagne. She could really get used to this lifestyle, which was why she'd come to an important decision. 'I'm going to pack some things later. Then tomorrow morning, I shall speak to my father and tell him about us.'

'Do you want me to come with you?'

'No! It'll be better if I speak to him alone first.'

'What about Tommy?'

'I might just leave him a note. I actually think he's met somebody himself, please God. I'll tell him he can see Robbie whenever he wants to, within reason. That's OK with you, isn't it?'

'Yeah, course. What about the lad's schooling though?'

'I can't be doing that distance twice a day, so we'll have to look into schools around here for him.'

'OK. I got a couple of pals with kids Robbie's age. I'll have a word with them; find out what the best school is.'

'Thanks, Josh. I love you so much.'

'Love you too.' Josh patted Donna's stomach. 'And that little one in there.'

Scratch propped her elbow in the sand. Without any prompting, Tommy had been opening up about his marriage. 'So, why do you stay with Donna?'

'Because I ain't got much fucking choice.'

'What do you mean?'

'The Darlings are Catholics, Scratch. I wouldn't be allowed to divorce her. This is why I'm hoping this bloke she has on the firm is the real deal. I think he is. She seems much happier than she has in years. I pray every night that she'll just fuck off with him. Robbie's gonna be the issue though. I ain't letting another geezer bring up my son. If she wants to leave, fine. But that boy stays with me.'

'What would happen if you left Donna?'

Tommy lay back in the sand, the sun on his face. He hadn't felt quite as relaxed in years. 'I dunno. It wouldn't be pleasant though.'

'Oh, don't be so overly dramatic,' Scratch laughed. 'Lots of couples get divorced.'

'You don't know the Darlings like I do. You wrong 'em, you're a dead man walking.'

Scratch feigned surprise. 'You're kidding me? What, have you actually seen them kill someone?'

Realizing he'd already said too much, Tommy stood up and held out his hand. 'Nah, course not. Come on, I'm starving. Let's go get something to eat.'

'Can I ask you something, Tommy?'

Tommy smiled. Unlike Donna, she was so easy to be around. The conversation flowed naturally. 'Go on.'

'How have you coped over the years, ya know, dealing with what happened to us as kids? We don't have to talk about it if you don't want to. But I haven't coped well at all and it's not a subject I can talk about with anybody else. You're the only person I've ever really told.' And part of her was telling the truth there, that was the hard part here, remembering what was Scratch and what was Kim Regan.

'I haven't coped well either. I saw him again, ya know – my uncle. He was in a pub not far from where I grew up.'

'Oh God. That must've been awful for you. Did he recognize you?'

Tommy cracked his knuckles. 'Nah. I wanted to kill him, even went back to the boozer a few times and waited outside so I could find out where he lived. But when push came to shove, I couldn't go through with it. Just the thought of being in close proximity to him again gives me the heebies. I did consider telling the Darlings – they would have been only too happy to rid the earth of the scum – but it would've meant coming clean to them. They know bits and bobs about what happened, but not, ya know, the full story.'

'You never told me the full story either. It's hard to open up about something so personal, isn't it? I've not even had sex with anyone else since you.'

Tommy turned to her in shock. 'No way!'

'It's true. I swear,' Scratch lied. To be honest, it wasn't a massive lie as there had only been Jay.

'But why not? You're so pretty. You must have blokes falling at your feet.'

'Not really. I don't trust men. Lee says I'll never meet one, cos I come across as too standoffish.'

Tommy looked into her eyes. 'I am truly sorry for letting you down that time. If I had one wish in life it would be to turn the clock back. I'd do everything differently now.'

Scratch gently rubbed his arm. 'It's OK, Tommy. I've forgiven you. Let's make a pact never to talk about the bad shit that happened to us again. It's depressing, isn't it?'

'Sure is. That sick bastard had even changed his name to mine, ya know.'

'What! Who?'

'Uncle Ian is now called Tom.'

'Oh, Tommy. That's dreadful,' Scratch replied, genuinely meaning it.

Tommy looked Scratch square in the eyes, 'He did rape me. But only the once. He was gonna do it a second time, that's why I stabbed him.'

'I kind of guessed that. I'm sorry, Tommy.'

'What doesn't kill us only makes us stronger, eh?'

Scratch squeezed Tommy's hand. 'Sure does.'

'Do you want to come in for a tea or coffee? Lee'll probably be home, but you'll like her. She's ever so funny and nice,' Scratch said as they approached the flat.

'No, but thanks anyway. I promised Robbie I'd read him a bedtime story before he goes to sleep. I always try to, when I can.'

Instead of pulling up outside the actual block, Tommy parked on the corner and took a cassette out of the glove compartment. 'Remember this? I've never forgotten it. It's like, our song.'

Scratch shuddered. The song was Johnny Nash's 'Tears on My Pillow'. How could she ever forget it? She'd sobbed for days, playing it over and over, before smashing it to smithereens.

'You cold?'

'No. This, it takes me back, that's all.'

'Do you remember buying me a copy before I left Maylands? You said we should always remember one another when playing it.'

'Of course I do.'

'I've still got the photo you gave me too. The one of me, you, Smiffy, Dumbo and Benny sunbathing in the garden.'

'Listen, I was wondering, would you like to come round for dinner one evening next week?'

Tommy grinned. 'You try stopping me. How about Saturday?'

Thinking of the first excuse that came to mind, Scratch said, 'I can't do Saturday. It's Lee's mum's fiftieth birthday party. How about Monday?'

'Not gonna poison me, are ya?' Tommy smirked. 'Monday's fine by me.'

'Of course not,' Scratch chuckled. 'That lady I used to work for learned me how to cook.'

Tommy turned to Scratch and moved her hair away from her face. 'I am so glad we're back in touch.'

'Me too.'

When Tommy leaned forward to kiss her, Scratch shut her eyes and responded.

Feeling his useless penis suddenly rise from the dead, Tommy felt ecstatic. He put Scratch's hand on it, but she quickly snatched it away. 'I'm sorry,' Tommy said.

'It's OK. But well, you know, I need to take things slowly, Tommy. I can't be rushing into anything like that.'

'I understand. Honestly I do. I won't put any pressure on you. I'm just happy to spend time together.'

Scratch smiled. 'I'll see you on Monday then. Does half seven sound OK?'

'Yeah, fine. Is it all right if I call you tomorrow, when you get home from work?'

'That's if I still have a job after throwing a sickie today,' Scratch laughed. 'Yeah, call me tomorrow – and thanks so much for the lovely day. I thoroughly enjoyed it.'

Tommy winked. 'Me too.'

CHAPTER TWENTY-EIGHT

The thing about love is it blindsides you. I had been a hard man for years, had shut my feelings off — you've got to when you're kicking the shit out of someone, can't be thinking about their kids, or who they are . . .

Scratch made me feel alive in a way that only violence had. And yep, you could say I was falling hook, line and sinker . . .

Meanwhile, the Darling firm was floundering, keeping a handle on Ronnie was becoming a full-time job. His mood swings had turned him into a proper nut job. Danny was just playing dad of the fucking year and Jack wasn't the same since his stroke. And Donna, well whoever said women were the answer to all evil clearly hadn't met Donna!

But the family was relying on me to keep up the Darling name. And it was a job I took very fucking seriously . . .

'You're up early,' Tommy said to Donna.

'Yes. I've got a lot of running around to do this morning.' She'd already packed some of her and Robbie's clothes, and other necessities, put them in the boot of her car while Tommy was out yesterday. 'I'll drop Robbie off to school. Why don't you go back to bed, have a lie-in.'

Tommy looked at Donna suspiciously. She'd been

extra nice to him when he'd got home last night and the lazy cow never usually got out of bed before lunchtime. He always took Robbie to school and Donna would pick him up. 'OK. Cheers.'

Tommy went upstairs, got dressed and as soon as he heard the front door slam, ran down the stairs and jumped in his car. Donna hadn't wanted him to read Robbie a bedtime story last night and when he'd insisted on doing so, the lad had slipped up. 'I didn't go to school, Daddy. We went to Mummy's friend John's house and I had a ride in his sports car and swam in his pool. It was ace.'

Tommy had somehow managed to hold his temper, but was determined to find out what that bitch was up to today. She could fuck off with John tomorrow for all he cared, but no way was she taking Robbie with her. Over his dead body.

Scratch met Hunter in the same place they'd met the previous day. She handed him a list of all she'd found out so far.

'Well, this ain't enough to get any fucking convictions, is it?'

'I know that, Guv. Slowly, slowly catchy monkey. He will open up to me, I know he will. He's coming to the flat for a meal on Monday night. I'll ply him with booze to loosen him up a bit.'

'Why wait until Monday? Can't you cook for him beforehand?'

'This is Jay's first weekend off for ages. We've arranged to go house-hunting and booked a hotel in

Hertfordshire on Saturday night. I've hardly seen him for weeks. I should imagine weekends are the busiest time for Tommy in his line of work anyway.'

'Ask him and see. Work before pleasure. You know the drill, Regan.'

'OK.'

'You spoke to your snout?'

'Yeah. All good.'

'All systems go then. But you need to start getting more info out of your childhood sweetheart, sharpish. I don't care how you do it. Give him a wank if need be.'

Scratch looked at Hunter with distaste. He truly was a vulgar man.

Tommy knew immediately that Donna wasn't taking Robbie to school as she headed in the opposite direction. He hung back and was shocked when she stopped near Churchill's. She got out of the car, leaving Robbie inside, locked the doors and pressed the buzzer. Jack opened the door and ushered her inside.

Tommy tapped on the window of Donna's Volkswagen Beetle. 'Why aren't you at school? What's Mummy doing here?'

'She said she needed to talk to Granddad, then we could go to John's house again. You should see his car, Daddy. It's a Ferrari.'

Tommy was livid. 'You wait here. You'll be spending the day with me, OK?'

Using his own key, Tommy crept inside Churchill's. He could hear voices coming from upstairs, the area they used as their office.

As he tiptoed up the stairs, the voices became clearer.

'No way, Donna. Tommy's not just my best pal, he's like a brother to me. You can't do this to him. It'll break him,' Danny said.

'Stupid little cow's lost her marbles. Who is this fucking geezer?' Jack bellowed. 'You've got a good husband. Tommy's one of our own. You married the man; you make your marriage work. Understand me?'

'Tommy'll go apeshit if you take Robbie away from him,' Eugene added.

'I'm a grown woman, not a fucking child, and I'm sick of living in an arranged loveless marriage. Don't you think I deserve to be happy? For your information, Tommy has been unable to get an erection for years and we sleep in separate bedrooms,' Donna screeched.

Tommy felt mortified, and what did she mean by 'arranged marriage'? He barged into the room. 'Donna's right, guys. Our marriage has been dead in the water for a long time. If Donna has met the man of her dreams, then good luck to her. Robbie will live with me, mind. But Donna can see him on certain days. We'll work something out.'

'I don't fucking think so,' Donna laughed manically. 'Tell him the truth 'cause if you don't then I bastard-well will.'

Jack glared at the bane of his life. 'Shut your trap, you. Or else.'

Tommy turned to Danny. 'The truth about what?'

Danny couldn't reply, looked at his shoes. He had never wanted to be part of this conspiracy in the first place, had said it was wrong at the time. But his father and Ronnie had insisted, so that was that.

Ronnie put a comforting arm around Tommy's shoulders. 'Come down to the bar. You look like you need a drink.'

Tommy shrugged Ronnie's arm away. 'Nah. I wanna know what the fuck is going on 'ere.'

'Danny, go downstairs with Tommy while I have a chat with Donna,' Jack ordered.

'Come on, mate,' Danny said.

'I ain't going nowhere until I find out the truth. What did you mean by "arranged marriage", Don?'

'She didn't mean anything. She's talking bollocks, ain't you, Donna?'

'Tell him. He needs to know the truth,' Donna hissed.

'The truth about fucking what?' Tommy shrieked.

'Robbie isn't your son. I was pregnant before we got together. I'm sorry,' Donna wept.

'You've got to be fucking kidding me. This is some kind of joke, right?'

'Go and get a bottle of brandy, Ronnie. I think we all need a drink,' Jack ordered, glaring at his daughter.

Tommy prodded Danny in the chest. 'Please tell me this ain't true, mate.'

The cat well and truly out of the bag, all Danny could mumble was, 'Sorry, mate. None of this was my idea.'

Tommy sank to his haunches and put his head in his hands. He could not believe this was happening to him. That little boy he'd loved and cherished since birth wasn't even part of him.

'Drink that,' Ronnie ordered, handing Tommy a large brandy.

Tommy took a sip, stood up and smashed the glass against the wall. 'Whose fucking kid is it?' he bellowed, his eyes fixed on the slut he'd married.

'Tek's,' Donna wept. 'Tek was the Turkish lad I dated before we met. He doesn't know Robbie is his. I never told him. You can still be part of Robbie's life. You've been such a good dad to him, I would never stop you seeing him.'

'How could you do this to me?' Tommy stared at Jack. 'I fucking loved you like a dad. I trusted you.'

'Donna's not leaving you. She's not taking your son away. I won't allow it,' Jack bellowed.

'But he ain't my fucking son, is he?'

'And you,' Tommy pushed Danny in the chest. 'My best mate. The brother I never had – or so I thought. How could you betray me like that? I trusted you with my life.'

'It weren't like that, Tom. I had no say in the matter. Dad and Mum wanted you to be part of the family. They love you like a son,' Danny explained. He was very near to tears, felt awful.

'No. I'll tell you what you saw. A care home kid who you could easily manipulate to do whatever you fucking wanted.' Tommy pointed at Donna. 'I bet that slag didn't even love me in the first place. No wonder our marriage was a shambles.'

'I did love you,' Donna sobbed.

'Shut up, you fucking slapper,' Tommy spat.

'No need to speak to Donna like that, Tommy. I know you're upset son, but we need to all calm down and sort this situation out properly, like a family,' Jack said.

'Go fuck yourself,' Tommy pointed at Jack, Ronnie, Danny and Eugene. 'Family? It was only muggins 'ere thinking you mob were my family. Well, you can all go fuck yourselves now. You're dead to me, the lot of ya.'

'Go after him, Danny,' Jack urged as Tommy bolted down the stairs.

'Daddy! Daddy, where you going?' shouted Robbie. His mum had left the car window half open.

Ignoring the son that wasn't his, Tommy leapt in his Merc and as he pulled away very nearly ran his treacherous so-called best mate over.

'Where's Dad gone?' Robbie asked his mother.

'You go home and you sort this out with Tommy. Do you hear me?' Jack yelled. He stood in front of his daughter's car. 'I mean it, Donna. You'll do as I fucking say,' he said, punching the windscreen, his gold sovereign ring chipping the glass.

Donna nodded, then pulled away from the pavement. She had no intention of going home. Everybody needed to calm down a bit. She'd had enough of her family ruling her life. It was about time she decided what was best for her, not them.

'Where we going, Mum?'

'John's house. Want to go for another ride in his car and play in the swimming pool again?'

'Is Daddy coming too?'

'No, love. He isn't.'

* * *

Tommy dashed home, chucked some clothes in the boot, his stereo and other personal belongings.

As he was about to lock up the phone rang. Expecting it to be Danny or Jack, he ignored it. Then he heard the answerphone message. 'Hi, Tommy – it's Ray from Maylands. Can you call me on this number?' Ray rattled off a number that Tommy scribbled down. Ray then ended the call by saying, 'It's rather urgent.'

Tommy contemplated driving to Clacton to spend some time with his sister. But not only would she be at work, he didn't want to burden her with this. She'd grown very fond of Robbie, was bound to be devastated by the news. Linda had her own life now anyway. A happy one, thank God.

His head all over the place, Tommy drove through the Blackwell Tunnel. He needed to get out of South London. He only had one true friend now. Scratch would understand.

Jack Darling was furious. Suzie had driven around Donna and Tommy's house. Neither were at home. She'd also rung the school and Robbie wasn't there. 'We need to find Tommy first, then we'll deal with your sister and her bit on the side afterwards,' Jack said to Danny. 'Who's that fucking plum your brothers are talking to?'

Danny put his forefinger to his lips. 'Tommy's mate. You said he could start work here today. Be nice to him, for Christ's sake. We need to get Tommy back on side, Dad.'

Jack marched over to the lanky-looking streak of piss

and held out his right hand. 'All right, lad? I'm Jack, the owner.'

'Nice to meet you. I'm Dumbo. Where's Tommy? He promised to be here to show me the ropes.'

'Tommy had some urgent business to attend to. But don't you worry, Eugene 'ere will show you the ropes,' Jack replied, slapping his youngest on the back. It was obvious just by looking at Dumbo he wasn't the full shilling. Even his suit looked five sizes too big.

Eugene put an arm around Dumbo's shoulders and grinned at his brothers and father. 'He reckons he's an expert on making cocktails, even better than Tom Cruise. Trouble is, the name Dumbo don't exactly suit our establishment, eh, lads?'

'Button it, Euge, will ya?' Danny felt embarrassed. There was no need to blatantly mock the poor sod.

Not taking the hint, Eugene grinned at Dumbo. 'Seeing as he looks like a certain Trotter brother, I think we should call him Dave after Rodney.'

Ronnie creased up laughing. 'Brilliant.'

Dumbo grinned like a Cheshire cat. '*Only Fools and Horses* is my favourite programme. I'd be honoured to be called Dave.'

Tommy stopped at an offie, bought four cans of lager and a half-bottle of brandy, then parked up near Central Park. Without the fairground there, it was hard to know exactly where Smiffy had died, so Tommy picked a spot randomly, sat down and took a swig of brandy.

How could he have been so stupid, especially when all the signs were there? Yes, he'd been young. But Jesus, he must've been thick. Looking back now he could see it all so clearly. Donna throwing herself at him. Jack and Suzie encouraging the relationship. Ronnie booking that caravan holiday for the pair of them, when they'd only been dating five minutes. Robbie being born early and Suzie telling him that was normal with a first-born child. Robbie's dark skin and nearly black hair. No wonder he looked so Mediterranean if his real father was Turkish. Jack showing him photos of himself and his father from donkey's years ago insisting Robbie had their colouring. What a load of old bollocks.

Tears streamed down Tommy's cheeks as he remembered how proud he'd felt when he'd held Robbie for the very first time. How Robbie had clung to his hand, not wanting to be parted from him on his first day at school. How he'd gently dabbed calamine lotion all over the poor little sod when he'd had a bad case of chickenpox. 'Dadda' was the first word Robbie had spoken. Lies, lies and more fucking lies, Tommy thought bitterly.

Cracking open two cans of lager, Tommy poured one on the grass beside him. 'This one's for you, Smiffy. Wherever you are, it has to be better than where I am. This is fucking hell down 'ere, I'm telling ya, pal.'

Tommy downed his lager and punched the grass with frustration. Even Danny had lied to him and that hurt badly. He'd thought he could trust Danny more than anybody, but obviously not. He must be as manipulative as the rest of the Darlings. Any true friend would have told him the truth, not allowed him to raise a child that wasn't his.

Tommy visualized Robbie's innocent face. The lad was a great kid, didn't deserve this shit. Robbie was bound to miss him, but there was no going back. Tommy had already made his mind up never to see the lad again, or Donna. He'd been bored with his job for a while now, had wanted out, so perhaps this was an opportunity to part company with the Darlings? Jack knew he could be trusted. He'd been involved in too much skulduggery himself to ever open his trap. A clean break, that's what he craved.

Glugging another mouthful of brandy, Tommy lay back on the grass. He had to try to look at the positives, not the negatives. At least if he was a free man, he and Scratch could be together.

'Fancy a takeaway tonight?' Sam asked Scratch.

'Yeah, whatever.'

Sam sat on the edge of the sofa. 'Come on then. Spit it out.'

'What?'

'Whatever it is that's bothering you.'

'Nothing's bothering me. I'm fine,' Scratch fibbed. She wasn't going to tell her best mate that Tommy had kept her awake last night and she'd begun to have second thoughts about Operation Sting. That would make her look weak. She'd signed up for this; the whole reunion had been her bloody idea in the first place. She had to put her head down and get on with it now.

'What's that mark on your arm?'

'I accidentally cut myself while cutting the bread,' Scratch lied.

'What, on your arm?'

'Yes. On my fucking arm.'

'You can talk to me, mate. You know that,' Sam urged.

'There's nothing to talk about,' Scratch insisted.

When the phone rang it was Sam who answered. 'Oh, hi, Tommy. This is Lee, Scratch's flatmate. Hang on a tick. I'll see if she's out of the bath yet.'

'Scratch, Tommy's on the phone. You out of the bath, mate, or shall I tell him to call back?' Sam shouted out, walking over to Scratch. 'He sounds agitated, said it's urgent,' she whispered in her pal's ear.

'Coming,' Scratch replied, pausing for a few seconds before picking up the receiver. 'Hi, Tommy. What? Slow down. Yes. Yes, that's fine. OK. Give us half an hour or so though. I've only just stepped out of the bath and I need to dry my hair and get dressed.'

'He's coming round?' Sam asked.

'Yeah. Right, where's me pager? I need to message Hunter. Actually, can you shoot down to the phone box and call Hunter for me?' Scratch scribbled down a number. 'Tommy's only in the Albion pub and I can't risk him seeing me. Grab some beers while you're out. If he's here when you get back, I'll pretend I sent you out to get them. Oh, and I think it's best if you go out anyway. Something's happened. Something terrible, he said. He won't open up if you're here. He's definitely been drinking and sounds upset.'

'No. SO10 said I was to stay in my room if he comes to the flat. I ain't leaving you alone with him.'

'Tommy isn't dangerous, trust me. Listen, when he gets here, stay in your room. If I want you to leave, then I'll come in and ask if you're going out for a drink, OK? Now go and tell Hunter all this and give me your pager. I need to put it with mine in the hidey-hole soon as I've messaged Hunter. I'll tell him to keep his phone line free.'

'Hunter won't want you left alone with Tommy, mate. Not if he's been drinking.'

'Then don't fucking tell Hunter he's been drinking. Look, we need a result and sharpish. Only I don't think I can do this much longer. Now go, and if you can't get hold of Hunter, call Banksy. Oh, and watch what you say when you come back, Lee. No slip-ups. Only I'm flicking the switch on in a bit.'

'OK. See you soon.'

Scratch paced up and down the flat. The switch was hidden behind the TV, had been made to look like an ordinary plug socket, but Scratch couldn't bring herself to switch it on yet. She was a bundle of bloody nerves and the thought of the team watching and listening to her every word filled her with dread.

Remembering she had a couple of beers in the fridge, Scratch took one out and drank it quickly to calm herself. She couldn't let the cat out of the bag, not now. If she acted like she felt, Tommy would soon realize something was amiss.

'Did you get hold of Hunter?' Scratch asked when Sam got back. 'I haven't turned the equipment on yet, so you can talk,' she added.

'Yeah. He said "Do what you got to do", but he wants me to wait nearby in the car and he's sending back-up too. He's gonna be watching live, so if you feel you're out of your depth at any point, he wants you to offer Tommy a cheese and pickle sandwich. Oh, and give me my pager. Only he'll need to message me to arrive home if that were to happen. I told him we didn't need back-up, but he was insistent. He said if it got too heavy, I was to act a bit pissed and pretend I'd invited a couple of lads back from the pub.'

Scratch scrambled underneath the cupboard below the sink, lifted the false bottom and handed Sam her pager. 'Shit!' she mumbled as the buzzer sounded. 'Right, get in your room and I'll flick the switch on. Oh, and play some music so he knows you can't hear us. But not too loud, obviously.'

Scratch said a silent prayer as she flicked on *that* switch. If she fucked this up, not only would she lose Hunter's respect, that piss-taker Banksy would never let her live it down.

The buzzer sounding hadn't been Tommy, it had been a pizza delivery by somebody who'd got the address wrong.

Scratch sat in the lounge, her heart beating wildly. She'd been filmed on other undercover operations, but never with her own team watching her. She wasn't sure if it was that or the fact she was trying to set up Tommy that was making her feel physically sick.

Thankfully, the only camera was in the lounge, hidden in the plant pot, so Scratch went to the bathroom and splashed some cold water on her face. She needed to get a grip, swiftly.

* * *

The buzzer sounding a second time made her jump. She answered it. 'It's me,' a familiar voice said.

Faking a smile, Scratch opened the door to him. 'This is a nice surprise, Tommy.'

Tommy put his arms around Scratch and held her close to his chest. 'I'm in bits, babe. I've been done up like a kipper. Those Darlings ain't to be fucking trusted.'

The whole flat was wired for sound, but Scratch led Tommy into the lounge where the camera was. She could tell her first love was extremely inebriated, but knew from past experience that the drunker a man was, the more liable he was to spill his guts. 'Sit down, Tom. I'll get us a drink. Then you can tell me all about it.'

'Is that your mate playing Bowie? I can't listen to it. It reminds me of – ya know.'

Scratch put her head around Sam's door. 'You going out for a drink, Lee?'

'Er, yeah.'

'Cool. Turn the music off, will ya?'

Lee said a quick hello to Tommy, then left the flat.

Tommy drank a can of lager before explaining to Scratch what had happened earlier. He looked dishevelled, had stains on his white shirt and he smelled of sweat, brandy and the salt and vinegar you got on chip-shop chips.

Scratch couldn't help but feel sorry for Tommy. 'Will you go back to work with them?'

'Nah. Once that trust is gone, it's gone. I've got a few quid stashed away. I can live on that while I decide what I'm gonna do next.'

'You still gonna see Robbie?'

'No fucking point, is there? I'm not even related to him. That poor little mite's gonna be devastated when he learns the truth, and I'm going to make sure that bitch tells him. I don't want him to think I've deserted him.'

'You said the Darlings weren't to be messed with, Tommy. Say they come after you?'

'Tough shit. We got many secrets between us. They know I'll never grass as I'd only be dobbing myself in it. Jack ain't stupid. That's why he made me do stuff over the years.'

Scratch held Tommy's hand. 'God Tommy. What did Jack make you do?'

'Loads of stuff. Heavy shit.'

'Like what?'

'You know I'd tell you anything babe, but I also want to protect you. I don't want you to think badly of me.'

'Tommy Boyle.' Scratch took a deep breath. 'You are the love of my life, we've lived through all the shit the care homes could throw at us, we are in this together.'

'It's bad though, I can see now I was only a pawn in their game. Jack would've hated Donna getting up the spout by a Turk. Hence silly bollocks 'ere being forced to marry the slut. So yeah, I did what they needed me to do. I've also had to dismember bodies and all fucking sorts. I've shot a man in the head for them, I thought they were my fucking family Scratch. But I want out. All I want out of life now is an ordinary job, an ordinary life and you.'

When Tommy leaned in to kiss her, Scratch responded. They were getting somewhere at last.

'Can I stay here tonight? On the sofa, of course. I haven't got anywhere else to go.'

'Erm, yeah. But you'll have to leave when I go out in the morning. I've arranged to go shopping with the girls from work.'

'That's fine. Thanks.'

Scratch cracked open another couple of beers. 'So come on, spill the beans, why were you running round the East End killing every Tom, Dick and Harry?'

'It weren't only me. We all did it. And it wasn't anyone Scratch, you don't understand. It was the geezers who got on the wrong side of Jack, who threatened the family. It was all about the family.'

'Did Jack get his hands dirty too then, or just get you to chop 'em up?'

'No. He killed most of 'em, then we had to do the honours and get rid of the bodies.'

'Oh Tommy. What were their names?'

'You wouldn't know any of 'em. They were from the other side of the water.'

'How did you do it?'

'Burnt 'em, then buried 'em. Can we talk about something else? I'm depressed enough as it is.'

'Yeah, course. What do you want to talk about?'

Tommy locked eyes with Scratch. 'Us. Now I'm officially single, will you be my girl?'

Scratch smiled. 'Yes. But I will need to take things slowly.'

'I get that. I swear to you though, I would never let you down again. Biggest mistake of my life that was. You're not only my soulmate; you're my best friend too.'

Lee came home at eleven and went straight to bed. Tommy was understandably angry and as the evening entered the early hours he told Scratch that Ronnie was uncontrollable at times and had recently killed his one-time best pal because he'd started working for a rival firm. 'He was a good lad was Griff. He didn't fucking deserve to die. Got two little kiddies an' all. Bang out of order, Ronnie was.'

'It sounds as if getting away from that family is the best thing you can do, Tommy. Say they try to kill you for walking away though?'

Tommy shrugged. 'That's a chance I'll have to take. I'll go and see Jack later, tell him my decision. I'd rather part on good terms. For all their faults, that family took me in and treated me like one of their own.'

Scratch yawned. 'I'm going to have to go to bed now. You gonna be all right with that blanket and pillow?'

'Yeah, fine. Thanks again for letting me stay.'

'Night then, Tommy.'

'Where's me goodnight kiss?'

Having little choice, Scratch duly obliged.

Scratch lay in bed, her mind racing. She didn't want Tommy to go to prison, he didn't deserve to. Tomorrow, she would speak to Hunter. Perhaps if Tommy turned QE, gave evidence against the others, he could be put on the police protection programme. A new name, move miles away. A complete fresh start.

Lies and deceit have an awful way of rearing their ugly head when least expected and Scratch had no idea what was about to happen next. If she'd even had an inkling, she would have called Operation Sting off there and then.

CHAPTER TWENTY-NINE

Tommy had a bath and changed his clothes at Scratch's, then headed to a local café. As he pulled out his money to pay for the full English, Ray's phone number dropped on to the floor. 'Where's the nearest phone box, love?' he asked the woman behind the counter.

'Go out of here, do a right and it's on the corner. That's if it's working. It wasn't the other day.'

'Thanks. If my breakfast is ready before I'm back, just put it on that table,' he pointed. 'My newspaper and jacket are there.'

Tommy jogged down to the phone box. It was working, so he dialled the number. A woman answered and said the word 'Hospice'. 'Erm, can I speak to Ray Clarke, please?'

'May I ask who's calling?'

'Tommy. Tommy Boyle.'

'Hang on a tick.' The lady returned a minute or two later and told Tommy she was wheeling the phone into Ray's room.

'Tommy.'

'You all right, Ray?'

'Not at me finest, lad. That bastard cancer returned with a vengeance. There's nothing they can do but keep me comfortable now. That's why I'm holed up in here.'

'Oh, Ray. That's proper shit news, mate. I'm so sorry. I truly am.'

'I need to see you, Tommy. In person. It's extremely important.'

'OK. What's the address there?'

Ray rattled off the address and Tommy scribbled it down. 'I'm in Rainham right now mate, so I'm not that far from you. I've ordered some breakfast, I'll eat that, then I'll come straight over, if that's OK?'

'That'd be great. But don't tell anyone you're visiting me, Tommy. This is only between us.'

'I won't. Do you want me to bring anything in for you?'

'No, thanks. See you soon.'

Tommy was racking his brains as he replaced the receiver on the cradle. Whatever Ray wanted to say sounded very cloak-and-dagger.

Tommy couldn't believe the change in Ray. He'd lost loads of weight, was a shadow of his former self. His face was gaunt and his skin looked yellow. 'I brought you the *Racing Post*. I know how you like to study those nags,' Tommy grinned, chucking it on Ray's bed.

'Thanks, Tommy. Sit down on that chair, lad.'

Tommy sat down. Ray had a serious expression on his face which was rather worrying.

'I couldn't go to my grave without telling you the truth, son. You have every right to know, in my opinion.'

'Go on.'

Ray sighed. 'There is no easy way to say this. But when Scratch left Maylands, she was pregnant with your child.'

'No! Never! Nah, she couldn't have been. We're back together now. She would've told me. That's bollocks. It has to be.'

'It's true, Tommy. I swear to ya. Connie arranged for Scratch to go and live with her sister Caroline and her husband Keith. Caroline couldn't have children, had already adopted a little girl called Fiona many years ago. It was decided that Scratch would have the baby and Caroline and Keith would raise it as their own.' Ray handed Tommy a photograph. 'That's your son, Tommy. His name is Mikey.'

Tommy stared at the photo, dumbstruck. Only yesterday he'd found out Robbie wasn't his, and now this bombshell.

'Scratch isn't what she seems, Tommy. She's a police officer and has a fiancé. She's getting married this summer.'

Tommy shook his head repeatedly. 'Nah. She works in an office along the A13. Scratch ain't Old Bill.'

Ray handed Tommy another photo he'd pilfered out of Connie's drawer. It had been taken at Hendon at Scratch's passing-out parade.

Tommy leapt up and repeatedly head-butted the wall. 'The fucking bitch. What is she planning to do then, bang me up? I loved her, Ray. Really loved her. How could she do this to me?'

'I don't know what she's up to at present. But if

she's sniffing around you asking lots of questions, chances are it's a work thing. Her name is Kim Regan now.'

Tommy sank to his haunches and put his head in his hands. He'd told the bitch only last night that Ronnie had killed Griff, and he'd admitted to murdering a man and dismembering bodies. He'd even told her Jack had killed a couple of men. You could bet your bottom dollar that flat was wired for fucking sound and, thanks to his stupidity, he'd dobbed them all in it. He'd trusted Scratch. What a mug he was.

Ray handed Tommy a piece of paper. 'That's Caroline and Keith's address where Mikey lives. Be careful though, Keith's Old Bill an' all. Don't go round there like a bull in a china shop. Act sensibly and tell them you're the lad's father and you have every right to see him on occasions. Threaten them with court if they fail to agree.'

Tommy stared at the photo of his son once more. No wonder Connie had snatched a similar photo out of his hand once in her office. Mikey looked like him, was standing at the garden gate with a football under his arm. 'Thanks, Ray. For telling me.'

'You're welcome, lad. Every father has a right to know his son, and vice versa.'

'Does Scratch see him a lot?'

'I don't think so. Not since she moved out. Connie says very little to me now. She'll never speak to me again when she finds out I've told you. But what have I got to lose? I've only a few weeks to live anyway.'

Tommy hugged the man who had raised him for part of his life. 'I'll come and see you again soon.'

'I'd like that. You were always special to me, Tommy. Like the son I never had. Be lucky and happy.'

Tommy felt anything but lucky and happy, but nodded nevertheless.

'Good work, Regan,' Hunter grinned as he stepped inside his colleague's car.

'Thanks, Guv. I feel bad about Tommy, mind. He isn't like those Darlings. He's got a good heart deep down. Can't we strike a deal with him? Put him in witness protection?'

'You think he'll grass on 'em all?'

'I don't know. What I do know is he won't be able to handle a long stretch inside. It would kill him.'

'That's the way the cookie crumbles, unfortunately. Don't do the crime if you can't take the time. When is he back round at yours?'

'Monday. I'm cooking him dinner.'

'Very romantic. You need to get him to tell you where those bodies are buried, Regan. Once we find them, we can drag the whole Darling mob in.'

Scratch felt torn between the devil and the deep blue sea. The hatred she'd harboured so long had disappeared since spending time with Tommy again. If anything, she felt sorry for him. He was still that same mixed-up lad she'd fallen for at Maylands. Whereas, she had a job to do. That's what she needed to keep reminding herself. She was DS Regan, not bloody Scratch.

'Well?' Hunter grunted.

Scratch forced a smile. 'I'll do my very best, Guv.'

Tommy ordered a large brandy and sat in the corner of the pub. Scratch's betrayal had all but ripped his heart in two. Surely she knew the Darlings would kill him? Did she honestly hate him that much that she wanted to see him dead or doing life behind bars? Obviously, she fucking did.

A plan forming in his mind, Tommy finished his drink and rang his landline from the call box. Nobody answered, so he leapt in his car and headed towards South London.

Aware that Jack might have sent somebody to watch the house, Tommy parked around the corner, leapt over a couple of his neighbours' fences and entered his house via the back door.

Everything looked the same as it had the other day, so he guessed Donna and Robbie were staying with her new bloke. Good. The poor fucker was welcome to the no-good treacherous whore.

Tommy ran upstairs and took a sports bag out of the airing cupboard. He packed a black tracksuit, black trainers, a balaclava, jeans, a couple of shirts and some underwear. He then got a ladder, clambered into the loft and removed the fake panel. He put all the money in a separate bag, along with a big hunting knife, a gun, masking tape and some rope.

Tommy took the photos out of the bottom of his

wardrobe and sifted through them. He chose the ones he wanted, then packed the framed photo Scratch had given him when he left Maylands.

About to leave the house, Tommy spotted a letter on the table. The handwritten envelope read:

TOMMY
PLEASE READ
DANNY

Tommy put the letter in the bag, then grabbed a bottle of brandy out of the drinks cabinet.

Satisfied he had all that he required, Tommy left the house the same way he'd entered.

The traffic was a nightmare. Two lorries had collided on the A13, so by the time Tommy got to Barking it was late afternoon.

Finding a quiet spot, not too far from his destination, Tommy changed into his tracksuit and began plotting. Fish and chips were one of the fat bastard's weaknesses. When he'd lived with him, they'd have it every Friday or Saturday as a treat.

Tommy took a swig of brandy and turned the radio on. 'Can't Get Used to Losing You' was playing. Scratch reckoned she loved The Beat. Was that a lie too? Tommy thought back to their recent conversations. Every band he'd said he liked, she'd said she liked them too. Every topic they'd spoken about was probably riddled with fucking lies on her side, he fumed.

Remembering Danny's letter, Tommy ripped that open.

Dear Tom,

I can't tell you how sorry I am about Robbie, but please hear me out before ripping this up.

As you well know, my mum and dad adore you. They also don't believe in abortion. So when Donna got pregnant with Robbie, it was originally Dad's idea to pass the baby off as yours.

Donna was really into you at the time, so she agreed. Ronnie also thought it was for the best, as did Eugene and Mum.

I was the one who wasn't on board. I told Dad it was wrong, but he and Mum were genuinely thrilled that you would become part of our family.

Unfortunately, Donna's a law unto herself, but don't worry, we're gonna sort the situation out. We haven't found out who the geezer is yet. When we do, it'll be dealt with, trust me.

Robbie worships the ground you walk on. You're the only father he wants or needs.

Ring me mate, day or night. Let's chat man to man and sort this shit out. I know you must be in shock right now. But believe me Tom when I say the whole family is on your side. You've always been like a brother to me, and a son to Mum and Dad.

Love you, mate,
Danny

Tommy ripped the letter into small pieces and slung it out of the window. By trusting Scratch, he'd opened an enormous can of worms. There was no going back. Not now. Not ever.

It was a small block of flats, only three floors high. It was dark now, but Tommy put his hood up anyway and was pleased to find the communal door had no lock on it.

Fish and chips in his left hand, Tommy put his sports bag out of sight of the spy hole and rapped on the door of flat number 2. The pretty Irish barmaid had been rather loose-lipped when Tommy had enquired about the arsehole. 'He only comes in here in the daytime. His wife died a while back. He's a nice man, polite and friendly. I feel a bit sorry for him, to be truthful. He seems lonely,' she'd explained.

Tommy had no idea if the beast of a wife was actually brown bread. His guess would be she'd left the scumbag.

'Who is it?'

'Your nephew,' Tommy replied. The flat next door was playing reggae music at full blast, which was handy, considering the circumstances.

The door opened only as far as the security chain. 'Is that you, Tommy? What do you want? Are you alone?'

Tommy held up the bag of food. 'I bought us cod and chips, your favourite. I didn't forget the onions or wallies. Yeah, I'm alone. I thought we were long overdue a catch-up. I can't find any photos of my mum as a kid and was wondering if you had some I could borrow. I'll get 'em duplicated and give the originals back to you.'

Ian smiled. Even though he'd changed his name to

Tom Harris by deed poll, friends and family still referred to him as Ian. He undid the chain. 'What a lovely surprise. Come in. I'll put the kettle on. My, my, haven't you grown.' Ian was hopeful. Usually, if a lad came back in later life, they wanted more. That had actually happened to his friend Cecil only recently. 'Go in the front room, Tommy. Make yourself comfortable. Do you want a plate for your food?'

'No, thanks.' The front room reeked of cigarette smoke. There was a two-seater dining table squashed in one corner; two armchairs, a TV and an old radiogram were the only other furnishings; there was no room for anything else.

'Do you still take two sugars in your tea?'

Just hearing his voice again made Tommy want to chuck his guts up. Did he remember everything about him? The filthy piece of shit. 'Yes, please.'

As Ian walked into the lounge, Tommy leapt out from behind the door and pointed the gun at his head. Ian, stunned, dropped both mugs on the floor. The tea splashed everywhere.

'Move. Sit on that fucking chair,' Tommy spat, nudging Ian in the back with the gun.

Having never had a gun pointed at him before, Ian held his arms aloft like they did in films. 'What have I done wrong? I always thought the world of you, Tommy. You know that.'

Tommy held his breath as he tied his uncle to the chair. He still had that distinct smell about him. A mixture of sweat and cigarettes. It was a stench Tommy would never forget.

Tommy opened up his cod and chips. He was starving, hadn't eaten since this morning.

'What are you going to do to me?'

Tommy ignored the question and sat legs crossed on the floor opposite Ian. He'd wanted to come here and do this for years and now he'd finally plucked up the courage. He had nothing to lose now. He'd lost everything he'd ever cared about. 'What happened to Sandra?' he enquired, as he washed the last of his food down with brandy.

'We separated.' Ian was trying his best to keep calm. Surely Tommy wouldn't kill him? Not here in his own home.

'You hungry?' Tommy asked, unwrapping the other meal.

'I can't eat with my hands tied up.'

Tommy stood up. 'I'll feed it to ya. Open your mouth. Make sure you enjoy it an' all, seeing as it'll be your last meal.'

Suddenly terrified, Ian screamed 'Help!' but as soon as he opened his mouth, Tommy rammed a handful of chips inside. 'Why did you rename yourself Tom? After me, was it? You disgust me. People like you shouldn't be breathing the same air as normal people,' Tommy hissed.

Ian's face reddened as he tried to talk but instead started to choke. Tommy had black leather gloves on, so he prised Ian's mouth open once more and stuck a big lump of battered cod in, and the wally.

Realizing Ian might actually choke to death, Tommy

shoved the cheap plastic chair forward. It did the trick. Pieces of fish and the wally flew across the threadbare carpet. Ian gasped, spluttered, then managed to steady his breathing. 'Tommy, please don't hurt me. I beg you. I feed this little cat every day of the week. The neighbours have kicked her out because she's carrying a litter. She won't survive without me. I'm not a bad person, honestly I'm not.'

Used to people lying to him, Tommy guessed Ian had made up this story as he remembered he was an animal lover. 'Into bestiality an' all, are you? Ya fucking weirdo,' Tommy spat, as he placed the duct tape across the filthy bastard's mouth. He had heard enough. Never wanted to hear that voice again.

He took the hunting knife out of the bag, turned the chair over and hacked at the waistband of his uncle's stained grey pleated trousers. The material was cheap and thin, and ripped easily.

Ian began rolling his head from side to side as if he were having a fit. He was trying to plead through his nose, but sounded as if he was deaf and dumb.

Tommy looked away as he fiddled around in the filthy Y-fronts to find the cock that had haunted him for years. Thank God he had thick gloves on. No way would he have been able to touch the thing otherwise. When he grasped it, he turned to the quivering wreck whose eyes were now bulging out of his head. 'Won't be ruining any other kids' lives, will you, Uncle Ian,' he grinned as he began hacking at his member.

Ian lost consciousness almost immediately, which was a shame for Tommy. He'd wanted to taunt and torment him for much longer.

When the cock was fully dismembered, Tommy drank some more brandy before taking a good look at it. As a child, it had seemed enormous. But looking at it now, it was no bigger than a small pork sausage.

Tommy wasn't finished yet. He checked the perve's pulse: he still had one. He'd crapped himself as well, the filthy pig. Tommy untied Ian's hands and hacked at the right one. It took him a good five minutes to dismember it. The years of practice were coming in handy now. He could practically do this with his eyes closed. He started on the left.

Splattered in blood, Tommy checked the pulse again. This time there wasn't one.

Smiling, he took another sip of brandy and stood up. He gathered up the chip wrappers, the machete, the gun and packed his stuff away carefully. Not that he was bothered about getting caught. Not in the long run, anyway. But he had stuff to do first. People to meet.

Tommy swigged the last of his brandy, then put the bottle in his bag. He'd worn gloves throughout. There would be no fingerprints.

Picking up the dismembered penis, Tommy had great pleasure in ramming it down the back of his dead uncle's throat. 'Rot in hell, nonce-case.'

Checking around the flat for anything that might incriminate him, Tommy was satisfied there was nothing.

He picked up his bags, pulled up the hood of his track-suit and quietly let himself out of the flat.

He knew his next destination. He was off to Kent to meet his son.

CHAPTER THIRTY

Tommy showered, then got dressed in a white Fred Perry polo shirt, dark Levi jeans and beige desert boots.

Having made himself a cup of tea, Tommy put the TV on. After leaving Barking yesterday, he'd driven straight to Kent. He'd burned the tracksuit and trainers in a field, then booked into a hotel for the night. Rather than use his real name, he'd signed in as Tom Smith.

There was no mention on the news of his uncle's murder, which didn't surprise Tommy. He doubted Ian had many visitors and reckoned it might be a while before his body was found. Perhaps the Irish barmaid in the pub would alert the police? Or the postman would notice a bad smell drifting through the letterbox? Whatever the outcome, good riddance to bad rubbish. Tommy had no regrets.

Taking one last glance around to make sure he'd left nothing, Tommy turned off the TV and picked up both sports bags. He'd grab some breakfast on the way.

'Did you enjoy your stay, sir?' asked the receptionist.

'Yes, thanks.'

'Any plans for today? The weather is meant to be gorgeous.'

Tommy smiled. 'Yes. I'm going to pick my son up.'

Scratch arrived back at the flat around noon. 'Has Tommy called?' she asked Sam.

'No. Although I haven't been home long myself. No messages on the answerphone. How did your house-hunting go?'

'Yeah, good. We finally found somewhere we both like,' Scratch grinned. It had been lovely spending the day and night with Jay. They'd gone for a romantic evening meal. Then made love until the early hours of the morning.

'What's it like then? Which area?'

'Broxbourne, Hertfordshire. It's really nice, Sam. Three bedrooms, detached, decent-size garden and the kitchen's big. The neighbours seem nice too. Lovely couple next door – we got chatting to them.'

'Sounds perfect. You put a bid in?'

'Jay's going to tomorrow. Right, I need to get my head back into work mode. What shall we cook for Tommy?'

Sam chuckled. 'You mean what should *you* cook for Tommy. He's your guest and ex-lover, not mine.'

'Bitch.'

Having already read the *News of the World*, Tommy flicked through the *Sunday Mirror*. The news lately was always the same old, same old. Thatcher had called an election in June and politics bored Tommy rigid.

Another headline was about wheel clamps being introduced in London. Tommy turned to the sports pages. Manchester United were playing Brighton in the Cup Final next weekend, but Tommy had little interest in football any more. He had little interest in anything at all these days.

He sipped his can of Coke and watched the house for a while. Over three hours he'd been parked here now and in all that time he hadn't seen any movement.

It was a nice house in a nice street. Young children were playing outside. It had a safe feel to it. Obviously, Tommy had no idea whether Mikey was allowed out alone. But if he wasn't, he was determined to snatch the boy anyway. He'd threaten the parents with his gun if need be, or tie the bastards up. He was hoping he would get the kid alone though. That would give him more time with him.

When a couple who'd walked past earlier paused to stare suspiciously at him, Tommy debated whether to park elsewhere. He hadn't wanted to sit right outside the house Mikey lived in, so had parked up on a corner opposite. He'd had two sets of false registration plates made up after going back home the other day. One set was already on the car and he would swap with the other set after grabbing Mikey. That should throw the police or any nosy bastards off the scent.

Thinking back to the past, Tommy felt a pang in his heart. He could remember the first day Scratch had arrived at Maylands as though it were yesterday. How the hell could a shop-lifting skinhead end up joining the police force? It beggared belief. As for fitting him up, that hurt like fuck. He wasn't just anybody. He was the lad who'd poured his heart out to her, the one she'd lost her virginity to, the father of her child. She must have no conscience whatsoever.

Tommy sat bolt upright. His son was walking up the path with a football under his arm. The boy walked up next door's path and knocked on the door. Tommy doubted anyone was in, as he'd seen two adults and three boys go out earlier.

Getting no answer, Mikey walked down the road, alone. Tommy turned his ignition key. This was perfect.

'Hey, Mikey. Can I talk to you for a minute?'

Heading for the small park down the bottom of his road, Mikey spun around. 'I'm not allowed to talk to strangers.'

'But I'm not a stranger. Look, I'm a friend of Scratch's.' Tommy held out some photographs that Mikey warily took.

'We're not allowed to call her Scratch any more. We must call her Kim now.'

'Kim then,' Tommy smiled, thinking how well spoken the boy was. Looking at him up close melted Tommy's heart. Mikey very much resembled himself at the same age. 'What football team do you support?'

'Liverpool.'

'Don't tell me, let me guess. I bet Ian Rush is your favourite player.'

Mikey's eyes widened. 'How did you know that?'

'Because he's the best.'

'What team do you support?'

'Millwall.'

Mikey turned up his cute little nose that had a

sprinkling of freckles across it. 'Millwall aren't as good as Liverpool.'

Tommy chuckled. 'Yeah, I know.' He sank to his haunches. 'Will you come for a drive with me, Mikey? I promise I'm not going to hurt you.'

Mikey shook his head and fearfully stepped backwards. 'No. My dad says I'm never to get into a stranger's car.'

'But I'm no stranger. Keith isn't your real dad, Mikey. I am.'

As the terrified lad began to run, Tommy chased after him, lifted him off his feet, then bundled him inside the boot of his car.

'Whey-hey,' laughed Ronnie Darling as their thick new employee mixed up another cocktail. Dave actually wasn't a bad barman and the regulars had already taken to him. Naturally a few took the piss out of him, but that was to be expected.

Dumbo handed the cocktail to Ronnie. 'Taste that. Tell me what you think.'

Ronnie sipped the drink. 'Not bad. What we calling this one?' They had little demand for cocktails, but it was fun getting Dave at it.

'Dave's Delight,' grinned Dumbo.

'Dave, 'ere a minute,' shouted Danny. There was still no word from Tommy, even though he'd obviously picked up his letter as it was gone. Danny was worried. He could understand Tommy being upset, but he'd never gone AWOL before.

'What's up, Dan?'

'Do you know where Tommy's sister Linda lives?'

'Clacton.'

'Yeah, I know that. But whereabouts in Clacton?'

'By the seaside.'

Danny rolled his eyes. 'OK, thanks.'

Tommy pulled over by some garages and opened the boot. Mikey was understandably hysterical. It broke Tommy's heart to tie his son's ankles together, his hands behind his back, and lay him along the back seat like a small roll of carpet. He had little choice though, not until the lad calmed down. Tommy secured the seat belts, so Mikey couldn't fall off. 'I'm not gonna hurt you, boy. I promise you that faithfully.'

'I want my mum and dad. I have to be home for my dinner at three,' Mikey sobbed.

'I'll get you something to eat. No shouting now,' Tommy ordered as he quickly changed the registration plates.

Tommy kept a picnic blanket in the boot of his car, so chucked that over Mikey in case other motorists spotted the lad was tied up. Then he leapt back in the driver's seat and headed towards Clacton.

'What we going to watch now?' Scratch asked Sam. They'd just caught up with their favourite programme, *The Sweeney*.

'We've got *Minder* on tape. Let's watch that, eh?'

'OK. I don't know about you, but I can't be arsed going out for a pizza later. Shall we order a takeaway instead?'

'Fine by me.' It was rare the two of them got a day

off together where they could laze around watching TV and doing little else.

When the phone rang, Scratch leapt up to answer it. 'Hi, Tommy. You all right? I'm looking forward to tomorrow. Do you like spaghetti bolognaise?'

Tommy had turned off the A12 to find a phone box in a quiet spot. He didn't want to pull up in a service station with Mikey tied up in the back. 'You can stop with the bullshit, Kim Regan. I know everything.'

Scratch's face drained of colour. Her heart raced and her hands shook.

Sensing something was seriously wrong, Sam stared at her pal in horror. *What's up?* she mouthed.

Scratch was so taken aback, for once she couldn't think of anything to say.

'Right, listen to me and listen very carefully. You know our son who you forgot to tell me existed? Well, he's sitting in my car as we speak. Now, I don't intend to hurt him or run away with him. All I ask is to be allowed to spend a few days with him. You owe me that much at least.'

Scratch couldn't believe what was happening. How the hell had Tommy found out about Mikey? 'Where are you, Tommy? You can't just take Mikey. His parents will be beside themselves and you'll get into terrible trouble.'

'Very funny. As if you weren't trying to fit me up and put me inside anyway. Wired for sound was it, your flat? How could you do that to me? I trusted you, you slippery slag.'

'Tommy, I'm sorry. But it's not what you think. You're

not in any trouble, I promise. But you will be if you hold Mikey hostage. Tell me where you are and I'll meet you. We can chat properly then. I'll explain everything to you.'

'I'm calling the fucking shots 'ere, not you,' Tommy spat. 'Holding him hostage. Don't make me laugh. He's my fucking son. I've every right to get to know him.'

'You can't snatch him. He doesn't even know you.'

'Well, he fucking does now. I ain't lying to the lad. I've told him the truth. So best you keep his so-called parents off my back. Same goes for your pig colleagues. Because I'm telling ya now, Scratch, Rosie, Kim, or whatever your cunting name is today. If you send a search party out for me, I swear on my life, I will kill Mikey. A couple of days, perhaps three, that's all I'm asking for, then you can come and collect the lad. Stay by your phone. I'll be in touch again tomorrow – and don't even think about tracing my calls, as I meant every word I said. Understand?'

'Yes,' Kim mumbled. 'Tommy, can I—'

Scratch didn't get to finish her sentence. Tommy had already hung up.

By the time Tommy reached Clacton, Mikey had sobbed himself to sleep.

Tommy parked in a remote spot, not far from where his sister lived, and gently woke his son. He untied his hands and ankles and held him close to his chest. 'I rang Kim. She's going to let Caroline and Keith know where you are, so they won't be worried. Kim said it was all right for us to spend a couple of days together,

403

then she'll pick you up and take you back home,' he lied.

Mikey's lip trembled. 'I want my mummy.'

'Caroline isn't your mum, Mikey. Not your real mum. Kim is. Now I know this must be difficult for you to understand, but it's the truth. Kim is your real mum and I am your real dad.'

Six-year-old Mikey didn't understand, so said nothing.

'So, what do you fancy doing? Shall we get something to eat then go to the beach? We can play football and have a paddle in the sea. Then we can get an ice-cream. How does that sound?'

Not knowing what else to do, a confused Mikey nodded.

Kim paced up and down. Scratch was no more. She never wanted to hear or be referred to by her old nick-name again. She must've been mad even contemplating bringing Scratch back to life. Now she was paying the price. She had royally fucked up, that was for sure.

'You've got to tell Hunter,' Sam insisted.

'How many more times? No, Sam,' Kim snapped.

'Tell SO10 then.'

'No. We need to deal with this. Just you and I.'

'We can't. A young child has been snatched. We'll both lose our fucking jobs if we don't follow the correct procedure.' Sam was completely thrown by Kim's behaviour since Tommy's phone call.

'Pass me the phone. I need to speak to Caroline. If she wants Mikey back safe and sound, then she's gonna have to trust me.'

'I doubt she's gonna see it that way. Caroline's bound to lose the plot. What mother wouldn't?'

Kim picked up the plant pot with the hidden camera inside and slung it against the wall. If only she could turn the bloody clock back. 'Caroline isn't Mikey's real mum. I am.'

'You what!'

'It's true. Mikey's my son and Tommy is his father.'

'No way! Does Hunter know this?'

'No. Of course he doesn't. Nobody knows. Not even Jay.'

'For fuck's sake, Kim. You don't do things by halves, do you, girl?'

'Now you know why I didn't want to get involved in this case. But thanks to you opening your big trap, my son has been kidnapped. Well done, Sam. Fucking great work, love.'

Mikey munched on a hamburger as Tommy tried to clarify the situation by using language that a six-year-old might understand. The lad had stopped crying, thankfully, and seemed willing to listen.

'Do I have to call you Dad too?' Mikey enquired.

'Not if you don't want to. You can call me Tommy if you like. Kim, your real mum, was very young when she gave birth to you. She and I grew up in a children's home together and sort of became boyfriend and girlfriend,' Tommy explained, handing Mikey some more photos as proof.

'Is that Kim?' Mikey asked, pointing at the framed photo Scratch had given him when he left Maylands.

'Yeah. Not long after that was taken, Scratch – sorry, I mean Kim, fell pregnant with you. She never told me about you, Mikey. We lost contact. We were only teenagers ourselves. That's why she found you another mummy and daddy. Which means you're a special boy really. Not many lads have two mums and two dads who love 'em dearly.'

For the first time that day, Mikey actually smiled. 'Can I have an ice-cream now, please?'

Tommy held his son's hand and stood up. 'You can have whatever you want, boy.'

'Well?' Sam asked Kim.

'Caroline was understandably hysterical. But she's agreed to let me deal with the situation.'

'And Keith?'

'Playing golf, thank God. She isn't going to tell him. As far as Keith is concerned, Mikey is staying with me for a few days.'

'Surely Keith will smell a rat? Shouldn't Mikey be at school tomorrow?'

'Caroline is going to tell him I've taken Mikey to a holiday camp with you. Keith knows I get little time off work and I rarely get to spend time with Mikey. What can he say?'

Sam shrugged. She'd heard Kim admit they'd been working undercover to Caroline and she was worried. She'd grafted so hard to get as far as she had in the police force. No way was she risking losing her job. 'I'm sorry, mate. But you're on your own with this one. Best you tell Hunter that Tommy has blown out dinner tomorrow and I'm staying at my girlfriend's until we hear from him again. As much as I love you, I can't be ballsing up my career. It means too much to me.'

Kim was disappointed. 'Cheers, pal. This is all your fault and now you want to bail out on me. Go on then, fuck off.'

'Thirty-one, thirty-two, thirty-three,' Tommy counted. Mikey was doing keepy-uppies with his football and Tommy was stunned by how good he was for his age. Robbie couldn't do them and he and Mikey were close in age.

'Ah, dropped it,' Mikey said, as he finally lost control of the ball.

Tommy clapped wildly. 'That was brilliant, boy. You're gonna be a professional footballer one day.'

'Do you think I might be as good as Ian Rush?'

'Better. You've either got it or you haven't – and you've definitely got it.'

Mikey planted himself next to Tommy on the sand. He had been truly scared earlier when he was tied up, but he didn't feel scared any more. His other dad Keith didn't like football. He only liked cricket and golf. 'Can we get a fishing net and go fishing in the sea?'

Tommy smiled. 'Of course we can. But first we're gonna ring Linda. She's your real auntie.'

Mikey didn't reply. He was confused again now.

After Sam left the flat, Kim paged Hunter to inform him she thought she had food poisoning as she was spewing up and shitting through the eye of a needle. Hunter only understood things that were written or said in his own foul language.

When Hunter messaged back immediately, asking if Tommy was still coming around tomorrow, Kim said she'd have to postpone the date until she felt better. She then rang Jay from the landline and told him the same lie. This was her problem and she knew Tommy better than anybody. But it broke her heart to think how upset and confused Mikey must be right now. Once again she cursed herself for agreeing to be part of Operation Sting in the first place.

Where had Tommy taken Mikey? she wondered. He'd mentioned his sister lived in Clacton. Had he headed there? All she could do was wait by the phone as he'd told her to. Surely Tommy wouldn't hurt his own son? But he obviously wasn't thinking straight to have abducted Mikey in the first place. Very few people knew the truth about Mikey, so how Tommy had found out was a mystery.

As requested, Linda met Tommy alone at the beach. Tommy briefly explained about Robbie and the fallout with the Darlings, then pointed at the small lad who was paddling with a fishing net. 'That's my real son, Mikey.'

Linda looked at her brother as though he'd lost the plot. 'Whatever are you talking about?'

Tommy told Linda what Ray had told him. 'Look, I need your help, Sis. I need somewhere quiet to stay for a couple of nights. Paul's family got any unoccupied caravans at present?' Linda had told him Paul's family owned half a dozen caravans in a local holiday park and rented them out.

'The family one is free. Paul and I stayed there the weekend.'

'Perfect. You got the key?'

Linda fished in her handbag, handed him the key and scribbled down the address. 'I'll have to tell Paul you're staying there.'

'I'd rather you didn't tell anyone. Just in case the Old Bill come sniffing around. Or the Darlings.'

'Oh God! You're not in any trouble, are you, Tommy?'

'A bit. Nothing I can't handle though. Anyone asks if you've seen me, you just say no. I got a sports bag in the car I want you to take home with you. Hide it somewhere and don't open it until I tell you to. Don't worry, there's nothing dodgy inside.'

At that moment, Mikey skipped towards them to show off what he'd caught.

Linda gasped as she saw the lad up close for the first time. 'It's like looking at you as a little boy, Tommy.' She smiled. 'Hello, Mikey. I'm your Auntie Linda.'

Mikey eyed Linda suspiciously. 'Hello. I've not got to be tied up again, have I?'

Linda turned to Tommy. 'Please tell me you haven't abducted him?'

'It's all fine. His mum knows where he is, I swear. Do you know of a shop around here that sells Subbuteo? Mikey's never played it and I know he's gonna love it. I need a fishing tackle shop too. He's never been proper fishing, I wanna take him tomorrow.'

'I can show you where to get both. But I do hope you know what you're doing, Tommy.'

'I do. Trust me. Come on, let's go back to the car, pick up the stuff I need. Then I'll drop you near home.'

On the journey back from the shops, Tommy spoke glowingly about the past and how happy they'd once been as kids.

Tommy's words were heartfelt. Some memories were vivid to Linda, others less clear, and as usual when she remembered their loving, kind, beautiful mother and Hazel, Linda felt tearful. How she wished her mother and Hazel would be there for her wedding. Paul's mum had offered to accompany her dress shopping, but it wasn't the same.

Tommy parked up on the corner of the Pipers' road. Mikey was fast asleep on the back seat. Tommy took his sister in his arms and hugged her tightly. 'Thanks for today. You're the best sister I could ever have wished for. Never forget how much I love you, will you?'

'Why are you being so soppy?'

Tommy pushed Linda's fringe out of her eyes. 'I'm not. Can't a brother tell his sister he loves her? Look at you, all grown up and engaged to be married. Mum would be so very proud of you.'

'She'd be proud of you too,' Linda insisted.

Tommy took the sports bag out of the boot. 'It's locked. I forgot the key. I'll pop it in the post to you.'

'OK. Take care, Tommy. When you've finished with the caravan, just put the keys in an envelope and post 'em through the Pipers' letterbox.'

'Will do.'

'I love you too ya know.'

Tommy smiled. 'I might need another favour soon. If I do, I'll be in touch.'

If only Linda had known at that point what Tommy had planned, she would have moved heaven and earth to stop him.

CHAPTER THIRTY-ONE

Let me tell you something for free. In this world, everything is smoke and mirrors. Trust no one, don't even trust what you see, I learnt that the hard way.

I recall going through every emotion I could think of as I watched Mikey sleep beside me for the first time that night. We were so alike. He had my long eyelashes, sprinkling of freckles across his nose and he also slept curled up in a foetal position as I tended to, even now.

But I felt so bitter. I barely knew the lad, had been forced to kidnap him to spend time with him. I couldn't stop thinking about Robbie either. I loved that lad, couldn't turn my feelings off like a tap, even though he wasn't my flesh and blood.

I remember tossing and turning all night. My mind was all over the place. I was more angry with Scratch than Donna. I had never really trusted Donna, but Scratch I had with my life. I'd even disclosed my biggest secrets to her. What a callous bitch she'd turned out to be. The snake of all snakes.

Well, nobody fucks with me and gets away with it.

I'm Tommy Darling and I call the shots. Literally.

'You all right?' Sam asked, as she unexpectedly returned to the flat the following morning.

'Yes,' Kim lied. She was anything but all right. She'd

barely slept a wink last night and had spent the entire morning staring at the phone, willing it to ring. Every hour that passed seemed like a day. The waiting was truly unbearable.

'Well, I'm glad you're OK, 'cause I'm bloody well not. I barely slept last night for worrying. I'm truly sorry, mate, for everything. It's all my fault.'

'No. It isn't. I should have told Hunter where to shove Operation Sting, not let him bully me into it. To top it all, I had Caroline on the phone first thing. She reckons if Mikey isn't home by tomorrow evening, then she'll have to tell Keith the truth.'

'Brilliant.' Sam rolled her eyes. 'That'll be the end of both our careers then.'

'No. It won't. No matter what happens, this isn't your fault. If the shit hits the fan, you pretend you knew nothing, OK?'

'Thanks, mate. I couldn't leave you in the lurch you know.'

'I appreciate that. I'm sure things will work out OK, mind. I've already planned a story to fob Hunter off.'

'What?'

Kim began to explain.

'Look, Tommy. Look.'

Aware that his son had got a bite, Tommy stood behind him and showed him how to reel the fish in.

Mikey's eyes widened. 'I don't want to eat it.'

Tommy chuckled. The fish was a small carp. 'Don't worry. We'll be putting it back in the water, so it can swim free again. I'll get you some proper fish and chips later from a shop.'

'I don't like fish.'

Tommy put his arm around his son's shoulders and felt sad as the lad wriggled away from him. He knew everything about the boy he'd raised who wasn't his. Yet knew so little about Mikey. 'What do you like then? Do you like chips?'

'Yes. When am I going home to my real mum and dad?'

Tommy sighed. The lad had perked up yesterday afternoon, but hadn't enjoyed the Subbuteo so much in the evening. Tommy had also heard the boy crying early this morning, which had made him feel terrible. 'We'll ring your mum later, Mikey. Your real mum, Kim, will pick you up tomorrow and take you back to your other mum and dad. But in the meantime, just try and enjoy the time you're spending with me. I am your real father and after tomorrow, you won't be seeing me again.'

'Why?'

'It's complicated. So what do you want to do now? Do you want to go back to the beach? Or the amusement arcade?'

'Both,' Mikey shouted.

Tommy stood up. 'Let's make a move then. We'll leave the fishing rods here for someone else to use.'

Jack Darling shook hands with his bent detective inspector pal. 'Not a word to anyone about this, obviously,' Jack said, handing over an envelope that contained five grand.

The DI tapped his nose. 'Mum's the word. You let me know if you need anything else, Jack.'

'Will do. Thanks, Lenny.'

'Well?' asked Ronnie when his father reappeared at the bar. Donna had phoned his mum yesterday to let her know she was OK. 'I'm living in Essex and I'm not coming back to South London. I have never been happier and you should be happy for me,' Donna had stated.

Suzie had demanded to speak with Robbie and the lad had let slip John had a red Ferrari and a swimming pool. Jack had got straight on the phone to his contact and requested a list of everyone in Essex who owned a red Ferrari.

Jack laid the list out across the bar. There was only one owner called John, but he was sixty-two, so it couldn't be him.

'I bet it's this geezer,' Ronnie said, pointing to the name Josh Palmer. He was the youngest name on the list and lived in Loughton.

'Perhaps Robbie got his name wrong, Dad. Or knowing how devious Donna is, she's told Robbie his name's John to throw us off the scent,' added Danny.

'A possibility,' Jack replied. 'It's quiet in here. Who wants to drive over to Loughton and have a sniff around?'

'I will,' Danny replied. He still hadn't heard a word from Tommy, and Churchill's wasn't the same without his pal. He could do with a change of scenery.

'I'll go with Dan,' Ronnie said.

'Where you off to? Anywhere nice?' asked Dave the barman.

'Bit of business. I expect you to have a cocktail waiting for me on my return. I want a Drippy Dave,' Ronnie chuckled.

Dumbo grinned. 'OK. I will make you one.'

Tommy dialled the number. Scratch answered immediately, as he'd known she would. 'Meet me tomorrow morning at eleven at the Kings Arms in Clacton. It's along the Colchester Road. I want us to spend the day together as a family and I want you to tell Mikey the truth about everything. Then you can take him home with you in the evening, OK?'

Kim was surprised. Tommy no longer sounded angry with her. 'I'll be there. Is Mikey OK?'

'Yes. He's fine. Be warned, Kim, you bring back-up with you, you'll never see Mikey again – and I mean that. You've messed with my head enough as it is. I'm armed and I will shoot him if I have to.'

Kim felt a shiver run down her spine. 'I promise I'll come alone. I have a lot of explaining to do, I know that much.'

'You can say that a-fucking-gain. Tomorrow, eleven, Kings Arms. See you there.'

'What did he say?' Sam asked.

Kim repeated the conversation.

'You aren't going alone, not if he's got a gun. I'm coming with you.'

'No, Sam. Nobody knows Tommy like I do. If I go against his wishes, he might do something stupid. You know nothing about all this, remember? If you're with me, you're implicated. I want you to wait here and I'll call you if and when I can throughout the day.'

'I hope you know what you're doing, Kim. My big worry is he takes you and Mikey hostage. How d'ya know that isn't his plan?'

'Tommy's not that silly. I'll be fine, honest I will. Now I must ring Caroline and let her know what's happening.'

'Your pager's going off again.'

Kim had called Hunter earlier. Apparently a new witness had come forward with information regarding the Dean Griffiths murder. Hunter was debating whether to drag Ronnie in for questioning now, or wait until he had a tad more on him.

'Who is it?' Sam asked.

'My snout. He's got some info. Wants me to call him urgently on some number. Probably a call box. I'll ring him from here.'

'All happening today, isn't it?'

'You could say that.'

Mikey was excited. Tommy had informed him that Kim would be spending the day with them tomorrow and then he'd be going home in the evening to his other parents. He was still confused over the whole shebang, but didn't feel as though he was in danger now. Tommy had been nice to him all day, had even bought him some clean clothes, underwear, and a Liverpool football kit. 'Can I wear my new kit tomorrow, Tommy?'

'Yeah. We'll get up early and go over the shower blocks. You wanna be nice and clean when you go home. Your hair needs a wash too.'

'Are we going to play Subbuteo again tonight?'

'No. I thought we'd just chat. I've got some photos to show you of your real family. Wanna see 'em now?'

Mikey nodded.

'Go and wash your hands at the sink then. You've got chip grease all over them.'

Mikey did as he was told and plonked himself on the sofa next to Tommy. 'Who's that?'

'That, Mikey, is your real nan. She was my mum and she was such a beautiful lady. She would have loved you.'

'What's her name?'

'Valerie.'

'Will I meet her one day?'

'Unfortunately, you can't. She died years ago, in a car accident.'

Mikey's lip trembled. One of his nans lived in Australia and his other dad's mum was dead too.

'What's the matter?'

'I wanted to have a nan. My friends all have one. Some have two.'

'Oh well. You've got two mums. You can't beat that.'

Mikey jumped up and down. 'And two dads.'

Tommy smiled and for the first time felt guilty over what he planned to do.

'Bingo!' Ronnie Darling grinned, as he leaned against the bar in Churchill's.

Jack raised his eyebrows. 'You found Donna?'

'Yep. First attempt. Her car was parked on Josh Palmer's drive. Massive fucking gaff he's got. No wonder her head's been turned. She always was a materialistic one, our Donna.'

'Did you see the bloke?' asked Jack.

'No. His car weren't there. So unless he parks it in the garage, they must've been out,' explained Danny.

'So what now?' Jack asked.

'Gotta go, ain't he? That's the only way we're going to get Tommy back on the firm and he's going to get Robbie back,' Ronnie replied.

Danny and Eugene glanced at each other. Both were thinking the same thing. They hoped it would be a drive-by shooting, as neither were keen on chopping bodies up. It turned their guts.

Sipping from a bottle of brandy, Tommy listened to the news on yet another radio station. Still no mention of the dead pervert. He imagined something like that would make national news. Not often a bloke was found with both hands chopped off and his cock rammed down the back of his throat. He probably hadn't been found yet was Tommy's guess.

Mikey was fast asleep in bed. Overall, it had been an enjoyable day. But Mikey was ready to go home, Tommy could sense that.

Putting his favourite cassette on, the one with all the music that reminded him of Maylands, Tommy took the pad and pen out of his sports bag. No matter what had happened, he could never hate Danny Darling. He deserved an explanation, at least.

Afterwards, Tommy would plan his outfit for

tomorrow. Just because he felt like shit on the inside, he still wanted to look good on the outside. 'People judge you by what you wear, Tommy. The smarter you look, the further you'll go in life,' his dear mother used to say – and she was right.

CHAPTER THIRTY-TWO

'You sure you don't want me to come with you?' Sam asked the following morning.

'No.'

'What about if I follow you in my car?'

'Nope. This is my problem and I'll sort it. I need to talk to Tommy privately anyway.'

'Please take your pager then.'

'No, Sam. After what I've done to him, Tommy is bound to be hurt, upset and wary. As I said to you last night, I reckon he'll frisk me for a wire and who's to say he won't lose his rag if he finds my pager. I'm not risking it. Getting Mikey home safe and sound is my priority.'

Sam hugged her mate. 'Good luck. I'll stay here all day and wait for you to call me.'

'Thanks. See you tonight.'

As Kim left the flat, she hadn't a clue she wouldn't be returning that night.

Tommy wasn't unduly worried Scratch would turn up at the Kings Arms with an entourage. She might be a lot of things, but she certainly wasn't stupid. Nevertheless, he drove up and down the Colchester Road numerous times to check there were no suspicious vehicles parked up. He knew what to look for. Jack Darling had shown him the ropes, after all. Fake gas/electric men, road workers or a pretend accident were always enough to put you on red alert. Common set-ups that the Old Bill used.

Having spotted nothing untoward, Tommy plotted himself up in the Kings Arms' car park. Scratch would have a fit when she realized Mikey wasn't with him. Good. She deserved a taste of her own medicine.

Her little car, that the filth had obviously supplied her with, pulled into the car park at 10.45. Tommy gesticulated for her to get into his car.

Kim was immediately alarmed. 'Where is Mikey?'

'Like I can trust you to not set me up. You wired?'

Kim took off her thin jacket and lifted up her T-shirt. 'No. I swear.'

'I'll be searching you thoroughly before I believe that. Tip out your handbag,' Tommy barked.

Kim did as he asked. As always, he'd made an effort to look smart, was dressed in a tan Lacoste T-shirt, beige tight-fitting cords and his trademark desert boots. He also reeked of expensive aftershave, but that didn't hide the stale alcohol fumes on his breath.

'You OK?' Tommy asked.

Kim nodded. He seemed very calm, considering. Too calm in fact.

'We'll drive to a quiet spot. No need to worry. I won't be touching you up or anything like that. You're getting married soon, aren't you? To Jay?'

The sarcasm in his voice was clear. 'Yes,' Kim mumbled. Wondering if she should have taken Sam's advice and told Hunter everything, Kim said a silent prayer as she put her seat belt on. She had the distinct feeling she was in for a bumpy ride.

Kim glanced at Tommy. She'd expected a barrage of questions, not silence. He'd said nothing as he searched her and only mentioned the journey and the weather since.

Tommy bumped his car up a kerb and put the handbrake on. 'Wait here while I get Mikey. Don't you dare get out of the car, OK?' He'd left his son at the Pipers' house. Catherine was looking after him.

'I won't. I promise.'

'I want today to be the perfect family day out, even though we're not the perfect family. For Mikey's sake.'

'Yes. Fine by me.' Kim nervously chewed at her fingernails as Tommy disappeared out of sight. She couldn't believe he knew absolutely everything about her, found it unnerving. Connie must have told someone. That was the only explanation she could think of.

Minutes later, relief flooded through Kim's veins as she spotted Mikey holding Tommy's hand, skipping happily by his side.

'Kim!' Mikey squealed, overjoyed to see a familiar face.

'That's not just Kim. That's your mummy. Your real mummy. Tell him the truth. Now!' Tommy ordered.

'I will. Can I sit in the back with him?'

'Yeah. Course you can.'

Kim wrapped her arms around Mikey and gently began to explain the situation. Caroline and Keith weren't going to be happy, but she couldn't worry about them. The cat was already out of the bag.

'Do I have to call you Mum too?' Mikey asked innocently. He still couldn't quite grasp what he was being told. He already had a mum and dad.

'No, darling. You can call me Kim.'

'Or Scratch, or Rosie,' Tommy said sarcastically.

'We're having a picnic,' Mikey informed Kim.

'Are we?'

'Yes. Tommy and me made the sandwiches.'

Kim smiled. Mikey seemed quite chirpy, all things considered.

Tommy drove towards the beach. The kids were at school, so it shouldn't be too busy.

'Wow! What's all this?' Kim exclaimed, when Tommy opened the boot of the car. There was a large cool-box, a big picnic hamper and numerous carrier bags.

'I meant what I said. I want us to have a proper family day out. Not too much to ask, is it?'

'No. Of course not.'

'Good. Can you grab those bags? I'll carry the rest of the stuff. Mikey, take your bucket and spade, and your football.'

Tommy waited until Mikey was out of earshot, then showed Kim the inside of his Harrington jacket. 'Any funny business and I meant what I said.'

Kim's mouth dried up as she stared at the gun. She'd thought he was bluffing.

* * *

Her intense police training had taught Kim how to deal with difficult situations and although this wasn't like anything she'd tackled in the past, she was determined to allow Tommy to lead the conversation.

Surprisingly, Tommy had yet to bring up her working for the police. He asked numerous questions about Mikey and her pregnancy instead.

'I cried for days you know, when you didn't turn up. I already knew I was pregnant by then. Connie had made me do a test the week before. She'd tried to warn me not to hold out much hope of you keeping your promise. Your letters had dwindled by then. But I was so young and naïve, I honestly thought you would come back for me.'

'I'm sorry. I truly am,' Tommy said earnestly.

'There's no need to apologize, Tommy. I did hate you for years, but that was my immaturity. Since we've met up again, I can see things from your point of view too. You'd only just turned sixteen, for Christ's sake. What lad wouldn't be flattered by a pretty older girl offering it to him on a plate?'

'So, did you hand Mikey straight over to Caroline after the birth?'

'Yes, but don't fucking judge me. It was the toughest decision of my life, I was totally on my own thanks to you! And I was so young back then, I could barely look after myself, let alone raise a child alone.'

Tommy cracked open two lagers and handed one to Scratch. 'Do Caroline and Keith look after Mikey well?'

'Yes. They're great parents. I've never regretted my decision to allow them to raise Mikey as their own. He's got a great life, wants for nothing.'

'Good. I'm pleased.' Tommy glanced at his son, who was busy building sand castles with a dainty little girl. He seemed much more at ease now Scratch had arrived. 'You hungry yet?'

'I'm a bit peckish.'

Tommy lifted the lid off the hamper. 'Tuck in. I bought far too much of everything. But as I said, I wanted today to be special. I brought *our* cassette too.' Tommy pressed the play button. 'Where and who does this remind you of?'

The song in question was the Bee Gees' 'Stayin' Alive'. 'The Catholic club disco. Benny had all the moves to this, didn't he? I remember Dumbo trying to copy them. He was useless,' Kim laughed. 'Did he start the new job you got him, by the way?'

'No idea. Not been back there.'

Kim delved inside the hamper. There was a whole cooked chicken, a hock of ham, a large lump of cheese, numerous pickles, tomatoes, a large Spanish onion, pork pies and three crusty French sticks.

'The butter's in the cool-box and there's paper plates, plastic knives and forks and serviettes in that blue carrier bag,' Tommy explained.

Kim was perplexed. Tommy had gone to so much effort. But why? It seemed odd that he was being so calm and nice to her, having found out the truth. Something wasn't right, that was for sure.

* * *

'God, I'm stuffed. I can't eat any more. Thanks for going to all that trouble, Tommy. It was a lovely picnic.' Kim hadn't been at all hungry, but had forced herself to eat as much as she could.

'You're welcome. I should've brought some suntan lotion. Mikey's shoulders are red, look. He's got my skin colouring, hasn't he?'

'He most certainly has. Tommy, can we talk about the case I'm working on? I've got some important things to say to you.'

'Not now. We'll talk about that later. Tell me about Jay. What's he like? Where did you meet him?'

Kim gulped at the lager. This was awkward. 'I met Jay at Hendon, when I did my police training. We started dating a few months after we left there and have been together ever since. Apart from you, Jay's the only bloke, ya know, I've ever got close to. By choice, that is.'

'Does he treat you well?'

'Yes. He does. Jay's a good person.'

'I'm pleased for you. What about Mikey, is Jay good with him?'

'Yes. But he doesn't know Mikey is my son.'

'*Our* son, I think you mean. Why not? Because you're embarrassed of me?'

'Of course not. I made a promise to Caroline and Keith not to tell anybody. We decided when Mikey was born not to tell him the truth either, at least until he was old enough to truly understand. Fiona, Caroline and Keith's daughter, doesn't yet know she was adopted, and she's fifteen. They are going to wait until after she finishes her studies to tell her.'

'Fair enough.'

'Can I ask you a question, Tommy?'

'Fire away.'

'How did you find out about Mikey and all the other stuff?'

Tommy began cracking his knuckles. 'None of your fucking business, I'm afraid.'

'Sorry.'

'I'm hot now. Let's dump the picnic basket and take a walk down the pier. Then afterwards, I wanna take you somewhere, show you something.'

Kim glanced at her watch. It was 3 p.m. already. 'I promised I would take Mikey back to his adopted mum tonight, Tom. She knows he's with you and is obviously worried sick. If I don't return him, she's threatened to tell Keith everything, and I really don't want you getting into serious trouble. Keith will involve the police.'

'Bit late for that, isn't it?' Tommy spat. 'Call her from a phone box. Let Mikey chat to her; tell her what a good time he's having. Then tell her you're gonna be back later. As I keep telling ya, I want this day to be special.'

Tommy squeezed inside the phone box with Scratch and Mikey. There had been a time when he would have trusted her with his life, but not any more. She rang Caroline, insisted all was fine, then put Mikey on the phone to her.

'Why is Mummy crying?' Mikey enquired, as he handed the phone back to Kim, who then explained to Caroline that she would be bringing Mikey home later

428

than they'd arranged. 'No, everything is fine, honest. Tommy made us all a lovely picnic. Delicious, it was. And he's bought Mikey his first Liverpool kit. Looks so cute in it, Caroline. We're off to the amusement arcades now.'

'She all right?' Tommy asked, when the call ended.

'Fine. Do you mind if I give Lee a ring now?'

'Lee who?'

'Lee, who you met. My flatmate. I need to let her know I'm OK, that's all. We're best friends and she is the only other one I have told about Mikey being with you.'

'Got a secret code, have ya? You say a certain word or sentence, then she sends the entire police force down 'ere.'

'No, Tommy. Honest. I wouldn't do that.'

'Can't trust you though, can I? So I will word what you are going to say to Lee. That all right with you?'

'Yes. That's fine.'

The pier was fun. Mikey loved the amusements. Kim couldn't stop winning on a one-armed bandit and Tommy showed his son how to play Space Invaders. To onlookers, they must have resembled a happy family enjoying a day out at the seaside, but Kim felt edgy. Why wouldn't Tommy discuss the case she'd been working on? And what did he want to show her? She couldn't stop thinking about the gun he was carrying. Did he plan on using it? Or was it just a ploy to scare her?

'Ready to make a move?' Tommy asked.

Kim nodded and at the same time said another silent prayer for herself and Mikey. Instinct told her something was amiss. She only wished she knew what.

Tommy drove for about forty minutes, then started heading uphill on what looked like a cliff. Kim glanced at Mikey on the back seat. He was soundo, away with the fairies, thank God. 'Where are we going, Tommy? Only I haven't seen another car for the past ten minutes.'

Tommy squeezed her hand. 'It's OK. Don't panic. I found this place a while back when I brought Robbie here. It's stunning. I won't hurt you, I swear. Unlike yourself, I'm not a deceitful person. If I say you can take the boy home tonight, I truly mean it.'

For the first time in years, Kim hated herself. She'd become so focused on her career and impressing those male chauvinists, Hunter and Banksy, she'd let slip what truly mattered in life. 'Tommy, I'm so sorry. I thought I hated you and I was wrong. You will always be my first love. I could never hate you.'

Tommy glanced at her and smiled. 'Glad to hear it.'

They drove for another ten minutes, then Tommy stopped the car. Kim had no idea what area they were in, but they were certainly a quarter of the way up a cliff.

'Where we going now?' Kim asked, her voice betraying her concern. She was suddenly feeling out of her depth.

'Nowhere. Leave Mikey sleeping. I'm gonna get the picnic blanket and booze out of the boot and we're gonna watch the sun go down together. It's a lovely sight from up here. Truly spectacular. We can talk here too. No earwiggers. But first I got something to tell you.'

Kim sat opposite Tommy on the tartan blanket and gratefully accepted another can of lager. 'What do you want to tell me?'

'My uncle – you know, the pervert – I killed him the other day.'

Kim looked into Tommy's eyes and immediately knew he was telling the truth. At that point, she realized that it was her betrayal that had tipped him over the edge. He'd been haunted for years, just as she had been. Only an abused child would understand that. You learn to live with what happened to you, but you can never stop the nightmares. This was all her fault.

'Oh my God! Tommy, no. Where?'

'Inside his flat. He asked for it. He ruined my life. He must have ruined the lives of other lads too. People like him don't deserve to breathe the same air as people such as you and I.'

'Has he been found, do you know?'

Tommy shrugged. 'Not heard nothing on the news and I'm sure they would have covered the story. I cut both his hands off and his cock. I rammed that down the back of the dirty bastard's throat.'

Kim flinched. 'Have you told anybody else this? Did anyone see you enter or leave his flat?'

'No and no. I wore gloves, so there won't be any fingerprints. I've no regrets at all. I should have killed him years ago.'

'Why are you telling me this, Tommy?'

'Because you were the only one I ever really spoke

to about him. I even admitted to you last week that he raped me. That's because I thought I could trust you, Scratch. More fool me. Wrong again,' Tommy laughed.

'Tommy, I'm so sorry. About everything. But I swear, I won't say anything about this. I don't intend getting you into any trouble,' Scratch said. She meant it too. Sod the consequences. She would take this secret to the grave with her.

Tommy smirked. 'You're having a laugh, ain't ya? You've already handed me a death sentence.'

'Meaning?'

'The Darlings. I take it that flat I visited you in was wired? Shame I was so pissed. Unusual for me to shoot my mouth off like that. So, how did this little operation of yours come about? It all falls into place now. You approaching Dumbo to arrange a Maylands reunion. I fucking trusted you, Scratch. Whereas you must have sensed I was some desperate mug and you were right.'

'You're not desperate. Neither are you a mug, Tommy. You've just been misguided in life.'

'What do you mean by that?'

Kim explained that Ronnie and Jack Darling in particular had been on the police's wanted list for some time. 'As you well know, Tommy, a lot of men have gone missing during that time. Those men's families are desperate for some kind of closure. If we could unearth their remains, it would bring peace to many people.'

Tommy took the lid off a bottle of brandy. 'Want some?'

'No. I've got a long drive later. Listen, Tommy, if you were to give evidence against the Darlings, you'd be free to start a new life. You said when we went to Southend for the day that you'd like to have a normal job now and live by the sea. I could sort you out a new identity and you can start afresh. This is your chance to make something of your life.'

'I might be a lot of things, Scratch, but I'm no fucking grass.'

'Not even after the way the Darlings all lied to you about Robbie? They're not your true friends, Tommy.'

'Danny is. He's always been there for me. So have the others. They gave me a home and a job. Yes, they were wrong to deceive me about Robbie. But other than that, they've been like family to me. No way would I ever testify against them. They're more fucking loyal than you.'

'Ronnie's a danger to society. We know it was him who killed Dean Griffiths. How many more lives is he going to ruin, eh?'

'Ronnie can't help the way he is. He suffered a brain injury. So, was that flat wired?'

Kim stared at her hands. 'Yes, and there was a hidden camera. The only night I switched it on was when you turned up drunk after you found out about Robbie. I'm so sorry.'

Tommy put his head in his hands. 'Brilliant! I take it you'll be using that in court?'

'I honestly can't answer that question. That won't be my decision. But, Tommy, I seriously want to help you. I'm offering you a lifeline here. You'll have a new passport, driving licence, a whole new identity. The police will protect you. I will make damn sure of that.'

'So if I was to take you up on your kind offer, would I get to see Mikey regularly?' Tommy asked, his voice laden with sarcasm.

'Unfortunately not. If you sign up to the witness protection programme, you cannot keep in touch with anyone from your previous life. You literally start again as a different person.'

'Yep! That's what I thought. So why the fuck would I even consider that shit?'

'Because you're brave, a survivor, and like myself, you have little family to leave behind. This would be a walk in the park for you after what you've already been through in life. Trust me on that one.'

Tommy forced a smile. As if he would ever trust her again. 'Tell me, how did you feel when we kissed again after all those years? I bet you wanted to vomit, didn't ya?'

Kim was rather taken aback. 'No. Of course not. Nobody forgets their first love, do they?'

'Really? So you enjoyed it then?'

Kim felt uneasy. Tommy was swigging the brandy like water and she could sense a change in his earlier pleasant mood. 'It's been a lovely day, but we'll really need to leave soon. Mikey's shattered, bless him.'

'You'll leave when I say you'll fucking leave,' Tommy hissed. 'You haven't answered all my questions yet.'

'What do you want to know?'

'I can't get my head around what possessed you to set me up like that. Yes, I left you in the lurch. But bloody hell, Scratch. I could never have done something like this to you if the boot was on the other foot. Never

434

in a million years. We were such good pals, had an unbreakable bond – or so I thought. When Smiffy died, we were inseparable. And what about the good times at Maylands, all the laughs we had? Did those days mean that little to you?'

Kim's eyes welled up. 'Our days at Maylands were great. But after you left, everything went horribly wrong for me and I chose only to remember the bad times. Ever since my passing-out parade, I've thrown myself into my career. So much so, I barely see Mikey or Jay lately. Women aren't treated equally in the police force, we have to work harder than the men to prove our worth. When this operation was set up, I wanted to prove all the doubters wrong. But I was the one in the wrong. Never should I have got involved or involved you. I cannot apologize enough. You don't deserve it.'

'Thanks. But it's a bit late now. Did you ever love me?'

'Yes. I was besotted with you and at one point wanted to spend the rest of my life with you.'

'What about now?'

'You'll always have a special place in my heart, Tommy.'

'Trying to get me shot or banged up isn't exactly the term of endearment I was hoping for when we met up again. Does Connie know about this operation? What's it called, by the way? Operation ex-boyfriend?'

'Connie doesn't know. Very few people do. I can't tell you the name of it.'

'Jack has Old Bill on his payroll. I bet he's already been tipped off. He'll find out what it's called.'

'Who has Jack got on his payroll?'

'None of your fucking business who. Pass me that black bag. There's another bottle of brandy in it.' Tommy pressed play on the cassette recorder. 'Reminds me of you, this.' The song was Janet Kay's 'Silly Games'.

'Tommy, I really must make a move now. Caroline will be pulling her hair out if I leave it any later.'

'No. Not until we've watched the sun go down. You can ring Caroline from a call box later.'

'You can't drive the car, Tommy. You've had too much to drink.'

'I wasn't intending to. You can drive it.' Tommy held his hands out. 'Dance with me. Our song's on next.'

Kim felt she had no option other than to take his hand. Earlier she'd felt she had the situation under control. But now she was cursing herself. She was in the middle of nowhere with her drunken, armed ex-boyfriend. A known villain who was in a volatile state of mind and reluctant to let her leave.

Tommy held her close to him as he crooned the words to Johnny Nash's 'Tears on My Pillow.'

Kim stared at his jacket. It was lying on the ground. The gun was in the inside pocket. She felt scared now. If Tommy could kill his uncle in the way he had, what might he do to her or Mikey? His head obviously wasn't in a very good place. Killing someone was one thing. But chopping their hands and penis off was psychotic behaviour.

As the song neared the end, Kim knew this might be the only chance to get away. She lifted her knee and caught Tommy hard in the groin. He fell to the ground, but grabbed Kim's legs and tripped her up too. 'You fucking bitch. You've spoiled my day now,' he hissed as he snatched at his jacket and took the gun out of the pocket.

'Tommy, I'm sorry. But I need to take Mikey home. Please can we leave now?'

'When I say so,' Tommy shouted. 'I enjoyed today. Now you've ruined everything. You're not the person you once was. You're a fucking snake. What was you gonna do? Take the car and leave me here to die?'

'No. I would have come back for you.'

'Liar!'

Having been woken by the conversation, Mikey got out of the car. 'What's happening?'

'Get back inside the car, son. Now!' Tommy ordered.

Mikey's eyes widened as he clocked the gun. 'Can we go home now, Kim? Please. I miss my other mum and dad.'

'Just do as Tommy says, Mikey,' Kim urged.

'Daddy not Tommy. I'm his fucking father,' Tommy spat.

Kim crouched next to Mikey. 'Everything is going to be OK. Please get back inside the car though and stay there.'

'OK,' Mikey wept.

Tommy downed more brandy before pointing the gun at Scratch's chest. 'Walk. Behind the car. Then keep walking,' he ordered.

Scratch had been in numerous dangerous situations in the past, but never like this.

She thought of Jay, the lovely new home they'd had a bid accepted on, and their wedding plans. She'd been an absolute idiot to come here alone today; if the wedding she'd so been looking forward to didn't take place, she had only herself to blame. 'You're frightening me now, Tommy. Please don't hurt me. For Mikey's sake.'

'Shut up and take your clothes off.'

'No, Tommy. Please God no. You're not thinking straight. We were raped ourselves. You know how that feels.'

'Do as I fucking say,' Tommy yelled. She was right. He wasn't thinking straight. He was seething and very inebriated. He'd had to get sozzled to carry out his plan.

Tears ran down Kim's cheeks as she undressed.

Tommy paced up and down, gun in hand. 'That was our song as well. You chose to knee me in the bollocks while *our* song was playing. How low can you go? After everything you've already done to me. I can't believe you was going to drive off and leave me here to die.'

'I'm so sorry.'

'Too late for fucking sorries. Take your bra and knickers off an' all.'

As he sauntered towards her, Kim cowered. 'Move over there,' Tommy pointed, before scooping her clothes and underwear under his left arm.

Kim hugged her knees to her breasts to try to cover her nakedness. Memories of her awful childhood came flooding back. She recalled sitting in this position as a kid when her mother rented her out.

'Feel exposed, do ya?'

Kim stifled a sob. She was sure Mikey was looking out of the back window of the car. 'Yes. Of course I do.'

'Now you knows how it feels then, don'tcha? That's what you've done to me. You exposed me and at the same time ruined what little life and friendship I had. I can never look the Darlings in the eyes again, not after being duped by you. Does that make you feel good about yourself, does it?'

'No. It doesn't.'

'Put your clothes back on.'

'What!'

'You heard. You didn't honestly think I would rape you, did you? As if! God, it's as if you don't know me at all. Unlike you, Scratch, I have never forgotten my roots. You've changed, for the worse. A part of me will always love the old you, that cheeky, ballsy skinhead bird who used to make me laugh. But I don't like the new you. In fact, I despise the new you.'

'I'm so sorry, Tommy. Please forgive me,' Scratch wept.

'And so you bastard well should be. You'll be living with the guilt of what you've done for the rest of your life. There won't be a day goes by you don't think of me. You mark my words. I'll make sure of it.'

Gun in hand, Tommy walked over to the car. He took a bag out of the boot and urged Mikey and Scratch to sit on the picnic blanket with him. 'This is for you,' Tommy said, handing the bag to Mikey. 'There's twenty grand in there for you to spend any way you want when you get to seventeen. I know it sounds a long way off, but I'm hoping it might pay for your driving lessons and your first car.'

'Oh, Tommy. You don't have to do that. Honestly,' Kim said.

Tommy glared at her. 'Oh yes I do. I'm his fucking father. Your mum, this one here, the real one,' he pointed at Kim, 'will open up a trust fund and put it in there for you.'

'Thank you,' Mikey said. He didn't have a clue what twenty grand was and couldn't stop staring at the gun. It was freaking him out.

'Did you enjoy spending time with your dad?' Tommy asked, ruffling his lad's hair.

Mikey flinched, which saddened Tommy. 'Yes. Apart from when I was tied up.'

'I'm sorry about that. Really sorry. Can I have a hug?'

'Give your dad a hug,' Kim urged, trying to work out where this was leading.

Tommy hugged the lad, then turned to Kim. 'When he's old enough to understand, I want you to tell him all about our days at Maylands and the great fun we once had. Can you do that for me?'

'Yes, Tommy. I dare say when he's older you can tell him yourself, mind.'

'No. That won't be possible. I never want him to forget me though.'

'He won't. I'll make sure of it.'

'Right, you get back in the car, Mikey. It was a pleasure spending time with you. Oh, and when you make it as a professional footballer, don't you forget to tell the press who your real dad was. Your mum will take you home in a bit. I just need to have a quick chat with her first.'

'OK. Bye, Daddy.'

Tommy's face lit up. The boy had called him 'Daddy'. He got to his feet. 'Walk over this way. Away from the car. Look at that sunset – ace, isn't it?'

'Yes. It's lovely,' Kim replied.

Tommy sat by the edge of the cliff and urged Scratch to do the same. 'Want some?' he asked, offering her the brandy.

Her nerves shattered, Kim gratefully drank some then handed the bottle back to Tommy. She didn't like heights. Especially as she was sitting near the edge of a cliff with a drunken deranged man who had a gun.

'Do you know what, Scratch, I don't reckon I was ever destined to be happy. I know you had it tough as a kid too. But at least you've come through the other side, found some serenity in your life. That's never happened to me. Not properly, anyway.'

Kim had to think of her words carefully. She couldn't afford to say the wrong thing. 'Now you and Donna have split, I'm sure you'll find love, Tommy. The woman of your dreams must be out there somewhere.'

'Don't fucking patronize me,' Tommy hissed. 'All through my life I've been let down by people. People who I mainly trusted. I loved my mum and sisters. It was great when it was the four of us. But then he'd come home from the oil rigs and start knocking seven bells out of my mum again.'

'It must have been awful for you.'

'Shut up and fucking listen for once, will ya? I don't want your sympathy, that's for sure.'

'Sorry.'

Tommy swigged at the brandy. 'As if me mum dying wasn't bad enough, Hazel then gets done for murder and taken away. Then I get told my dad isn't my dad and that horrible old cunt Nanny Noreen isn't my real nan. So I get pushed out my own home and sent to live with that fucking pervert. I didn't even get a proper chance to say goodbye to Rex before that bastard Alexander took him to the knacker's yard. I loved that dog. Broke my heart in two, that did.'

Tears streaming down his face, Tommy paused and angrily wiped them away. 'When I moved to South London, I hated it there at first. Until I met Danny Darling. His family were so kind to me, used to invite me round for dinner. They really took me under their wing. Ronnie was great back then too. A real dude. We used to go over Millwall on a Saturday. Good times. Suzie Darling was like another mum to me. Jack was in prison in those days. Apart from living with that pair of weirdos, I was actually moving on. Until one night when that stinking bitch Auntie Sandra decided to stay over her sister's house. That's the night that dirty fat cunt made me share a bath with him. I knew it was wrong, but tried to convince myself he was harmless. But of course he weren't. Worse then happened, so I ends up stabbing him and was carted off to Maylands on my thirteenth birthday. What a way to celebrate becoming a teenager, eh?'

Kim said nothing. But was crying now herself. Operation Sting could go fuck itself. She wanted no more part of it. Poor Tommy.

'Do you remember that night Smiffy died? When we ran towards the fairground and his lifeless body was all screwed up on the grass.'

'Yes. I had nightmares over that for a long time afterwards.'

'Well, I still have those nightmares. I dread going to sleep at nights. If it's not Smiffy, I see my uncle looming towards me.'

'I feel your pain. I still dream of that monster my mum rented me out to. These things never truly leave you, do they?'

He was in his own world now, lost in the story of his past. 'Then, after Smiffy died, we became closer. I never truly forgave Benny and Dumbo for running away that night, ya know. I get that they were scared, but I would never have left him alone with those evil shitbags. But you helped me grieve. We got through his death together. You were my rock back then.'

'You were mine too,' Kim said in earnest.

Tommy turned to her. 'Marrying Donna was one of the biggest mistakes of my life, ya know. I could never open up to her like I could you.'

'I can't open up to Jay like I did to you either.'

'Really?' Tommy was pleased by this snippet of information.

'As I've already told you, he doesn't know Mikey is mine. I have never told him I was abused either. Or how bad my mother actually was.'

'Why?'

Kim shrugged. 'He comes from such a normal family.

His parents and his sister are lovely. It's embarrassing, isn't it? Only people who have been victims of abuse can truly understand.'

'When Robbie was born, Donna wasn't exactly the maternal type,' Tommy continued. 'It was me who'd get up in the night and see to him when he cried or was ill. Soon cracks began to appear in our marriage. Donna would go out with her mate a lot, which didn't bother me at all. But if I fancied a night out, there'd be murders. She'd hunt me down wherever I was, sometimes with the baby, and accuse me of all sorts. I never cheated on her, not once. You and Donna are the only two women I've ever slept with. We plodded on for the sake of Robbie. Jack and Suzie were against us separating, sort of forced us to stay together. But then finally Donna found a bloke and you came back on the scene. For the first time in years, I felt a spring in my step, a reason other than Robbie to get up in the morning. I was so excited to be seeing you again. Obviously, I was distraught to find out Robbie wasn't mine. But do you know what, a part of me thought: That's my ticket to get away from Donna. I have no ties now. You and I can be together.'

Tears pouring down his cheeks, Tommy drank the last of the brandy. 'But that wasn't to be, was it, DS Regan? You stitched me up like a fucking kipper and threw me to the wolves.'

'Tommy, I can't tell you how bad I feel. I am willing to resign. I'll tell my boss everything. I will do anything to sort this shit out. I swear on Mikey's life.'

Tommy stood up. 'It's too late for that. I'm done

with this shit life of mine. One thing I'm grateful to that old cow Nanny Noreen for is her religious ramblings. Don't get me wrong, I doubt she's gone to heaven. She'll be in hell. She used to teach us about the most Holy Trinity, the Virgin Mary and the angels. Her actual words were "Heaven is the ultimate end and fulfilment of the deepest human longings, the state of supreme, definitive happiness."'

'No, Tommy. Noooo,' Kim screamed, as her first love placed the gun against his right temple.

Tommy chucked an envelope towards Scratch and smiled. He wasn't scared. He wanted the misery to end. 'I told you you'd think about me every day from now on, didn't I? You were the final nail in my coffin, Scratch. Please don't let our son ever forget me. Be happy in life.'

A second later, Tommy pulled the trigger . . .

CHAPTER THIRTY-THREE

Nine Months Later

Danny Darling glanced at his watch: 5 a.m. Too early to get up, but he knew he wouldn't get back to sleep. Today would've been Tommy's twenty-second birthday. It was also the day he was going to get revenge for the pal whom he missed so much.

Danny glanced across the room. Eugene was still asleep, snoring like a pig, as per usual. They were meant to be on holiday in Spain, had been until yesterday morning. They'd travelled back with dodgy passports, would be returning to Spain this evening, providing all went well.

He could remember receiving *that* letter as though it were yesterday. It had chilled him to the bone. Sobbed on his knees in front of his wife and kids, he had. He'd read it numerous times until it was imprinted in his brain, before burning it.

Dear Danny,
*   Please don't be angry with me, but by the time you read this I will have taken my own life.*

I know this must be a shock for you, but my head's been all over the place and I've had enough, mate.

There's stuff you don't know about what my uncle did to me. I could never really talk about it, except to Scratch. She'd been through similar shit. But you'll be happy to know that, earlier this week, he got his comeuppance. I went round his flat, cut his cock off first, then his hands. Then I rammed the nonce's cock down his fucking fat throat.

Obviously, finding out Robbie wasn't mine broke my heart. But, believe it or not, a day later I found out I did have a son after all. Scratch conceived him while at Maylands and then proceeded to sort of give him away. He has a decent life though. Lives in a nice house, goes to a good school. Mikey, his name is. I snatched him the other day so I could spend some time with him before I did the deed. He's lying next to me fast asleep as I write this.

Which brings me to Scratch. Turns out she's Old Bill and she gave me a tip-off. The filth want the Darlings behind bars big time. For fuck's sake get rid of anything untoward and tell your dad, Ronnie and Eugene to do the same. I think you're all being watched. I also think they know who killed Griff. Be on your guard and please don't contact or hurt Scratch. She came up trumps in the end, even though she lied to me at first.

Please DO NOT mention Scratch's involvement or Mikey's existence to your dad or brothers. You *know how hot-headed Ronnie can be. I plan to put a bullet in my head in front of Scratch tomorrow. That's enough payback for her deceiving me. The press won't print jack-shit. Bound to cover up my death if the filth are after your family.*

I'm rambling now, so best I say my goodbyes. I need to write to my sister next.

There's fifty grand in a sports bag in the loft at my old house, mate. Can you put twenty grand in a trust fund for Robbie, please? For when he turns seventeen. Twenty is for you. Treat Lucy and kids out of it. And the other ten grand, give to Maylands.

Please thank your mum, dad and brothers for all they've done for me, Dan. Apart from my mum and sisters, you were the only family I ever had. As for Donna, she can rot in hell for all I care.

Thanks for all the memories and the good times, bro.

Until we meet again.

Tommy.

PS Burn this letter as soon as you've read it.

Feeling an overwhelming surge of sadness, Danny's expression hardened.

He owed it to Tommy to stay strong. Today of all days.

Paul Markham hovered awkwardly by the lounge door. 'Are you sure you're OK, Lin? Silly question, I know.

But I will ring my dad and blow work out if you need me to come with you.'

Linda Boyle dabbed her eyes with a tissue. 'No. You finish the job, Paul. I'll be fine, honest. Alice offered to come with me too. But this is something I need to do alone.'

'OK then. If you're sure. I'll be back by lunchtime. Love you.'

'Love you too.'

Linda waited until she heard Paul drive off before taking the large framed photo out of the bubble-wrap. She'd only picked it up yesterday. Thanks to Tommy leaving her a sports bag full of cash, twenty thousand pounds in total, tomorrow she would be having the wedding of her dreams.

It had been Paul's idea that they bring their wedding forward and it was her idea that they marry the day after what would have been her brother's twenty-second birthday. It seemed a fitting tribute somehow and Linda knew it was what Tommy would have wanted.

To say Linda had been hysterical when the police knocked on her door that awful evening to break the tragic news was putting it mildly. Her screams of anguish must have been heard half a mile away. Then she'd had the horrendous task of identifying her brother's body, a task she would never get over. She was confused, upset, shell-shocked, heartbroken. Why?

But when her vile uncle's body was discovered shortly afterwards, it soon became apparent why. The story made the national newspapers. Now her brother was seen as a hero. There'd been no photos of Scratch, but she'd given her name as Scratch and stuck up for Tommy. She'd told the press that she and Tommy were friends at Maylands and he'd confided in her about the abuse he'd received at the hands of his uncle. The fact Tommy had once stabbed him only backed up those claims. PC Kendall had even given an interview to the *Sun* and *News of the World*. He'd been their local bobby when they'd lived in Barking. He'd spoken so highly of Tommy and had told reporters what had happened. The case had never got to court apparently because, after his house was set on fire, Ian had disappeared into thin air. He'd even since changed his name to Tom. How sick was that?

The thought of what her brother must have gone through sickened Linda to the stomach. She could understand why Tommy had never told her though. He'd have known how upset she would be. But that was Tommy all over. So thoughtful and kind. She was glad her wonderful brother had killed that monster in the way he had. Good riddance to bad rubbish.

'Bye, Caroline. See you on Sunday,' Mikey waved.

Kim gave Caroline a hug then held her son's hand. 'Did you write Daddy's card?'

'Yes. It's in my bag.'

'Good boy.'

It had been tough for Mikey since that fateful night. He'd witnessed everything, had seen Tommy lying on that cliff with half his head blown off. Understandably, he'd been traumatized, and so had she. They'd both had counselling and Mikey seemed to be coping better now. He still had nightmares, wet the bed on occasions, but his school work had improved and he seemed happier in himself.

Keith had been furious when he'd found out what had happened, had been arsey with her for ages afterwards, but they were on good terms again now. Caroline had been far more understanding. She was so relieved to have Mikey home in one piece.

Kim had told Keith the same story she'd told Hunter, Jay and the press. Tommy had killed himself after murdering the uncle who'd abused him as a child. Only Sam knew the truth. She'd had to tell someone. Tommy had most certainly killed himself over her deceit. How she loathed herself for what she'd done, would never truly forgive herself. It would haunt her until her dying day.

Hunter had been thrilled with what they'd found at the address Tommy had thrown at her before he'd shot himself. The scene inside Ian Taylor's flat was as gory as they come. It was like something out of the TV series *Hammer House of Horror*. A real coup for Hunter, as the press were all over it like a rash. He even appeared on *Thames News*, which boosted his already massive ego no end.

The next development Hunter was anything but thrilled about. Kim had told him her cover had been blown, but had lied and said she'd only found out on the evening Tommy had died. Sam had agreed to back her up and both would take their lies to their grave with them.

Kim now reckoned that Tommy had somehow

warned the Darlings the police were after them, as Ronnie had done a moonlight flit and had not been seen since. Hunter had been ready to haul him in for the murder of Dean Griffiths as a new witness had come forward. So he was well pissed off. He had no idea where Ronnie was now. Abroad, most probably. But he hadn't used a passport to leave the country. Not his own anyway.

Hunter had given her a massive telling off over meeting Tommy alone, but she'd told him Tommy had threatened to harm Mikey if she involved the police and had now admitted to all and sundry that Mikey was her and Tommy's son. Hunter had reprimanded her for not disclosing that information too and Banksy was still dining out on the story. She didn't care though. Mikey called her 'Mummy' now and she was extremely proud of that. Her son still lived with Caroline and Keith, but spent weekends and school holidays with her. They were very close and Jay doted on Mikey too.

Her wedding had still gone ahead as planned last August. Sam had given her away. Sam looked like a bloke anyway. Jay's sister and two of his cousins were bridesmaids, along with Fiona, and the friends they'd made at Hendon all attended. Billy, Jay's best mate from school, was best man.

It was a lovely day, but tinged with sadness as Kim was still struggling to deal with her part in Tommy's death. The two-week honeymoon in Barbados was what the doctor ordered and it was while she was there Kim made some important decisions regarding her future.

She'd been off work with stress anyway and after everything that had happened, she knew her heart was no longer in the police force. What was the point when the likes of Jack Darling had bent cops on his payroll? She'd worked with some great officers herself, but corruption was rife elsewhere.

If Tommy's death had taught her one thing, it was to put family and friends above work. She'd fallen pregnant within two months of getting hitched, much to Jay's delight, and they were eagerly awaiting the birth of their first child together. The baby was due in July.

Linda, Tommy's sister, had organized and arranged his funeral. Kim hadn't attended, could not bring herself to go. She often visited Tommy's grave with Mikey though. He was buried in a cemetery in Upminster.

'You OK, Mummy?' asked Mikey.

'Yes, darling.' Only yesterday Kim had informed Hunter she wouldn't be returning to her job. She'd lost out on raising one child and wasn't going to make the same mistake twice. No longer was she Kim Regan, she was now Kim Delaney. A pregnant housewife who lived in Broxbourne. She enjoyed the normality, having the dinner ready when Jay came home from work, and listening to what crimes he'd dealt with that day.

Perhaps one day she'd take another career path. But she wouldn't rejoin the police. Not ever.

'The lads ring from Spain today?' Jack Darling asked his dense but likeable barman.

'No. Nobody's rung.'

'Probably on the piss with Ronnie,' Jack grinned. His eldest son was holed up in the Costa Brava and wouldn't be returning to England anytime soon. Jack had heard through the grapevine that if Ronnie were to land on British soil he would be arrested for the murder of Dean Griffiths.

Jack opened his newspaper. He missed his eldest son, but life was calmer without Ronnie around. He didn't fancy doing another lump inside at his age, so had scaled the business down. He still had the gaming machines, but had knocked the pub protection on the head. That wasn't worth the grief any more. Jack had made his money over the years, so lived off the proceeds of Churchill's now, and his doorman business. That was doing OK.

Tommy's death had been a shock to Jack. In his opinion, suicide was a coward's way out. Young Robbie had been devastated, as were Suzie and Danny. A waste of a young life. Why hadn't Tommy spoken to him? He would have sorted that uncle of his out for the lad.

Donna seemed happier now. She and Robbie lived in Loughton with Josh Palmer and their baby girl, Charlee. Danny and Eugene refused to have anything to do with Donna or Josh, but himself and Suzie did. Josh had a few bob, was pleasant enough and owned a nice gaff. Sometimes in life you had to let bygones be bygones.

Dumbo turned the radio on and sang along to Frankie Goes to Hollywood's 'Relax'. He was very relaxed himself these days. In fact, life was grand.

* * *

Having watched his prey for the past few weeks, Danny knew that after lunch on a Friday, Josh Palmer left his used-car lot to do his banking.

The bank was on a busy high street, so Josh parked over the road in a car park situated behind the shops.

Dressed in black leathers and a black crash helmet, Danny sat in wait. Eugene was parked a couple of miles away in a white van. The van had a ramp, so the plan was to drive the bike up it, then they'd be on their way.

At 2.20 p.m., Josh's red Ferrari pulled into the car park. Danny fired numerous bullets at the car and saw blood splatter everywhere inside.

Hearing a woman scream, Danny put his hand on the throttle and sped off down the road. Tommy was like a brother to him. Always.

'Hello.'

Kim looked around.

'Mikey!' the woman squealed. 'Do you remember me? I'm your auntie.'

Mikey clenched his mum's leg and nodded.

'Hi. I take it you're Tommy's sister. I'm Scratch.' Kim felt awkward as she held out her right hand.

'I'm Linda. It's lovely to finally meet you. Thank you so much for all the lovely things you said about my brother to the press. He was such a beautiful, kind person. I miss him dreadfully.'

'I can imagine. So sorry for your loss,' Kim replied. There had been no mention in the press of her being a policewoman and she doubted Tommy had told Linda. Her demeanour was too nice.

'Mikey looks so much like Tommy did at his age, you know. He's got the same eyes, nose and smile. Do you come here to visit Tommy often? I've seen fresh flowers here before and wondered who'd left them.'

'Twice a month we visit Daddy, don't we?' Kim said to her son.

'Yes. Do you remember when we went to the beach, Auntie Linda?'

'I do. How could I forget? It was the only time I got to meet you. Have you come far?' Linda asked Scratch.

'We've come from Kent, but I live in Broxbourne. I'm married now and expecting my second child in August.'

'Congratulations. I'm getting married tomorrow,' Linda announced. 'Tommy was meant to be giving me away. It certainly won't be the same without him, but I've set him a place at the table next to me. I've had a photo of him blown up.'

Thinking that was a bit morbid, Kim said, 'How lovely. I'm sure he'll be looking down on you with pride.'

'I do hope so. Erm, please don't think I've got a cheek, but would it be possible for us to stay in touch? Mikey is all I have left of Tommy, so I'd love to see him from time to time. That's if you're OK about it – and if Mikey wants to see me.'

'You'd like to keep in touch with Auntie Linda, wouldn't you, Mikey?' Kim asked.

Mikey nodded.

'Let's swap numbers,' Kim suggested.

'Brilliant. Tommy used to talk about you all the time to me, Scratch. He really did love you, you know.'

'I thought the world of him too. He was my first love.'

'I know and I am so glad you were with him that night. I would have hated him to be all alone. Did you have any inkling what he was going to do? Did he seem depressed or anything?'

'No. He seemed fine,' Kim lied. 'We'd best get going now. Give your Auntie Linda a kiss, Mikey.'

Linda handed Kim her phone number and vice versa. 'I'm so pleased I bumped into you today. I'm sure it's fate. I reckon Tommy organized this. I know he'd want us to be friends,' Linda said.

'Yes. He would.'

'It's weird, you know. How Tommy's become a bit of a national hero. My friends are always telling me to turn the radio or TV on as Tommy is being spoken about. I even saw some graffiti on a wall the other day – *RIP Tommy Darling. Top lad*, it said.'

'I've seen lots of graffiti too mentioning Tommy. I think people see him as some have-a-go hero who took the law into his own hands. He'll never be forgotten,' Kim replied.

'No. Then again, Tommy always did do things in style.' Linda walked towards Kim and hugged her tightly. 'Thank you so much. For being there for Tommy and everything you've done for him since.'

Kim walked away in tears. Tommy's words to her on that fateful evening were, 'You'll be living with the guilt of what you've done for the rest of your life. There won't be a day goes by when you don't think of me. You mark my words. I'll make sure of it.'

By Christ, Tommy was right.

* * *

Six hours after shooting Josh Palmer, Danny and Eugene were back in Ronnie's apartment in Spain washing the temporary blond dye off their hair. They'd looked a right pair of plonkers at the airport, dressed in Hawaiian shirts and bright shorts. Like Bros gone wrong.

Ronnie liked his new life in the Costa Brava. There were a fair few familiar faces on the run out here. Old school villains from South London. Ronnie knew a couple of them and had made friends with their friends. Life was laid-back out here, not a hundred miles an hour like it was in London.

Danny had been in bits over Tommy and was adamant that finding out Robbie wasn't his was what had actually tipped him over the edge. Ronnie had to agree. He also agreed to help Danny get revenge.

Ronnie had sorted the fake passports and arranged for a pal of his, Les Sharp, to pick the lads up from the airport and put them up at his for the night. Sharpy had also sorted the van and motorbike. Both of which had now been disposed of.

'Hurry up. I'm starving. The restaurant's booked for half nine and we need to ring Dad first,' Ronnie said. They'd kept their father in the dark about today's shenanigans. Ronnie knew he wouldn't approve. Neither would their mother.

The restaurant was a ten-minute walk away, the phone box situated nearby. The three men gathered inside. 'I'll do the talking,' Danny said.

Danny dialled Churchill's number. Drippy Dave answered. 'Is me dad there? It's Danny,' he said, holding the phone slightly away from his ear so his brothers could listen in.

'No, Dan. Something terrible happened. Something really terrible. Your dad's with your mum and sister. I'm running the bar.'

Danny winked at Ronnie and Eugene. 'What's happened then? Donna all right, is she?'

'There was a shooting, Dan. Someone on a motorbike shot your sister's boyfriend.'

'Fuck! No way! When? Where?'

'I dunno. But he got rushed off to hospital in an ambulance.'

Danny glanced nervously at his brothers. 'So, is he dead or alive?'

'Alive. But you ain't heard the worst part yet. Robbie was sitting next to him in the car and a bullet went straight through his head.'

Shocked to the core, Danny dropped the phone.

Danny, Ronnie and Eugene were back at the apartment. There was an eerie silence, only broken by the odd slurp of brandy.

Deciding to take charge, Ronnie paced up and down his newly laid floor tiles. 'Right, what has happened is sickening. But, it was an accident. There's nothing we can do now to change it. So we're gonna have to live with it, OK?'

'I'm gonna have to live with it, you mean. You two ain't done fuck all,' Danny wept. Robbie had never been in the car previously when Josh did his bank run. Why wasn't the lad at school?

'You can't blame yourself, Dan,' Eugene reiterated. 'It's just one of those things.'

Tears running down his cheeks, Danny glared at his youngest brother. He had Ronnie's genes, was hard as nails, but he didn't have the excuse of being one sandwich short of a picnic. Only he had cried. 'Your car breaking down or your fridge blowing up is just one of those things. Not blasting your nephew's brains out.'

'In fairness, we never saw that much of Robbie, did we? And if Donna would have stayed with Josh, we'd have probably never seen him again,' Ronnie replied. He was trying to think of things to make Danny feel better.

'Today was for Tommy and I've cocked everything up,' Danny insisted.

'Nah, you ain't,' Eugene replied. 'Look on the bright side. Tommy will be reunited in heaven with Robbie. He'll take good care of him. Thanks to you, they're together again.'

Sharon Nelson stuffed handfuls of cheese balls in her mouth while catching up with her favourite programme *The Young Ones*. She loved her video recorder, the latest gift from her wonderful man after he'd had a windfall on the horses.

Bursting out laughing at Neil's antics, Sharon nearly choked, before coughing all the cheese balls over the coffee table. She heard a noise and turned around. She'd obviously woken the naughty twosome. 'Caleb, Malik, get back to fucking bed. Now!' she bellowed.

From an early age, Sharon had realized she wasn't destined for greatness. She was born big and, as the years passed, she got bigger. She'd hated school, was forever getting picked on because of her size. But that didn't stop David Manning and Johnny O'Shea wanting a wank and blow-job behind the bike sheds. Thankfully for Sharon, unlike her mother, she had a pretty face.

Sharon left school with no exams, then was forced to take a job in the Butterkist factory in Blackbourne Road. She hated it. As much as she loved food, that sickly smell of popcorn turned her stomach no end.

Deciding to get up the spout so she would get her own flat and claim benefits, Sharon and her pal Denise headed up to the Princess Alice in Stratford. Denise was big too and the girls had read in a magazine black men liked big women.

Their cunning plan worked a treat. Not only were they spoilt for choice, within three months both were pregnant. Four months later they both had their own council flats.

Leroy was Caleb's dad. Sharon had told him she was pregnant, then never seen him again. She wasn't bothered though. He'd given her what she wanted and she would never have to take on another boring job.

Malik had been an accident. She'd got drunk in the Royal Oak in Green Lanes one night, then gone for a kebab. She'd only asked for extra chilli sauce, but had got more than she'd bargained for. The Asian bloke behind the counter had offered to take her to his flat above to drink vodka. That's how Malik was conceived. She hadn't even bothered telling Mohammed she was up the duff. She was just grateful for the extra child allowance.

Sharon patted her stomach. Now she was pregnant again and this little one was not only set to secure her that council house she so badly wanted, he or she also had a daddy who couldn't wait to meet them.

'Surprise,' a voice boomed.

'Shit! You made me jump. I didn't hear you come in. Why you home so early?'

Dumbo planted a fat kiss on the lips of the woman who had made him so very happy, then picked up Caleb and Malik as they ran to greet him. 'Jack told me to close the bar early and I got the whole weekend off with full pay,' Dumbo grinned.

'How comes?'

'I'm not sure. Jack's got family problems, I think.' Dumbo never told Sharon anything important because unfortunately her mouth was even bigger than her body.

'Shall we do something tomorrow? Can we take the kids to the seaside? They've never been to the seaside.'

Dumbo held his woman in his arms. He knew when they went out as a family, people laughed and stared. He was tall and lanky with massive ears, Sharon ginger and fat, Caleb half Jamaican, Malik half Asian. But having been raised in numerous children's homes, Dumbo didn't care. Maylands in particular had taught him how to grow crocodile skin. 'Seaside it is then, Sugartits. I was thinking, I know it's gone ten, but how do ya fancy going clubbing tonight? It's been ages since you and Denise had a night out. Tell Den to drop Denzil round 'ere. I'll babysit the kids.'

Sharon squealed with delight as Dumbo handed her a fifty-pound note. 'We'll go Lautrec's and I'll bring you a kebab in from Lazet's. I won't drink too much cider. I'll stick to halves, not pints.'

Dumbo smiled. He had work to do.

Even though his brothers had hearts of stone in comparison to his own, Danny Darling knew they were speaking sense. He and Eugene had flown out to Spain last Monday with their own passports, and would be flying back next Monday with their own passports. Nobody knew, bar Ronnie and Sharpy, that they'd even left the country in between. Therefore, they should be in the clear. Sharpy used to box with Ronnie, was as trustworthy as they come.

'The other option is to go home, act normal, then tell Mum and Dad you liked it so much out here, you wanna move out here with me. That way, you won't have to look Mum, Dad or Donna in the face for much longer,' Ronnie suggested.

'I'm for that. South London ain't what it used to be,' Eugene said. 'What would we do for wonga though?'

'I'll buy us a bar out here. You two can run it,' Ronnie replied.

Danny thought about his own family. Lucy loved the sun and his kids would have a better life in Spain. He raised his glass. 'To new beginnings – and Tommy and Robbie. Gone but never forgotten.'

Ronnie and Eugene followed suit. 'To new beginnings, and Tommy and Robbie,' they said in unison.

* * *

Dumbo waited until the kids were asleep before lifting up the carpet, then the floorboard. Sharon had no idea about his 'Little Black Book'.

Writing down the events of today, Dumbo grinned as he thought of his telephone conversation with Danny. Danny had dropped the phone in shock when he'd told him Robbie had been shot in the head. Not that Dumbo thought Robbie dying was funny, but it served Danny right.

A couple of weeks ago Dumbo had been earwigging when Danny and Eugene hatched their plan to shoot Josh. They hadn't noticed him hovering. Nobody ever did. They all saw him as the simple barman everybody laughed at.

That was the good thing about having massive ears. Dumbo had better hearing than most. Scratch had called him her top snout, but Dumbo preferred to think of himself as a police informant. That made him feel ultra important.

Getting the job at Churchill's was all part of his and Scratch's cunning plan. He was to be her eyes and ears in the bar. But now Scratch had left the police force, he'd decided to keep the job anyway. He liked working at Churchill's and it paid quite well. Jack gave him cash in hand, so he could still claim his benefits.

Previously, he'd helped Scratch put away a murderer, numerous drug dealers and armed robbers. He'd even grassed up Benny and his boss. Two grand, he'd got for that job. He had no regrets. Benny had changed since their days at Maylands. He was rude and flash. Served him right.

Since he started working for the Darlings, Dumbo had written down every piece of juicy information in his Little Black Book. Churchill's was full of villains who spoke too loudly when inebriated. Extra-marital affairs, illegitimate children, armed robberies, who'd murdered who – Dumbo knew everything.

Checking his dates and times were all correct, Dumbo snapped the book shut and put it back in its hidey-hole. For now, he was happy with his life and job. But if the Darlings ever wronged him, he would work for Scratch's husband Jay and grass the lot of them up.

Dumbo checked on the boys, then poured himself an orange juice. On the lounge wall, amongst numerous other photos, there was one of himself and Tommy taken at Maylands. Dumbo raised his glass. 'Happy Heavenly Birthday, Tommy. You're a legend and I got you to thank for the man I am today. You always told me to believe in myself and now I do. People might think I'm thick, but I'm not. I'm fucking clever.'

EPILOGUE

I smile as I watch Linda walk down the aisle.

'Doesn't she look beautiful, Tommy?' my mum says to me.

I stroke Rex, my beloved Alsatian. 'She looks amazing,' I reply.

'Paul looks nothing like Little Jimmy Osmond,' jokes my big sister.

I put an arm around Hazel. Seeing her again was a lovely surprise when I arrived here. No wonder Linda and I hadn't been able to trace her. She'd committed suicide in 1978.

I can't wipe the grin off my face when I see the place set for me at the table. The photo of me is a nice one.

I put my other arm around Robbie. What happened to him was truly tragic. But at least we are together again.

My mum asks me if I'm OK.

'I'm sound, Mum,' I assure her. 'Happier than I've felt in many years.'

I've now come to the conclusion that the place we leave behind is hell. Heaven is a far better place to be.

As for me becoming a national hero, I fucking love it. Nobody will ever forget Tommy Darling/Boyle.

Thank you for reading my story and please don't have nightmares. Life is what you make of it.

Look out for the
explosive new novel from

**Kimberley
CHAMBERS**

QUEENIE

Meet the woman behind one of London's
most notorious gangland families

COMING EARLY 2020

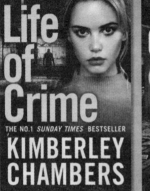
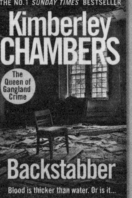
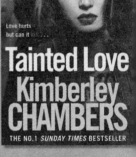